Father Divine's

Bikes

A Novel by
Steve Bassett

Print ISBN: 978-1-54392-336-0
eBook ISBN: 978-1-54392-337-7

*By inspiration, information will come. The thing
we vividly visualize, we tend to materialize . . . and
that which we materialize we will also personify.*

Rev. Major Jealous Divine
a.k.a. Father Divine
a.k.a. George Baker Jr.
c. 1876–1965
Founder of the International Peace Mission Movement
November 15, 1936

---

*When you have mastered numbers, you will
in fact no longer be reading numbers, any
more than you read words when reading
books. You will be reading meanings.*

W. E. B. Du Bois
Sociologist, historian, civil rights activist, and author
1868 to 1963

For my wife, Darlene, without whom this book would have never been completed.

Chapter

1

It was almost nine o'clock on a Monday morning when Police Lieutenant Nick Cisco and Sergeant Kevin McClosky pulled up in their unmarked cruiser in front of the Broome Street tenement. The meat wagon from the morgue was already there, its rear doors wide open to accept the latest human jetsam to be scraped from the Ward's streets.

The stiff, a Negro man probably no more than twenty-five, was sprawled across the pavement, feet on the lower tenement step, his head a few feet from the gutter. The killing was not high profile enough for Coroner Walter Tomokai to handle so an assistant was given the thankless task of collecting the necessary forensic evidence.

A brown wooden handle above the man's chest stood strong against the mid-morning breeze indicating where an ice pick had skewered his heart. Blood that had pooled around the body had already begun to harden at the edges. About a dozen onlookers, young and old alike, displayed the indifferent curiosity common to those who have seen it all before. A uniformed cop stood between them and the body.

"Jesus Christ, it's Frank Gazzi. So this is where they buried him," McClosky said as he switched off the ignition and stepped out to the street.

"He's still got his badge," Cisco said. "Come on, let's get started."

The two homicide detectives examined the body while the ghouls from the morgue snapped their pictures. McClosky turned to Gazzi, "Frank, you the first one at the scene?"

"Yeah. I was around the corner when I heard a woman scream, so I came running. Took about thirty seconds. When I got here he was still breathing, coughing up blood, but breathing. Two uniforms got here a few minutes later," Gazzi said nodding over his shoulder to the police cruiser. "They're upstairs now."

"Good luck with that," Cisco said. "Doubt if they'll get much. Whatever it is, we'll want it."

"You heard a woman scream, so there's a witness," McClosky said. "Where the hell is she?"

"What you see is what I found," Gazzi said. "Beats hell out of me how quick these people can run and hide."

It took Cisco and McClosky less than an hour to wrap it all up. Nobody heard a scream. Nobody saw anything. And nobody knew the victim's name or where he came from. That was remedied when they emptied his pockets. There was forty-seven dollars in his wallet along with a U.S. Army ID card stating that Staff Sergeant Wilbert Locklee was honorably discharged at Camp Kilmer only two weeks earlier. A 1942 driver's license had been issued to Locklee in Clarkdale, Mississippi. There was an unopened pack of Camels, eighty cents in change, and a Zippo lighter emblazoned with the crest of the 92nd Infantry Division.

"I'll be damned," Cisco said. "This guy was a Buffalo Soldier."

"Buffalo Soldier?"

"Yeah there was a big article in LIFE magazine, how the 92nd , an all Negro division, went all the way back to the frontier Indian wars. Did pretty damn well this time around in Italy. Quite a history."

"So what do you think?" McClosky said.

"Hunting for poontang," Cisco said. "What else would get him up here on the hill. He had plenty of green, just picked the wrong pussy."

"My guess, it was her pimp," McClosky said. "They love the ice pick. When his whore screamed, they panicked and hauled ass. Left behind a stuffed wallet and wristwatch."

"We'll contact the cops in Mississippi, see if there's a Locklee family still living in Clarkdale."

"Poor son of a bitch. Put his ass on the line for Uncle Sam and ends up this way."

They watched the meat wagon pull away with Locklee's body, then turned to Gazzi and the other two uniforms.

"Tell me what you've got," Cisco turned to the two patrolmen. "Your names…."

"James DeAngelo," the older one, probably about thirty and clearly in charge, said. "My partner's Dave Hurley."

"Come up with anything worthwhile?" Cisco was aware of a common tendency of street cops to embellish their reports in order to put themselves in the center of homicide investigations. He had been there himself.

"The same old shit," Hurley said. "Everyone was deaf, dumb and blind."

"How long have you had a badge?" McClosky said. "Got it all figured out, do you."

"Long enough to know there aren't any niggers in this Ward talking to cops," Hurley said.

"Hell, we almost had to kick-in some doors to get them out in the hall to talk at all," DeAngelo said.

"Life can be a bitch," Cisco responded sarcastically. "Just let us know, do you have anything?"

"Just names." DeAngelo said. "Had to pry one of them out of the landlord. Seems a gal named Ruby West was nowhere to be seen this morning. He unlocked her first floor flat to give us a look-see."

"And…." McClosky said, his impatience evident. "Is this Ruby West a whore or not?"

"With all the trappings," Hurley said. "Big fancy bed, velvet sofa, big pillows all around and even carpets on the floor. Beer in the ice box, gin and rye. Not the best, but pretty good stuff. Fancy duds, his and hers in the two closets."

"This bitch looks like a real moneymaker with a live-in pimp," DeAngelo said.

"Whatever you've got put it in writing, then get it down to homicide by tomorrow," Cisco said.

"Frank, it's good to see that you're still kicking," McClosky said. "Hang in there."

The two detectives drove away. Their first stop would be the Tenderloin to see if Ruby and her pimp also worked the downtown streets. Their curbside space was taken by a Fire Department truck. Two firemen had already begun unwinding a high pressure hose to flush blood off the sidewalk and down a storm drain with other gutter debris.

They were waiting for the light to change on Waverly when Cisco broke open a fresh pack of Chesterfields, tapped one out for McClosky and lit up for both of them. Cisco took a deep drag and exhaled. "You know, I've just been thinking about Gazzi, from wop golden boy to rousting voodoo scam artists along the black belt."

"He's been around a long time, longer than me, and just as long as you," McClosky said. "Clue me in. How was it that he fucked up?"

"Goes back to when the goombahs started flexing their muscles downtown," Cisco said. "Gazzi linked up with Tony Gordo's bunch from Messina. He saw how Richie the Boot and Longy had divided the city. Learned real fast how the game is played, and when to put the blinders on. It seems he took his blinders off at the wrong time and the wrong place."

"I heard it was a simple vice bust," McClosky said. "That he had picked up a whore. Jesus Christ, if that's all it was, he's really paying big time for it."

"It didn't end there," Cisco said as the squad car pulled to the curb in front of the Picadilly. "In fact, there was a second bimbo, the same thing, wrong time, wrong place."

Chapter

2

That morning Officer Francis Gazzi had just completed his swing through his Third Ward beat. After a few seconds at the call box, he was on his way to Bloom's Deli for a cup of coffee when he heard a woman scream from around the corner. Not knowing what to expect and fearing the worst, he felt for his Smith & Wesson, but left it holstered. He poked cautiously around the corner entrance to the Zanzibar Lounge. Four of the bar's patrons ducked back inside as he brushed past them. He found the sidewalks and tenement stoops, generally teeming with Negroes of all ages, completely empty.

Gazzi spotted a man's body on the sidewalk, and broke into a cautious trot. He realized, when he was within fifteen feet of the body and saw the spreading pool of blood, that this was going to be his first homicide. He turned his gaze back to the corner just as a Negro couple was leaving the Zanzibar. "Call the police! Do it now!"

The man stopped in his tracks, and turned towards Gazzi. But the woman kept going as fast as her tight skirt and heels would let her. "They's already on the phone inside," he shouted back, then turned and followed his lady already a half-block up the street.

Five minutes later the patrol car arrived, followed in short order by the meat wagon, and Cisco and McClosky.

Gazzi was only the second gentile cop to work a beat that included the heart of Newark's Jewish immigrant community, adjacent to the "nigger belt" with its stabbings, shootings, fire-trap tenements, voodoo parlors, numbers banks and staggering infant mortality rate.

The beat was the latest price he was paying for screw-ups dating back to his years as a rookie. His best friend, Lt. Tony Gordo, got him into the department. Tony was like an older brother to him. Their families had shared steerage from Messina. He was the best man at his wedding. Tony had joined the force just before the war, and worked his way up. Since the force was fifty percent Italian, it had been easy for him to pull Frank along with him. He showed him the ropes and told him to keep his nose clean, not to rock the boat. He even convinced his uniform boss to give Frank a soft, downtown cruiser beat even though it would mean screwing over cops with more seniority.

All he wanted was to do a good job, be a good cop back then. That was his first mistake. It all turned to shit toward the end of his first year in the squad car.

He would never forget the morning in Tony's office. "*Buon giorno, Francis,*" Lt. Anthony Gordo said "*Comé sta? E Maria?*"

"*Bene, grazie. E tu?*"

"*Molto bene, stiamo tutti bene,*" replied Gordo, motioning Gazzi to a battered chair in front of his desk.

"Let's talk about the arrest outside the Paradise Club last night," Gordo said.

"A whore and her pimp rolled a guy in an alley," replied Gazzi.

"Remember her name?"

"A broad named Golpe, Sublime Golpe. Her boyfriend got away. There's a pickup out for him. I took her in."

"Good piece of police work, huh?"

"Nothing special. We were cruising down Broad when this guy staggers out of the alley and stops us. He was bleeding real bad over the eye."

"How'd you find the slut?"

"He described her. She was sitting inside the Paradise, just like nothing happened, working another sucker at the bar."

"When was the last time a whore was picked up along that section of Broad?"

Frank shrugged. "Why, what's the problem?"

"You're the fucking problem! When you took over Dirk's cruiser, I told you that all vice complaints go directly through me to Captain Orsini, right?"

"But Tony. . .it was just a simple pickup."

Gordo got up from behind his desk. He was a big man. Swarthy. He stalked about the room trying to control his temper.

"But the guy was bleeding real bad. It was my duty to…"

"Your *duty* is to protect your ass and mine. Orsini's got his balls in an uproar. Golpe belongs to Zwillman." He moved closer to Frank and whispered. "So does Orsini."

Frank never saw his friend so mad. "Shit. How was I supposed to know."

"*Stupido!* Thought you got the message. Everyone else does."

"What can I do?"

"Nothin' at this point. I got to go and see if I can fix it. Orsini's out for your badge."

"I can't lose the job, Tony. Maria'll kill me."

Gordo's features softened. "Yeah, I know. I'll see what I can do. You're on desk duty until further notice."

The following week, Gordo broke the news to Gazzi.

"You still have a job, Francis. That's the good news."

Frank crossed himself. "Thanks, Tony. You saved my ass. So what's the bad news?"

The following week, Gazzi was reassigned to a walking beat near Rupert Stadium, only yards from the stinking city dumps. Smoke from the burning garbage thickened the air but never blurred his belief that he was in the right.

He was shifted to his downtown beat eighteen months later. Gordo, now commander of the night uniform division, had pulled some strings. It could have been worse.

For fifteen years, he smiled a lot with that tight little smile of a public servant adrift among the Philistines. He checked store doors, directed traffic, handed out tickets, and gave street directions. There were plenty of Christmas presents for Gazzi, and he was on a first-name basis with many of the city's business leaders. He had it made. Even his wife, Maria, agreed with him. These perks reinforced his mediocrity, willingly accepted and nurtured.

With the exception of a handful of robberies, the most serious crime Gazzi was called upon to handle was shoplifting. It was, in fact, a shoplifting case that had provided him with his most memorable day. It also provided him with the hate he could envelop and cherish with his whole being. It drove him to his confessor.

One afternoon, Gazzi had been standing idly on a street corner when a salesgirl from Bamberger's summoned him. He followed her to the entrance on Bank Street where a floorwalker waited with a pretty colored girl, no more than a teenager. She gazed squarely at Gazzi as he approached.

The girl, who had none of the docility usually found in teenagers caught stealing, looked pissed. When she saw him coming, she immediately lashed out.

"Hey, I didn't do nothing. That bitch's tryin' to pin it on me."

"Settle down, Miss," Frank said, and turned to the salesgirl. "What's the problem here?"

"We caught her with her hand in the costume jewelry case, already had some earrings and a necklace in her purse." She showed them to Frank.

"What's your name?" Frank said.

"Cherry."

"Okay, Cherry. Here's how it works. We go upstairs and file a formal complaint. Then you and Miss…"

"Elise Smith."

"Then you and Miss Smith will take a ride to the station."

The three of them went to the manager's office, where the saleswoman filled out the form and signed the complaint. Gazzi then took the girl down to a seldom-used entrance on Bank Street to await the patrol car he summoned from the precinct. They were alone.

Gazzi stood by the glass door, the girl beside him.

"I got no time for this bullshit. Do you know what the fuck you're doing? Who I work for?" the girl said.

"But you steal, you get booked."

The girl's expression softened as she looked at Gazzi. "Hey, ain't there nothin' I can do to get outta this?" she said, moving closer to him.

Gazzi could smell her perfume. She was wearing a thin, low-cut linen dress and no bra. He could see her nipples. This was no innocent kid. She smiled, a bold smile, a full-toothed smile, a hard smile. Her eyes darted toward the door. The meaning was clear to Gazzi as he tried to focus on the sparse traffic outside.

"Honey, there's got to be somethin'...," Cherry said. "You know what I do, and I do it real good."

The girl moved her right hand across Gazzi's chest.

Gazzi's brain exploded, thoughts spilling out in all directions.

"Come on," she purred as her hand strayed lower to his crotch. "Ooo, you are a big, hard man."

He felt the zipper of his fly pull down. The girl put her hand inside his pants. Her cheek was against his shoulder.

Gazzi was sweating. He was breathing heavily as her hand started to move. *Geesh, it felt good. This girl was a pro.*

"Oh yeah, Baby. Oh yeah." Her hand was moving faster. "You like it, don'cha?"

Gazzi grit his teeth.

Suddenly, the girl stopped. "I can make you happy, officer. Just let me go and I'll give you a good time later."

Could he let her go? Would it be possible? They could arrange a meeting later. Yeah, that's it. But would she keep her end of the bargain and keep her mouth shut?

Suddenly, he heard the door open and high heels clicking on the stairs. Cherry backed off just as the salesgirl appeared. Gazzi zipped his fly.

"Can we get this over with, officer? I've got to get back to work."

"Uh...sure. The squad car should be here any minute, Miss."

A few minutes later, the squad car arrived.

"What's the beef, Gazzi?" the officer said.

"Shoplifting at Bam's. This lady will file the complaint."

"Gotcha."

Gazzi put the two women in the backseat with another officer. His job was not over until he completed his shift on the beat. He would fill out his report at the precinct later.

"See ya later." Gazzi shut the door and the car took off.

He let loose a torrent of *mea culpas*. It was his second time dealing with a hooker. This time he had nearly compromised his duty because of that little Nigger slut. He could have lost his job. He'd know better next time. He'd just handcuff the bitch and be done with it.

The next day, he reported in and his friend, Tony Gordo, now a captain and head of the entire uniform division, caught him in the locker room.

"Frankie, you're at it again. What the fuck is going on with you?"

"Good morning to you too, Tony."

"I heard you made an arrest at Bam's yesterday."

"Yeah, some Nigger whore, she was just a kid. She wasn't working the street, just shoplifting."

"What's her name?"

"Cherry. Probably fake."

"It's been a long time and I thought you learned your lesson," Gordo said. "First, you fucked up with one of Longy's whores, and now it's Richie the Boot's bimbo. You could have let her go. You know the territory and that your beat includes Boiardo's stable."

"And you?"

"Don't go there, Francis."

Gazzi turned pale. He knew about all the cops on the take. It had slapped him in the face all those years ago when he arrested Sublime Golpe at the Paradise Club. And now his friend Tony Gordo.

"You need to wise up. It don't look good for me—or you."

"Won't happen again."

"You got that right."

The following week, Gordo broke the news to Gazzi.

"It wasn't so easy this time, Francis." Gordo said from behind his desk at headquarters. "Had to make three phone calls to set it straight. They wanted to can your ass. I'm doing this as much for Maria as you, families count. You still have a job, that's the good news. The bad news is that you'll be doing your walking in the Third Ward."

Gordo's words were a hard punch in the gut. Gazzi realized that any attempt to explain or protest would be useless. He knew they, whoever "they" were, had made up their minds, and Gordo was merely their mouth-piece, and that he had taken a big chance speaking up for him.

Gazzi knew this would be his final warning.

"Geez, Tony."

"Shut the fuck up. That was the best I could do. Just watch your ass. Don't be a hero. Maybe someday you'll get another chance to dig yourself out." Gordo said.

So for Gazzi, it was this shithole of a beat dealing with niggers, low-lifes, old Jews blocking traffic with their pushcarts, and voodoo fakes offering a sure thing to numbers players and God knows what else.

He steered clear of any criminal activity. Zwillman's numbers drops were everywhere, but Gordo had clued him in to ignore them if he wanted to keep his job. So until a few weeks ago, he put in his eight hours and went home. That's when he started hearing that Richie the Boot might be moving into the Ward. Twice he did what he thought was his duty, only to be kicked in the ass and put out to pasture. This time, if he worked it right, a Zwillman/Boiardo vendetta could be his ticket out.

Chapter

3

Sgt. McClosky knew Nick well enough to see that he was close to boiling over, and when he exploded somebody would pay for it. They had made the rounds of the Tenderloin's jazz clubs with no success. The Piccadilly, the Alcazar and the Nest were favorite haunts of pimps picking the deep pockets of servicemen on leave and defense workers with money to burn.

The two detectives were staked out in their car on Waverly a half-block from the Alcazar and well into their second cigarette when McClosky said, "You know, Nick, we're not really sure it was the whore and her pimp."

"I'm sure," Cisco said.

"Let's look at what we've got," McClosky said. "Everyone's buttoned up, no witnesses, nothing. Only that a slut named Ruby West and her high-fashion pimp, if in fact he was her pimp, worked the neighborhood."

"Just getting started," Cisco's irritation was evident as he took a final deep drag, and without looking flicked his cigarette out to the sidewalk. It bounced off the highly-polished shoe of a black pedestrian.

"Jesus Christ, man, watch what the fuck you're doing," a thin and wiry man about forty, who was obviously dressed to kill for a night in the Tenderloin, spun around to confront Cisco. He quickly sized up the two men in the car and pulled up short. "Just flew off, that's all. Didn't mean nothin', no offense."

"No offense taken," Cisco said. "Don't go off mad, but first tell me if the name Ruby West rings a bell? Ruby's in no trouble, just want to talk to her."

"Ruby West? Nope don't know no Ruby West."

"Ever hear her name anywhere? You know, here at the Alcazar or at the Nest?"

"No sir, never," the man was smiling now, "and Amos Slack is ready and willin' to help the police whenever he can. You can bet on that."

"Nice to know," Cisco said. "We'll be seeing you around."

They watched the Negro dandy stroll casually in the direction of the Alcazar, stop briefly to chat with two well-dressed young ladies, then changed direction and crossed Waverly on his way to the Piccadilly.

"Okay, back to where we were," Cisco said. "I figure Ruby and her pimp are new in town. Don't belong to either Richie the Boot's or Longy's stables. We should get a fix on when they got into town when we see the uniforms' report in the morning."

"Freelancers don't last long in Newark," McClosky said.

"They've got to know that, and if they don't, they're pretty damn dumb."

"They've already proved that, or why else would they ice pick a trick in broad daylight. With reformers breathing down their necks, Boiardo and Zwillman can't afford to have any casual corpses laying around."

"We've got to get twenty-four hour surveillance," Cisco said.

"How about Gazzi? The poor son of a bitch is aching to get involved."

"I was thinking the same thing. It's part of his beat, so why not. He may be the dullest, most sanctimonious cop on the force, but he's honest. I'll talk to his shift sergeant, shouldn't be a problem."

"Sanctimonious? Sounds like you really know the guy. Fill me in."

"Goes back to his first fuck-up with a mob whore. Orsini wanted his ass, but Gordo talked him out of it. Gazzi and I were rookies together in the Sixth before Gordo planted him in a police cruiser after only a year on the bricks. He was tough to be around. He let you know about him being family with the big shot wops downtown, and you can guess how the rest of us dagos felt about that."

"Pissed, probably wanted to strangle him."

"Yeah, and that goes for everybody, including the micks. He jumped over eight with more seniority. To be honest, I was glad to see him pull his holier-than-thou ass out of the Sixth."

"Here, take one." McClosky tapped out an Old Gold from its pack and offered it to his partner. "You need it."

"Christ, it's been years since I've given Gazzi a thought." Nick took a deep drag and exhaled through his nose just as the first drops of rain hit the windshield. "Now the rain, just right for the luck we've been having."

Kevin warily eyed Nick who had pushed back in his seat, and was staring blankly into space. They had been partners for almost ten years, going back before their days on the robbery squad. Nick, at forty-three, was five years senior to Kevin, both in age and on the force. They made an odd couple. Their rise from robbery to homicide was made possible in 1943 when Mayor Vincent Murphy decided to make a run for governor. Reform of the notoriously corrupt police department would be his ticket to Trenton. The two detectives were just low-profile enough to survive the shake-up, despite time-after-time skirting the boundary between rogue and honest police work.

Neither was connected. Nick was not Sicilian. His stevedore father and mother were born in Calabria, and arrived in steerage at the turn of the century. The McCloskys were third generation, having fled County Cork when Kevin's great-grandparents were evicted from their Skibbereen home during the fourth year of the potato famine.

Every cent of Angelo Cisco's stevedore wages that could be spared went toward Nick's tuition at Rutgers. An education cut short when Nick met, fell in love and married Constance Sophia Margotta. From the first day Nick joined the force, his father's disappointment, although never expressed, was palpable. His father never questioned the eighteen credits in electives Nick had collected toward an art degree. He didn't know that his son had grown to hate his job, knowing that his dream of a career as a museum curator or art critic had vanished.

Victor and Rose McClosky were overjoyed when their son Kevin secured one of the few rookie spots to open up during the depression. He had briefly considered the military as a way out from behind the counter of his parents' grocery store on Springfield Avenue. He saw how they worked from dawn to dusk to keep the doors open and wanted none of it. Turning in his uniform for mufti and a slot on the robbery squad, then getting sergeant stripes thanks to Mayor Murphy's police clean-up, were cause for great family celebration. They never suspected that their son's stripes helped fuel his obsession with the fight game, with its mob-controlled palukas, whores, bookies and even a few managers not willing to throw their pugs to the wolves for a quick pay-off. He had no trouble cashing in on a fixed fight.

Victor and Rose never questioned where their son's money came from, only too happy when he picked up most of the rent for a two-story house he shared with them on Hickory Street. His De Soto convertible, Botany 500 sports coat, and high-priced ladies he sometimes brought home for dinner were met with a wink and a nod from his dad and naïve shrugs from his mom.

Kevin could see by Nick's sullen expression that his partner was in one of his black moods, hopefully it could be assuaged before violence erupted. He had seen it all before. Today it was the discovery that a former Buffalo Soldier had been left to die on the sidewalk with an ice pick in his heart. Kevin could never forget that Friday night in the Ironbound, only their second call as a homicide team almost three years earlier.

"All in the kitchen and bathroom," a uniform sergeant said as they entered the third floor tenement through the front room door. "The coroner's on his way. The guy's in the kitchen, the wife and kid are in the bathroom. It ain't pretty. His name is Wonski, Mike Wonski."

Wonski, a big muscular man with graying blond hair, sat sobbing at the kitchen table, his forehead resting on his right forearm, his bloody left hand dangling. His sleeveless undershirt was drenched in sweat. Dirty cord workpants, scruffy Army surplus boots, and an almost empty bottle of Imperial rye next to the sink completed the picture. Two uniforms stood behind him.

"Mother of mercy, I don't know why I did it," Wonski said raising his left arm to inspect his bloody knuckles. "Never before, I swear to you on our Blessed Lady, never before I did this."

Kevin followed Nick into the bathroom. A little blond girl, no more than four years old, was face down in a pool of blood near the sink. Her mother was in the bathtub, her head under a faucet that dripped water on her badly bruised and puffy face. She was barefoot and clad in a brassiere and slip.

"I swear on the newborn Jesus, it was not me, but the devil," Wonski's mumbled entreaty was punctuated with sobs from the kitchen.

"That's a fucking bunch of bullshit," the sergeant, who had followed the detectives into the bathroom, said. "We've been here before, so has the social worker. He's been beating up on his wife and kid since he lost his job. She never signed a complaint so our hands were tied."

Kevin recalled how he came close to puking. It was nothing like their first homicide, a white drunk sliced ear-to-ear during an argument outside a Market Street saloon. He settled himself against the door jamb while Cisco bent first to inspect the little girl, and then turned to the bathtub and tightened the faucet that had been dripping water on the mother's face. The medical examiner arrived a few minutes later, did his business as pictures were taken, and gave the okay for the bodies of Sheila Wonski and little Anna to be carted away. Kevin looked at his partner who returned his gaze. He had wanted to say something, but remained silent in the face of unadulterated hatred.

"We'll take it from here," Nick told the sergeant. "Wait downstairs, first I want to have a few words with this piece of shit," he said as he strode over to the now handcuffed Wonski.

"How many times did you hit them, six, seven, eight." Nick pulled Wonski from his chair, kicked his feet out from under him, dragged him into the bathroom, and pushed his face into the bloody floor. "Did you kick them, too? Or was it the devil?"

"Yes, yes, that's it, the devil," Wonski lifted his head from the floor. His right cheek covered with his daughter's blood.

"And the whiskey, that's also the devil at work?"

Before Wonski could answer Nick kicked him in the face. He coughed out three front teeth and a mouthful of blood. "Don't say another word, you son of a bitch, and I'll show you how the devil really works."

Damn, Kevin thought, *it's never going away that night in the Ironbound.* Looking at his partner as they sat in the car with the rain outside, and the gloom inside, Kevin hoped his premonition was groundless. He relived the helplessness he felt that night and feared that it would be coming around again. It would always be with him, in bloody color.

"Jesus Christ, Nick, that's enough!" he had shouted that night.

"Stay where you are, Kevin. You're not part of this," Nick held up his hand and pointed toward the door. "Best you stay outside."

"No fucking way I stay outside. I'm your partner, god damn it. There's no way I'm going to let you kill this bastard." Just as quickly as Nick's paroxysm of hatred and revenge had erupted, it ended with a crooked smile.

"Yeah, you're right, but first we have to clean up this piece of shit. And there's only one way to do that," he said as he dragged Wonski over to the toilet, pushed his head into the bowl and flushed it.

For Kevin, that first time watching Nick working over Wonski was the worst. How many other self-righteous flare-ups were there over the years, three or maybe four, it didn't matter they were all ugly. He couldn't help wondering if it was a coincidence that Nick's violent mood swings started shortly after he began bedding down Grace DeMarco after almost fifteen years of his childless marriage to Connie. They never discussed it, but he would have to be blind not to see that Grace had become an obsession that Nick no longer attempted to hide. Sitting there in the Tenderloin with his partner, Kevin watched the whores, pimps and assorted "good time Charlies" scamper from door-to-door to avoid the rain.

With the windows closed, the combination of cigarette smoke and humidity had turned the detectives' car into a sweat bath. "Getting hard to breath, and I'm soaking wet," Kevin said. "I say we call it a day."

"I agree, drop me off at headquarters. It's still early enough to call Gazzi's boss and line him up for surveillance at that tenement first thing in the morning."

Frank Gazzi's early elation that he had been pulled off the street to be included in a murder investigation turned to depression when he realized that the rain clouds were here to stay. He knew his state of depression, at its lowest point, would border on the irrational. After a few minutes at the call box, Gazzi took up his surveillance position in the hall of a tenement across the street from Ruby West's apartment.

Gazzi was a religious man, and he liked to think that rain dampened not only the skin and by shutting out the sun, the spirit as well. At forty-five, he found it increasingly helpful to rationalize his paltry hates with metaphysical justifications. Gazzi was like many men faced with the onus of mediocrity. He lightened his burden with whiffs of heavenly ether. His devotion, simplistic and deluded as it was, remained.

Metaphor was Gazzi's best friend. The New Testament was his favorite. It was a mother lode. Gazzi accepted his assigned place among the humble standing in the back of the Temple, but from time to time was irked that he had not once had a chance to strut his stuff up front among the Pharisees. Perhaps Ruby West was his Mary Magdalene, a fallen angel destined to lift him off the squalid streets of the Third Ward and put him back into a squad car.

If so, it would be a rare stroke of good fortune, and it couldn't have come at a better time. It was an open secret that Boiardo was about to use *Beacon* paperboys as runners to expand his numbers racket onto Zwillman's turf. Gazzi had sniffed it all out. White kids were being recruited by three black bookies posing as barbers, then pushed into battle by Frank Marsucci, the punk circulation manager. If true, it would end the uneasy truce that had kept mobster bloodshed to a minimum.

He had been warned by Tony to be blind, deaf and dumb when it came to mob crime in the Third Ward, but the ice pick murder had freelance written all over it.

Chapter

4

About a year earlier, Richie Maxwell began a habit he had grown to hate. He was once again about to sneak around corners to get a haircut.

That morning Richie closed the door to the family's third-floor apartment behind him. He had taken only a few steps when the door popped open, and his mom warned him for at least the thousandth time to stay away from the cheap candy at Milt's Confectionery. His teeth would rot and the family could not afford a big dentist bill.

Geesh, he thought. *I'm not a baby. I'm almost fourteen.* He just nodded as he always did, then crossed the landing and headed down the stairs. His deception started when his dad gave him fifty cents to get a haircut at Top to Bottom, the local barbershop. He decided to take a shortcut through the Negro part of the Third Ward. He started to turn back, when a big black man in a starched white, loose-fitting coat greeted him from a storefront doorway. *Damn,* Richie thought to himself, *a black dentist?* He never imagined that there could ever be such a thing around here.

"Peace, little brother! Peace!" the smiling man bellowed. "Never seen ya'll around here before."

The man beckoned from the open door of a shop, whose fresh white paint, blue-trimmed windows, and white Venetian blinds made it a stark counterpoint to the drab, rundown buildings around it. "PEACE" was centered atop each of the two front windows on either side of the door in six-inch gold letters.

"You come to the right place. We're snappy an' good, real good. Get ya'll trimmed, good lookin', and outta here in ten minutes. An' for jes' a dime. Ten lonely pennies."

This guy isn't a dentist at all, Richie thought. *He's a barber and a cheap one at that. Only a dime.* He fingered the fifty-cent piece in his pocket. *Why not take a chance? If this guy is as good as his word, I'll walk out with forty cents in my kick.* Richie looked around and saw that there were no other whites on the street. It was safe for him to risk it so he stepped inside. He didn't want to be seen patronizing a Negro shop and be labeled a white nigger.

"Peace, little brother, in the name of Reverend Major Jealous Father Divine, we welcome you. Take a seat, right here." Two other Negro men in white coats were standing around the shop. The smallest of the three took a spotless white cape from the back of a barber's chair, snapped it twice, and spread it open to cover Richie.

All that Richie knew about Father Divine came from the streets, and from his father, who called him "an uppity nigger fake." Richie could see for himself what was closing in around his neighborhood, and Father Divine was a big part of it. "Peace" signs on diners that served ten cent meals, even some of them free, grocery stores that beat hell out of A&P's prices, and "Father Divine's Peace Mission" signs on old hotels and factories, now "Heavens on Earth."

From the very beginning Richie had doubts about these three guys, and he didn't know exactly why, just a creeping thought that everything wasn't on the up-and-up.

"Father Divine's sort of a big deal around here, ain't he."

"Not just here but around this great country of ours." The three black men said "Amen."

"What your mammy an' daddy call ya, son?" his barber asked as he draped and fastened the cape over Richie's shoulders.

"Richie, Richie Maxwell."

"Fair exchange needed here. Right here'n now, if ya be one of our regulars. So, here's us. I be Darn Good Disciple."

"Darn Good Disciple?" Richie responded, thinking that he had wandered into a loony bin and wondered if the forty cents was worth it.

"Yes, little brother. And that's 'bout as strong as our talk gets. No profanity is tolerated by the Divine Father," the big man said. "He's our messenger, and there ain't no room in his message for cursing and the like. That brother over there is God's Tall Timber." He was seated in the middle of three chairs watching Darn Good Disciple at work.

The third starched coat was sitting in one of the four customer chairs, two in front of each of the front windows. His legs were stretched out as he looked Richie over. He seemed reluctant to give Richie his name, hesitated, and said, "I'm Righteous Reckoning."

"Now, let's see to that haircut," Darn Good Disciple said and set to work.

After his haircut he handed Darn Good Disciple his fifty-cent piece and got a quarter, nickel, and dime in change. "Ya'll come back. Been open only a month now, and you be our first white customer," the tall black man said with a wink.

"Uh…Okay. Thanks," Richie mumbled and left.

That's how it started and he'd been going back every two weeks. If his father knew, he'd be in big trouble. His dad feared the blacks, convinced that it was only a matter of time before they took over Newark.

Chapter

5

Richie had just finished serving novena at St. Mark's. As he walked out of the church, he saw the caravan of cars squeezing its way up Market. The parade was headed uphill through a throng of salutation-shouting Negroes and some whites who were pressing into the center of the street from both sides.

That morning the *Beacon* had written it up:

Father Divine Welcomes

Wounded Negro Vets

Into His Heavens

The *Evening Clarion*, which had become concerned over Father Divine's growing strength in the city's Negro community, heralded the upcoming event as a white man's worry. Ever since Germany's surrender in May, there had been a steady trickle of wounded Negro veterans returning from Europe with their Purple Hearts. Editors, with no evidence to support their claim, hinted that black veterans were squandering their mustering-out pay and allowances on cheap booze and women, making them easy targets for Father Divine to showcase.

Discharged Negro Vets

Wounded and Jobless

Join Growing Movement

The caravan of uniformed veterans, white-gowned sisters, and dark-suited brothers edged its way up the hill. Richie could see that for the people around him, there was no movement, no horde of disgruntled black veterans, but only one drawing card, a small, skin-headed black man in the back seat of the biggest convertible he had ever seen. There were dozens of cops spread out along the route.

The black woman beside Richie was wringing a blue and white handkerchief in her hands. Beads of sweat had formed on her face and her breasts heaved in deep, labored breaths.

"Peace! Peace! Our great Father has given us Peace!" she screamed. "I was a sinful woman, a lustful woman, until Father Divine accepted me!" She was jumping up and down. "Father, father, you've shown me the way!"

"It's the Holy Way, the way to salvation, sister!" a big, Negro man in patched Levi overalls responded with roaring enthusiasm.

Then Richie thought someone had turned a radio on. Glancing at a pocket of dancers on the other side of the street, he realized it wasn't a radio at all. Their song was contagious.

"Accentuate the positive, eliminate the negative, latch onto the affirmative, don't mess with Mr. In-Between. . . oh yeah, don't mess with Mr. In-Between."

A tall Negro man noticed Richie's enthusiasm, and together they sang out, "Oh yeah, don't mess with Mr. In-Between."

"Peace, brother!" shouted a chorus of euphoric faces, a throbbing black universe engulfing a now-you-see-them-now-you-don't galaxy of white and gold-capped teeth.

"Peace! Peace! Ah done found peace!" squealed a woman, a thin reed slapping against a vast wind of emotion.

Richie was bewildered, fascinated. It was like a happy nightmare. From where he stood he could see Father Divine's car a block away. The man was engulfed by grasping faithful who crowded around his convertible.

The Cadillac convertible was followed by a line of other open cars and flatbed trucks loaded with Negro servicemen. A few white faces also bobbed above their uniforms. The first of the trucks had already passed Richie. Each veteran had a Purple Heart prominently displayed on his chest.

Women in flowing white walked beside the vehicles. It was bedlam all up and down the line. The chanting worshippers could not contain themselves. The men in uniform responded, extending their eager hands into the crowd.

Singing was going on all the while. The crescendo became a frenzied cry of liberation.

Listen, we want you to know,

Father Divine is our Prophet.

We were blind but now we see.

He opened our eyes.

Praise God for His Holy Prophet!

It was an anthem sung on friendly shores. Richie was caught up in the excitement. Father Divine's car was still a few hundred feet from Richie when he found himself eagerly joining the other worshippers as they pressed from the sidewalk out onto the street, straining against a human chain of chanting, black-suited men who tried desperately to keep a path open for the motorcade.

Upper windows along the street were crowded with the cheering and the curious. Fire escapes were crammed with the young and the old. Gray-haired men and women, black and white alike, nodded in wonderment.

People poured out of the stores. Richie found himself being pushed toward Father Divine's convertible as it passed slowly in front of the bursting knot of people. He still couldn't see the man, but some of the others could, and their happiness inspired everyone.

"Peace! Peace is ours for all time!" screamed a big Black man on one side of Richie.

"Peace, brother," came the chorus of those around him.

"He's got a sickle in one hand and a hoe in the other!" shouted a fat black woman on the other side of Richie. "The sickle of retribution and the hoe of the harvest! Vengeance and life!"

"Vengeance and life!"

The fat woman's ponderous body shoved against him as she tried to get closer to Father Divine. He followed in her wake. She would clear his way to the Divine chariot.

Propelled forward by the surging crowd of followers, Richie was thrust against the rear left fender of Father Divine's car. He got a good look at the Divine One up close.

The driver was a young white guy, dressed in a white suit. There were three husky Negroes, one in the front seat and two in the back. They were dressed in black and they seemed tense and alert.

Standing to the left of center in the back was a black man little more than five feet tall. The squat black man wore a tan tropical worsted suit that was neat as a pin. A bright red tie was neatly in place, its knot parting the ends of a starched white collar. Next to him was a tall, blond white woman. She was young. She wore a white dress. She silently nodded to the crowd, always smiling.

What impressed Richie the most was the man's head. It was hairless. His eyes were bright and shiny in a fierce sort of way. His wide mouth was always smiling.

Their eyes met for an instant.

"Peace, my little white brother. Peace!" Father Divine intoned.

Richie was pushed from the side of the car by a white-gloved, black-suited man.

"Move on, little brother. There's others who want to glimpse God's Prophet!"

Richie stumbled back just as an open Ford convertible was passing. A white-robed woman in the front seat was breaking open rolls of pennies and passing the loose coins to two men standing in the back. Every five yards or so they would each toss out a handful.

"Peace Pennies! Peace Pennies!" they shouted. "Pennies from Heaven right here in Newark!"

The kids were generally too fast for the grown-ups, darting quickly through the crowd and sliding through people's legs if necessary to reach the heavenly largesse.

Teenagers were the big winners. Just as fast as the smaller kids, but stronger, they muscled their way from one coin to the next. All the while there was a constant squealing of happy voices, as brothers and sisters of all ages gathered their treasure.

Richie regained his balance just in time to spot a fistful of pennies heading in his direction. His first reaction was to duck. Some of the coins bounced off his back and shoulders. One of them went down the back of his polo shirt and fell out the loose end to the street. Two of the pennies were within inches of each other only a few feet away.

Richie bent down and was about to pick them up when a big black kid pushed him out of the way.

"That penny ain't for you, white boy! Ah ought's to kick yer ass jes for the fun of it. Now git."

The joyous crowd swirled around them in happy pursuit of the motorcade. Nobody bothered more than a quick glance at their white brother as he picked himself up from the ground. Richie hightailed it home.

Chapter

6

Over the next few months, the ten-minute haircuts at the Peace Barber Shop stretched to fifteen minutes and included, at no extra charge, a Father Divine catechism lesson.

"You be a Catholic, right?" Darn Good Disciple began.

Richie nodded.

"Big churches, idols all 'round, and man-oh-man, you people surely do like the crucifix. Got poor saintly Jesus hanging all over the place. Seen some of ya'll's goin's on Sunday at St. Mark's. Great big costume parties."

"Now here's for you to understand," God's Tall Timber said. "We create our heaven right here, right on this street, around the corner, and across the land. Take this little shop here. It was a rundown paint store, but no more. We took it, changed it, and followed the Divine One's message that shows us that even the most humble, dirty, and abandoned buildings are our temples. Our Heavens."

And so it went, haircut after haircut. At first reluctantly and then with increasing ease, Richie found he was enjoying the hell out of their Heaven on Spruce Street.

Richie also learned that nobody should mess with Father Divine's Heavens. God's Tall Timber many times over the months would talk of the first Heaven at someplace on Long Island, wherever that was. White people didn't like it that Divinites came by the thousands to the big Peace Feasts and that the Divine Father drove around in a big Cadillac convertible.

"They couldn't abide by it, them uppity whites," Darn Good Disciple said. "Would ya'll believe it, they called in the police and had the Blessed Father arrested. Even claimed he had a harem."

"God-fearing with peace and love for everyone filling their hearts, black and white," said God's Tall Timber, "were jes' too much for them to accept. They be seein' a Peace Heaven grow amongst 'em, and 'stead of love, in return they wanted war."

Righteous Reckoning chimed in when describing that there was no reckoning equal to Father Divine's when he felt he was wronged. "Justice Lewis J. Smith couldn't imagine what he was callin' down from Heaven when he gave the Divine One a big fine and a year in jail. Nope, had no idea.

"Justice Smith couldn't see that he was looking into the face of peace in his courtroom. Couldn't understand the message, no matter that it floated right before his eyes. It was peace, brother, peace!" God's Tall Timber said. "Justice Lewis J. Smith died four days after messin' with the Divine One in *his* Heaven."

"I remember exactly what Reverend Major Jealous Divine said with sadness in his heart after Justice Lewis J. Smith passed. I memorized every word. Those words made me the believer I am today and put righteous fear in my heart: 'I hated to do it. I did not desire Judge Smith to die. I did desire that my spirit would touch his heart and change his mind that he might repent and believe and be saved from the grave!'" Righteous Reckoning stood tall and straight while reliving his epiphany.

"That poor Justice Smith, if he had only opened his heart. A harem indeed! He should have known that our International Peace Mission Movement has the strictest morality code on earth," God's Tall Timber intoned.

Richie had just been treated to a bravura performance of a blasphemy the trio rolled out whenever they met a genuine true-believer. They hadn't figured this kid out yet, if he fit into their plans, but he had listened transfixed so their bullshit was still working.

Richie was surprised to learn that there was no greater patriot than Father Divine, who gave his blessing to the good work of the Founding Fathers and the men who fought in the war, gave advice to Franklin Delano Roosevelt himself, and, in fact, decided to be an FDR neighbor of sorts when he purchased an estate across the Hudson from the president's Hyde Park home and called it Krum Elbow. Richie was bombarded by the Scripture according to Father Divine: segregation was wrong, lynching must end. FDR's welfare was a handout that weakened men's spirits.

"A man gots to work," Righteous Reckoning chimed in. "Else he ain't no man."

Funny, Richie thought. *That's what Dad always says.*

Aside from the sermons, he enjoyed their stories about Father Divine. Mostly he just accepted them. But one day, he heard the one about Johnny Mercer, the big time song writer and just couldn't believe it.

"Ya'll know that he be a Southern white boy, I mean Deep South, down in Savannah, Georgia," Darn Good Disciple said as he draped the barber's cape over Richie's shoulders. "Ya'll know he got the words of the song you hear right this day, right now and everywhere di-rec-lee from the Divine Father."

"What song?"

"Ac-cent-tchu-ate the Positive, son."

"That's the song they were singing at the parade."

"Yep," he said. Pinning the cape behind Richie's neck, Darn Good Disciple began singing the song in a low purring voice.

Righteous Reckoning chimed in from his perch near the front door, "Oh, yeah, don't mess with Mr. In-Between."

"Are you kidding, those words are from Father Divine?" Richie said.

"It be all true when we tell you about the Divine Father," Righteous Reckoning said, taking over the conversation. "Johnny Mercer, the big man his self, was humbled down a piece to accept the Divine word and pass it on."

"But he's at the top of the charts," Richie said.

"And the Divine one done put him there."

Richie was skeptical. How could a Negro preacher be behind a hit national song? It wasn't even religious. That's when he started to have second thoughts about Father Divine and his followers.

Chapter

7

As time went on, things started to fall into place for Richie about the Peace Barber Shop. Like their Southern talk. Richie knew one Negro kid from the neighborhood, Marvin Davidson, and he didn't talk like the Divinites did. He didn't know where Marvin's family came from before they bought their house on Morton Street, but he thought it was someplace in the South. If they came from the South, wouldn't he sound like Darn Good Disciple and the rest of them?

But Marvin never sounded like these guys. He'd never forget the first time he met him. It was in Milt's Confectionary just after he moved to Newark. Richie and Mary MacDonough, widely admired in the neighborhood as the "Profanity Pump," because she swore like a drunken sailor, were sipping Cokes in a front booth. Mrs. Sedworth sat in a back booth, enjoying a seltzer with a twist of lemon. She always stopped by on her way to the market. Mrs. Sedworth lived in a Victorian around the corner on High and was always elegantly dressed when she went out, usually with a pearl necklace and matching shoes and handbag. Business was slow that day.

The door opened and in walked this tall Negro kid. He was wearing cords, a blue T-shirt, and Converse sneakers. He took a stool at the soda fountain. No one said a word, not even Milt. Black kids just didn't wander into Milt's and everyone was shocked.

"I'd like to have a tall glass of Spur, sir," the kid said. He took a quarter from a front pocket and put it on the counter. "Spur beats Coke or Royal Crown any day."

Richie just stared. *This kid really knows what he wants*, he thought.

Milt, a short man with elfin features and mannerisms nodded, not saying a word, poured the Spur and gave Marvin fifteen cents change.

"Thank you, sir," he said and slowly sipped his drink. When he was done, he swiveled on his stool and turned to Richie and Mary. "I'm Marvin Davidson. Me and my family just moved into our house across the street, but I'm thinking you already know that."

"Uh…Hi," Richie said, a little embarrassed although he didn't know why. "I'm Richie Maxwell and this is Mary MacDonough."

"Nice to meet you. I'll see you around."

He stood to leave just as Mrs. Sedworth passed on her way to the front door. He walked quickly to the front in time to open the door for her. "Please, let me get it for you," Marvin said as he stepped aside to let her pass.

The middle-aged woman slowed for a moment, looked searchingly at the Negro boy, and struggled for a reply. "Thank you, young man. Thank you very much."

Marvin followed her outside, closing the door behind him, and while she headed toward High, he walked across the street.

After he left, Profanity Pump finally got her voice back. "Can you beat the shit outta that?" she said, living up to a well-earned reputation. "Who the fuck does he think he is? He better watch his ass around here."

No one knew for certain who dubbed Mary "Profanity Pump." It could have been Milt, but most probably it was one of the older kids from the Prep. They would have noticed her with her dark hair, blue eyes, really great skin, and straight teeth.

Nobody doubted that she was still a virgin, and everyone believed that her first time had better be good. Or else.

"That guy better know what he's doing or he'll pay for it," eighth-grader Leo Baldoni said, grinning as he described his fantasy. "If Pump was pissed off, she'd probably slap his monkey around real good." Smiling listeners agreed.

She was a year older than Richie and the others in his gang, was a year ahead of them at St. Mark's, and would probably end up at Central High.

No one could picture her at St. Mike's or St. James with their nuns, priests, and limp-wristed lay teachers who were probably all 4-F draft dodgers.

When Pump got going she could rattle it out like a machine gun. Quite simply, she was great. The best. Pump set the standard as to which guys had a pair of balls and who didn't, and she let you know it. And boy, could she string it all together without taking a breath.

Her crowning glory was the time Stan Wysnoski put his hands roughly on her shoulders during a spat. She pushed them off, glared defiantly, and set him on his heels: "Never put those cock mittens on me again or you'll be jerking off with your feet. Getit!"

Richie was not alone in admiring how those two little words once clamped together said it all. When she said "Getit!" you knew she was through with you and don't forget it.

Like Richie, Pump had watched Marvin in open-mouthed silence. By keeping her yap stuffed when she could have shot it off, Pump was saying with her silence that Marvin had balls.

Richie just nodded. But he had to admire Marvin's style. Here he was a new kid, a new *Negro* kid, in a white neighborhood, acting like he had lived there all his life. He just might be okay.

He talks normal, like the rest of the kids in the neighborhood. *The guys in the barber shop seemed to be putting on some kind of "jive" Nigger talk just for him. Why?*

They opened the Peace Barber Shop at seven o'clock every morning except Sunday. Richie was usually there at seven-thirty for his haircut. He could remember only four or five other haircut customers during the times he'd been there. But there was always a steady flow of Negro men and women, entering the shop from the side to the back door.

One morning, after Darn Good Disciple had finished Richie's haircut, some Negro men and women entered the shop through the side door. Richie caught Righteous Reckoning's nod in their direction as they covered the few steps to the back of the shop. Through an open door, he saw at least a dozen men and women seated at three long tables. Some were sorting coins. Others were counting bills. At least half of them were working with little bits of paper.

A few weeks later, Richie turned onto Spruce on his way to the shop for his twice a month trimming. Five Negroes, two of them women, had just turned down the alley leading to the shop's side door. At first glance, it was nothing he hadn't seen before, but a closer look pulled him up short. *Holy shit*, he thought, *what happened to them? Looks like somebody really worked them over.* The two women wore Band-Aids on their faces. One of the men had a bandaged right hand, and another sported a bandage over his left ear. The third man had a homemade sling, looked like a kitchen towel, supporting his left arm.

Richie took two deep drags of his Lucky, before stubbing it out and dropping the butt back in the pack and went inside.

Righteous Reckoning sat in his usual spot by the front door, and Darn Good Disciple sat in a barber's chair.

"Mornin', Richie," Darn Good said as he snapped open a fresh cape and motioned him to the middle chair. He draped the cape over Richie's shoulders and snapped it closed behind his neck.

After finishing up, Darn Good Disciple spun Richie around so he could admire his haircut in the big wall mirror. The rear door was partially opened, enough for Richie to see and hear what was going on in the backroom. One man was yelling while the others were nodding in approval.

"They was waitin' on us! Damn near busted my arm," the man said. "Can hardly lift it. Ain't no way a nigger's gonna pick up policy slips from a white man's parlor and walk away as big as you please."

Righteous Reckoning got up and shut the door.

"Hey, Darn Good, sounds like you've got an angry bunch here today," Richie said.

Darn Good Disciple looked at the other two barbers. "Nah, them folks is just doing Father Divine's business for the mission. They ain't customers. They's just volunteering for the Lord."

"I guess," Richie said, still playing dumb. "That guy seemed pretty mad."

Darn Good gave a glance at Righteous. "Always some problems with good work. Some folks don't take kindly to our ministerin' in the neighborhood."

"Especially the white folks," Righteous added.

"It looks pretty serious anyway."

"The sin of greed be an ugly thing. The Devil's poison. Makes folks do bad things. But it ain't nothin' the Divine One can't handle."

"Amen!" the other men said.

Darn Good looked at Richie in the mirror. "Son, you are one smart white boy. I always knew you was special. I said so, the day you showed up here. Ain't that right, boys?"

The two men nodded in agreement.

"We're like family here. And after all this time, we'd like to think you feel the same way."

What happened to all that Southern talk? Richie wondered. "Thanks. I like you guys too."

"And families take care of their own."

"Amen!" the other men said

"Father Divine says knowledge is a good thing. A golden blessing. But you got to know what's what. What's important and what's not. He says that knowing don't always mean sharing, especially outside the family. You catch my drift?"

"I ain't no snitch, if that's what you mean."

Darn Good Disciple smiled and took off the cape. "Now, that's what I'm talking about." Richie stood and gave him a dime for the cut.

"No need for that, son. It's on Father Divine today. After all, you're part of the family now."

"Thanks, see you next time." Richie left the shop, feeling that something big and nasty was happening at the Peace Barber Shop.

Chapter

8

Everything seemed to be back to normal when Richie returned two weeks later. That is until God's Tall Timber walked over as he was getting comfortable in Darn Good's chair.

"You know, Richie, we been worried about you," God's Tall said.

"Thanks, but I'm fine."

"Glad to hear it. But you've become a real big question for a lot of the folks in and around this part of the world," the tall man said. "Tell me, they got a track team over at St. Mark's? Maybe cross country, you know, long distance?"

Richie wondered what was coming. "Yeah, kind of a track team, only three CYO meets a year, the big one at the Armory, and a couple against other parishes over at Branch Brook Park. Why?"

"Now, that's interesting. You said you live on Morton between Quitman and High, and that's close. No more than ten minutes. But on the mornings you come here you've been spotted all over the ward, taking the long way but never stopping anyplace until you get here, at our side door. We all thought you were on the team and did all that walking to stay in shape," the big man said, his voice low and confidential almost in his ear.

Righteous Reckoning was in his usual position, paying close attention to the back door that had been left ajar about three inches.

They've been watching me? Richie was nervous. His stomach fluttered. "Nah. I'm not on the team. It's just that…"

"No, Richie, no need to talk," the big man said gently. "We know. Your friends are important to you. Sometimes even friends can be hardhearted. It wouldn't do for them to know that you come here for your haircuts."

Richie nodded.

"That's just fine. No need to rock the boat. But we care about you, son. Since you are going to come cross country for a haircut, we've come up with an idea. Actually, it was Righteous Reckoning. Tell him about the great idea you've cooked up, brother."

"My brother is very kind. But I can't take the credit," Righteous Reckoning said. "No sir. It's the inspiration from Father Divine that gave me the idea. All the time it takes you to get here, we figured you need a bike. You know how to ride, don't you?"

A bike? Richie thought. *How the hell am I gonna get a bike?* "Sure, learned as a kid. It would be swell to have a bike, but my folks don't have the dough."

"Now, we thought about that. Times are hard. But Father Divine is generous to his family. He wants to help you get a bike to lighten your load."

"What's the catch?"

"Lord almighty, did I tell you this boy was smart?" Darn Good said.

"You did, brother. You did," Righteous said. "Now, Richie, it ain't nothing much. Just a favor from one family member to another. There's even some extra money in it for you."

"Yeah, I'm listening."

"You know all them people in the back? They're doing the Father's work, collecting money from folks around the neighborhood to help out. But most of the black folks around here don't have much. Father was inspired to extend his work over to our white neighbors."

"So you need someone to collect from the whites, and that's where me and the bike come in. Do I get that right?"

Righteous Reckoning smiled. "You got it. And you can pick up a few dollars for your trouble."

"I appreciate it. I really do. There's just one problem."

"What's that, little brother?"

"If I get a bike, how do I explain where it comes from? My folks and my friends will ask."

"Good thinking. Father loves a deep thinker," Righteous Reckoning said. "We got that all figured out."

"How does a *Star Beacon* paper route sound to you? I think your folks will like that."

"*Star Beacon* routes ain't easy to get. I've got buddies been waiting months for a shot at one of them, so I never bothered. Besides the wop guy Marsucci who does all the hiring is a slime bag. What I heard, he's got twenty kids under him and gets a buck a month kick-back from each."

"Frank Marsucci has his faults. A man with faults always has debts to pay. So Richie, let's just say Mr. Marsucci owes us. There's a route waiting for you, that is if you want it."

"Okay, so far. So what about the bike?"

"Father Divine's got lots of friends. Like the old Jew Simon. I'm sure he has a nice used bike in his shop he's more than willing to donate to the cause."

"Just like that?"

Darn Good nodded. "He's a good friend of ours, always willing to help our good work."

Richie's wheels were turning. "What do I tell my dad? Simon's so tight, he'd never give me a bike."

"Let's just say you convinced him to let it go 'on time.' You be paying off from the newspaper money. Ain't nothing wrong with a little misleading now and then."

"What about the collections?"

"On your route, you pick up the donations at the twelve places we give you along the way, then bring 'em back here. You get five-cents each pick up."

"It sure sounds good…okay, I'm in."

Darn Good slapped him on the back. "It's a deal, my little brother. Tonight you can bring Father Divine's tidings home to your folks. That you are now a *Star Beacon* delivery boy with a route right in your own neighborhood. I can just see the big smile on your daddy's face."

The three men stepped aside to allow Richie to slide out of the barber's chair. There were smiles all around as they shook hands. Richie felt as light as a feather as he headed out the side door. He didn't notice that the back door to the betting parlor had been ajar.

They turned just as a trim, olive-skinned man, about thirty years old, pushed open the rear door, and with a twist of his right hand indicated that he wanted the front door locked. "And close the blinds," he said.

With a shrug, he straightened his navy blue, pinstripe suit coat, fingered the Windsor of his silk, blue tie and pulled down the starched cuffs of his white shirt to expose two heavy garnet and gold cufflinks. He glided into the center chair, rested his Florsheims on the footrest, scanned the three black faces and smirked, "Really laid on that Father Divine bullshit, don'cha think?"

"Come on, Vinnie, give us some credit. We only use what works, and we've been working this kid for weeks now. You like what you heard?" God's Tall Timber said.

"The kid can smell money, but does he have the *coglioni* to pull it off?" Vinnie Scarlatti said. "We agreed to take it slow like you asked after five of your people got busted up. Don't prove us wrong."

"Jimmy Rossi gave you the skinny on us," Tall Timber said, "that we're not just three dumb niggers from Georgia."

"Okay, so you're three smart spooks. Talk to me, tell me what I want to hear."

"For now, we're set up pretty," Righteous Reckoning said. "But we'll be moving the parlor outta here. Gotta great spot picked out, right in the middle of the action."

"What's this shit about moving out," the mobster said. "I'm going to say it one fucking time. You don't do so much as fart without clearing it with me. You did good by Rossi in Atlanta, that's why we're even talking. But this ain't Atlanta. When does this kid start?"

"Soon, real soon," Darn Good Disciple said. "We'll let you know when we put things in play."

"Don't mess it up. This is payback time for Richie the Boot. He's got eight shotgun slugs bouncing around inside him, thanks to Longy. He figures the Third Ward is ripe for the picking, and he handed me the job. The boss isn't a forgive and forget kinda guy, and neither am I."

Scarlatti got up, paused briefly to admire himself in the rear mirror, and walked out the side door.

How far can I trust these three coons, he thought as he walked to the black Buick parked behind the barbershop.

Scarlatti was still trying to sort things out when he slid behind the wheel of his car, turned on the ignition and slowly idled out the alley on his way downtown.

Rossi's a made man and you've got to take his word, he thought. *Let's just hope it isn't bullshit. Says they were real smooth in Atlanta with a barbershop bookie operation and a big bucks policy parlor. We'll see how they fit into a Third Ward turf battle.*

Scarlatti turned onto Broadway and parked his Buick in an alley that ran along the north side of Caffé Palermo. He entered through a side door for an early dinner of scungilli over pasta, antipasto broccolini with anchovies and garlic, a nice bottle of chianti, and grappa to tamp it all down. He was not about to let his anxiety affect his appetite.

That evening Richie waited until they were well into dinner, and his father was cutting into his second helping of meatloaf when he broke it to them. "It's not for sure yet, but it looks real good that I've got a *Star Beacon* route. I'll know for sure tomorrow afternoon when I see the circulation manager."

"That's great news," Andy Maxwell said as he reached out with his right hand to clap his son's shoulder. "How the hell did you get it? From what I hear they're hard to come by?"

"I got lucky, I guess. Seems the top of the list just sort of dried up and I was next in line," Richie lied.

"You never told us you put your name in for a paper route," Alice Maxwell said. "I'm so proud of you. Do you know when you'll be starting? Do you know where the route is? And how big it is? Remember, you'll have to work in your altar boy commitments and school work."

"Don't worry, Mom. The route is right around here. I start next week."

"There's no problem that our son can't work out," his father said. "From what I've seen, bundles are dropped off real early. I've spotted kids rolling their paper as early as five. How you going to get around?"

Richie paused. "I'm going to Simon's. He's got used bikes there. Maybe he'll let me pay it 'on time' once he knows I've got a route."

"I'm impressed," his mother said as she reached over and lightly ruffled his hair. "Seems we have a real operator under our roof."

"Step aside, Rockefeller, here comes Richie Maxwell," his dad said. "I don't think you'll have to worry about that greedy old Jew going for it." He smiled, "Now you can pay for your own haircuts."

Chapter

9

At thirty-five Alice Maxwell retained the Gaelic beauty that had captivated her husband fifteen years earlier. Her maturity was the firm-fleshed kind that came with planning well and loving wisely. After she had Richie, she had looked at the girls she knew from the neighborhood and had been appalled at their lives. A house full of kids, frumpy house dresses, Tuesday novenas, no money and husbands that spent more time in the pubs than at home – the fate of a good Catholic wife. She was determined that she would not become one of them.

As an unflagging disciple of Margaret Sanger, she was a member of Planned Parenthood. Each Sunday, she attended Mass at St. Mark's under the black cloud of mortal sin for not following the Church's teaching about birth control. Richie was the Maxwells' only child. There would be no more. Her friends were horrified, but she didn't care. They all had loads of kids. Alice wanted more out of life than diapers. On Andy's limited salary, they'd never get ahead with more mouths to feed. It was hard enough.

With Richie about to enter the eighth grade, they were giving serious thought to his high school. A good high school education meant he had a shot at going to college, maybe even a scholarship. They were in the Central High School District, but the school was out of the question. With all the blacks moving into the Ward, they never felt comfortable about sending him to Central. Catholic Prep was too expensive. So they set their sights on the more affordable tuitions at St. James, St. Michael, and Good Counsel, but found that since they weren't parishioners, tuitions at all three were too steep for their budget as well.

Without telling Andy, she went to St. Mark's rectory for help. Father Schneider sympathized, then passed her over to his new assistant Father Nolan. The young priest heard her out, and said he would make some phone calls.

From the start, she doubted this would go anywhere. The young priest was new in town. He probably didn't yet understand the problem. That the city's parish high schools were feeling the enrollment crunch as white Catholic families fled the public schools. The following week after mass, Father Nolan stopped her as she was leaving church.

"I talked to the principals at all three schools, even put in a call across the river to St. Cecilia's in Kearny," he said. "I got the same story from each of them. Their classrooms are bursting and money is tight. Father McDonough at St. Cecilia's said they could squeeze in your son, but at double the parish tuition."

Alice Maxwell studied the priest's face, and was convinced that he had done his best. He had not brushed her off, and she was thankful for that. Maybe there was some fresh blood pumping at St. Mark's.

"Thanks for your effort, Father. I couldn't ask for more than you've done."

"I'm sorry it didn't work out," Father Nolan said, then turned to acknowledge other exiting parishioners.

That past August salvation came in the person of Ruth Zellman. As volunteers at the clinic, Alice and Ruth had developed a kinship of sorts. Both had a secular outlook toward their religion that they openly shared during coffee breaks. Both also agreed that there was only one public high school in Newark still worthwhile, Weequahic, out in the south part of the city. The city's student population was exploding, and it was almost impossible to transfer from one district to another without a valid reason. Ruth supplied Alice with a real beauty.

"From what you've been telling me about your son Richie," Ruth locked eyes with Alice over the lip of her coffee cup, took a sip, leaned back and said, "learning Hebrew has always been one of his driving passions, and Weequahic will make his dream come true."

"Hebrew?" Alice stammered.

"I don't care if you and your family know only a few words of Yiddish," Ruth said. "They've got to be persuaded that for your son, a world without Hebrew is no world at all."

"Just exactly how do I do that?" a perplexed but hopeful Alice responded, as she tingled with anticipation.

Over three cups of clinic coffee, Alice learned that Weequahic offered four years of Hebrew with class size limited to twenty students. Four of the desks were for non-district kids, and it was Alice's job to make sure Richie was in one of them.

"I have a few strong contacts at the school. I'll make some calls. Lay the groundwork and see if I can get a date for you to meet with Seth Greenberg, the department head. That'll probably take two or three weeks. Prepare yourself—Seth is convinced he has a mandate from God."

Alice found that Ruth was right; Seth was a tough nut to crack, but she was confident she opened the door wide enough for Richie to jump district boundaries next fall to the best high school in Newark. But my God, Hebrew, Alice thought. She could just see the explosion that would rock the Maxwell apartment when she broke the news to the men at home.

Two weeks later her fears were justified.

"Richie, how much Yiddish or Hebrew do you know?" she asked in her breezy best as she set down plates of spaghetti and meatballs in front of her son and husband.

"Hardly anything," Richie said. "Just *mentsh, putz* and *shnuk*. Milt throws them around all the time. Why do you ask?"

"Because it looks like you're going to be learning a lot more."

"What the hell does that mean?" Andy asked.

"It looks like we found a high school for Richie, and learning Hebrew is his ticket. Weequahic High, the city's best, offers a course. I think I've convinced them to give Richie one of the four spots open for non-district students."

"Convinced them, who the hell have you been talking to?" Andy demanded. "And why the hell am I just now learning about all this?"

"The teacher's name is Seth Greenberg. I met with him two times, and yesterday I got a note in the mail from him saying he would recommend Richie for a spot in his class."

"How about me, don't I have any say?" Richie said. "That school is loaded with kikes, and how the hell am I gonna fit in? Have you figured that out?"

"How long have you been a Jew lover?" Andy said, his face a deep red and the veins in his temples clearly visible. "With everything now going on, you're saying we've got to kiss a Jew's ass in order to get our son into a good school. Is that what you're telling us?"

"Yes, you're damn right. That's what I'm saying. I'm not ashamed of it. You, more than anyone, know what a good education can mean. And you Richie, you're only going to get one shot at it, and this is probably it. We've got a lot more to talk about, so everyone calm down. Let's eat."

College was a touchy subject in the Maxwell home. Her husband had attended St. Peter's College, a Jesuit school, for a year and half. That's where they'd met. She was Alice Doyle then, a nineteen year old secretary in the administrative office. He'd wooed her for the first year and they got serious. He had a part time job and worked hard to finish his studies. He planned to be a teacher. Then tragedy changed everything.

Andy's father, Kenneth Maxwell, was shocked to death while troubleshooting faulty electrical cable in the Hudson & Manhattan Railroad tunnel under the river. It hit Andy hard. Alice went to the funeral tried to comfort his mother, Valerie. She was devastated.

At least they didn't have to worry about money. It had taken decades for his father to reach senior supervisor status with the railroad, and this lofty position carried with it a tidy life insurance compensation package. It was enough to pay their expenses and Andy's college tuition. But several months after his father's death, Andy's mother started to go downhill. Crying all the time. Drinking. Then she got really sick. She descended into a world of delusional gloom that squeezed out reality. All she did all day was sit and stare out the window. Andy didn't know how to help her. He called a doctor, but he didn't help much. When Valerie had reached the point where constant care was necessary, Andy realized he couldn't cope.

Valerie's sister, Agnes, and her husband, Hugo Sandifer, stepped forward. Andy had never been close to them, but they were all the family his mother had. His dad was an orphan. They offered to take her in to live with them outside the city in Monmouth County, but at a price. Andy agreed that all of his mother's compensation package, still considered substantial in the midst of the Depression, would be signed over to the Sandifers. The furniture from the Maxwell apartment would be sold, with Andy's aunt and uncle getting the bulk of the money. The Sandifers had given Andy $100 to find a place to live. St. Peter's tuition was not discussed, and the school did not offer a scholarship. Andy had to drop out, his dream shattered. But Alice stuck by him and they continued dating. He found a cheap boarding house on York Street, not far from the college. She visited him there.

He worked part time at the neighborhood market to make ends meet and tried to visit his mother as much as he could. Every time he saw her, she seemed to get worse. His aunt and uncle said she was getting the best of care, but he didn't believe them. Later that year, the Sandifers sent word to Andy of his mother's death, due to natural causes. They buried her in All Hallows Cemetery deep in the Pine Barrens of Ocean County, not far from Tuckerton. Alice had gone with him to her grave where he collapsed in grief. They cried in each other arms. He never spoke to his aunt and uncle again.

Andy took a succession of day laborer jobs to pay the rent. There was a twelve-month deckhand job on a Hudson River cruise ship. The job came to an end when the company became yet another Depression casualty. Would-be river cruisers would rather spend their money putting a meal on the table than ogling the New Jersey Palisades, and the cannon at West Point.

In January, Alice matter-of-factly told him he was about to become a father. Two months later, they were married at Jersey City's City Hall. She wore her mother's white lace wedding dress, simple and a bit yellowed with age. Mr. and Mrs. Patrick Doyle, two married aunts, another aunt who was a nun, two unmarried uncles, and a hard-drinking stevedore cousin who couldn't stop hiccupping and burping witnessed the ceremony. A wedding reception followed at her parents' small frame home in Weehawken.

It was decided that the happy couple would live with the Doyles, temporarily, of course, until he got a steady job. Alice would continue at St. Peter's until the baby was born, then return afterwards if Andy didn't find a job. Andy tried desperately to keep a modicum of self-respect as his confidence dwindled. Times were hard and he couldn't find a job. He did a few turns on the docks, thanks to her cousin, but that was about all. Richie was born at the Hudson County Medical Center on August 20, 1931. Alice went back to St. Peter's and her mother minded little Richie.

In April 1935, the Works Progress Administration became their salvation. The WPA's purse strings in New Jersey were controlled by Jersey City mayor Frank Hague, and he liked to make sure his local boys were first in line. The WPA didn't pay much, but the paychecks were steady and carried with them a veneer of pride that Andy and thousands like him badly needed.

On one of the projects, he'd overheard that Cracroft Pump & Steel out in Harrison had just gotten a government contract and was hiring. Andy got the job, and they'd moved out of her parents' home and into an apartment across the Passaic River from Cracroft in Newark's East Ward. Alice quit her job and stayed home with the baby. Cracroft supplied the military with badly needed turbines enabling Andy to get a 2B draft deferment for the duration.

When the war effort dwindled down after VE Day, Cracroft began cutting back and Andy was among the skeleton crew keeping the company alive. A pink slip in his pay envelope was inevitable. With all the vets returning from the war, good jobs would be hard to come by.

Alice and Andy Maxwell were survivors. They wanted more than that for their son. Alice was convinced that Weequahic High would be the first step in shaping a better future for him.

After that spaghetti and meatball dinner, Richie was more confused than ever. Weequahic was a crosstown commute by bus. Where would he get the time? All around him money was scarce, and the only people he knew that had more than a buck or two in their pockets were shady characters at best. He had made three commitments that he hoped would put him on easy street. He couldn't go back on any of them without going back on all of them, the numbers, Marsucci, and the three black bookies. He had to figure it out, and he had some time. His first Hebrew class wasn't until next September.

Chapter

10

Clear, chilly autumn mornings in Newark have a sort of transcendental beauty that lifts the city out of its blighted self. The expectant warmth of the first rays of the sun cut the drabness of the city in which most of its 430,000 souls lived. The smell of autumn in the air and the rich amber color of the fallen leaves gave people a kind of renewed hope for the future. These delicate, but forlorn traces of beauty, no less magnificent for their setting, enthralled Eli Simon on his daily walk from his apartment to his business.

This Friday morning the sparkle of weak sunlight reflected from a tenement window, glistened on a dewy branch of oak leaves. Simon paused for a moment to enjoy the sight, and then went on. Another sight along the way was less pleasant. The sunlight that caressed the oak tree also bathed a bent old man rummaging through garbage cans. His filthy fingers retrieved a rotten scrap of meat, wiped coffee grinds from it and threw it on the ground for his mangy dog to eat. The dog worked the meat to its back teeth. It moaned in pain as it chewed. All the time, the man patted the dog on the head. "Timmy, Timmy. There, Timmy, Timmy."

Simon paused briefly. He'd seen horrible sights during the war in his native Germany. Poverty, hunger, dehumanization. He wanted to reach out to the man, to help somehow. The old bum spotted Simon. "What you looking at, you Kike cocksucker. Fuck off!" Words formed on his lips, shaping thoughts that in Simon's world were better left unsaid.

Shaking his head, Simon moved on. The walk from his four-room third-floor Lido apartment took him past block after block of the Ward's "Black Belt." He arrived at the store and looked up at the sign as he did each morning.

SIMON'S

WE BUY, SELL AND TRADE FOR JUST ABOUT ANYTHING

His shop, a low, brown-painted wood building that had taken on an L-shape with two recent additions stood in the center of a large lot on Quitman and Waverly. The remainder of the lot was enclosed in rusty chain-link fencing. Three parallel strands of barbed wire four inches apart spanned the entire length of the fence. The yard was filled with the rotting but still usable debris of a neighborhood that itself was becoming the swollen flotsam of a city cast adrift.

As he unlocked the metal gate and entered, he looked around at the mountains of junk he'd accumulated over his years in business in America. It was a far cry from the small, elegant art gallery he once owned on Berlin's Pariser Platz, a short walk from the Academy of the Arts, and even closer to the Adlon Hotel, the city's finest. His late father, David Simon, had been a professor of art history at Berlin University. His mother, Anne Loepke Simon, was an operatic voice teacher whose students were among the most gifted in all of Germany. Their music filled the family's fourteen-room home in the fashionable Bayerisches Viertel area. He remembered the sophisticated lifestyle they lived before Hitler took control.

His family was among the Ashkenazim who saw no need to flee Germany during the early years of the Nazi takeover. They were used to the political upheavals in Germany since the Great War. This new party was no different than the others. His mother, up to the moment of her death in 1936, believed there was nothing for an educated Jew to fear. She would proudly recite names of Jewish academics, physicians, scientists, financiers, entrepreneurs, and even ranking military officers.

"Our people fought in the trenches, died in the trenches," his mother said. "We collected our share of Iron Crosses. We are Germans. We have nothing to fear."

Simon's family and other members of Germany's artistic Jewish community had become delusional in their denial of the inevitable.

After graduating the university, Simon became involved in the rich tradition of art in Berlin, making friends among the young artists at the time. He opened his gallery with the help of his uncles, and showcased their work with growing success.

However, Joseph Goebbels, Hitler's hate-filled propaganda boss and cultural czar, despised the new artists and used the Reich Culture Chamber as his bludgeon against them. Only racially pure artists were allowed to show their work. Simon's gallery showcased artists who refused to pander to Hitler's regime.

Unlike others in his family, Simon refused to wear blinders about what was happening around them. Simon realized he no longer had the moral resources to confront the inevitable. Was it cowardice that conflicted him? This question first began to eat away at him in the most unlikely of places, his safe sanctuary in Berlin that after the deaths of his mother and father contained the only things that mattered to him. Simon's doubts were confirmed the day his landlord, Kurt Hoffman, strode cockily into his spacious second-floor gallery. The gallery's rent had gone up four times in three years, the bad tidings delivered each time by a contemptuously smiling Hoffman.

"Hello again, Eli Simon," Hoffman said, smirking. "Things must be going well for you. Your stock appears to be low. Lots of buyers, I presume."

"It seems so."

"You know, Herr Simon, that if you weren't such a good tenant, I would have turned you in a long time ago for the smut you sell."

Simon didn't address that veiled threat. "And I take it that before you leave today I'll need be an even better tenant."

"How perceptive of you; how perceptive indeed. But we'll get to that later. I always find a visit to your gallery rewarding."

Hoffman strode about the gallery inspecting Simon's painstakingly collected treasures. He paused and peered closely at two small, beautifully framed abstracts by Paul Klee. "Ah, I see you have Klees. Controversial these days. Is he still around?"

"You know as well as I do he's a sick man and has been in Switzerland for the past five years."

Hoffman continued his tour. "You are well aware, Herr Simon, that the Fuhrer has declared that there is no place in the Third Reich for modernist and experimental art. Only the simple virtues of our beloved Fatherland are acceptable."

"Heir Hoffman, with respect, what is the reason for your visit. Come on, out with it. As if I didn't already know."

Simon had been seated at his desk during Hoffman's cruel word game. The man now stood stiff and correct in front of the desk. "Your rent is now doubled starting in July. I trust you will continue to be an excellent tenant." Hoffman hissed the words out, nodded, and headed toward the gallery entrance.

Simon knew it was only a matter of time before Hoffman tired of playing his little mocking word games, and decided the ever-bigger rent checks were no substitute for Nazi accolades awarded for exposing a subversive Jew.

That evening, Simon made plans to get out of Germany. He disposed of his collection piecemeal. First to friends, and then through contacts in Switzerland and France. The art world was filled with sharks that sensed instinctively when there was blood in the water, and Simon was bleeding. It was all over in three weeks. By late July, Simon had his passport in hand, and cash and some jewelry sewn into the left lining of his overcoat. Inside the right side were two Klee's, flat without frames.

Under the sponsorship of his cousin Isaac Weinstein, he boarded a tramp steamer at Hamburg bound for the United States, and a week later landed in the port of New York. His cousin met him at the dock and took him in until he got on his feet.

To have a gallery in New York had been Simon's dream. His timing couldn't have been worse. The depression had taken its toll. By 1938, the one hundred forty art galleries in Manhattan had dwindled to thirty. Polarization had set in. The Upper East Side galleries catered to the ultra-wealthy, while in the Village the avant-garde galleries offered the more affordable works of up and coming artists. There was no place for Simon.

His cousin Isaac came to his rescue. He had heard that the elderly widow of a Jewish pawnbroker in Newark was anxious to sell her husband's shop. The blacks were taking over the area, and she wanted out as quickly as possible. The money Simon had stashed in the lining of his coat was more than enough to close the deal. The old woman moved in with her daughter in Irvington on the other side of town.

Times were hard and pawn shops did a brisk business. Simon, a bachelor, devoted all his energies to his new enterprise. He developed a reputation for fair dealing and people trusted him.

Less than four months after his arrival in New Jersey, he read in *Aufbau,* the Jewish newspaper from New York, that Herschel Grynszpan, a seventeen-year-old Jewish émigré living in Paris, gained access to the German embassy and pumped three bullets into diplomat Ernst von Rath to protest his family's expulsion from Hanover to Poland. Von Rath's death propelled the Gestapo, SS storm troopers and the Hitler Youth onto the streets of every city in Germany. It was *Kristallnacht,* the Night of Broken Glass. Simon's cultivated stoicism evaporated when he called his cousin Isaac. Isaac's voice cracked several times, and he was obviously having trouble getting the words out.

"Eli, can you believe? Can you even imagine? Synagogues by the hundreds destroyed, all gone. Gone! I never thought the Nazi swine would go this far. Thousands of shops and homes were ripped apart and looted. So far, almost a hundred Jews have been killed by those strutting SS and Gestapo pigs."

A cold sweat drained Simon. The memory of that June afternoon encounter with Hoffman crystallized and hardened to hatred. He could imagine the servile little man first currying favor with the Gestapo, then happily leading the way as they pillaged his beloved gallery.

"We both know this is only the beginning," Simon said. "They aren't finished with us yet."

Simon had surprised himself with his involuntary "us." His father was a freethinker and didn't believe in religion at all. If it wasn't for his mother and her love of tradition, his family would not have followed even the most rudimentary Jewish orthodoxy. His mother did not keep a Kosher home, even for the holidays. They were members of a temple but only to keep up appearances with their neighbors and friends. They hardly attended. He had a bar mitzvah, but his religious training ended there. Yet, when all was said and done, they still identified as Jews.

Simon gently placed the receiver in the cradle of his newly installed telephone. He walked across the living room of his Lido apartment and gripped the fireplace mantle until his fingers turned numb in anger and disgust. That was a year before Hitler's war machine invaded Poland and the Holocaust began.

Inside his shop Simon kept furniture and other large items on the floor and in a back room. In a dusty glass case, he displayed smaller objects such as tarnished wedding rings; religious icons; fake baubles; medals from long lost heroes; and a few antique handguns. Rows of combat plane cards, each taken from a pack of Wings cigarettes, lined the wall behind Simon's desk. Kids collected these cards, and traded them for used issues of Batman or Superman comics. Simon had switched to Wings, with their atrocious flavor, when he found that a P-51 Mustang had value. After the war ended, interest in fighter planes dwindled and Wings stopped offering them as nicotine inducements. Simon switched back to Camels.

Chapter

11

Simon had developed a tough but fair method of dealing with his customers. Black or white, he treated them all with respect. The cops who patrolled the neighborhood knew he ran a good, clean business. He prospered. Until the day two of Longy Zwillman's thugs stepped through the front door.

The smaller of the two was neatly dressed with a gabardine suit, freshly blocked hat, and gloves. His companion was big, dark and forbidding, and carried a leather briefcase. His blue suit was rumpled and his tie was food stained. He had a wide smile that could be described as friendly until Simon noticed his expressionless eyes. "What can I do for you gents?" Simon said with some hesitation.

"We got something for you to push."

Simon looked at the little man. "I'm sorry, but I have enough merchandise."

"You'll like this stuff. It's like printing money. Hy, show the man."

The big man lifted the briefcase onto the counter and opened it. It contained pornography, magazines, pictures, cards, even 8 mm films.

"It's all top quality, a lot of it's from Argentina, the best. They do more than tango down there." Simon glanced at the cards and at the other crude wares. He knew two things: he could sell them at a good profit, and they were illegal.

"I run a clean business. I can't use these things. I don't want any trouble."

"No trouble. Just take it."

"Why me?"

"Let's just say we've been watching you. Longy trusts you."

Simon knew all about Abner "Longy" Zwillman, and his gang of Jewish hitmen. Zwillman's specter had been hovering over Newark's Jewish community for decades when Simon arrived. Zwillman had come a long way since hawking fruits and vegetables from a horse-drawn wagon on Prince Street. The old-timers with their pushcarts had long ago staked out Prince Street as their own, and Longy suffered probably the only setback of his life. Then the policy racket came to his rescue, and he found that selling numbers to better-off Jewish housewives on Clinton Hill was just his ticket. It wasn't long before he and Mafia Boss Richie "the Boot" Boiardo sliced up Newark between them. Boiardo staking out the north precincts, with Zwillman controlling gambling, prostitution, and labor racketeering in the rest of the city. He dated Hollywood bombshell Jean Harlow while setting up legit businesses and coughing up a quarter million for slum clearance. He even offered a reward for the return of the Lindbergh baby.

It took a while, even a stint with Murder Incorporated, before Zwillman would inherit the title "the Al Capone of New Jersey" after Dutch Schultz was gunned down in a Chinese joint in downtown Newark.

Simon saw him every Sunday at the Mercer Shvitz, billed by owners Gussie and Isador Goldberg as the most modern sweat bath in New Jersey. His weekly steam bath was his only pleasure. It did more than clean Simon's pores and drain his sinuses. It returned him to his roots and a time when his life made a difference.

Every Sunday night he shared the steam room with Zwillman, whose retinue included a coterie of thugs, politicians, and some legitimate business types. It was hard for Simon to visualize the florid, pink-skinned Zwillman pushing his weight around with the Mafia Ruling Commission.

After shvitzing, Simon was a fly on the wall in Gussie's dining room, watching Zwillman hold court with his cronies. He watched and listened furtively while enjoying Gussie's thick vegetable soup, boiled chicken, and her surprise specialty, Greek salad. Nobody seemed to notice him. He was just another solitary Jew at the shivtz. But Longy's men must have asked the owner about him.

"Please, mister. This stuff is illegal. I could lose my business if the cops find out."

The man laughed, "Don't be a schmuck. We've got an arrangement downtown. No cops are going to be sniffing around. You get 40 percent. We'll send a guy around every month," he said with finality and closed the briefcase.

"But…" Simon stammered.

"I guess you don't hear so good," the big goon said. "This ain't no negotiation. You don't want nothing to happen to this dump you call a store, right?"

"Yeah, just make sure we got something to collect every month," the little man said. "*Zeit gezunt.*"

The two men turned and walked out the door. They strode down Quitman Street to High Street and disappeared around the corner. The intensity of Simon's frustration grew.

It was only after the two thugs had left that Simon conjured images of honor restored. Nearly six feet tall with heavily muscled shoulders and arms, and a 47-year old body hardened after seven years of hoisting, dragging and pulling junk in to and out of his shop, he could have held his own with the big thug. At least for a while, until the commotion attracted attention.

Instead, he now looked at the briefcase with fear and loathing. It was like the old days in Berlin. Thugs telling him what to do or else. Even in America, from his *own* people. He shrugged. World weary and jaded, he took the briefcase and put it on the floor. What choice did he have? He had become a master at bartering for goods from desperate people. Chipped mahogany chairs, tarnished jewelry, old clocks and broken bicycles – everything had a price and his customers knew he could help them get through. Catering to their darker urges was no different. The cellophaned boxes, glossy magazines, and cheap-papered, crudely drawn smut were no different from his other wares. It was all the stuff of broken dreams.

Pornography became part of a business that, at best, was an unholy alliance with that final degradation—the calculated profiteering on man's misfortune. It was a sickness that he first saw at the start of the war and had now reached epidemic proportions. It engulfed all of Newark but had recently become localized in the Third Ward, where the disease had surfaced as a crusty, self-inflicted wound.

Simon knew his customers and selectively sold his new line. Business was good. He thrust the neatly wrapped packages across the counter with solemn regularity, often to nice people and generally in large quantities.

"I like to keep something like this on hand for my special customers," explained a suburban bookstore owner on one of his monthly visits. "You know, the James Joyce and D.H. Lawrence fans, and all."

A nicely dressed man from the West Orange Elks Club figured some of Simon's playing cards could really "stoke up the old coals" at the club's regular stag smoker.

Each month a Zwillman runner came for the money. And each month Simon handed over a good chunk of change. True to their word, the cops never questioned him about it, and except for the times Officer Frank Gazzi nosed around, the police were never a bother.

Simon couldn't quite figure Gazzi out. He guessed him to be about forty or so, and at that age, probably a police veteran who was still walking a beat in a miserable part of town. It was obvious to him that Gazzi hated it all, the old Jews with their pushcarts blocking traffic on Prince Street, the Zwillman-protected whores, the bar fights that emptied onto the sidewalk, switchblade knifings, swaggering numbers runners, wife beatings, and voodoo priests illegally casting spells on street corners at twenty-five cents a pop. And now police protected pornography.

"Name's Gazzi, Frank Gazzi. Just took over the beat and to let you know I'll be around from time-to-time to see how things are going," Gazzi informed Simon that Saturday he first came around. "You've got a lot of stuff to keep your eye on."

"Thanks for stopping by," Simon was taken by surprise that afternoon. "Good to know we now have an officer on the street, not just cruising by in a squad car. New policy?"

"No, just extended the beat down the hill a few blocks, that's all."

From then on, Simon was careful how he talked to Gazzi. He didn't know if this cop was aware of how much money rolled into his shop each month from pornography. Or that his superiors and Zwillman made it all possible. He would play their relationship by ear and wait to see where Gazzi was coming from.

"Not much for small talk, but I can always find time for the police," said Simon, wondering if a two-bit shakedown was on its way.

"I'll be seeing you. Don't have to worry about that."

Simon knew one thing for certain, Gazzi hated this godforsaken neighborhood, and a man who hated his job could be dangerous.

Later that afternoon Simon gave little thought to Gazzi as he prepared for his weekend ritual. Adrift in an inner-city world of Philistines and having nothing in common with the Yiddish vendors on Prince Street, Simon hungered for even a small taste of what he had left behind in Berlin. He found it five years earlier in front of the Essex County Courthouse, the soul balm he was looking for.

Gutzon Borglum's *Seated Lincoln* beckoned Simon to sit beside him. Borglum's bronze sculpture was magnificent, and Simon found it impossible to resist. He climbed the stairs to share the bronze bench with the Great Man. Resident pigeons swarmed into the air and alighted a short distance away. Simon rested his left hand on Lincoln's extended right arm. He caressed the cool, hard surface. His elation was immediate.

Honest Abe was a magnet that pulled Simon to his cherished spot on the bench every Sunday morning. Each Saturday night on the way home, Simon would purchase a loaf of bread at an A&P Market and break it into pieces to feed the pigeons.

At exactly seven-thirty he could be found with his bag of bread crumbs in one hand climbing the steps to greet his friend Abe while the pigeons cooed with ravenous delight. Simon long ago accepted that Honest Abe was one of the only two friends he had.

The other was an abiding love of music inherited from his mother. The recorded melodies of Mendelssohn and Liszt that emanated from his apartment each night exposed Simon for what he was—an incurable romantic.

Chapter

12

Not long after he moved into his Lido apartment, he discovered the Fuld Hall monthly concerts at the YMHA on High Street.

It was during a recital of Mendelssohn's Sonata for Brass Septet that a woman took a seat next to him and introduced herself. She wore a two piece, blue jersey suit and white blouse. The only adornments were a small gold broach pinned to her lapel, a pearl necklace, and a wristwatch. Her auburn hair was upswept into a French twist. She wore only enough make-up needed to accentuate her high cheekbones and full lips.

"May I?" she said as she slid past him and took the seat to his right. "I'm Gail Dolan, and you are?"

This was Simon's tenth concert, and up to now, no one had ever spoken to him. At first glance, he figured her to be about forty-five and well taken care of in a subtle sort of way. He liked what he saw.

"Eli Simon," he said and awkwardly extended his right hand. A furtive peek at her hands disclosed no rings. "These recitals have been a big surprise for me. I live nearby, only a pleasant walk away. And you?"

"The same for me, but it's a little bit of a walk to get here," she said. "I live on West, just off William. I prefer smaller recitals like this rather than a full symphony orchestra, they're much more relaxing. How about you?"

"It depends on what kind of month it's been," Eli said, "and this month has been tiresome."

"Business?"

"Yes, business."

"Do you mind if I ask you what kind of business?"

"No, not at all. I have a pawn shop on Quitman, just off Waverly."

"Oh yes, I know it. Quite a big operation."

The musicians had finished warming up, and were settling into their places on the presidium stage. Two were women. All six were obviously accomplished and the Mendelssohn Sonata was performed flawlessly. Eli and Gail were immediately drawn in. They waited until the applause ended before resuming eye contact.

"Wonderful, just wonderful," Gail said. "It's my first time with this Mendelssohn piece. I loved his *Scottish Symphony*. And his piano works, especially *Capriccio Brillante*."

"Then you must love Schumann," Eli said. "I never tire of his *Symphony No. 1*. And the way he mastered the piano. My favorites are *Arabeske* and his four-handed *Scenes from a Ball*."

Eli could go on, but figured to do so he would only come across as a boring pedant. He didn't know why, but Gail Dolan seemed to be someone special. It had been a long time since he had made any attempt to impress a woman, and he somehow knew that in this case only a subtle approach would work.

On their way out to the street, they stopped briefly in the lobby to check the schedule of upcoming events.

"Ahh, Franz Liszt, another Romantic," Eli said. "A collection of his *Symphonic Poems*. Are you game?"

"Certainly."

Reaching the sidewalk, there was a momentary awkwardness before Gail said, "It's a beautiful spring evening. Just right for a stroll. Are you game?"

"Certainly," Eli said. "May I walk you home?"

"Certainly," a smiling Gail reciprocated.

It had been a long time since he had felt so much at ease with a woman. His cousin Isaac and his wife, Rachel, had three times invited him to dinner at their Manhattan apartment, thinly disguised attempts at matchmaking that were dismal failures. After the last failed attempt, Isaac walked him to the door and slipped a piece of paper into his jacket pocket.

"These two ladies are young and pretty and they've been around," Isaac said, adding with a wink, "and they're available, if you know what I mean."

Eli gave it a try with both of them, only to reaffirm that empty sex had lost its appeal. Could it be possible that this woman walking beside him would fill the void?

He filled her in on what had happened during 1938, his final year in Berlin. He described in loving detail the accomplishments of his parents, and the veiled threat from Hoffman, his Nazi slob of a landlord, that sealed his decision to flee Germany.

"Now how about you?" Eli said. "I've been babbling on for blocks."

"Well, to start, I'm a widow, have been for close to four years. That would be about the time you arrived here from Germany. I live alone, and like it that way. Oh sure, there's been men, but nothing serious. For work I guess you could say I've been lucky. I run the upscale jewelry concession at Hahne's."

"Hahne's, 'the store with the friendly spirit,'" Eli said. "How did you pull that off?"

"My background," Gail said. "My husband owned a very successful downtown jewelry store, Rossmore's. It was strictly carriage trade goods. I closed it down after he died and moved all of the good stuff over to Hahne's. I still don't know if it was a coup, or if they felt sorry for me."

"Why would they feel sorry for you?"

"Because of the way he died," Gail said, seemingly reluctant to embellish her answer any further.

"Which was?"

"He was murdered. It was Saturday night, two men shot him down just before closing, then grabbed four or five trays of diamonds and jewels, stuffed them in their pockets and then ran like hell. I saw it all from the back of the store. They never saw me, and I'm convinced that if they had, they would have killed me too."

Eli searched for the right words, but came up empty. Anything he said would be banal and insulting. He decided to give it a try.

"Did they get the two killers?"

"Oh yes, it didn't take long. Shot down a few days later when they were cornered in a North Ward parking lot. No loot though. Word was that it was in Richie the Boot Boiardo's safe in Vittorio's Castle."

"So they were mobsters."

"The police thought so, but there was no way of proving it."

"Family? Friends? Anyone at all you could lean on?"

"Yes, there were condolences from everyone. But to tell you the truth, Eli, I just wanted to be alone. So they left me alone."

By this time they reached the corner of High and William. "Look Eli, my apartment is just down the block, you don't have to walk me to the door...."

"Okay, no need to go on, but I do want to see you again. What do you say?"

"I say sure."

"I'm glad, you name the time and place."

"Next Friday, five o'clock, the Pine Room at Hahne's. They treat me like a princess, we'll get great service and a great table. See you then."

That night was the start of what would become Eli's happiest year in America, almost twelve months to the day it was a bewitching phantasmagoria that blended hope, dreams, illusion and finally love. It took a month for Eli to get up the nerve to ask her to bed in his apartment at the Lido. Their lovemaking was never imposed, always soft and sharing. His music collection was put to good use. Gail was a good cook and insisted on doing the shopping.

They never missed a concert at Fuld Hall and made four trips to Manhattan for matinees at the Met. They shared bread crumbs with the pigeons on Sunday morning, took the Stanton Island Ferry, viewed the Manhattan skyline from the Statue of Liberty, and were the oddest couple to attend the Ash Wednesday ceremony at St. Mark's.

"Why not, you're inquisitive about everything. Everyone knows how we Catholics love sack cloth and ashes. You'll see how we do it now, just use your imagination."

Eli watched from their pew as Gail squeezed into the aisle, and joined a long procession winding its way to the altar rail where a tall young priest used his thumb to brush their foreheads with ashes.

"No sack cloth, but we still have the ashes," Gail said as they left the church. "But you get the idea."

They had six obligatory dinners with Isaac and Rachel, three at the Weinstein apartment, and three at Rockefeller Center after movies at Radio City Music Hall. Five visits to Montclaire netted three lunches and two dinners at various restaurants. Gail had warned him what to expect. Eli never saw the inside of the Dolan home.

He was impressed by the size of her jewelry concession at Hahne's, surprised when he had to discover for himself that she had two full time female employees. Gail twice visited his pawn shop, never passing judgment.

It was on a Friday afternoon that Eli decided that they should celebrate their one year anniversary. He would surprise Gail at closing time. They hadn't spoken since Tuesday and it would be nice if they could share the shopping on the way to his apartment. He took his usual route through the store and came up short when he saw that all the lights at Gail's jewelry concession were off.

"Why no lights? What's going on?" he said out loud to disinterested passersby.

A floor walker came over. "I'm sorry sir, but hadn't you heard?"

"Heard what? What are you talking about?"

"Gail's dead. Struck by a hit and run driver as she was crossing Broad Street. The man was drunk, crashed into a light pole after hitting her."

"When did this happen?"

"Wednesday at noon. She had just gone out to get some fresh air."

My Gail dead. It can't be. Run down in the street by a drunken swine. The thought of it was like a hard punch to the stomach. He came close to vomiting. He found it impossible to speak. His grief turned to rage and hatred. His knees began to buckle. He fought for balance when two steadying hands grasped his shoulders.

"I've got you. Steady now," the floorwalker said. "Take some deep breaths."

A sympathetic crowd had gathered around them. The few who recognized him offered empty condolences. He gave them nothing in return.

"You'll want to attend the funeral," the floorwalker said. "Her family has made all the arrangements. There will be a requiem mass at their parish in Montclaire next Tuesday at ten. Visitations begin tomorrow at the Carlisle Funeral Home. We'll all try to make it."

Eli stared silently at the tall young man in his well-tailored brown suit, adorned with a white carnation in the lapel, and a tri-tip handkerchief protruding from its pocket. He turned, choked down a sob and barely restrained himself from putting his fist through the glass front of a jewelry case.

A funeral parlor visitation and requiem mass would be abominations, and he wanted no part of them.

Chapter

13

The sun was setting as Simon stepped into his office and walked to his cluttered desk. He switched on the desk lamp and he was about to record the day's receipts in the ledger when he heard the small bell attached to the front door jingle.

"Oy, now what," he sighed and went to see who it was at this relatively late hour. A tall, slender Negro was standing at the counter and introduced himself.

"Blessings to you, Mr. Eli Simon from Father Divine. My name is John Travers, but my friends know me as Righteous Reckoning." He reached out his hand.

With his white, long sleeve shirt, black bowtie and matching white pants, he could easily be mistaken for a Good Humor man.

Simon doubted that he was here to sell him ice cream.

"Nice to meet you," Simon said, shaking the man's hand.

The man briefly eyeballed the contents of the two glass display cases that took up most of the space in the small store. "Many sad stories," he said. "Bet you've heard them all, many times over."

"What can I do for you?" Simon said, ignoring his comment. "Please take a seat."

"Thank you," Righteous Reckoning said. "I believe in getting right to the point. We understand you have some mighty fine bikes for sell."

"I do, and you're here at the right time. I just got in an Army surplus bike. It's just like new. Are you interested?"

"Can I see it first?"

"Of course. I'll bring it right out."

Simon appeared wheeling the bike to the front. It was olive green with "Property U.S. Government" stenciled on its handlebars, equipped with a canvas tool bag, and a headlight on the front fender.

"Looks like a fine vehicle," Righteous Reckoning said, after giving the tires a squeeze. "Might need a new paint job though. Don't want too many questions about where it comes from."

Simon nodded. "That's not a problem, for the right price that is."

"Ah, right to the point. You're a man of business. Are you aware of Father Divine's standing in this fair city?"

"Sure. I've seen his parades, read about him in the paper and all his soup kitchens. Why?"

"Father Divine feels it is his mission to support local business. You have a fine reputation among his followers for your honesty. When they are feeling the pinch, they come to you with their worldy possessions and you give them a fair price. The bike, I'd say it's worth fifteen dollars."

"I was thinking more like twenty-five. I'm sure you can handle that amount."

"No problem at all. But that's not the only reason I'm here."

"What else do you have in mind?"

"It's simple. Many of Father's followers donate their valuables to support his mission. What if he gave you first pick of these items? Could be some serious money in the long run. All it would take is for you to donate this here bike."

"I'm not saying no, and I'm not saying yes," Simon said. "How do I know that these donations are worth anything?"

"Sure 'nuff." Righteous reached into his pocket, pulled out a lady's hat pin and put it on the counter. "Here's an example of the kind of valuables we get as donations."

Simon examined it. It had several small garnets set in what appeared to be a silver plated setting. He knew he could sell it for a good price.

"How would it work?" Simon said.

"We get word to you where and when we receive donations. You take what you want."

"For how long?"

"Let's say 'bout six months or so. God's got no timeclock."

"Well, Mister, if the rest of the items are like this, you've got a deal." He handed it back.

"Oh, keep it, my brother. A little gift of good faith."

"When do you need the bike?"

"A tall white boy will be stopping by tomorrow afternoon to pick it up. His name is Richie. He needs it for a paper route."

"It'll be ready."

The men stood and shook hands.

"Nice doing business with you, Brother Simon," the black man said, and then with a patronizing smile added, "We've had our eye on you for a while now. No promises, but I think we'll have some big things in store for you. Have a good evening. We'll be in touch."

Simon followed the man as he left the store and locked the door behind him. He flipped over the OPEN sign in the window to CLOSED.

Even the schvartes know how to work an angle in this town, he thought. *It could mean some easy money for me, but damn if I don't feel trapped. First Zwillman's filth crammed down my throat by that smirking little thug, and now who knows what's in store for me. I don't need another Kurt Hoffman in my life.*

Chapter

14

The morning after he told his parents about the paper route, Richie was cutting across the intersection of Broome and Kinney on his way to Frank Marsucci's grimy office. He saw that the door to the circulation office was open, took three deep breaths, and walked in.

The office was a dump. The floor and a long wooden table were littered with undelivered newspapers, some still in bundles. A man was at the rear of the office, his legs extended over a battered wooden desk, as he focused on cleaning his fingernails with a small pocket knife. His unshaven face added at least a decade to his twenty-two years. He was short and muscular, with the dark, crooked features of a guy well-equipped to bully a bunch of kids. He shifted his gaze to the door where Richie stood uncertain what to do next.

"Want something kid?"

"Mr. Marsucci?"

"Yeah."

"I was told I was next in line to get a paper route."

"You got a name?"

"Richie Maxwell."

Marsucci slowly swung his legs down from the desk, stood up, folded his pocket knife, dropped it into his front pants pocket, and opened the top desk drawer. He took out a ledger.

"Yeah," he said. "You're next in line."

Richie breathed easier.

"But I don't take no bullshit. You're on time every day or you're out. You do collections on Saturday and bring them here. You got a bike?"

"Yes, sir. When do I start?"

"Meet me here at five tomorrow morning. You'll ride with me tomorrow and Sunday in my car to learn the route. Monday you're on your own. Don't be late."

"Thank you, Mr. Marsucci. See you tomorrow."

You've got to hand it to those three niggers, using Father Divine as a shill. Sweet set-up, Marsucci thought. *But they ain't fooling no one. Been playing the bug for months now and really moving out. Even sweet little Milly next door is writing policy for them. And now they're cramming a snot-nosed numbers runner down my throat. They're crazy if they think I don't want in, and they'll find that out pretty god damn fast.*

Marsucci retrieved the knife from his pocket, thumbed out the smallest blade and resumed work on his fingernails. It all began with yet another one of his fuck-ups. They saved his ass when he got wrong side up with a Boiardo pimp down on Broad. With a general Army discharge "under other than honorable conditions," and no mustering-out pay, he was flat broke when he hit the streets. All because the MPs discovered that Army hospital linens and blankets were disappearing from their warehouse, and ending up at hotels in and around Cherbourg, France. Sgt. Marsucci, the warehouse dispatcher, was the prime suspect. They had the goods on him, but couldn't prove it. So they dropped the case and shipped him home.

Downtown Newark offered opportunities galore for a guy like Marsucci. He had to get started fast. True to his nature, he fucked up again. There were plenty of hot broads to choose from, so it came natural to him to pick the wrong ones. He tapped into two of Boiardo's whores. It was a rare bit of luck that John Travers, alias Righteous Reckoning, Buck Barton, alias Darn Good Disciple, and Wilber Fontaine, alias God's Tall Timber, were working the downtown scene that night.

They'd arrived in Newark two weeks earlier, fresh from being run out of Atlanta by the cops. They had been playing the bug from a three chair barbershop and running a backroom policy parlor until a rare police crackdown padlocked their operations. Streetwise, their names on long police sheets, they knew the rules never changed from town-to-town. You had to find the crooked cops on the take, and in Newark, you didn't have to look very far. In less than a week, they had a get together with Captain Tony Gordo. A few days later they had just left Swifty's Bar and Grill when they stumbled on Gordo, in plain clothes, pounding the hell out of Marsucci in an alley while two other goons held him. Gordo recognized the three blacks and motioned the other two cops to release the semi-conscious Marsucci.

"You didn't see nothin'," Gordo said as the three cops pushed past the three blacks. "You're blind as bats. Make damn sure of that."

Marsucci was convinced that Gordo would have beaten him to death if not for the three interlopers. That was a few months ago. Since then he had moved in with his folks on South 8th, conned his uncle out of two hundred dollars for an old Plymouth, talked his way into a circulation job with the *Beacon*, and set up shop on Kinney. He had no idea how the phony barbers had tracked him down.

The joke's on them, Marsucci thought, *they've got no idea there's a real kick-ass circulation war going on right now. This kid is getting a new route straight into Clarion territory, and those fancy apartments. First time ever for the Beacon. If Richie the Boot and Longy are gonna knock heads for the Third Ward, no matter to me, just so long as I get part of the take.*

Marsucci's delivery boys were streetwise enough to know that kissing his ass even a little could pay off. They fed him juicy tidbits picked up along their routes, and pieced with what he saw himself, left little doubt that the numbers game was changing and the three phony barbers were part of it. He spotted the big guy, God's Tall Timber or Wilber Fontaine, whatever you call him, going into Milly's Beauty Shop several times to set her up as a policy writer. Business was brisk and he wanted his piece of the action.

Another tip-off that the policy game was changing was how often the new beat cop, Frank Gazzi, came snooping around real innocent like.

"Just letting you know I'll be poking my head in from time-to-time," Gazzi explained on his first visit. "No big thing, just getting a feel for my beat. Already talked to Milly next door. She's got something real good going, don't you think?"

"I'm kept kinda busy with all these kids I got working for me," Marsucci said playing it innocent, "but yeah, I guess you could say that. Lots of people coming and going, even guys."

"For manicures no doubt," Gazzi said. "Seems like clean and polished fingernails are a big thing in this neighborhood. Be seeing you, gotta hit the call box."

"Be seeing you."

Marsucci knew that Jim McDuffie did more than just deliver the *Evening Clarion*. Some of his kids, the oldest and toughest, carried with them a little pull apart notebook and pencil. By the end of their route they would have at least a dozen number slips and wagers to drop off with McDuffie for delivery to the Zwillman policy bank on Clinton. These kids would be lying in wait for Richie, especially after learning that he would be double-dipping into their numbers territory.

The *Clarion* was a class act, and its affluent subscribers had money enough to include tips for the delivery boys, and even something extra at Christmas. There was no way they would allow a fish-wrapper like the *Beacon* to take any of this away. McDuffie had fifteen kids on the street, their routes included the Lido, Westmore, Crayton Arms, and the Armstrong Apartments. The gem was the Riviera Hotel where Longy Zwillman had an entire floor.

Richie retraced his steps across Kinney to Broome, then stepped it up on his way to the Peace Barber Shop on Spruce to find out about the bike. The three Divinites were waiting for him. Customers were getting trimmed by Darn Good Disciple and God's Tall Timber, and Righteous Reckoning was in his usual spot near the front door. There were smiles all around.

"Richie, my little brother. You set?"

"Yeah. Marsucci's driving me around this weekend to show me my route. I start on my own on Monday. But I need the bike."

"No worries. Righteous Reckoning has taken care of everything. Eli Simon has a bike waiting for you. Ain't that right?"

"Just like new, a Columbia Military," Righteous Reckoning said. "Sturdy with a fresh coat of paint. You got your story straight with your folks?"

Richie nodded. "As far as anyone knows, I'll be paying it off a little each week to Simon, just like you said," Richie said. "My dad ain't easy to fool, so I need to know what's a good price for a used Columbia Military."

"Did we pick the right boy," God's Tall Timber said. "You bet we did. The Jew said fifteen dollars."

"Sounds good. Don't worry, I'll pull it off," Richie said.

"Once you get your route down, we'll talk business," Righteous said.

As Richie headed to Simon's, it sunk in that, for better or worse, there was no turning back. A deal was a deal. He had already lied to his parents, and that bothered him, but not enough to turn down the Divinites' offer. He turned off Waverly to Quitman and went into the shop. The Jew was sitting behind the counter.

"Yes," Simon said, looking up at the tall teenager.

"My name's Richie. I'm here for the bike."

"Ah, I've been expecting you. I hear you got a paper route."

"Yeah, I got lucky."

"Luck is knowing the right people, boychik. Wait right here and I'll get it for you."

"Here you go," Simon said as he wheeled the bike around the corner. "It's all yours."

Richie was impressed. The bike had a strong look about it. The dark blue paint job really made the chrome headlight on the front fender stand out. It looked almost brand new.

"Thanks."

"*Mazel tov.*"

"Huh?"

"Good luck with it."

Richie pushed the bike out the front door, jumped on and pedaled back home. His folks would be impressed. So would the guys.

Simon, once owner of a Monet and an envied collection of German impressionists, sensed that his future was about to spiral out of control. Already the purveyor of pornography, he feared that the "something big" inferred by John Travers, alias Righteous Reckoning, might easily be translated into "something bad." And that the kid who had just left his shop would somehow be at the center of it all.

Chapter

15

Marvin poked his head from under a faded, heavily mended quilt. The clouds sweeping in over Newark from the northeast were still a long way from the lush green field where he and his family had spent that chilly night in early September of 1939. The feel of rain was already in the air.

Marvin focused across U.S. 22 at the silhouette beside the highway. He didn't know why, but it looked different this morning. Somehow bigger and stronger, not at all like the tired '31 Hudson it was yesterday.

Marvin rubbed the sleep from his eyes, reached over and shook his brother, Benjamin, who, at six, was three years his junior. Their bed had been the thick grass matted under and around a split-rail pasture fence.

"Look at that, Benjamin. It looks like a statue."

Benjamin peeked out from under the quilt and followed with half-closed eyes his brother's extended arm. The index finger seemed to rest on the roof of the Hudson.

"Sure do," replied Benjamin, his reply a mere expedient, as he promptly ducked his head back under the quilt.

"That's what it looks like, a great statue like the ones in Birmingham and all those places we just passed. Only this one moves when we want it to."

The lump under the quilt quivered slightly and contracted into a tight mound.

"Yeh, man, that's it," Marvin continued, an idea shaping in his sleep-muddled mind.

"It's our great rollin' statue that's going to take us down this road, past all the green fields and all those oil tanks Uncle Josh said we'd be passing on our way to Newark. It ain't far now. Then maybe we won't need this old statue anymore."

A muffled snort came from under the quilt.

The Hudson, all 153,275 miles of it when he checked last night, did indeed seem a thing of grandeur. Framed against the rising sun, its rusty shell candied with early morning dew, the car smiled benignly.

Marvin placed his foot against the breathing part of the quilt and shoved.

The brown sedan had cost Bill Davidson five months' wages spread over a year's time. Each week for twelve months, he and his wife divided his meager pay from the Alabama mine boss into pathetic little piles on their linoleum-covered kitchen table.

Through the good and lean months, two piles remained unchanged in size: there was always enough for the First Ebenezer Baptist Church and for The Trip, in that order.

Davidson and his wife left unsaid their fear that if for one week, only one week, the visit to Old Man Crawford's General Store and Gas Station was put off, their dream would die. Every Saturday, with The Trip money and handwritten payment sheet wrapped in a handkerchief, Davidson walked the six miles to Crawford's.

It had all come about, this unheard-of thing, after Davidson learned the car was for sale. He waited until Crawford was alone. Walker County niggers don't ask white folks about buying their cars. Davidson had earned a reputation among the whites as "one of the good coons, not uppity at all." He wanted no redneck hangers-on in the store when he talked to Crawford.

"Ah hear the ol' Hudson of yours is for sale."

Crawford was behind his cash register. He looked lazily at Davidson. "Yep."

Davidson hesitated, then in a voice a little too loud, too bold, said, "Ah want to buy it."

Crawford, suddenly interested, walked from behind the register.

"Can ya drive?" asked Crawford, his face all smiles at Davidson's interest. "Well, hell, sure ya kin. Yur that number one handyman over at the mine, ain't ya?" They walked outside.

"Bill, it's more than good enough to get y'all out of this gawdawful Walker County coal dust," said Crawford, leaning comfortably against the Hudson. It was perched on cinder blocks in a shed behind the store.

"Sure it ain't been used for a year. But don't go poor-mouthin' this ol' beauty. Guarantee it's had the best o' care. Why ya s'pose I put it in the shed? Ta keep it out o' the elements, ya know, rain 'n all."

Davidson came close to turning his back on the old man and the relaxed way he had of talking down to him. He had been in the store many times when Crawford was talking to his own kind. And he had seen other white shopkeepers, like the one in Jasper, talking to white men. There wasn't any of the molasses-smooth "y'alls" and "yah suh boys" that punctuated Crawford's mocking nigger talk.

"Ain't just an ordinary Hudson, it's a Great Eight." Crawford sensed he might be losing a chance to finally unload the rusting relic. "Cost big money when it hit the road back in '31, almost a thousand Yankee dollars. But that was then, and this is now, and we got some bargaining to do."

Crawford tugged on Davidson's sleeve drawing him closer to the car.

"C'mere," said Crawford, "Know how these two holes got up there in the ceiling, don't ya?"

Davidson had heard the story, how the white mine foreman and his high yellow would park out on the bluff over the Southern tracks. Folks said they'd spend two, sometimes three hours out there, going at it all the time, her with her sharp high heels poking through the car's overhead lining. The foreman left a few years ago, a promotion they said. He took his woman with him. He left the car behind for new owners to take their shots at the backseat. As with Davidson, the car's path to Crawford's shed had not been an easy one.

Crawford, still holding Davidson's sleeve, reached through the rear window with his other hand, poked a finger into one of the holes in the upholstery and grinned. "Always put them in the same place."

Davidson, unable to gracefully free his arm, peered into the rear of the car, clearly annoyed.

Crawford misread the black man's troubled face. He released his hold. "Come up with $150, and I'll guarantee it'll kick over."

It was more than Davidson expected to pay. A small fortune. "I don't think . . ." The words trailed off as Crawford pulled him once again to the side of the Hudson.

"An' lookee here, at these tires. Good rubber 'n even a spare. A chariot to the promised land. Lordy, yeh."

Davidson turned and strode slowly from the shed. He was disheartened. Could it be done? Could he get the $150?

"To the promised land. Lordy, yeh," Crawford's mocking words followed Davidson all the way home.

That night, long after the kids had been put to sleep, Davidson and his wife discussed Crawford's offer. But their two sons and one daughter had been affected by their parents' unspoken anxiety. They huddled in their bedroom, their ears pressed against the door.

Elizabeth Davidson, who, like her husband, had stretched her education through the sixth grade. Her knack for figures served the family well. She jotted figures on pieces of paper, some were discarded, while others were transferred to a large notebook, the family ledger.

Elizabeth had developed the cynicism and craftiness common to poor men's wives. While their husbands, faced with the tradition of menial labor, toiled at humble tasks or ways to avoid them, the women were cursed with a different fate.

Home with a growing brood of children, day after day of decay and growing despair, the women have ample time to question their doomed existence. The honest poor man dies with the unanswered, eternal WHY on his lips. His wife had always known why and cursed the reasons for it.

"Bill, can we trust 'im? This ain't some grub for the week. This is $150."

"He's as honest a white man we kin expect. He said no interest, jes a straight $150. That means somethin', don't it?"

"Lordy, won't ya ever learn? No interest on a piece o' rusty junk. Won't ya ever learn?"

"We got a chance to get somethin' better?"

"No."

"Crawford ever done us dirt?"

"The stones in the bottom of the feed bag? Ten pounds' worth. An' how 'bout the chopped stalks and roots in the loose burley?"

"Woman, that's only stealin' our pennies. He ain't yet gone for our blood. Or any other nigger's that I know of. I think we kin trust 'im."

So after a last check of their meager budget, the Davidsons decided. Their children went to bed. But there was little sleep for anyone that night.

The first Saturday of September 1939 was the long-awaited day. Final payment was made, and true to his word, Crawford got the car started. He even greased it, changed the oil, and filled the gas tank—free.

It took more than a week for the Davidsons to put together all the loose ends and cut them. One of the first things Elizabeth did was send off a letter to Bill's brother in Newark, New Jersey. Joshua Davidson had taken his family north four years earlier, and had been asking his brother to join him for some time now. The last letter exchange was a month earlier. A second floor flat in the tenement had become vacant, and Joshua was ready to put down some money to hold it if Bill and his family were on their way. His wife, Lucretia, would tidy it up and get it ready.

The next day, Elizabeth took the early bus into Jasper, went to the post office and handed over twenty-five cents for a registered, special delivery letter to Joshua giving him the go ahead. Four days later, she received confirmation, and the next day Joshua's return special delivery informed her that he had slapped down twenty-five dollars to hold the flat for them.

The Hudson burned almost as much oil as gas. It was in a continual state of near-disintegration. It held together amid a cacophony of rattles, the variety increasing with each mile. Absence of a familiar metallic whimper led to the greatest of fears—that a part of the car had fallen off. But as the miles ticked off, the children discovered to their delight that the orchestration shifted back and forth across the car. A timid squeak, now gone from the front right fender, became a grating screech in the left rear.

The family, never before out of Alabama, gaped incredulously as the old car carried them through one state after another. Not fast, but steadily. Bill Davidson occasionally allowed himself the luxury of a few low-whistled notes, as he guided the car through Georgia, across the Carolinas, up through Virginia and across the bituminous tail of West Virginia. Then they rattled through Pennsylvania, crossing the Delaware on a Thursday night. Right on schedule. Davidson had planned to arrive in Newark on the last Friday of the month, giving him a weekend of rest before he looked for work.

Now, Friday morning, the entire family began to stir beside the road. Marvin had finally succeeded in prodding Benjamin from under the quilt.

Then the seeming impregnability of the Hudson's silhouette was suddenly broken. It caught Marvin by surprise. Blankets placed over the windows during the night were lowered. A beam of sunlight burst through the car and broke itself on the cracked highway. A window lowered.

"Marvin! Benjamin! Come over here 'n wash up. There's water up the road a piece. C'mon, hurry." The boys' mother didn't get, nor did she expect, an answer. Only action.

"Shake it, brother," the older boy said, feeling excitement once again. He was wound-up so tight his stomach jumped. Marvin wondered if Benjamin felt the same way. He doubted it.

Marvin, in undershirt and shorts, rolled from under the quilt onto the grass. He shivered when the cold wetness touched his legs and arms. He saw that his brother had once again retreated under the quilt and angrily pulled the cover from him. Benjamin sat up. The two boys began putting on their clothes.

It didn't take long. Benjamin, with one oversized, high-topped work shoe already on, grew impatient with his lack of progress with the second. He stood up, slammed his foot twice on the ground and felt with satisfaction his sole slapping against the makeshift cardboard bottom.

Marvin grabbed the quilt, walked to the shoulder of the road, groped for his brother's hand, and stood frozen as a semi-trailer rig rumbled past. Once across, Marvin couldn't resist a last glance to the other side.

"Our last night before Newark," he said airily. His words were lost in the chill morning air. Benjamin had already disappeared behind the car to join his sister.

Bill Davidson, as had been his practice throughout the trip, did not sleep in the car. The vehicle was shared by his wife and daughter. He had found himself a comfortable spot under a nearby elm. His blanket was an old brown greatcoat that had been his father's.

Elizabeth Davidson walked to the tree, reached down and lightly touched the shoulder of her husband. The effortless way that Davidson awoke, slowly opened his eyes, and yawned was instinctive.

For seventeen years, half her husband's life, Elizabeth Davidson had awakened her man the same way—a light touch of the shoulder. The last few weeks were no different. But they had moved fast, faster than she had wanted. They had also come farther than she would have ever hoped possible, if not for this man. She was frightened.

This was not the little sharecropper's cabin near Pinckard, nor was it the three-room shack that came with the handyman's job at the mine. Elizabeth Davidson peered knowingly into her husband's face. Not once had his features shown the anxiety that she knew gripped the man behind them. Her husband opened his eyes.

He was immediately awake. "This is it. A few more hours, then Newark."

The wife said nothing. She stooped and picked up the greatcoat, then turned and walked back to the car.

Davidson relieved himself behind a tree. In the distance, maybe a quarter mile away, some black angus were being driven through pasture gates. Prize stock. He could see that, even from where he stood. The bulky, well-fed black beasts were the pride of their dairyman owner. They were his clenched fist against the Teamsters and the increased cost of bringing milk to market. Things were easier once.

In an adjacent pasture a dairy herd was feeding on lush grass. Davidson gawked at the greenness, comfortably enclosed behind a damp white fence. He reached out and touched the upper rail with his right hand. He pulled it back and looked at the beads of dew on his fingertips. He pressed his fingers together and the water trickled down the calloused gullies to his palm.

Davidson lifted his hand to his lips. The water was sweet.

The excited chatter of his children snapped Davidson from his reverie. He pulled out his tarnished pocket watch. It was 6:35. Davidson turned abruptly, strode quickly to the car, and took a piece of toweling from the back seat. He walked to the creek.

His suddenly quiet sons walked beside him.

Chapter

16

Bill Davidson didn't know how it happened. He had been real careful the entire way through New Jersey. Now he was on a bridge crossing a river to . . . to where? Once across, he picked up a road sign that said Newark was that way, to the south. The road ran along the east side of the river. The sun popped through the dark threatening clouds to the east. Bill hoped they would reach Joshua's place before the rains came.

"Can't be long now, can it?" Marvin's impatience underscored every word. He couldn't wait to tell his cousins all about the trip.

"Hush down. Your father will get us there best and fast as he can," Elizabeth Davidson admonished her son.

The tired old Hudson wheezed its way past an East Newark city limits sign. The road had veered away from the river and the Davidsons were now driving past the biggest factory they could ever imagine.

"Look at that, will you?" Bill wondered aloud. "Bet there'll be plenty a' work there." Up ahead and to the left was a Sinclair gas station, and the needle on the dashboard gauge was almost down to the E. "We'll buy jes enough to get us to Joshua's."

The Hudson pulled up to a pump. A white gas jockey in coveralls strolled lazily over and skeptically asked, "How much?" He hoped he hadn't gotten up for only a couple of gallons.

"Well, we're in Newark now," Bill said with his first grin in miles, "so I guess a dollar will do us jes fine." The young attendant peered through Bill's window, saw the two kids in the front seat, a woman and little girl in the back. God only knows what's stuffed into the trunk of this old relic, he thought.

"You ain't in Newark yet. This is East Newark," the attendant said. "Newark's over there across the Passaic River. The bridge is straight ahead. Can't miss it. Then you'll be in Newark when ya cross it."

Another attendant, this one no more than a kid, had come over with a rag and spray gun and was cleaning the windshield. He leaned toward Bill's window. "Need anything under the hood? Pop it, and I'll take a look."

"Nope. No help needed there. Everything's jes fine." Bill's amazement was reinforced once again, that white men all down the line in New Jersey washed his windshield, wiped the side mirror, and twice filled the radiator.

Bill paid for the gas and asked, "Once we get across, do you know how we get to Avon and Clinton Avenues? That's where my brother's place is."

"I can tell ya how to get to Broad and Market. Can't miss that. But nope, after that, not much help," the older attendant said.

The attendant felt five pairs of eyes on him. "Wait a minute. Be right back." He returned with a map on which he had clearly marked Broad and Market.

"Here, take it. I've circled Broad and Market," the attendant said, wondering if they could read. "Once you cross the bridge you're on your own."

A somewhat bewildered Bill took the map and handed it to Elizabeth in the backseat. "Thanks kindly, we truly appreciate it."

Both attendants stepped back as the Hudson coughed to a smoky start and pulled out toward the bridge. "You gave him the map free? Sometimes I don't get you," the younger one said. "I know how you feel about niggers, but you gave 'em a fifteen-cent Sinclair city map for nothin'."

"Don't worry yourself. If they'd run into some wise-ass nigger-hater over there, they'd probably be sent to Bloomfield or Irvington," the older one said. "I don't know. Just something I felt like doing."

They were right on schedule to reach Joshua's before noon. Elizabeth used a pencil to trace the streets as the Davidsons made their way through downtown rush-hour traffic to Broad and Market. With his wife directing him, Bill edged the Hudson into the far left lane and prepared to turn onto High Street.

A strong and steady rain had begun. It had started just as they crossed the bridge from East Newark. The Hudson's worn windshield wipers could make only a feeble attempt to do their job. Bill cracked the two front vent windows. It didn't help much; fog misted the windshield. With his son Benjamin helping him, they used rags to clear the glass as best they could. Horns were blaring, drivers were cursing.

Marvin bent over the back of the front seat to monitor his mother working with the map. "Here's where we are, and up here is Clinton and Avon." Elizabeth was using the eraser end of the pencil as a pointer. "Appears to be not far, just up here."

"Not far now, we're just about there." Marvin lit up. "Can't wait to see everybody. Lots to tell them."

The Hudson moved slowly forward, and with this kind of city driving, Bill hoped that the radiator wouldn't start blowing steam.

Twenty minutes later, the over-heated, steam belching Hudson pulled to a stop in front of a three story tenement on Clinton. Joshua and Lucretia Davidson and their twin, ten year old sons Nathaniel and Paul, had been standing vigil for more than an hour at the front window of their first floor flat. They raced out the door to the curb, and despite the steady rain nine members of the Davidson clan were reunited with hugs and a chorus of "Glory be's."

By the end of the day, the family's belongings that Elizabeth reckoned to be worthwhile were unloaded from the Hudson's trunk and carried up to the second floor flat. The electric would not be turned on until Monday morning, so some important matters had to be tended to before nightfall.

"Able to get them both, like I described to you?" Joshua said. The four adult Davidsons were relaxing at the kitchen table after supper, the five kids were jabbering like crazy in the back bedroom.

"These do?" Bill said taking two envelopes from Elizabeth and pushing them across the table to Joshua. "Ate some real crow, had to perform the nigger's humble shuffle to get the one from the mine. For Elizabeth it was easy."

Joshua opened the envelope bearing the Warrior Mining Company logo, and pulled out a single typewritten page. He had cleared the company's coal dust from his lungs four years earlier and never stopped urging his brother Bill to follow him. "Pay no mind that Carter Jennings made you crawl before signing this paper, you got it, and that's all that counts." The note read:

"Bill Davidson is a good boy. He has been on our payroll for six years, and is trustworthy. Performed his duties as instructed and handled men well enough to be boss of our seven man tailings crew. He has some education, and handles numbers and work schedules well. Carter Jennings, Foreman, Warrior Mining Company, Carbon Hill, Alabama."

The second envelope contained a letter from the Reverend Wilbur Joiner, First Ebenezer Baptist Church, RFD, Walker County, Alabama. The Reverend heaped it on real good, praising Elizabeth's bookkeeping skills and handling of the church's soup kitchen that served more than fifty indigent church members daily.

"Aim high. Everyone says won't be long before the shooting starts," Joshua said. "That means jobs, even for southern niggers. Lucretia and me, we're set up just fine at Bambergers. Four years under our belts, we're staying put."

Armed with the Reverend Joiner's letter, Elizabeth made the rounds in Newark looking for work. She wore her best Sunday dress, her only pair of heels, and her sister-in-law Lucretia did up her hair. Her timing couldn't have been better when she got to the Ronson plant on Mulberry. War was on the horizon and Ronson was girding for the shift from consumer goods to munitions. More help was needed. She filled out an application form, and was the only Negro among the five women ushered into a windowless room for verbal and math testing. After scoring was completed, she had a job as a checker in the shipping department. A job that would last for the duration.

My big brother sure knows what he's talking about. Can't go wrong listening to what Joshua has to say. He figures if there be shooting overseas like the last war, then there be a big need for ships to get there. Let's hope that old Hudson of ours will keep breathing. First, I got to do some sprucing up myself.

"You're next big fellow, step right on up and take a seat," the skinny, little black man said as he snapped his shoe buffing cloth twice, laid it aside, and nodded toward one of the two chairs on the elevated shoe-shine platform. "Ain't seen you before. New around here?"

"Family moved in last week, a flat around the corner on Clinton. Time to start looking for work, and it pays to look good. Shoes are a good place to start."

"How right you are, big fellow. And no better for the job than right here with ol' Willy. What's your name?"

"Bill Davidson. Up from the coal mines in Alabama with my wife, two boys and a girl."

"Okay, Mr. Davidson, sit back and relax, and ol' Willy will give your brogues his very best shine, a job huntin' shine. Here's something to read while I busy myself."

Bill was handed a dog-eared copy of a newspaper, its front page masthead reading *Newark Herald,* and learned from Willy that it was owned and operated by Negroes, for Negroes, and came out every Saturday with news you didn't find in the white man's papers.

"Good place to start if you be lookin' for work. This one's a week old. Better you mosey over to their office on West Kinney. Ain't far, and if there's any jobs out there, it's a good place to look."

Joshua sure knows his stuff. No jobs listed, but Lordy how this story backs him up. Says that the Federal Shipbuilding and Dry Dock Company is going to need men to meet the government contracts that are coming in. Now, if my rusty friend down at the curb is still alive, Federal Shipbuilding can expect a black man from Alabama to come driving to its door.

Bill was not about to give all the credit to Carter Jennings' note for him catching on at the shipyard. He could read. He could write. He was good with numbers. And other black men listened to him when he gave an order.

Starting as a hot-rivet heater-boy, Bill quickly mastered the three remaining, teeth jarring steps needed to complete the hot rivet operation: catcher, riveter and holder-on. He was one of a growing number of blacks at the shipyard, a mandate from FDR that if you want Uncle Sam's bucks, you better hire any able body man who applies regardless of color.

Bill packed in all the overtime he could get, and within six months, he was an Assistant Shift Foreman, and within a year he bossed an entire riveting crew. Everyone, black, white and brown, liked him, and a few months after Pearl Harbor, he just barely lost the election for Shop Steward.

By the time January of 1945 rolled around, Bill and Elizabeth had salted away enough money in their joint account at the New Jersey Fidelity & Trust for a down payment on a house. After two weeks, they found what they were looking for on Morton, a two-story with a good roof, attic and a rebuilt coal-burning furnace in the basement. It took a month for the paperwork to clear, and with the help of Joshua and friends the Davidsons moved their furniture and belongings into their new home.

Chapter

17

By this time the Hudson was history. Bill caught a bus to downtown Newark where he transferred to a Public Service electric trolley to Kearny Point, and his job at Federal Shipbuilding. Elizabeth was making good pay and as much overtime as she could handle as junior bookkeeper at a Ronson plant converted entirely to munitions. The Davidson kids just made the deadline to transfer from Somerset to Morton Street Elementary School.

Somerset was still fifty-percent white during the war years, so the transfer to Morton Street was a shock to Marvin, Benjamin and their sister, Melissa. Their new school was almost all black, and they found it hard to fit in. Ben and Melissa found new Negro friends, but Marvin wanted more.

The day he sashayed into Milt's and astounded everyone when he took a seat at the counter and ordered a glass of Spur was the starting point. It didn't take long for him to notice three of the white kids were buddies and about his age, so he gave them a try. He didn't much care that Richie Maxwell, Joey Bancik, and Billy Spratlin were Catholics, he hadn't known any before. By March and the warmer weather, they were tossing a ball around together and Billy even asked him to partner up in a stoop ball game.

The three white boys were a mixed bag, and Marvin wondered why they pal'd around like they did. Richie was the friendliest, but only up to a point. He saw early on that Richie was always careful not to talk with him too much so that the other white kids hanging around Milt's, especially Profanity Pump, would not have a reason to come down hard. The Pump's mouth could be wicked, no doubt about that.

Billy didn't seem to care about anything. It was almost like he was there, but not really there. Everything seemed to be a joke. He didn't live on the block, but lived on High Street the other side of Court, in one of those big old homes. Billy was always generous with the change he had in his pocket, and wore really fine duds that Marvin's folks could never afford. And he seemed to be along just for the ride, a take it or leave it kind of thing that Marvin couldn't understand.

Joey was different from the other two, the only one that Marvin could see really had it in for Negroes. It was easy to see why. The Banciks were one of three white families still living in that rundown tenement near the corner. It was no secret they were having it tough, and for the first time Marvin saw how cruel white kids could be to their own kind. He had never heard anyone say "white nigger" before. It was just outside Milt's when bully boy, Stan Wysnoski, spit the words into Joey's face after mocking his family for buying their groceries at a Father Divine Peace store. Joey took it and with several other kids looking on silently walked away. Marvin couldn't get those two words out of his mind whenever Joey was around.

One Saturday morning Marvin was sitting on the stoop of his house minding his own business when he spotted two young white ladies stroll into Milt's. Their clothes were tight and their make-up heavy. He was old enough to recognize sex when he saw it.

Inside Milt's, Richie was sitting alone, sipping a lemon coke while studying the latest *Baseball Digest*. It was a habit for Richie, coming into Milt's at midmorning, buying a five-cent coke, helping himself to one of the new magazines, then sprawling out in the rear booth.

As he was going through the latest stats, two pretty young women strode through the front door, and plopped themselves down on two swivel stools at the counter. Richie had never seen them or anyone like them in Milt's before.

"Hi, sugar," said the big-titted, peroxide blonde in a purple blouse and white skirt.

"What can I do for you ladies," Milt said, his eyes stroking her chest.

"Eyes up here, hon. How about coupla Cokes?"

"Yeah and could you squirt a little vanilla in mine?" said the other babe, a hot little redhead. Her hair reached her ass. She put her hand inside her blouse and scratched her left tit.

Richie sneaked a few glances up from his magazine.

The redhead swung halfway around her stool, and crossed her legs slowly in Richie's direction, showing off her bare legs. She smiled at him, "Like the view, killer?"

Richie huddled behind his magazine.

Milt placed the Cokes in front of them, "Leave the kid alone."

He called over to Richie, "Richie, why don't you take a hike? Your soda's on the house."

Richie slid across the booth and was about to stand up when he noticed it, a huge hard on clearly visible in his jeans.

He had to walk past the counter to the magazine rack. The practiced eyes of the two girls caught everything.

"Shame on you, honey," said the blonde, laughing.

"You're in big trouble if a door slams on that thing. You'll be needing it for a long time, stud," the redhead said.

Richie, his face flushed, limped toward the front, threw the *Baseball Digest* back on the rack and went out to the street, without even closing the door.

The two whores giggled as they sucked down their Cokes, then got up from their stools and confidently minced their way toward the door.

"Hey, that'll be two bits...ladies," Milt called out after them.

"Put it on Longy's tab, handsome." At the mention of Zwillman's name, Milt's facial muscles tightened as he clenched and unclenched his teeth.

"Get the fuck out. I don't want you within a mile of me or this shop."

"No worries. Sort of lost our way. Thought this might be a shortcut to the Riviera Hotel," the big-titted blonde said. "Guess we were wrong."

"God damn right you are!"

"Damn if you ain't cute when you're mad, little man," the redhead teased. "There ain't no business here for us anyway. Horny kids don't pay the rent."

Milt's glare followed them to the door. The blond turned and wiggled her fingers, "Bye, handsome."

The two whores were still giggling as they watched Richie cross the street, then they turned toward High Street and barely missed running into Father Nolan.

"Whoa there, ladies," the smiling priest said holding up both hands while backing off to take them in. "You took me by surprise. Have to admit I never saw anyone quite like you coming out of Milt's."

"Just asking directions, Father," the redhead said as she gave him a professional top-to-bottom sizing up. "Did I get it right, you are a priest ain't you?"

"My collar must have been the tip-off," he said. "Yeah, I'm a priest. Father Nolan, but you can call me Terry."

"Well Father Terry, it's been nice meeting you," the blond said, "but it's got to be short and sweet. We have to get going."

"So it's hello and goodbye, such a shame, you've really changed the scenery around here," he quipped as blondie and the redhead brushed past him.

Milt had witnessed the exchange from his shop's door, surprised at the easy way the priest had handled the two bimbos. "Never saw them before Father, and you can be sure you won't be seeing them again."

"Really dressed things up around here, wouldn't you say."

"I run a family soda shop, Father, and can't have broads like them around."

"I understand." Father Nolan took a stool at the counter, and took a sip of the coffee Milt had poured. He studied the troubled expression on Milt's face, smiled and quipped, "We in the church call them Occasions of Sin."

Chapter

18

Aftеr leaving Milt's, Richie took a deep breath and tried his best to be nonchalant as he crossed Morton toward a smiling Marvin who sprawled leisurely on his front porch. He was thinking of wheat fields. He had heard Terry McDivit say that always worked for him. The flowing fields of grain began to have their effect: slowly, but surely his hard on receded.

"Those two beauties a little too much for you," Marvin joked.

"Shove it, just shove it." Richie planted himself next to Marvin on the front step. The two of them sat silently as they watched the two whores disappear around the corner onto High.

"Quite somethin' ain't they," Marvin said. "But you know that, dontcha. Game to go back? Looks like the whole gang's arrived. Come on, the Spur's on me."

They were challenged by Bob and Stan Wysnoski as soon as they walked in the door. It was prime stoop ball weather and the twins were looking for some exercise.

"Hey, you two, how about some stoop ball?" Stan said. "We got the balls, you got the money?"

It was the first of many challenges that would soon be going out, house to house, one side of the street to another and from block to block. You didn't need much, just two guys on a team, a good stoop, preferably a solid stone one, and enough balls to get through the game. That was the rub. The challenging team supplied the balls. Pink, high bouncers were the favorite. If you were any good, you could zing them off the point of a step so they were only blurs as they rocketed past the opposing infielder's ear.

If you were really good, you could put English on the ball, making it dip to the left or right, or with over spin soar over the outfielder's head to the other side of the street—a home run.

Then there were the cuties. Didn't use the high bouncers, only nice, fluffy tennis balls. Mainly, it was because they didn't have much for arms. They'd cozy the ball over the edge of the gutter, just out of reach of the infielder—a single. With their little tricks—reverse spin, over spin, and all—they'd single you to death. You didn't dare pull in the outfielder to cut down on the singles, because they'd lob one over your head for a double and two runs. The cuties were more a pain in the ass than a threat. Once you got onto their rhythm, it was all over.

But take a team that knew all the tricks, had power, and could catch the point of the step with a good shot about three out of five times, then you had a sure winner.

And in a nutshell, that's what you ran into when you took on the Wysnoskis. Each was a junior-size Bronko Nagurski. Eighth-graders, they were tabbed for sure-fire starters on the Prep's junior varsity football team in the fall.

It was sort of a gentleman's agreement that once you reached high school, stoop ball became a thing of the past. Once you left kids' games behind, that's it. So until the lots and parks dried out enough for baseball, the Wysnoskis would be the scourge of the Martin-Baldwin stoop ball circuit for one more spring.

They were the reigning bullies at St. Mark's. They feared only one person, Sister Regina, who was bigger, stronger, and, they were convinced, even meaner than they were. Before pushing around other kids, they made sure she was nowhere in sight.

The Wysnoskis, by making the challenge, supplied the balls. The losers replaced any that were split during the game. The brothers could be counted on to demolish about four balls a game. They once ran their total to seven. At eighteen cents a crack, it meant real money.

Richie and Marvin slipped past the twins and joined Billy Spratlin and Joey Bancik in their booth. Bob and Stan walked over to confront them, "What do you say? Any of you have the guts to take us on?"

"I got chores." said Joey.

"Shove it, chicken. Yer just yellow," Stan said.

"Bullshit, yellow. Fact is, I got to help my old lady."

"Momma's boy."

"Go fuck yerselves," said Joey and pushed past them.

"I'm out," Billy piped up, "I don't wanna pay for any balls today."

"You mean you don't have the balls," Stan said. His brother cracked up.

"You Polak bastard!" Billy said and stood up. Richie held him back.

Richie fingered the coins in his pocket, forty-five cents. And he had a plan, but he needed a partner. He turned to Marvin.

"Got any money?"

"Thirty-five cents."

"I got forty-five. Should be enough."

"Okay, Wysnoski," Richie said, "you got a game."

"You and who else?"

"Me," Marvin answered.

"The darkie, huh? Okay with us. Don't forget, this might cost ya," Stan said, laughing.

"Let's play over at the Exeter," said Richie, ignoring the taunt. The Wysnoskis shrugged with the confidence of bullies who knew they had easy marks.

Richie explained his plan to Marvin on the way. It was simple. He knew the nutty old janitor at the Exeter would be catching the matinee at the Empire Burlesque, so no trouble about using the apartment stoop. Directly across from the Exeter, sandwiched between two tenements, was an open lot. The ground was still a little soft, but free of junk.

Without a building for Bob and Stan to bounce their long shots off, an outfielder could play deep enough to flag down anything hit into the lot. There would be no cheap homers. The infielder could play a little deeper, to cut off the doubles and triples. Give them the singles, but take away the long ball. With a little luck, the Wysnoskis could be whipped.

"Sounds like it'll work," Marvin said.

"Want infield or out?" asked Richie.

"Infield. I'm probably faster than you."

This was the shit that Richie hated. The few times he'd gone out of his way to smooth things, friendly like, between him and Marvin, he got this attitude shit instead. It pissed him off.

Chapter

19

The teams stood in front of the Exeter. Stan flipped a coin to see who would be home team. The brothers won, electing to take last bats.

Right off, Richie nubbed a soft shot past Bob for a double, the ball glancing off his fingers as he jumped to his left in an unsuccessful attempt to make a grab. Before the top half of the inning was over, Marvin contributed two singles. One run.

It took only one out in their half of the inning for the brothers to realize that this game would be different. Stan sent a long, soaring shot about thirty feet into the lot. Richie had no trouble getting under it for the catch.

"Wise asses," sneered Stan, glaring at his opponents.

But when Bob sent a screamer, no more than three feet off the ground, Richie hardly saw it. The ball carried into the lot, a home run and tie score at the end of the first inning.

The pattern was set. Richie and Marvin kept pecking away, hardly ever scoring more than one run in an inning. The Wysnoskis refused to alter their power game, and there was no way you could keep them from scoring.

And the brothers were exacting a price.

One hard shot spun Marvin completely around as he reached off-balance with his right hand to catch it. The ball fell to the street for a double. Stan sent a ball off Marvin's right leg, raising a welt. Marvin's hands had become so swollen, he couldn't close his fingers. Richie tripped on a rock in the lot, falling hard on his right hand. A small stick punctured the heel of his thumb about a quarter inch. Later, a nail in a utility pole sliced the leg of his trousers as he ran for a foul ball. He'd catch hell from his mom.

The game drew attention of the whole neighborhood including Eight-Ten.

Eight-Ten—no one knew his real name—was a big, stooped retard who'd lived in the Ward his whole life. He was between twenty-five and forty-five. He had no family or home. He slept in an empty coal bin at the Armstrong Arms, elite apartments with underground parking and two elevators, one in the lobby and one for freight and deliveries.

For years, the freight elevator had been a good friend to Eight-Ten and *Clarion* paperboy, Gino Sharkey. Delivering the paper provided great cover for Gino's real task, picking up six to eight number slips and wagers to be dropped off at McDuffie's office each day.

Every Sunday morning was the same. Eight-Ten would be waiting for Gino to pull his wagon full of the heavy Sunday *Clarion* up to the freight elevator at the rear of the Armstrong. While the carrier stood back, lit a cigarette and watched, Eight-Ten off-loaded fifteen bulky copies into the elevator, then held the door for Gino to join him. Starting at the top floor of the seven-story building, their routine rarely changed. The big dullard, smiling to be part of an operation he barely understood, held the freight door open while he watched Gino make his rounds. At some stops, Gino simply dropped the paper in front of the apartment door. At others, he rang the bell, waited for the door to open, handed over the *Clarion* and was given a slip of paper and some money in return. A rare policy payoff provided the only break in the routine.

"Okay big guy, so what's it gonna be?" Gino couldn't understand why he had taken a liking toward the big oaf. During the more than two years they had been sharing the freight elevator, they had exchanged no more than a couple hundred words except, of course, for that idiotic cackle. "Feel lucky? Or do you want the dime?"

"Aheh, Aheh. I feel lucky, aheh, aheh."

"You want me to mix 'em, or you want to?"

The imbecile's numbers combo played off his name. The eight was a constant. The ten was divided into two numbers to fill out the three number combination needed to play "the bug."

"My turn, my turn," Eight-Ten giggled. "I want three, eight, seven. Aheh, aheh."

Gino tore the top page from a small pad, scribbled a five-point star in the upper left, and two XXs on the bottom right, his runner's code, then scrawled 3-8-7. He made sure Eight-Ten had eyeballed the paper before stuffing it into an envelope with his other numbers, then fished a dime out of his pocket for inspection.

"Your lucky dime," the carrier said, then added "You know you have a better chance if you don't use an eight every time. Why the fuck do you always need an eight?"

"My first name, it's what they call me. Aheh, aheh. Always need my first name."

Gino shrugged, reached for the handle of the wagon, and turned up the alley to the street.

The Armstrong was the only home Eight-Ten had. He earned his keep by doing all the unpleasant, backbreaking janitorial work the super didn't want to do. He used the water spigot in the basement to bathe and wash the hand-me-down clothes the janitor's wife gave him.

The dullard got help from another source, Profanity Pump. About a month earlier, on a scorching hot day, she spotted Eight-Ten shuffling down the street on a pair of shoes barely more than tattered uppers and shoelaces. The sidewalk was hot enough to raise blisters if you touched it long enough. Without letting anybody know, she had walked him over to Oscar's Shoe Repair shop on Prince Street to pick out a couple of pairs of shoes left unclaimed by their owners.

"You're all set now," Pump said, handing over a brown paper bag containing the shoes.

"Why do you help me?" Eight-Ten took the package and studied Pump's face. "You're not my friend. You make fun of me at Milt's and everybody laughs."

"Just take the shoes and head on home. Go on now, get lost. And keep your god damn trap closed about this. Getit?"

Pump stood outside the shoe repair shop and watched the big, clumsy oaf shuffle across the street with his booty. She had just gone through two months' of her allowance, and another three bucks lifted from her mom's purse and dad's wallet.

Eight-Ten scratched out a few bucks a week by selling the *Evening Clarion* in front of the Empire Burlesque. But selling newspapers was only one reason Eight-Ten stationed himself in front of the Empire. Every other Friday, Cy Golden, the red-faced and corpulent stagehand, would slip out the alley door of the burlesque house with an envelope in his hand filled with eight-by-ten publicity glossies of the lovelies ending their run and moving out for that night's opening show at the Hudson Burlesque in Union City.

The two men never looked at each other. The fat stagehand took his four-star final edition of the *Evening Clarion* from under a rock that held the papers in place and went back into the theater.

Eight-Ten went back to his crib at the Armstrong and examined the pictures. He stayed there for hours, just gawking at the half-naked women.

He loved his prints, and in return the lovelies gave him his name. He had a whole collection, which he willing shared with boys in the neighborhood for a soda. He was the neighborhood's Pied Piper, leading a generation of avid boys into an erotic never-never land.

"Yul see. You Polak mother fuckers got it rough and don't like it. And a nigger too. Aheh, aheh," Eight-Ten called out.

A few of the Prep hotshots were also watching the game. Terry McDivit, Mike Suchi, and Jackie Conn, an all-city quarterback as a sophomore who, rumor had it, was already being scouted by Fordham.

"Nice play, kid," said Jackie, when Marvin speared a hard shot from Stan just as the convoy of critics arrived.

"Fast hands," said Mike.

"Yeah. I hear he plays pretty good round ball too," said Jackie.

"Conners can use him," said Terry. "Basketball's been shit at the Prep since Zubi and Gast graduated."

"You kiddin'?" mocked Mike. "A nigger at Prep. No way. I'll bet he ain't even Catholic."

"Sorry, wasn't thinkin'."

"Pisses me off sometimes," said Jackie. "Central picks up more good spades that way."

Neither team could gain an advantage. For the Wysnoskis, there was the added frustration of Eight-Ten. Each good play against Richie and Marvin was greeted by his obscene cheer.

"Lucky Polak fuckers!" droned Eight-Ten, when Stan raced in to catch a shot by Marvin.

"Ya god damned retard, if ya don't shut the fuck up, I'll ram a ball down yer throat."

"Hey, take it easy, kid. Not lettin' ol' Eight-Ten rattle ya, are ya?" chided Mike Suchi with a wink to his pals.

"Hell no," replied Stan. "Fuck him."

At the end of eight innings, the score was tied 9-all.

In the top of the ninth, Marvin managed a single. Richie added a triple, good for one run and a 10-9 lead going into the bottom of the final inning. Everybody was suddenly quiet.

"Wat'cha think?" whispered Richie as he and Marvin walked out to the street.

"Nuthin'."

"Nuthin' bullshit. I think we got it. So do you." Richie and Marvin were smiling as they took their positions.

The Wysnoskis, faced with their first defeat ever, resorted for the first time to the cute tricks they had always mocked others for using. And it looked like they would work. With two outs, the bases loaded, Bob took the ball from his brother. He approached the stoop with confidence that he could bring home at least one run, possibly more.

Then, instead of playing it cute, he spiked the ball off the bottom step with all the force he could muster. The ball hit Marvin and he fell to the ground, one hand clutching his throat, the other moving to his belly.

"Holy shit!" cried Terry McDivit.

"Didn't even see it," said Mike.

"They killed the nigger," intoned Jackie Conn.

"Fuck the coon, where's the ball?" shouted Stan, as everyone ran toward the fallen youth.

"Ya all right, kid?" Terry asked, leaning over Marvin.

Marvin remained motionless, flat on his back in the middle of the street. He cautiously moved his lips. No sound. An ugly welt was already visible beside his Adam's apple. He stared straight at the sky and moved his lips again, then smiled. Cradled between his right hand and his stomach was a pink high bouncer.

"Yer out, mother fucker. An' ya lose. Aheh, aheh." Eight-Ten yelled. The other kids were shocked.

"If ya don't shut your mouth, I'll kill ya," warned Bob, shaking a fist at the chuckling Eight-Ten.

"We did it! Hot damn, we did it!" shouted Richie, reaching down to grab Marvin's hand and help him up. "You can keep the game ball, you earned it."

Marvin nodded.

"Nice game. Lucky, but nice," Bob said to Richie. "You too," he added looking at Marvin as he rubbed his neck.

"Let's hit Milt's," said Richie. "A real victory bash."

Milt listened to the babbled accounts of the game that came from the big booth in the back of the room after he served them with a soda each, on the house. Everyone, including Profanity Pump, joined in. Everyone, that is, except Marvin, who silently rubbed the lump next to his Adam's apple. The Pump had nudged herself to one side of Marvin after pushing Eight-Ten aside and almost out of the booth.

"Jesus Christ," she said, "You got some big-ass lump." She tenderly pressed a bar towel filled with ice Milt provided against the spreading black and blue welt on Marvin's neck. "It looks like a big fucking hickey that's come out to say hello."

Everyone laughed. Even Marvin. The Pump always had the right words waiting.

"Now get yer asses outta here," Milt said to the kids an hour later. "Ya told yer story. I got a business to run."

Richie walked Marvin to the front of his house. "See ya later. Hell of a game. I had a feelin'. I just had a feelin'. Glad ya showed up."

Marvin didn't seem to hear Richie's words as he walked up the steps to his front door. Without saying a word, he opened the door and disappeared inside.

Richie was overcome by a swirling giddiness. "Bejesus H. Christ," he shouted. "Bejesus H. Christ. I did it. I did it." He shadowboxed with a utility pole, throwing two left jabs and a right cross.

Inside his house, Marvin stopped before climbing the stairs to his bedroom. He fingered the growing knot on his neck and giggled. He couldn't help himself. Three months earlier he was a stranger at Milt's, and today he had the seat of honor in the big middle booth.

Chapter

20

In 1919, Alexander Bancik, a thirty-nine-year-old uneducated Montenegrin, arrived in New York with his fifteen-year-old son, Josef. They were stupefied by what they saw at Ellis Island. Propelled by a dream that hard work and education would pay their fare on the dizzying ride to equality and democracy, it didn't take long before they learned how much the ticket really cost.

The father and son cleared customs and were met by two dumpy men in ill-fitting suits. Josef remembered that they had dark skin and moustaches. Each wore a hat with a small feather in it. Their dark suits, vests, high-button shoes, and stiff, high collars were identical. They seemed ill at ease. They spoke in Croatian, but with an accent Josef couldn't make out. Later he learned they were communists, and that his father was the ideal recruit worthy of being sponsored to help spread the movement across the Atlantic. Ten years of killing Ottoman Turks had earned Alexander Bancik a reputation as a fearless warrior.

From Ellis Island, the quartet went to a small Bulgarian restaurant in Manhattan. Josef was told to sit at a table near the front door. His father and the two men joined a fat woman in a black dress, black stockings, and no shoes at a rear table. She also had a moustache. The conversation was animated and lengthy. Finally, Bancik was given a piece of paper and some money. He and the woman arose at the same time. She put her hand on his shoulder and uttered the only words Josef was able to hear: "Sre̋cno, sretno," good luck.

One of the men accompanied them all the way to Newark, by ferry, train and trolley. It was dark when they arrived at the tenement on Morton

Street. Sophie Crno, a widow from Cetinje, greeted them. She had a Greek lover, Zerkorian, and a twelve-year-old daughter, Catherine.

The Crnos helped the Banciks with the grace of countrymen ushering their own kind through a labyrinth that they themselves were only beginning to understand. The widow gave them an old mattress, and kitchen essentials. Catherine taught Josef English, as much as she knew. The elder Bancik—proud, stubborn, and strangely reluctant— refused to learn any more than a handful of necessary words and phrases.

It didn't matter much.

The job he had waiting for him at the Pennsylvania Railroad freight yards required little human communication. Bancik, the red-bearded warrior hailed throughout Montenegro for his bravery, now retrieved paper and other debris from along the tracks. He watched for cinders from passing locomotives and was always available for the backbreaking tasks that others shirked. He was "Big Dumb Alex." Twice he was goaded into fights. The second time, he almost killed the man, a thick-necked Mick from Hoboken. Then they left him alone.

Three times the dumpy little men from Ellis Island came to the tenement, and Josef was told to go out and play. After the third visit, his father's spirits were higher than at any time since they had come to the new country. He picked up Josef and almost crushed him in his arms.

Day after day he waited for the two men to come back. Finally, after two weeks, Josef accompanied his father to the Bulgarian restaurant in Manhattan. The fat lady with the moustache told his father that the two men had to leave the country. He should go back to his job, and consider himself lucky.

Not long afterward, two other men came to the tenement. They spoke only English and talked to Bancik through the widow Crno. They said they were sent by the United States government. They worked for a man called A. Mitchell Palmer.

They said he was an important man in Washington, the attorney general. Josef watched from the top of the stairs as the widow Crno relayed this information to his father. No, his father told the widow, he knew nothing of the two men, hadn't seen them since that first day on Ellis Island. They left, but said they would probably be back.

They stepped to the sidewalk, and the smaller man tapped two cigarettes from a pack of Chesterfields, offering one to the other man. They lit up, inhaled deeply, and surveyed both sides of the block in a bored manner that showed clearly they had seen it all before.

"What did you think, Bolshies?" the smaller man asked.

"I don't know. Those Bolshevik bastards have gotten a lot smarter since we started shipping their asses back home. Christ, I'm still amazed they thought they'd get away with setting a bomb off outside the boss's digs."

They never returned.

Where once his father could stare down any man alive with pride, Josef noticed that he began to look mostly at the ground. His father once walked with the full-chested stride that was a boast of his manliness. Now he shuffled along, sullen and sad. Josef vowed that this would never happen to him. With Catherine's help, he learned English and got an eighth-grade education. He got a job at Pennsy and worked his way up to switchman. He and Catherine married and had a little boy, Josef. They got a larger apartment and his father came to live with them.

Josef and his wife decided to build their lives the American way. Except when speaking to his father, he and his wife spoke only English at home and didn't teach their son Croatian. They abandoned their Eastern Orthodox religion, became Catholics, and sent their son to St Mark's school.

By the age of twelve, Joey was just like any other American son of immigrants, complete with inherited prejudices and hate.

Chapter

21

"Ya want no breakfast?" asked Joey's mother as he burst into the kitchen. She was pouring coffee for the bent old man at the kitchen table.

"Didn't I tell you? I'm receiving this morning."

He and Billy Spratlin were serving as altar boys at the six-thirty Mass, and Joey had decided to take advantage of the opportunity to receive Holy Communion.

"This somethin' new, Communion durin' the week?" She brushed past him on her way to the communal toilet at the end of the hall. She carried a roll of toilet paper.

"No, Mother, it isn't new. I've done it before," replied Joey, speaking slowly, enunciating every syllable. More and more, Joey slapped his parents in the face with the correct diction of a son who was ashamed of his immigrant parents. Just as suddenly as Joey had turned on his contempt, he turned it off.

"Gimme a cupla sheets o' that," he said, reaching for the toilet paper. "Gotta little cold and no hanky."

"Be home after school?" she asked, ripping off some sheets of paper.

"Nope, saved a few cents for a coffee 'n donut. I'm meeting my friends."

His mother was at the door of the toilet, as her Negro neighbor was coming out. She'd never had to share a bathroom with anyone at their other apartment, and now they were sharing with niggers. She and her husband hated what was happening to them. He urged her to find a place for them to move.

For a few short months, Catherine Bancik and her son sampled the sweets of life. Joey accompanied his mother on most of her apartment hunting trips. It was always the same. They were either too late or the rent was too high. When the rent was out of the question, it only served to put her into high gear. No trip was wasted. She always wore her Sunday dress, and Joey's shoes were always shined.

"Make 'em think we got dough. Bring the kid. Let 'em know we got a kid. Don't mention the ol' man, though. What for? Everything above board from the start. Let 'em know we ain't goin' to screw 'em," advised Josef Bancik.

It was heaven. Apartment managers and owners ushering them through newly painted apartments well out of their reach. Catherine checked the stove, closet space, bedroom size, and whether the windows rattled. She asked questions about the schools, churches, and neighbors. She even perfected a little routine for the fantasy tour.

"I really don't know if we'd get all our furniture in. What's the size of the parlor again?"

"I wouldn't wait. It'll be gone by tonight. There's a war on, you know. A little deposit will hold it."

"Let me call my husband, see what he thinks. You're here all day? That parlor size again, twenty by seventeen?"

The excursions stopped when Josef Bancik lost his job at the Pennsy in late '43. The siding and right-of-way switches were now all electronically controlled, and Josef was forced to the loading docks. A slipped disc put him out of work completely. He was given a small disability pension and an introduction to despair.

During those first weeks, it was a daily, early-morning ritual for Catherine and Josef to pore over the Help Wanted columns, "Skilled and Unskilled Labor." This morning, the paper was on the kitchen table. Josef was still snoring in bed.

The old man had been no trouble. He had been more than able to take care of himself since he retired at sixty-five the year before. With his pension from the railroad, it was the old man and not Josef who kept the Banciks barely afloat.

Joey walked down the hall, past the door of the Fitzsimmonses—the door an obstacle that Joey would never get passed. "Fitzsimmons, what a god damned laugh. Whoever heard of an Irish coon?" his father said the day the black family moved in. The plight of the Banciks made his father's words an anthem to which Joey would march with increasing stridency.

"But Mr. Rogovin, the roof's been leakin' for a month now," said Catherine Bancik. Jacob Rogovin, a big, heavy-shouldered man, moved to the back of his jewelry store on Prince Street. "We never had to wait that long before."

"Things've been tough. It's 1943, there's a war on, and roofing materials are hard to come by."

"We're only askin' for a little patchin' on the roof. Give us the stuff, and my Josef'll fix it."

"Your Josef'll fix it? God damn right he'll fix it. Not only should he be happy to do that, but with what you're paying for rent, he should be kissing my ass. S'cuse me, Mrs. Bancik, if I sound a little pissed, because I am. The government takes the shirt off your back. Okay, okay, your Josef will get the stuff. Here's where he's to go. It's a warehouse down by the river. I'll phone." Rogovin handed Joey's mother a piece of paper.

"Thank you, Mr. Rogovin. My Josef will do a good job."

"I bet he will. This'll probably be the last time. I'm thinking of bailing out."

It wasn't long before Rogovin told his tenants that he would no longer repair broken mailboxes and windows, unclog toilets, or replace stolen garbage cans. And from now on, the rent would be either mailed or brought to his jewelry store by the first of the month. He wouldn't be coming down to the tenements any more.

"Bastard. God damned bastard," Josef Bancik snarled when his wife described her experience with Rogovin that afternoon. "I saw it comin'."

Chapter

22

"Wow, nifty. Let's take a look," said Billy Spratlin as he led Joey, Richie Maxwell, and Carl Schroder across the street to join the big kids.

"Hot damn, who's it belong to?" asked Mike Suchi.

"Dunno, but it's nobody's round here, ya kin bet yur sweet ass on that," said Terry McDivit.

"I think I saw it on Baldwin the last cupla weeks or so," said Carl. "A big guy, mean lookin' as hell, was in it.

Joey peered inside. It was big as a house. He backed away to take in its sweeping lines. It looked half a block long, a black, 12-cylinder, 1939 LaSalle. Its shiny spotlessness was accentuated by the smell of leather wafting through the windows—a classic. It was too big, too monumental for Joey to feel envy. He was awed.

"Hey, kid, see who drove it?" Mike yelled to the colored boy on a tenement stoop.

"Big white man. He's in Milt's."

They all turned toward the store. A shadow was just barely visible at the phone in the rear. They walked across the street to a porch to begin their vigil. They didn't wait long.

God, was he big. The kids began their appraisal. The guy wore a hat, son of a bitch if it wasn't a derby. A trench coat hung from his shoulders, cape style, and he wore a navy blue pinstriped suit with white shirt, vest, and light blue tie. It was a beautiful getup.

The man took a cigar out of an inner pocket and unwrapped it. The big man lit the cigar, spotted his audience through the smoke and smiled crookedly. He wondered how many of them he would see later, in their kitchens and living rooms or peering through the doors of their bedrooms.

He turned and walked toward High. The big man could feel the kids' eyes on him as he turned up the stairs of the corner tenement house.

"Wonder what he wants," said Joey, watching the big man disappear into the building.

"Who knows," said Billy. "Hell, with that car, mebbe he's buyin' the whole block for all we know."

They gave the LaSalle another long, admiring look and then went their separate ways. It was the first of the month, Joey was due at four that afternoon to help Sister Joan clean votive candle holders and to dust around the altars at St. Mark's.

Two hours later Joey was finished, closed the door of the church sacristy and headed home. Across town, the door of the Bancik apartment was opening.

"Mrs. Bancik? My name is Cyril Hennington. I represent the new owners of the building. My card."

Catherine was stunned and speechless. The huge specter filled the entire door. The heavy face atop the large shoulders smiled crookedly at her. A furrowed brow ended at the thick, black line of a single eyebrow that ran the width of the broad face. The eyes were small, just big enough to catch the light that flickered through the shadows of the deep sockets. In one hand he held a business card, in the other was a finely brushed brown derby.

The big man was amused by what he saw. He noted Catherine's cheap print dress and frayed cloth slippers, the thick ankles, tired face, and dull eyes. Her brown hair, now mostly gray, was pulled back severely in a bun. Her hands, one on the doorknob, the other holding a threadbare kitchen towel, were big-veined and thick-fingered. The fingernails were broken. Foreign scum.

Catherine looked at the card but didn't take it. A card. Did he take her for a fool? Anyone could have a card. The new owner, what new owner?

"It's the first of the month. You know what that means," the big man said. "I represent Property Managers, Inc. I can assure you that it is one of the top real estate firms in the city."

"Josef! Josef! Commere, hurry!" A kitchen chair scraped on the floor.

"Damn it, whadaya want? I'm eatin'."

"Mr. Bancik, my name is Cyril Hennington. I'm here to collect the rent."

"The rent? Wha'cha talkin' bout? Our rent goes to nobody but Rogovin, in person, at his store. Jes who're you? Get lost, mister," said Josef, emphasizing each point with a feeble jab of his right index finger.

"Here's my card. I offered it to your wife, but she didn't care to take it."

Hennington extended his hand. The small white card slipped from his fingers, fluttering to the floor. "I'm sorry. Here, let me get it."

As he bent down, the man called Hennington seemed to stumble. He fell forward, his enormous head catching Josef in the stomach. Josef was driven backward, landing on his back in the middle of the living room.

"How clumsy can a guy get? Let me help you." As he reached to assist Josef, the big man stumbled again, this time catching himself by throwing his right foot forward splintering the spindly leg of a straight-back chair. The chair remained stationary during impact, then collapsed when its underpinning was ripped from under it.

"There I go again. I don't know what's wrong. I'm sorry, truly sorry." Hennington righted the chair and propped it against the wall.

"Now about the rent, it's twenty-eight dollars, isn't it?"

"Ya know damned well it is."

"Well, here's some good news. We know you're having trouble, been out of work for a while. We're going to make it easier on you. From now on, you can pay by the week, in installments. So, beginning right now, it will be nine dollars a week."

"Nine a week? Ya can't do it and ya know it. There's rent controls. The OPA won't let you."

"The Office of Price Administration? Don't be a fool." The big man bent down and picked up the broken chair leg. He fingered the splintered end then tossed the leg onto a sofa across the room. "What can the OPA do? Really, what can they do?"

"Get it. Give it to 'im. God damn it, go get it," Josef ordered his wife as he arose from the floor. It was over in less than a minute.

Catherine came into the room with the rent money, and handed it to the man called Hennington. He extracted nine dollars and handed the rest back to her. "We'll be around every Friday." He closed the door quietly behind him.

A few seconds later the Banciks heard a knock on the door across the hall.

"Mr. Fitzsimmons? My name is Cyril Hennington. I represent the new owners of this building. My card . . ."

Alexander Bancik had been sitting at the kitchen table. From where he sat the old man could see to the front of the railroad apartment, through the two bedrooms into the living room. He witnessed everything from over his plate of beans and fried pork roll. He understood none of it.

Joey was half a block away when he spotted the LaSalle turning onto High from Morton. The big, black car idled past Joey, headed south toward Baldwin.

Joey sensed something was wrong when he stepped into the kitchen. The depression that had become standard mealtime fare at the Banciks seemed deeper than usual.

"Ya shudda seen the big ol' LaSalle that just cruised down the block. The guy drivin' it was big and mean-lookin'. Dressed real good though. That car, man, it was really—"

Josef Bancik was on his son like a flash, his open right hand coming down with great force across the boy's face. The blow knocked Joey against the corner of the coal stove. As he tried to regain his balance, his father was on him, raining at least a dozen blows on his son's arms and shoulders.

Joey covered his head with his arms and hands as he stumbled sobbing into a cupboard.

"Impressed by the guy, were ya? His big car. His clothes. How big he was. My son telling me this." The words spilled out of Bancik's livid, tear-stained face. The ache in his gut pushed the words out, the bile of frustration. "Ungrateful little bastard."

"Josef! Josef! God's sake, stop! It's enough. He didn't know," his mother screamed.

The beating stopped, but Joey wasn't sure, wouldn't move until he had some word from his father. He cringed in the corner, his head pressed against the cupboard.

"Git yer ass in yer room. No eats. No nothin'. Don't want t' hear or see ya all night."

Like a dog that had been beaten by its master, Joey slinked into his room, his eyes on the floor. Catherine Bancik stared at her plate. She sobbed. Alexander Bancik watched Joey leave the kitchen, then went back to his dinner.

"I ain't hungry no more," Josef said and walked to the living room.

Joey threw himself on his bed in the corner of the bedroom he shared with his grandfather. He hurt like hell. He didn't understand what made his father so mad at him. He was just talking about that guy with the big car.

Still awake three hours later, Joey watched as his grandfather went through his nightly ritual. He avoided it like the plague, staying up as long as he was allowed until the old man was asleep. It had been months since Joey had witnessed his grandfather's devotion. He took off his old work clothes and hernia truss, compliments of Pennsy, and got into his pajamas. The old man lit two candles on top of a bureau completely covered with old-time religion pictures and other crudely made religious objects, mostly cheap plaster-of-Paris statues of saints Joey never learned about in catechism. Crucifixes hung on the dirty wall above the table. The candles cast an eerie glow about the room. Throughout the weird half-hour ceremony, the old man continued a low, guttural chant. His eyes rolled from whatever object he was holding to the largest of the crucifixes directly in front of him, then to the ceiling above the pitiful shrine. The old man kissed the pictures as he passed from one to the next, crossing himself three times for each. When it was over, he blew out the candles, got in bed, and within a few minutes was snoring.

It was well into early morning before Joey dozed off.

Chapter

23

A month after Hennington's first visit to the Criolas, their downstairs neighbor called it quits. They had to leave because of the higher rent. At least that's what Joey's dad said. They were middle-aged with two grown children—a son in the Coast Guard and a daughter in the WACs. Joey was sad to see them go.

The Criolas were still moving their furniture out when the carpenters arrived. First a hole was knocked in the wall for a second door into the hall. The wall between the two bedrooms was closed up. A sink was installed in what had been the Criolas' parlor. An old stove was dragged over from Simon's.

It was an instant apartment, and cheap too, only nine bucks a week for each of the one-bedroom cages. The Lujacks were the first to arrive, taking the rear apartment. A few days later, the Johnsons, a black family, arrived.

"Hear ya got two nigger families on yer floor," Bob Wysnoski taunted Joey at Milt's.

"Real jigaboos too, from what I hear," Stan chimed in. "Like they can't even talk American. Hear they talk real coon, like there's still pig shit on their feet."

"Ya know it all, why the fuck ya askin' me?"

"Movin' out? Guess not; father's still lookin' fer work, ain't he?" Bob drilled the words home like a pink high bouncer to the throat.

Joey reddened. Some of the older guys were sitting in the booths. He knew they were looking at him. He could feel their eyes burning into the back of his head.

"Kiss my ass. Fer all ya know, my old man's got an interview downtown somewhere today. He got another one tomorrow. In fact, fer all yer s'posed to know, he's been offered a whole lot of jobs. Turned them all down. He cudda been workin' for months now, but he ain't taken' jes anything."

"Oh, I'm sorry, real sorry. I didn't know yer ol' man was in such demand," Stan kept boring in.

Joey wanted to smash the twins' ugly faces, turn them into bloody hamburger.

"You fuckers are gonna eat your words, you'll see."

Joey ran from the store. He didn't stop running until he got to the end of the block. Stan's final words were like a knife in his back: "Don't the stupid kid know he and his folks are nuthin' but white niggers?"

Joey ran most of the way downtown. He was furious. The tears didn't start until he passed the Hall of Records and turned down Market. He had to fight back, but how and with what? He couldn't dare the Wysnoskis to shut their god damn mouths or else. They'd kill him in a fight. Joey knew what he was looking for, something small but expensive. He tried Woolworth's and then Kresge's. In Grant's he found it.

Joey walked past the toys. He was now playing an adult game, it was payback time. He idled from one display to another, then peered past the cash register. The Negro woman was still alone at the other counter. She was changing prices on some items and had her back to his target area. Joey casually circled the store.

He approached the display, reached across the counter, and grabbed a tube of *Petulant Rose Petals* lipstick and a small bottle of *Evening in the Casbah* perfume. They were safely in his pocket when he walked past the nigger saleslady to the front door.

"Can I help you, young man?"

"No, just lookin' around."

She smiled and turned back to her work.

Outside on the sidewalk, he tossed the two objects into the first trash can he came to. "I ain't no white nigger," he mumbled to himself.

Some dough in his pocket could be the clincher. The loose change he got every week for helping Sister Joan at St. Mark's wasn't doing it. So instead of heading home, he detoured to Frank Marsucci's dump at Broome and Kinney to check where he was on the *Beacon* carrier waiting list.

"You back again, not giving up are you kid," the circulation manager looked up from the paperwork he had spread across the desk. "Nothin's changed since the last time. You're getting close."

"How close? It's been months since I've put my name in."

"Keep poking your head in here and who knows …. Someone might be quitting on me next week. Ain't likely, but it could happen."

Joey shrugged and walked out of the office. He'd be back again next week.

He didn't notice Eight-Ten standing in the shade of a doorway on the opposite side of the street. The man-child had tailed Joey from Morton Street. It was one of several times in the past few weeks that he had shadowed some of the gang from Milt's. He knew something was going on that wasn't good. Whenever this happened, it made his head hurt. They didn't look at his pretty pictures so much anymore. Richie even pushed them off the table at Milt's and when he stooped to get them, everyone laughed. When he looked up, Richie and Joey were laughing the loudest. And today, he had once again tailed Joey all the way to the same place he had followed Richie not too long ago.

Richie was the one to blame, Eight-Ten thought, *but for what. He goes to that nigger barber shop too many times for it to be good. And to that cheap Jew to get a bike. Everyone loves that bike more than my beautiful pictures. It don't look good that Joey is coming here, too. Does he want a bike like Richie? If he gets one, will they love it as much as Richie's?*

Eight-Ten rubbed both temples in an attempt to make the hurt go away. The throbbing only increased. *If they love two bikes, then what happens to my beautiful pictures?*

Stan Wysnoski's "white nigger" taunt hung like a heavy stone between Joey's shoulder blades as he headed home from Marsucci's. There was no way he would let them know at Milt's that nothing much had changed for more than a month, and it looked as though it would only get worse. There were more changes in the building, but after the initial shock, they were expected. The Kusliks moved out of their first-floor apartment. It was just like the Criolas. Another colored family moved into one of the subdivides. A white family took the second apartment.

Joey couldn't understand it. He wondered about it and was troubled by the fact that he was pissed off that niggers hadn't taken both units. They should have. Shit, that's all the apartments were good for anymore—niggers.

The former Rogovin tenements weren't the only ones the big man in the shiny car visited each week. Nor were they the only ones to know the carpenter's hammer, as lodgings were readied for newly arrived urban immigrants.

One Friday when Joey was walking up his stoop, he nearly bumped into a tall, well dressed black guy leaving the building.

"You got to look where you're goin', son."

Joey just ignored him and pushed right by him.

He had no way of knowing that ten minutes earlier the same black man had introduced himself to his mother at their apartment door.

"Hello, I guess you might say I'm Cyril Hennington the Second. And, I guess you know why I'm here," the man was as easily as big as Hennington. He never stopped smiling.

Catherine called her husband to the door and retreated to the kitchen.

"Like I told your wife, I'm here for the rent money."

Catherine strained to hear what her husband would say. Nothing.

"Well, thank you, Mr. Bancik. That wasn't too hard now, getting used to a new man. Well, until next Friday then, and you have a good week now. Give my regards to the missus."

Catherine peered from the kitchen. Josef hadn't said a word. He quietly closed the door and then stood with his head pressed against the jamb. His eyes were closed. He was still standing there when the big black man introduced himself across the hall.

Chapter

24

Everyday Catherine and Josef checked the Want Ads in the newspapers, "Skilled" and "Unskilled Labor." They seemed to be running out of opportunities until one day Josef informed them that out of nowhere they had caught a break. He waited until the family was well into supper before he casually broke the news. As he spoke, hope, fear, anxiety, perhaps love peered at him from over spoonfuls of lentil-and-ham-hock soup.

"I gotta chance for a job in the mornin'." Josef let the words drop into the middle of the table and lay there. He spooned some soup into his mouth. He savored it. A stringy piece of ham hock caught between his upper left molars. He loudly sucked it out, the only sound in the room.

He waited until he was sure everyone, including the old man, was listening before going on. Josef Bancik, except for an odd job here and there, never more than a week or two at a time, had been unemployed for thirteen months, nine days.

"Jim Palic told me about it this mornin'. A janitor's job downtown at Prudential. He gave me the guy's name. Now let me see." Josef pulled a crumpled piece of paper from his shirt pocket. The note had been folded and unfolded, read and reread many times during that day. Josef placed it on the table, and then smoothed it down flat.

"Mike Callahan, building custodian, room one-oh-one. Eight sharp."

Josef sat back and breathed deeply. He was excited. Hell yes he was excited, almost enough to be taken in again by hope, that eternal charlatan.

Catherine fingered the paper. She studied each word, moving her lips. "It's all jest like I read it," said Josef.

"What kind of job?" his wife asked.

"Janitor's. Pays seventy cents per. But Jim sez I can move up. That's where he started. Now he runs the building's supply office. Makes eighty-five cents after only three years."

"Jim thinks you'll get it?" said Catherine, sliding the paper across the table to Joey.

"The job opened up yesterday. Jim sez the guy who had it got promoted to the boiler room startin' next week. Only a few guys know 'bout it. He's already talked to Callahan 'bout me. So I'll jest be there at eight sharp. I'll get it, you'll see."

Catherine smiled. "I'll iron your good shirt."

Joey was up at six in the morning. He found his father, mother, and grandfather drinking coffee at the kitchen table. They were silent. Joey grabbed a cup from the cupboard, filled it with coffee, and added a squirt of Carnation evaporated. He watched his father. Josef Bancik stared into his cup. He wore his only pair of dress pants, brown gabardines with deep hanger creases across the knees. Dark brown suspenders cut across his open collared white shirt. His high-top black work shoes were newly shined.

"Gotta go," Josef said. He arose and lifted his Army surplus Eisenhower jacket from the back of his chair. Josef kissed his wife on the forehead and nodded to his father. "See ya later, boy," he said to Joey without looking at his son.

"Good luck, Pop. You'll get it."

Catherine Bancik hurried out of the kitchen after her husband. She caught him as he was about to close the door to the hall behind him. Joey could just barely hear their whispered conversation.

"Ya got any money?"

"Nope. Walkin' down and walkin' back. It won't cost nuthin'."

"It ain't right. Yur gonna see that guy Callahan like a man, with money in the pocket. Here take this. 'N after ya see him, after he gives ya the job, ya buy a paper, a coffee, and mebbe even a hot dog at Nedick's. Then come back 'n tell us. We'll be waitin'." She took a five dollar bill out of the pocket of her apron.

"I don't need this much."

"Take it. You don't need to spend it. At least you have it."

Joey ran home that afternoon, raced up the stairs, and plunged into the kitchen. His mother was alone. "He ain't home yet," she said without looking up from the potato she was peeling.

"Wonder why? He shudda had it all wrapped up this mornin'. Mebbe he's celebratin'. Mebbe he's started already. Ya know, learnin' the ropes before he starts for real next week. What d'ya think?"

"I don't know," she said. She knew her husband. She knew what to expect when he returned. "Why don't ya go out and play. First change your clothes."

Josef Bancik returned shortly before midnight. He reeked of cheap muscatel. Catherine and Joey woke up and joined him in the kitchen. The old man was asleep. Josef's jacket was open. There was a stain on his shirt where the wine had dribbled from his chin. His fly was partly unzipped. He staggered a bit, then plopped down into a chair. "What ya doin' up?" Josef took off his jacket and threw it across the kitchen.

"We were worried. What happened?" Catherine asked in a dull voice.

Josef's fist came down on the table hard. "I didn't get the damn job. That's what happened. I'm there at eight sharp. I mean eight sharp. This guy Mike Callahan's waitin' fer me in his office. Sort of like a storeroom. A big Mick, I mean a real big red-faced bastard. But a nice guy, mebbe too nice. We shake hands and talk. He hands me an application. I fill it out 'n give it back to 'im. He looks it over and sez, 'I see yer thirty-nine.' But he's smilin' so I know it ain't gonna go against me. Then he sez, 'Palic tells me ya got some back trouble, lost a job 'count of it. That right?' He ain't smilin' now. 'Watch,' I sez to 'im. 'Jest watch, I'll show ya.' So I take this big barrel in the corner, half filled with soap powder. It's gotta weigh a hundred pounds at least. I picked it up. I mean I picked that god damned barrel up real good, easy as shit. I carried it 'round his desk, not once, but two times. The first time he don't want to look up from his desk. The second time he's really lookin' me over.

"Then, real casual like, I put the barrel back in the corner and sit down in front of his desk. I ain't even breathin' hard. 'Ya see, that's how my back is botherin' me,' I say.

"Callahan's smilin' again. He sez, 'I gotta be impressed. Looks like ya don't even need the doctor's exam we give t' all the new guys. Tell ya what, ya come back 'bout eleven. See, this ain't my decision, I gotta boss too. But it looks good, I'll tell ya that. Be back 'bout eleven, okay?' He shakes my hand, but somethin' don't sit right."

By this time Joey had taken a chair at the table. His mother sat opposite him. She had one hand on her lap, the other on the table.

"Sonofabitch bastard, my head hurts." Josef walked to the sink and held his head under the cold water. His shirt quickly became soaked and the water seeped down to his pants. He turned from the sink.

"No doctor's exam. Who the fuck did Callahan think he was foolin'? I had a hunch. So I jes waited down at the end of the hall. Sure 'nuff, not ten minutes later the biggest, blackest fuckin' nigger ya ever saw walks into Callahan's office. Ain't in there long either, before he came out with a paper in his hand. They ain't pullin' no wool over Josef Bancik's eyes. I follow him. Know where he goes? I'll tell ya where he goes, to Doctor S.L. Brady over in the Kearny Building on Broad. He's so god damned stupid he had to run his finger down the list of names in the lobby, then check it with the name he had on that fuckin' paper. Bet the bastard couldn't even read. I got in the same elevator, to the twelfth floor. No mistake, it was right there on the door, sign says Doctor S.L. Brady, em-dee.

"I went back at eleven. Know what that lyin' sonofabitch Callahan said? He said, 'Sorry, Bancik. I didn't know, but the people upstairs already had a guy hired. Never even told me. Like I said, I gotta boss too. Sorry.' I din't say a word, just walked out. That jig got the job over me!"

Late that night, Joey heard his parents talking in Croatian. His father was crying and his mother seemed to be trying to comfort him with soft words.

Why are they doing this to us, Joey thought. *The niggers. If it ain't them, who is it?* He rolled over, buried his head in his pillow and sobbed himself to sleep.

Chapter

25

"Nigger meat."

"Nigger meat?" asked Catherine Bancik. "What's that?"

"You don't want those hot dogs, Mrs. Bancik," explained Abe Fishbein. "Hardly any meat in 'em, and what there is ain't worth eatin'."

Joey and his mother walked to the far end of the meat display case, past all the prime cuts. In three clearly marked trays were ox tails, 11¢; pig's feet, 9¢; cow brains, 12¢ lb. They had never seen them on display before.

"I got a deal down at the slaughterhouse for this kind of stuff," said Fishbein, leaning across the display case.

"I can't cook that," Catherine said.

"Look, Mrs. Bancik, you're one of my old customers. I don't want to pass this stuff off on ya. I feel I gotta warn ya. But I gotta start stockin' this stuff. All the other markets been selling it for months now. I gotta make a living."

"Okay, gimme eight of the twenty-cent hot dogs. 'N grind up a half pound of pork 'n half of chuck. It's for stuffed cabbage."

While they waited, Joey noticed that three of the ten customers in the store were Negroes. He couldn't remember ever seeing more than one at a time before.

"Here ya are, Mrs. Bancik. That all?"

"That's it. On the bill, okay? We'll catch up on it next week."

"Sure. Hey, by the way, how's Josef doin'?"

"Still lookin'."

"Yeh, I know. Things're really tight. No more war work. Hardly anybody at the shipyards anymore. Even Ronson is cutting back," the pale butcher said, nodding his head toward the three Negroes. "Tell him 'Good Luck' for me."

"Thanks."

As they walked out of the shop, his mother said, "It don't seem right."

Joey was silent. He carried the package of meat, along with two other bags. One contained marked-down fruit and vegetables from the "Ripe but still Dee-licious" produce counter at the A&P. The other held day-old bread and week-old cake from Fischer's.

"I hope your father don't mind that cake. Maybe I can heat it up. You know how he gets."

"It'll be okay, Mom. Don't worry."

One day after school, Joey came home and put his books on the kitchen table, next to a newspaper.

"Where's Dad?"

"Out with your grandfather. You want something to eat?"

"Nope, I'm okay." He sat at the table and glanced at the open newspaper his mother had been reading.

THE NEW DAY

National & International

The Works of Father Divine

36 pages — 5¢

"Hey, Mom, what's this?"

"What's what?" Catherine turned from the sink. "I picked it up at the store."

"Store? What store?"

"The Peace Store down the street."

Joey rolled up the paper and moved toward his mother. Frightened that her son was about to strike her, she stepped aside as he repeatedly slammed the newspaper against the lip of the sink. Tears of rage covered his face as he fell back into a kitchen chair.

"The Peace Store! The Peace Store! You went to one of that god damn nigger crook's stores? Why . . . why in hell d'ya do that? Sonofabitch!" Joey shredded the paper into tiny pieces. "Sonofabitch, Father Divine's Peace Store!"

"I was told about it by Mrs. Criola. I don't like goin' there, but we got it tough. We gotta take advantage. Ev'rythin's cheaper there. Even hard-to-get stuff. Margarine's five cents less. I been going there for a few weeks now."

"Gotta take advantage? Ya know what they're callin' us? D'ya know?" Joey got up from the chair and blasphemed through his tears. "White niggers! That's right! White niggers! And that was even before you started going to that god damn store."

"But Joey, ev'rythin's cheaper. 'N they got nice canned goods."

Joey reeled from the room and into the hall. "White niggers they're calling us," he mumbled, "and they're right!"

Chapter

26

Joey and Billy talked about the changes in the neighborhood one morning while sitting on the stairs of the Exeter Apartments. "What the hell's goin' on?" agonized Joey. "Everything's changing around here."

"Yeah, ain't no room for whites anymore."

"I don't mean that, the fuckin' coons an' all. It ain't that. But everything. Ya kin feel it. It's all changed."

"What the hell ya talkin' 'bout?"

"I don't know. All I know is . . . it makes me feel . . . hell . . . it . . . well it's like once on the Number 8 from downtown. One day I really busted my ass to catch it at Broad and Market so I could get a seat. No luck. I gotta stand in the back. Ya know, once the bus starts up the hill, yer ass is grass. Everyone pushes back and you get crushed. You can push back, but it ain't no use. They still keep squeezing you."

"You're nuts. What's a bus got to do with anything? Crowds are crowds."

"That ain't the point, you dumb ass. We're getting pushed out. All of us. And how about we now got a cop walking in the neighborhood. No more squad car cruisin' by without stopping. What's that tell you?"

"You tell me why don'tcha."

"More coons, more crime. Everybody knows that."

"I don't. Besides, the cop they put on the beat is hardly Dick Tracy," Billy said. "He's kinda old. Saw him in Milt's the other day freeloading a coffee. Name's Gazzi."

"Can't be much of a cop, should have some stripes on his sleeve but he don't."

"Sure does nose around a lot. Saw him poking into the Jew's pawn-shop more than once."

"Yeah, and he's been kicking some voodoo ass as well. Came down hard on those fake priests when he caught them peddling guaranteed numbers winners and chicken bones over on Montgomery," Joey said.

"Not touching the numbers runners or banks though," Billy said. "Probably too hot for him to handle."

"*Beacon* paper boys are more his speed. I was over at Marsucci's office last week when they walked out buddy-buddy like, all smiles."

"Still waiting for a route, how many months…?"

"Just forget it."

"Oh yeah, guess ya heard, Father Schneider is lookin' into the rent thing," Billy said.

"So what? No way he's going to stop that big son of a bitch from collecting."

"If Father Schneider can't do anything, nobody can," Billy said.

"I hear he's turned the job over to pretty boy Father Nolan. If that's right, kiss it off."

"At least he comes around," Billy said. "Even popped for some sodas at Milt's last week. Shot the shit with the gang. It was the longest I can remember that the Pump had to button her lip."

"Yeah, guess you're right. He's a big change from Father Koestler, and he's young, won't keel over and die on the sidewalk like the old guy, not for a while anyway," Joey said.

"Come on, let's get a soda," Billy was tired of talk that didn't concern him. "It's on me."

Joey's trips to the hated Peace Store became inevitable. He would not go to the Father Divine establishment on Baldwin. That was out of the question. Instead, he hiked the extra four blocks to Mercer and Howard, always sizing up the area from both sides of the street before going into the store. Was he really fooling anybody?

Joey had to admit that shopping at the Peace Store was a hell of a lot nicer than being pushed around in the other markets. It was that way right from the start.

"Peace, little brother, what can we do for you?"

Joey studied the black man who came from behind the front counter. He was probably about his father's age, more or less. Joey took in the starched, white, open-collared shirt, the spotless white trousers, and the worn, but clean, black shoes.

"I gotta list," said Joey, looking about the store as he fumbled for his mother's shopping list and the rationing books. The market, formerly McMillan's "Hardware and Anything Else You Can Think Of," was large. Everything had a scrubbed look.

"I don't recall seein' you here before, little brother," the man said. "I hope this will be the first of many visits. Oh, this is a fine list."

The man moved effortlessly about the store, taking a can of beans here, a package of spaghetti there, a two-pound bag of flour, two pounds of potatoes, a head of cabbage, two loaves of fresh bread (cheaper than the day-old stuff at Fisher's Outlet), a pound of margarine, oatmeal and dry skim milk.

Directly behind the counter, in large gold letters, was an emblazoned "Peace," and an inscription.

God and Country

Peace for All

The Divine Father Will Lead You

"Yes, it is a beautiful testimonial, isn't it, little brother?" said a startlingly beautiful woman's voice from behind Joey. "The Divine Father is never far from our thoughts."

Joey was awed by the light-skinned Negro woman. She was as beautiful as her voice.

"Oh, I see you've met Sweetness Charity," the man said.

"I haven't been formally introduced," said the beautiful woman. "Well then, little brother, won't you tell me your name?"

"Joey Bancik and I'm Catholic," he stammered.

"Well now, little brother, that certainly is a strange kind of introduction," said the man. "Sweetness Charity operates this store. She is the one who makes this fine food available to you, with the Divine Father's blessings, of course."

"His blessings? Sister Immaculata says Father Divine is a heathen who took a verse from the bible and screwed it up to make it look like he was God's messenger."

"Sister Immaculata? Then you must be a student over at St. Mark's," said Sweetness Charity, her mouth now frozen in a hard smile.

"Did the good sister also inform you, oh yes, she must have done so, that there are many people, good people, who call the Catholic Church the 'whore of Rome'? Certainly she told you that. But no, we won't go into that, little brother. It is slander of the worst kind. Father Divine exacts a harsh retribution from those who slander another soul, or another church.

"Instead let me, as a servant of the Divine Father, welcome you to this store," she said, placing the nine food items in a paper bag.

Joey placed four quarters in the woman's hand. Sweetness Charity rang up the sale, then put the ten cents change in Joey's hand, gently closing his fingers around a dime.

"Peace, little brother. We hope you'll return," she intoned.

Joey's mother sent him to the Peace Store at least once a week. Catherine Bancik unpacked the groceries when Joey got home that first time. Attached to the cash register receipt was a wallet-size card, obviously placed there by Sweetness Charity. On one side of the card was a picture of Father Divine, on the other:

Father Divine is my Father

He is walking in the land.

Got the world in a jug

And the cork in his hand.

PEACE!

No doubt about it, Joey thought, *I'm screwed. Sure be easier if I could get a Beacon route. Don't pay much, but a lot more than the pennies Sister Joan hands out. No sense trying for the Clarion, that's sewed up tight by the kids from St. Mike's, half of them dropouts. Al Sweeney, Christ how old is he? Bet he's already shaving. Mean son of a bitch. Says he'll kick our asses if we come looking for work. He ain't gonna get a piece of me, that's for sure.*

Joey and Sweeney had no way of knowing that trouble was brewing. Sweeney's boss, Jim McDuffie, got the word a month earlier that the *Beacon* was moving into *Clarion* territory, and that his district with its ritzy apartments, Riviera Hotel and stately homes was a prime target. It was two years earlier when one of McDuffie's kids got sick and he had to take over his route. This was no easy thing for him. Classified 4-F because of two bum knees, already turning arthritic at the age of twenty-four, climbing apartment stairs had become a painful ordeal.

Chapter

27

"Ain't you kinda old to be tossing newspapers around?" a short stocky man with a left cauliflower ear and bent nose asked from the open door of Zwillman's spacious Riviera Hotel apartment. "What happened to the kid? Got used to seeing him. Longy ain't much for strange faces around here."

"He's sick, so I'm filling in," McDuffie said. He handed the man, who was obviously one of Longy's prize fighters, the early edition of the *Evening Clarion* wrapped around a *New York Mirror*. Longy let it be known that when he was in town he couldn't live without his daily dose of Walter Winchell.

The pug took the papers and turned to go back inside, then hesitated, "What did you say your name was?"

"I didn't, but it's McDuffie. Jim McDuffie, and I'm the kid's boss."

"The boss, huh. What kinda boss is that?"

"Circulation manager for the *Clarion*. I handle fifteen kids working this part of the Ward. Your kid is Tommy Spencer, a tough cookie who's been supporting his widow mom."

"Not just a boss, but a manager. Are all your kids tough cookies?"

"Gotta be," McDuffie said. "Some of them the only ones putting bread and butter on the table. You ask a lot of questions. Any reason, or you just curious? What's your name?"

"You a fight fan?"

"Yeah, kinda. Take in the amateur bouts at the YMHA, and the downtown AC. Can't afford the Laurel."

"I'm Benny Switzer. My name ring a bell?"

"Hell yes, damn good lightweight. Held your own against some really good ones. Word was out that Ike Williams was ducking you."

"Ike is one of Blinky Palermo's pugs out of Philly. Blinky hand-picks every fight. Grooming Ike for the title. He'll get it okay. No way a dago mobster is going to take chances that a Jew boxer out of Newark is going to beat his boy."

Switzer lowered his gaze to his right hand, then raised it so McDuffie could see the three deformed middle knuckles. "That was then, Mr. Manager, and this is now," Switzer said.

"How'd you bust it up?"

"Against a second rate palooka in a six-rounder in Elizabeth. Felt the bones snapping in the second, kept my mouth shut and kept going. Got so swollen they had to cut the glove off. Washed me up."

"Too bad," McDuffie said, suddenly at a loss for words. "Anyway, I'll see you around, at least until Tommy's back."

McDuffie was amazed at the speed everything tumbled into place. He often wondered if the Spencer kid wasn't sick that week, would it have happened at all. It began on Friday when Switzer was waiting for him in the hall. After taking the newspapers from him, he got right to the point.

"You gotta record McDuffie?" the pug's heavy lidded eyes bored in. "No bullshit now, you got a sheet or don't you?"

"Nothing serious, boosted cars twice when I was seventeen. Slap on the wrist each time, so there's no record. That's it."

"Good you don't have a rap sheet. The numbers, ever play them? Know how the racket works?"

I wonder where the hell all this is going, McDuffie thought. *God damn this ain't a street punk grilling me. It's one of Longy's bodyguards. Here goes nothing.*

"Hell everyone knows the numbers. I drop a quarter every now and then. So, you gonna tell me what this is all about?"

"Come on inside. Longy's at his home in East Orange and we'll be alone. He only comes here for business meetings. I've told him about this talk we'll be having. He'll want to know how I size you up."

McDuffie followed Switzer into a large, thick carpeted living room. He was motioned to one of two stuffed club chairs that shared a coffee table, and Switzer took the other.

"Got a family?" Switzer asked, making eye contact while massaging the broken knuckles of his right hand.

"A wife, no kids."

"No other folks?"

"Mom and dad, don't see much of them anymore. Two older brothers, both overseas. The last I heard they were in North Africa."

"Your wife, I don't know her name, have anything against the numbers racket?"

"Maureen, but she answers to Mo. Never talk much about it. If I'm right about where you're going with this, I think she'll be all for it."

Their meeting lasted almost two hours. McDuffie explained his circulation territory to the mobster, the fancy apartments, the big homes, and how it was one of the blue chip districts in the city. Switzer was pleasantly surprised how much he knew about the numbers. How the runners, the writers and banks worked, and how the banks laid off their losses on big payoffs.

"Ain't much I got to tell you then," Switzer said. "Sink in yet what we're talking about?"

"You're asking me if I want in. If I'm right, the answer is yes."

"Okay, you'll be hearing from us. What we just talked about doesn't get out of this room, got it?"

"Sure."

"Any questions?" Switzer said. "If you do, get 'em off your chest now."

"This is small potatoes. Why would your boss stick his finger in when he's already got so much going on? Don't seem likely to me."

"It's where it started for Longy, and he's a sentimental guy. The numbers got him off his vegetable wagon on Prince Street. That's after he sized up all those fancy ladies who came down from their apartments to shop with plenty of money to burn."

"I still don't get it."

"Let's say he killed two birds with one stone. He took their money and they weren't bored anymore. Most of them are still hooked, but don't like leaving their expensive digs to place their bets. That's where you and your tough kids come in, working places that were once like home to Longy."

"Anything else?"

"Won't need all fifteen. I figure that three of your best will do it. Leave it to you to pick 'em."

During the next two weeks McDuffie met with everybody he needed to, and no one else. He shook hands with Sy Howard who ran the numbers bank over on Clinton to seal the deal. The three young punks he tapped for the job had been in and out of juvie court often enough to know the bailiff's first name.

McDuffie recognized right from the get-go that folding the numbers in with paper deliveries was a sweet deal. The money was great and could only get better. He dumped his '37 Ford for a '41 Chevy, for the first time could afford ringside at Laurel Gardens, took Mo to catch stripper Georgia Sothern at the Empire, and at her insistence, shelled out big bucks for a new stove and refrigerator. Zwillman had the cops in his pocket making everything neat and clean.

There was some clean-up needed now and then. Like the time those three coon barbers tried to squeeze their policy runners into his territory. That's when his hoods went to work. He laughed his ass off when they described how they laid in wait and picked off, one at a time, three guys and two women, kicking hell out of the men and slapping around the bimbos.

He couldn't imagine that in only two years this sweet deal would turn sour. Zwillman's nemesis, Richie the Boot Boiardo, had secretly called off their truce and was moving into the Third Ward. The Boot's first move would be disguised as a circulation war between the *Clarion* and the *Beacon*.

The Pulitzer Prize winning *Clarion* smugly accepted the sobriquet "the *New York Times* of New Jersey," and dismissed David Goldman's *Beacon* as a cheap throwaway.

Goldman had emerged from Manhattan's Hell's Kitchen three decades earlier, and almost immediately had financially strapped newspaper publishers running for cover. Like a shark hunting in bloody waters, he picked off one weak paper after another, either looting it or merging it with a paper of his own. In the end, it would be a city with one less newspaper, and hundreds of lost jobs. Goldman took no prisoners. Ten years earlier he'd brought the printer and editorial unions of one newspaper to their knees. The newspaper failed and everything was auctioned off.

Herb Bix was an arrogant man secure in the knowledge that his *Evening Clarion* was a king-maker. Every public figure in New Jersey realized his career could be made or broken by Bix's editorial writers. Four generations of Bixes had created an empire, with a dozen bureaus in New Jersey, another in Washington, correspondents on four continents, and a fleet of reporters covering the war in Europe and the Pacific. Bring on Goldman's *Beacon* with its underpaid staff, primitive layout and grasping owner. He was ready.

Bix had no way of knowing that the battle had already begun on two fronts, and that the combatants didn't give a damn about Pulitzer Prizes and foreign correspondents.

McDuffie had inherited his job on the frontline from his father, and like his old man, he treated his carriers like family. During the Depression, these kids helped keep their folks off the bread lines and out of the soup kitchens. These were tough kids and some of them, like Al Sweeney and Gino Sharkey, were down right mean as hell, but they toed the McDuffie line if they wanted to work. They were clean, neat, and courteous, giving their full names to new subscribers, and the customers were always addressed as mister this or missus that. To the kids it might be phony as hell, but the tips and gifts made it easy to swallow.

Joey might have ruled out ever working for the *Clarion*, but he still made his weekly trips to Marsucci's office to see if a *Beacon* route had opened up. He had no way of knowing that the job would put him in the middle of the Ward's numbers racket and a circulation street brawl.

All Joey could do was wait. He played it cool at Milt's, lying about his father's job prospects, while all the time haunted by Bob and Stan's racial taunts. His weekly trips to the Peace grocery store confirmed that the two bullies were right, the Banciks had become white niggers.

To his surprise, he found himself drawn to Billy Spratlin, the one gang member, who from the very beginning, had been a big question mark. Why the hell was a rich kid like Billy hanging out at Milt's? At first, Joey made no attempt to hide his envy, even resentment, for this intruder. It took a while for him to see that even with his nice clothes, a pocketful of change, and that big old house he lived in, Billy was someone he could talk to.

Chapter

28

From the beginning, Billy realized he was something of an outsider at Milt's, his family was different, he lived in a great house, had pocket money to spare, and better clothes. When he went along with the gang at Milt's, it was a take-it-or-leave-it sort of thing.

To get to this point of acceptance wasn't easy. His mother had pulled him out of Hackburne after he finished fifth grade at the upstate New York boarding school. She wanted him closer to home, to have a man in the house she jokingly told him, after his father was shipped to the Pacific. She broke the news to Billy in St. Albans while they were casting for lake trout from the Covington family dock on Lake Champlain.

"Things will be a lot different at St. Mark's," Margaret Spratlin said. "It will be hard at first, but you're a whiz and I know it won't take long for you to fit in."

"St. Mark's? I'm leaving Hackburne for St. Mark's?" Billy forgot he had a casting rod in his hand and almost dropped it into the water. He remembered the kids and their folks who shared Sunday mass at St. Mark's with him and his mom, dad and grandmother during the holidays. The clothes they wore, the way they acted up and even their haircuts were so different from what he was used to at Hackburne.

"Why mom?" Billy searched for the words to convey his dismay. "How about my plans for the summer? I've got invites to spend a week with Jason and another with Travis."

"You'll just have to tell them you won't be coming. It won't be all that bad. We still have three more weeks here at the cottage."

"Then what?" Billy said. "Golly, mom, I won't know anybody, or where they hangout. Have you thought of that?"

"Yes I have, and I'm not worried about you finding new friends. But the rules will be different, they always are when you switch from one school to another," his mother said. "Your new buddies won't be like the friends you're leaving behind."

"Rules, what rules? At Hackburne no one talked about rules, you just fit in or you didn't. And if you didn't, they booted you out."

"No matter where you go to school, you've got to be accepted. If they don't accept you, it won't be easy. You just have to remember they'll be looking you over, and that's when you start living by their rules."

Billy saw that his mother was averting her eyes, peering out over the lake as she reeled in her line. As she watched the bait skim across the surface of the water, she filled in the details. He would be leaving his new Schwinn racer at home and walking to school. The families of the kids he'd be paling around with can't afford bikes. Father Schneider, his new pastor at St. Mark's, had already been told to expect a new altar boy in the fall.

"Geez, mom, what can I say, seems you have it all figured out for me."

Billy reeled in his line, emptied the unused bait into the lake, and they headed up the grassy knoll to the Covington cottage.

It only took about two weeks, or was it three, before it all sunk in. September of 1943 was a hot one, lunchtime recess and after school stoop ball filled the void until footballs started flying. Billy had never played the game before, and it didn't take long for him to see that it wasn't a kid's game. Mastering it would not be easy. He did pretty well partnering with Richie Maxwell and Joey Bancik, but it wasn't until he and Carl Schroder almost knocked off the two kingpins, Stan and Bob Wysnoski, that he could sense the gang warming up to him.

"How much do you like watermelons?" Profanity Pump asked from the corner of the rear booth at Milt's.

"Watermelons?" Billy said as he slid into the booth next to Joey.

"What the hell did I say," Pump challenged. "Get the god damn wax out of your ears."

"Yeah, I guess so, never thought much about it, but yeah, watermelon is okay."

"Like it good enough to steal one?" Joey was looking him over. Their noses were no more than six inches apart.

"That's right, from Springer's Produce over on Springfield. You walk over, pick up one of those big babies, and then run like hell. Think you can do it?" Richie, seated across from him with Carl, said.

"Is this a joke?" Billy said. "It's gotta be a joke."

"Take a god damn look at us," Pump said, "look real good. Does it look like we're joking?"

Billy turned to Pump and fought off a smile as he tried to picture her bouncing down the street with her arms wrapped around a melon. "How about you, do you measure up?" he asked.

"Don't worry your sweet ass about me," she said, "it's you we're talking about."

Billy saw that it would be now or never with this bunch. As he scanned their faces, he realized that Jason, Travis and Hackburne School were gone forever.

"Okay, I'm in," Billy said. "Where does it go from here?"

"A couple of us will walk you over to Springer's so's you can size things up," Joey said. "Then we'll stand back and watch. Springer puts all of his melons on two big sidewalk stands. You grab two cantaloupes and run like hell. Pull it off and it's the watermelon next week."

"It ain't a kid's game," Carl said. "Get nabbed and Springer will press charges. You'll find your ass in juvie court."

"It ain't ol' man Springer who you worry about," Richie said, "he stays near the cash register next to the scales. It's his son, big and mean as hell, that you keep your eye on. No way you'll out run him. If he grabs you, it won't be pretty."

"Just ask Jerry Malone, he's over at St. Jude's now," Joey said. "That big son of a bitch caught him stuffing apples in his pockets. Grabbed him before he made it around the corner, got him to the ground, jammed a knee into his back and held him until a cop showed up."

"So what happened to Jerry?" Billy asked, at the same time kicking himself for agreeing to the melon caper.

"Went to juvie and judge orders his mom and dad to be there too," Carl said. "That's the worst part. The judge read them all the riot act. Warned what would happen the next time."

"Jerry's old man kicked hell out of him, could hear the yowling half-block away," Joey said. "Next thing ya know, they move away and Jerry's over in St. Jude's."

The following afternoon, Richie and Carl watched from in front of Gingold's Pharmacy next door, as Billy walked over to Springer's melon stands. He took a deep breath and failed miserably in his attempt to shake off his nerves. *Have to be cool,* he thought. *Like I'm just passing by, then real fast grab those two babies and hightail it outta here. There's the big guy over there in the back, coast is clear.*

Billy ran for two blocks and didn't stop until he was certain he was not being chased. He was drenched with sweat when he sat down on a tenement stoop to be joined by Richie and Carl.

"You did good," Richie said. "Same time next Tuesday for the big one. Now hand 'em over, they ain't for you."

It was mid-morning when Billy returned to Springer's the following Tuesday. The palms of his hands were slippery with sweat, so he rubbed them dry on his pants before grabbing a melon that had to weigh at least ten pounds. *Can't let this baby slip,* he thought. *Be nabbed for sure. I got it, right here against my belly. Not too fast now, get past the drug store and I'm home free.*

Billy never let on that he had hedged his bet from the beginning. Carl's warning about juvie court had sunk in. He made sure he had two bucks in coins in his pocket, just in case and had rehearsed what to say if the cops grabbed him. *"Gee, officer, it must have slipped my mind. Here it is, got the money right here. Just forgot, that's all."*

Richie, Joey and Profanity Pump were slurping sodas in the rear booth of Milt's when Carl burst in. "You can't guess what I just saw. Billy lugging a big ass watermelon over to the Exeter. Looked like he was about to cave-in when he sat down with the melon in his lap."

"A watermelon?" Joey said. "Jesus Christ, it's Tuesday. Did you ever think he'd really do it."

"Damn, I forgot all about it," Richie said. "More a joke than anything. Who'd a thunk it?"

"He snatched the two cantaloupes, that ain't so hard," the Pump said. "But a god damn watermelon, right in front of ol' man Springer and his big ox son, that's really the shits."

The quartet walked out to the sidewalk, clearly at a loss as to what to do next, "Let's say we go over and kiss his ass for the good job he's done," Pump said. "Unless you guys have a better idea."

Billy was resting with his elbows on the top step of the Exeter entrance. He studied the four faces in front of him, then much like a kid admiring his new puppy, reached down and patted the melon. "Gotta say it's a real beauty."

"So you pulled it off," the Pump said, "took a real pair of balls."

"There's a first time for everything," Carl said. "Bejesus H. Christ, a watermelon from Springer's and in broad daylight, tops it all."

"First time, what the hell do you mean 'first time,'" Billy said.

"We were putting you on, see what you were made of," Richie said. "It was Pump's idea at first, then we all jumped in."

"You're saying none of you ever stole a watermelon from Springer's, is that what you're telling me?"

"That's right," Pump said. "Maybe apples, pears, bananas, you know small stuff that we could put in our pockets. No cantaloupes either."

"What about Jerry Malone?"

"Nope, no Jerry Malone either. Made him up, too," Joey said. "Had to make it sound good so we threw in juvie, the judge and an old man who kicked hell out of poor little Jerry."

"The Pump gets most of the credit," Richie said. "We were laughing our asses off when we put it all together, how the new kid from the big house on Court Place would handle it."

Carl used his all-purpose Boy Scout knife to carve-up the watermelon, and they spent the rest of the afternoon spitting watermelon seeds onto the sidewalk. After the heist, none of the gang said "nice job" or anything like that, but Billy could feel the change. He showed them that he measured up, and they had to let him in.

About the time he turned thirteen, Billy Spratlin began to notice big changes on how he looked at things. Sex was the welcome intruder whenever he put two or three thoughts together. As Carl Schroder put it, "Well, kid, you now know why the good Lord gave you a right hand."

It seemed to Billy that the neighborhood thrived on sexual temptation. It was everywhere. You didn't even have to look for it, it just jumped out at you. Take the Good Fellows Lodge's stag smoker every third Friday night at the Krameir Mansion.

Taking buckets of beer money with them, the Krameirs long ago fled to the green hills of the Orange Mountains overlooking Newark. Their brewery still pumped out its "Beer of Cheer for People We Hold Dear," or "Ale for the Hale," and in the spring, "Krameir Bock for Men of Rock."

There were still a few people around who remembered the old days with the big parties, important people, and elegant carriages and automobiles. But to the handful of neighborhood kids in the know, the relic was important for its monthly stags.

During one of his nocturnal wanderings, the sweet sounds of Benny Goodman's clarinet and Harry James' trumpet pulled Eight-Ten to the east side of the mansion. He peeked through the ill-fitting drapes on one of the lower windows and discovered a pornographic bonanza. True to his calling, he tipped off a few of his young friends at Milt's.

The horny bunch would soon discover that a crack in a warped window frame presented another opportunity to further their carnal knowledge. By stacking themselves totem-fashion, two or three at a time, and squinting one eye and then the other into the basement below, they were introduced to tribalism, "69," bestiality, and just about everything else. The grainy black-and-white film was accompanied by Benny Goodman and Artie Shaw records. "Sing, Sing, Sing" was the Good Fellows' favorite for all the rock-em-sock-em gangbangs. "Begin the Beguine" set the mood for the more sedate offerings.

Only once did they come close to being found out. That was after the totem collapsed into the shrubbery when they were left gasping for air while watching three couples in a shower stall. Eight-Ten on the bottom got so excited he began to shake. Billy had been high man on the totem, he fell on top of Eight-Ten. Everyone held their breath. Finally, from beneath the pile there arose a mirthful, "Aheh, aheh. Aheh, aheh."

It had been quite a while since Richie, Joey, Freddy and Carl began piecing it all together. Reluctantly at first, they compared the sounds coming from their parents' bedrooms, and after debunking virgin birth, agreed that mom and dad had been fucking. With his father still serving Uncle Sam as an Army engineer on Okinawa, he could add nothing from home to the sexual stewpot boiling over at Milt's. Thanks to the monthly Good Fellows' sex shows, Eight-Ten with his glossies from the Empire Burlesque, and Profanity Pump and the crude jokes at Milt's, Billy soon caught up.

Despite all the second-hand knowledge he was collecting, Billy found it hard to picture his mother having sex with his father. Sure, his mom was beautiful, his dad was handsome, but as hard as he tried, it just didn't fit.

It was months ago that he first saw the guy from the window of his bedroom over the garage. It was about eleven at night. Billy saw the uniform, and with all those stripes he had to be at least a full commander. He automatically thought he was a friend of his father.

He changed out of his pajamas and ran to the house just as the drapes of his mother's bedroom were being drawn. When he entered the house, all the downstairs lights were off.

There were voices from his mother's bedroom. Billy took off his shoes and crept up the stairs.

"Jesus, you're beautiful," the man cooed.

"Come here and look at all of me."

"Yes ma'am."

There were giggles, then some muffled man and woman sounds.

Billy went all the way to the stairway landing. He saw that the bedroom door was ajar, but he couldn't get himself to go any farther. He thought of the stag movies at the Krameir Mansion. He didn't want to see his mom like that.

Chapter

29

Margaret Spratlin had been awakened by hands caressing her breasts. A warm glow was already beginning. It was getting light outside. They had slept longer than usual, it must be close to six.

The man beside her had already attached an electric vibrating massager to the back of his right hand. He was leaning across her body to a jar of Vaseline on the night table. He dipped a finger in, turned on the massager and then went to work between her legs.

"God. How I love you."

The man said nothing. His breathing became labored and he grunted as he pushed the sheet to the bottom of the bed with his feet. Margaret spread her legs even more, hooking one over the side of the bed, the other around her lover's waist.

"Be rough! Goddamnit, hurt me!"

The man rolled her over on her stomach, completed his busy work with the electric machine, and then mounted her from behind.

"Oh yes, do it. It hurts. Oh yes, it hurts. Keep fucking me that way. Keep it up. Do it! Do it!"

Afterward they dozed off. Margaret was awakened by sounds from downstairs in the kitchen. The refrigerator opening and closing. Billy flipping on the toaster, stumbling around for a juice glass.

She was glad they weren't fucking when Billy came over from his room above the garage in the back. It was a big, old house with great acoustics. Sound really carried and in all directions.

The man beside her was still asleep, breathing slow and easy. She propped herself on her elbow and looked about. The bed looked and smelled of sexual combat. This was the first time he had stayed past four o'clock, and the first glitch in Margaret's finely tuned trysting routine. That evening was one of two each month that her mother-in-law stayed over in New York after sharing dinner with family and friends. Two other nights each month she was never home before midnight after taking in a Broadway show with her college roommate. Four sexual trysts a month hardly made her a slut, Margaret reasoned.

Margaret laid her head on the man's shoulder and waited for her son to leave. He had been serving the six-thirty Mass this week, and it wouldn't be long before he left. She wondered if Billy knew.

He did.

It was last spring when Billy first spotted the gray Pontiac, a staff car from the Port Newark Navy Shipyard. He tried the driver's door, and to his surprise found it unlocked. He peeked inside, back and front, and saw in the middle of the dashboard a metal plate that looked like an oversized dog tag. The raised letters read:

USN Vehicle 46390

For priority use by

Cmdr Jacob Feinberg

A Jew, a god damn Jew, Billy thought, his temples pounding. And while my dad is still out there in the Pacific, this Jew is pushing papers around at the Navy base and sleeping with my mom.

Until now, he had nothing against Jews. Couldn't remember if he had even met one. What little thought he had ever given them was force fed by his grandmother. Sylvia Spratlin never felt it necessary to explain to Billy her distaste for Jews, only to say, "They're not like us, the less you have to do with them the better. As you get older, you will see why I'm telling you this."

The thought of Commander Jacob Feinberg in bed with his mother erased any doubts that his grandmother might be full of baloney.

And this morning as usual, Feinberg's Pontiac was parked halfway down the cul-de-sac. He instinctively looked for the car while walking across the backyard to the kitchen door. Billy's grandmother was staying with friends in New York. His mother had been alone last night.

This morning he would make it easier for them. Making all the noise he could so they'd know he was there. Billy rinsed out his juice glass in the sink, grabbed an apple from a bowl on the kitchen table, and made sure to slam the door on his way out.

Margaret stood naked at her bedroom window as she watched her son turn off the front path onto the sidewalk. Her naked lover came up behind her. Feinberg put his hand around her waist.

"I love you, ya know."

"Sure you do, stud. Sure you do."

She pushed his hands down to her groin.

"Isn't that what you wanted to hear?"

"Yeah. But over there. In bed I love everybody."

She took his hand and led him back to the sack. They were giggling as they disappeared under the sheet.

Billy had felt their eyes on him, but didn't turn around. Then everybody would know. He would never be able to face his mother if she knew that he knew.

Colonel Walter Spratlin was confident he would be coming home soon. His last letter said perhaps as early as late October. He had been heading up the Army Engineer contingent converting war-ravaged Okinawa into a huge military base. His job was just about over and his replacement was on his way.

Billy wondered what it would be like when his dad came home. How his mother would act. How things would never be the same between him and his mom. These thoughts of his mother and that man were forever haunting him. These images kept him occupied as he headed to St. Mark's.

Midway there, he paused for a moment, and stared intently at the front door of the synagogue his grandmother hated so much.

There's gotta be a way to get back at him. There has to be payback, Billy agonized. Pausing in front of the synagogue, an idea took shape. Newsreel images from Europe since VE Day provided the solution. He studied the double doors at the top of the steps confident he could pull it off.

Heading down High Street, Billy began to run, hoping this would crowd out the questions with no answers. *All these secrets. It will never be the same. When Dad comes home, we got to keep our mouths shut. I never kept anything secret from Dad, and I know he never kept anything secret from me. And what about mom? I'll have to keep all of this buttoned up forever, but will she? Where do I fit in? We'd be lying to Dad by keeping our mouths shut. God damn it! Now I'm crying, and I never cry. What the hell is happening to me?*

Billy slowed to a trot as he neared William Street, and the crying stopped as suddenly as it had begun, with two deep, gurgling sobs that forced snot from his nose. He pulled a hanky from his rear pocket, wiped his upper lip clean and dried his eyes. He stepped off the curb and walked across the street to St. Mark's, knowing he would find no answers inside.

The following Tuesday, Billy rummaged through his father's work shop in the garage below his room. He found what he was looking for, an unopened pint can of Dutch Boy red enamel, a large screwdriver to pop the lid, and a half-inch paintbrush. He waited until he was sure his mother and grandmother were asleep in the main house before crossing the driveway and heading down Court Place to High.

He walked past the synagogue to the next corner to be sure the street was empty, and retraced his steps to the Jewish temple. Certain there was no one around, he set the paint can down on the top step, popped it open, and dipped in his paintbrush. It took less than five minutes for him to assuage his anger. Bookending the words with four inch tall crosses, Billy spread his message across both doors:

+ KILROY WAS HERE +

The outrage remained on the doors for more than a month. People came to look at it; it got write-ups and pictures in the papers. Even the gang at Milt's took a gander. Father Schneider and Father Nolan used the church pulpit, and Sister Mary Margaret addressed St. Mark's school assembly to excoriate Billy's handiwork. Billy was both confused and oddly surprised by all the commotion.

Chapter

30

Ever since the watermelon caper and his acceptance by the gang, there had been only one time Billy went out on a limb. As a result, he was slapped down and laughed at. And it was because of Marvin, a black kid he hardly knew and would probably never understand.

That spring he'd watched Marvin and Richie hand the Wysnoskis their first stoop ball defeat ever, and with Marvin taking it in the neck to make it happen. Marvin was tall and fast, and word was out that he played a damn good first base for Morton Street Elementary.

Later that spring plans fell through to keep the St. Mark's baseball team intact for the coming PFAL season. The Wysnoskis had moved on to the American Legion, leaving shortstop and first base open. Freddy Urbanik took over at short, that left first base up for grabs.

"How about Marvin?" Billy suggested during a gab session at Milt's. "We saw what he could do against Bob and Stan. He's around, so why the hell not."

"Shit, what da we need him for?" asked Urbanik. "We can always pick somebody up. Besides, ya know what'll happen."

"No, wise guy, what'll happen?" asked Billy, suddenly defensive.

"Look, shit head, you barely made the team yourself," Urbanik said. "You even miss half the games when, la-di-da, your mother takes you on vacation. So who are you to put your two cents in."

To Billy's surprise, Joey jumped to his defense.

"What gives with that 'la-di-da' bullshit?" Joey said. "How about you? Why the hell are you here, won't the rich fruits at St. Jude's let you play with 'em?" Joey hated Urbanik, and his words showed it. "Why the hell you go there anyway?"

"You know why. The same reason my folks are lookin' to get the hell out of the neighborhood," Urbanik said. "Niggers. Christ o'mighty, look at Morton Street. Three years ago there wasn't any on our block. Now look—twenty, thirty families mebbe. My old man sez the fifteen bucks a month and car fare for St. Jude's is worth every cent."

"What the hell's all this bullshit got to do with the team?" Billy said.

"Let one of them on the team, and there's no stoppin' 'em. My old man sez it's just like pourin' black axle grease in yer hand. Make a fist and it squeezes out between the fingers. Let the coon play and all his Morton Street buddies will be shufflin' over."

"Shove yer old man and his black axle grease," said Billy. He knew he was defeated. Marvin didn't stand a chance.

"Shit, Billy, there ain't no way I can see myself throwin' to a jigaboo at first base," said Joey, the team's second baseman. "It just ain't natural. When Wysnoski screwed up, ya could call him a fuckin' Polak or anything, and he just laughed."

"It ain't natural," said Carl Schroder, a bench warmer who had been eyeballing first base for himself. "What d'ya say to the coon? Damn, he's ready to fight if ya even look at him cross-eyed."

Joey affected an effeminate pose, a limp-wristed right hand in front of him, his left hand on his buttock. "Oh, you neegrow, you. If y'all didn't notice, y'all dropped the ball."

Everyone, Billy included, laughed. The matter was dropped. Carl became the first baseman.

Billy's immediate reaction was regret for having made a rare unselfish gesture on behalf of a black kid he barely knew. And from that day on, he sized up Joey a lot differently for backing him up. He and Joey seemed to bump into each other a lot more than usual, even went over to Branch Brook Park a couple of times to hit fungoes.

As the weeks went by, Billy found it impossible to shake the memory of that night when he silently climbed the stairs and overheard the sounds of his mother's betrayal. Were the carnal images pulled from the basement of the Krameir Mansion any different from what was happening behind that bedroom door? He thought not. It didn't help that four times a month a gray Pontiac with U.S. Navy license plates was parked on Court Place.

And it didn't help that all of the gang's bull sessions sooner or later got around to sex. They laughed like hell when describing their trips to the confessional at St. Mark's. How they tried to disguise their voices while confessing their jerk-off sessions to Father Schneider and Father Nolan.

"Damn, you should have heard me mumble," Richie said. "Don't know if it did any good. I still think Father Schneider recognized my voice."

"You, too," Billy quipped. "How about you Joey? Were we all trying to mumble like Eight-Ten?"

"The same here," Joey said, "all except I left out 'aheh, aheh, aheh, aheh.'"

"We shouldn't have to hide what comes natural," Carl Schroeder added. "None of us believe anymore that we'll go blind if we keep it up."

"I ain't giving it up," Joey said. His avowal getting nods of approval from the others.

It wasn't long before they were tipped off by Jackie Conn and Mike Suchi that the Polak parish, St. Stanislaus, offered a safety net.

"So you'll have to walk a few blocks," Jackie said. "It'll be worth it. Hey, we all went through it. At St. Stan's, the priests barely speak English. Even if you raped a nun or murdered a priest, you'll still skate through with 'ten Our Father's, ten Hail Mary's, and a good act of contrition.'"

"Look at us, you don't see any hair on our palms do you?" Mike added.

For Billy, as she was for others before him, ever lovin' Linda Kosjak was the conduit that transported him from sexual fantasy to reality. She was only a few years older than Billy and the others, and kept the truant officer happily at bay with discreet sexual favors. She furthered their education that began at the Good Fellows Lodge stags.

She was the first girl to show him her "twat," and allow him to fondle her "boobs." She called them "tits," and "ain't they beauties."

Ever lovin' Linda and her round-heeled mother, Beth Kosjak, the biggest white slut in the neighborhood, lived a block over in a three-story tenement, long overdue for demolition. The horny guys who made their way up the rickety wooden staircase to their top floor apartment ignored a flaked yellow sign with red letters, "CONDEMNED PROCEED AT YOUR OWN RISK, by Order of the City Director of Public Safety."

It was Saturday morning and Milt's was busy. Billy spotted Leo Baldoni and Carl Schroeder looking very much like they were hatching a plot in the back booth. They were scrunched over their drinks on opposite sides of the table, and were whispering so no one else could hear. Billy was as nosy as the next guy, but there was no way he would bust in on them. Let them get it off their chests he thought as he took a stool at the counter and ordered a ten cent Spur.

"We better wrap it up. Billy just came in," Carl said. "Probably be heading over. My five bucks is burning a hole in my pocket."

"Same here," Leo said. "Let's get out of here, make it casual."

"What gives?" Billy asked as he was about to slide in next to Carl.

"Not much, just something we've been talking about," Leo said. "We'll let you know if it works out. Should be fun."

"Amen to that," Carl said.

Billy sized up immediately that he was on the outside looking in, and that he'd be a jerk if he pushed it any further. He waited until his two buddies left Milt's and then cautiously followed them out.

He watched them turn into the driveway of the Exeter. Billy waited a few seconds, then followed. By the time he got to the driveway, Leo and Carl were already half over the fence into the Kosjak's backyard. After they dropped out of sight, he ran to the fence.

Peering through the boards, he watched them climb to the top landing where a smiling Linda, barefoot and wearing only a white lacy slip, greeted them, and loud enough for him to hear, "Got it?"

"Right here," Carl patted his right front pocket.

"Same here," Leo said patting his pocket.

"Bet you busted your piggy banks to come up with the fin," Linda teased. "Ain't the only thing you'll be breaking today."

Linda took each of them by the hand and guided them inside. A disappointed Billy turned from the fence and walked back to the street. He wondered how long it took for Carl and Leo to raise the five bucks needed to bust their cherries. He caught Marvin as he was walking into Milt's and the two of them ordered sodas at the counter, then slumped into a front booth.

"You look lower than snail slime," Marvin said. "Don't suppose you want to talk to a black boy about it."

"You supposed right," Billy said, "and don't give me any of that 'black boy' shit. Just have somethin' on my mind. Talking won't help."

"Okay then, we'll just stare it out of your head. Nothin' like a good head-staring."

"I can feel it already," Billy laughed, surprised at their easy give-and-take.

"My old black magic worked its spell," Marvin said.

"Damn, I already feel that tingling up and down my spine," Billy said.

They both looked-up when Frank Gazzi walked in, nodded in their direction, and took a stool at the counter. "Time to give my tired feet a rest," the cop said to Milt. "How about a coffee."

"Just put a fresh pot on," Milt said. He was still getting adjusted to having a beat cop in his shop. "A little something if you're gonna keep our streets safe for the women and kiddies."

Gazzi pulled a paper napkin from its holder, wiped the sweatband of his hat, and swiveled around to take in the half-filled booths.

"You kids staying out of trouble?" His question to Billy and Marvin had an edge to it, putting both of them on guard.

"You betcha," Billy said, as he and Marvin slid out of the booth. "Time to get out of here and scare up some work for you."

Gazzi watched them walk outside, then turned to Milt, "Smart ass kids. I get the feeling there's something going on they know, and I don't."

"How's your coffee doing?" Milt knew it was best to play dumb when a cop was around.

Chapter

31

Fifteen minutes later the boys were sitting on Marvin's stoop when Leo and Carl swaggered back from the Kosjaks'. The two rakes gave acknowledging flicks of the wrist as they walked down the block. Billy watched with envy as they disappeared into Milt's for recuperative sodas. He glanced at Marvin, then followed his upward gaze.

"There it is," Marvin said. "I gotta get going."

"Don't tell me you're going to run around chasin' those shitty pieces of paper?" Billy said.

It was their first sighting of the U.S. Navy blimp, a fat silhouette that seemed to hang suspended against the sun behind St. Mark's steepled cross. A continuous stream of larvae poured from its underside.

"Yep, for my little brother Benji. He's got the mumps, gotta get him a fistful to cheer him up."

"What the hell, I've got nothin' better to do right now," Billy said. "I'll give ya a hand. Let's hike it to High. They'll prob'ly drop most of the stuff near downtown."

The wind had carried some of the droppings as far as Court Street. A few spun erratically to the ground on the other side of High. Billy and Marvin made backhanded grabs.

Another blimp, its U.S. Navy markings clearly visible, appeared not more than a mile away. It seemed to be heading straight up Court. You could even see the crewmen in the door, kicking out packets that exploded into thousands of fluttering bits of paper.

Kids raced across sidewalks, between cars, and into the street in pursuit of the bomb-shaped paper scraps.

At the corner of Court and Shipman, Lt. Col. Ret. Jonathan Quincy McAdams, his white air-raid warden's helmet strapped in place, stiffly saluted the passing dirigible.

Billy and Marvin were caught up in the excitement. Their pants pockets bulged with the worthless bits of paper. They speared the missiles in flight and retrieved them from atop cars and off the street and sidewalk.

"That was a hoot!" Billy shouted.

"Yeh, the same for me," Marvin laughed as they trotted down Court, shoving each other while weaving around passersby.

They had just begun to stuff some of the bombs inside their shirts when they realized they hadn't even read the slogan:

6th War Loan Drive

For Smashing, Unconditional Victory

And on the other side:

Your Stamps and Bonds Mean More Guns and Bombs

They shrugged, crossed Shipman, and stopped to catch their breath. Two blocks away loomed the burnt-out Herman's Potato Chip factory. With its roof still intact, the challenge was obvious.

"Lots of bombs up there, I betcha," Marvin said.

"Wanna try it?"

"Ever been up there?"

"Nope, have you?"

"Nope."

"Safe?"

"Shit, I don't know."

"Wanna try it?"

"Game if you are."

"Game."

"Let's go," Marvin said.

They vaulted onto a blackened loading platform, entered a side door and walked across the first floor toward the rear of the building. They gingerly sidestepped debris and the turds of kids and bums who found the building a handy outhouse. In back there was a fire escape that led to the roof of the three-story building.

What they found was not reassuring. The fire escape had been torn from the large steel plates welded to the building. The rusty steps were dangerously suspended from four I-beams that reached to the level of the roof. The carcass squeaked and swayed in a slight breeze as Billy and Marvin approached it.

"We really need any more of these shitty pieces of paper?" Billy said.

"We're here."

"I'm game."

"Sheeit, let's do it."

Their first steps, at best hesitant, became openly fearful after they reached the top of the second floor. The stairs paralleled the building as they crisscrossed between the I-beams. The higher they got, the more the vibrating skeleton swayed. The climb to the top became as much a battle of balance as progress.

"I'm gettin' seasick," said Billy, clinging to a rail.

"How d'ya know—ever been on a boat?"

"Yeah, a small one."

They finally made it to the top. By this time the fire escape was teetering about three feet from the wall. To make it to the roof they would have to rock it. Starting slowly, they put their shoulders first to the front, then to the back upper railing of the rusty structure. The whole thing got away from them. They began to gyrate in an ever-increasing circle. *Vringhh . . . vringghh . . .. vringghh . . .* came the grating sound of metal against metal, as the broken weld slammed against the metal plate from which it had broken loose.

Below, there was a cacophony of strange creaks and groans, as sheets of rust peeled away and floated to the ground.

"Sheeit," said Marvin, holding on for dear life.

"You can say that again," said Billy right beside him.

They looked down—the descent into hell couldn't be worse.

They agreed they would have to jump to the roof. Miraculously, they timed their leaps just right. Billy, then Marvin, stood poised at the edge of the fire escape. When it made its grating pass alongside the building, each leaped onto the roof, sprawling head over heels onto the soot-encrusted tar paper.

"Weeooh! Give me that ol' time religion!" wheezed Marvin.

"Praise the Lord and pass the ammunition!" Billy groaned.

They sat staring at each other. Smiles crinkled their faces. With heroic disdain, they turned their backs on the fire escape, now but a Minotaur reeling in death's agony. And what they saw was a bonanza. The roof was almost a blanket of propaganda bombs.

In the center of the roof, next to the hatch leading to the floor below, was an unbroken packet. It had failed to break apart in the air and was still intact after impact. Stuck under the twine was a label that read: "6th War Loan Bombs. Property of U.S. Govt. Count 1,000."

Marvin picked up the packet and placed it on the ledge that ran along the front of the roof. The ledge formed the upper part of a façade that identified the ill-fated company. As he turned, his elbow accidentally knocked the packet over the edge.

Directly below, followed by two of his aides, was Lt. Col. Ret. Jonathan Quincy McAdams. Billy and Marvin peered over the ledge just as the packet struck McAdams' helmet, knocking it askew over his left ear. The straining twine snapped apart. The bombs cascaded off his shoulders to the ground.

"Whereditcomefrom?" blurted McAdams.

"Dunno," said one aide.

"Up there," said the other, pointing to the two heads atop the building.

"Reconnoiter," ordered McAdams. "You there and you there."

The two men warily inched their way along either side of the factory. McAdams strode to the other side of Shipman for a better vantage point. Billy and Marvin ducked their heads.

"They comin' up?" asked Marvin.

"Shit no. Let's jes wait it out."

They glanced to the rear of the roof. The fire escape was still vibrating.

"You two punk kids know what's good for you, you'll come down," McAdams shouted.

Silence.

McAdams fingered the label from the bomb packet.

"Come down, and through the chain of command, we'll work something out."

Silence.

"Do you know what the destruction of government property during wartime calls for?"

Silence.

"Goddamnit, get down here, or when I catch up with you, I'll kick your asses from one end of Court to the other."

Silence.

After ten minutes of unanswered surrender appeals, the three wardens, McAdams in the lead, strode away, heads high, eyes clear, alert.

The two kids waited a few minutes before lowering themselves through the roof hatch to the third floor, then felt their way along the charred stairs to the main floor. Once outside, they breathed easier. Marvin headed home with his hard-earned booty, and Billy saved only a few of the paper bombs as souvenirs to show his mother and grandmother.

On his way home, Billy realized that it was getting easier and easier to get along with Marvin than with some of the gang at Milt's and most of his classmates at St. Mark's. He had tried several times to figure out why, but always came up empty.

Chapter

32

In the autumn of 1945, sixty year old Sylvia Spratlin had been a widow for five years. That's when the body of Guy Spratlin, an excellent swimmer, was found in only four feet of water not far from the family's summer cottage on Lake Champlain, just north of St. Albans.

There were two distinct lines of conjecture regarding Guy's death: that he had committed suicide, or he had suffered a heart attack. Sylvia, never one to take a chance, forbade an autopsy, and the certificate read "death by drowning."

Billy's grandmother was a vivacious woman who kept busy running the house for her daughter-in-law. She dined once a month with classmates from Bryn Mawr, attended opening night at the Met, and took in six Broadway plays each season, but only after carefully studying the nuances of every George Jean Nathan review.

Sylvia also doted on her grandson, transferring to him the same sort of attention in the same sort of way that she had lavished on her son up until the day he was married sixteen years earlier.

Sylvia Hargrave's Episcopalian roots dated back to the Revolution. The family could point with pride that Philo Hargrave shared a pew in Philadelphia's St. Peter's Church with James Madison and other Founding Fathers.

Sylvia had lost only one battle of note in her entire life. The prurient aspects of her defeat would forever shape her wary view of sexual abandon. It came during the summer before her final year at Bryn Mawr, when she shared a down quilt with a husky lifeguard amid the sand dunes of Cape May.

Guy Spratlin took her virginity at exactly ten minutes before midnight, making the first painful insertion at the same time the barroom gong at the Regency Hotel was tolling last call. He seduced her two more times before the weekend was over.

After the initial pain, she had thoroughly enjoyed herself. After the second time, she agreed to marry Guy. After the third time, she agreed with his demand that their children would be raised Catholic.

They had only one child.

Billy's defacing of the synagogue had gone a lot smoother than he expected. He had the whole street to himself, not so much as a passing car. He had thrown the paintbrush down the storm drain, and returned the paint can and screwdriver to his father's workshop. He couldn't find any turpentine to remove the paint from his right hand, so it would have to come off with some hard scrubbing at the kitchen sink. It was after nine o'clock by the time he burst through the kitchen door and rushed to the sink.

"You're later than usual for a novena night. Your grandmother had been waiting up for you. She just went to bed," his mother said from the doorway.

"I stopped off for a while with the guys," mumbled Billy without turning from the sink.

"Any place in particular?" asked Margaret, now leaning against the door jam as she eyed her son at the sink, curious why he hadn't turned to greet her.

She had just combed her long chestnut hair and was dressed in a nightgown and house robe. She dropped the comb into the robe's pocket and started towards her son. She was truly a beautiful woman, with the kind of beauty that needed little pampering.

Tall, fine-boned, armed with an English degree from Bennington, possessor of nice teeth and an honest arrogance, she seemed almost a caricature of that certain type of upper middle class beauty that is native only to the United States.

Her refinement began when Harold and Suzanne Covington decided their daughter, like her mother, would attend Miss Spence's School for Girls. The raucous hustle and bustle of mid-town Manhattan blended well with the music, dancing, drama and intellectual curiosity fostered by Miss Spence. Margaret loved all the sports the school offered, but fencing was her favorite, and by the time she had reached the eighth grade she had mastered the intricate footwork necessary to parry and thrust.

She met Walter Spratlin the summer between her junior and senior years of college. Their family eight-room cottages along the east shore of Lake Champlain were only a half-mile apart, but they had never socialized.

Margaret had just taken a dip and was strolling north along the lake front when she spotted a bare-chested Walter pushing off from the Spratlin pier in his centerboard dinghy. It was sunny, warm and windy, a great day for small boat sailing. He was pulling himself out of waist deep water and into the hull when he spotted her.

"Hi there," Walter smiled. He dropped the thin centerboard into its slot in the hull, then turned to size her up. "Where in the world did you come from?"

"Our family place is down by the cove just south of here."

"First time I've seen you, and you're hard to miss. That family of yours keep you locked up? By the way, what's your name?"

"You first."

Why not play it a little coy, she thought, *and see what happens. Tall, blond, probably blue eyes and doesn't mince words. Who knows, he might even be a Mellon or a Vanderbilt. We're here for another month and this could be interesting.*

"Nothing doing," Walter said as he lifted himself out of the hull and back into the water. "I've got first dibs, you missed your chance. So come on, out with it."

"Margaret Covington. So now, big boy, your turn."

"Walter Spratlin," he smiled as he waded closer. "My friends call me Walt, never Wally. I've another question. Want to go hiking?"

"It depends on how good you are. There's a strong wind. I'm not keen on chafing my ankles under hiking straps with a rookie skipper at the helm."

So she knows how to sail, and damn she's pretty, Walter thought. *There's a month of sailing left, and what better way to find out what she's made of. If I'm guessing right, this summer won't be the end of it. Let's get a little salty and see how she takes it.*

"You'll also be bouncing that pretty backside of yours in the water at the same time. Come on, Meg, get aboard! Show me what you've got!"

That sailing day was the first of several that August of '28. Meg and Walt competed in five regattas, winning two and finishing second in a third. When not sailing, they came close to wearing out their welcomes at each family's cottage. They coveted their times alone strolling the lake front, or huddled in their favorite St. Albans coffee shop booth. On three occasions, they beached Walt's dinghy in an isolated cove, removed a blanket from its protective tarp, spread it on the sand and made love. Labor Day proved to be awkward, neither wanted it to end, but agonized on how to say so. That week they would be off to their senior years, Meg to Bennington and Walt to Stevens Tech, in what she jokingly referred to as "godforsaken Hoboken." They would share holidays, and squeeze in as many weekends as possible. Neither Guy and Sylvia Spratlin nor Harold and Suzanne Covington doubted their kids' intentions. Walt and Meg held off any announcement until after graduation.

In the interim, the elder Covingtons and Spratlins were not idle. The attorney husbands and socially-attuned wives, enjoyed bridge up to a point, preferred scotch to gin, scoffed at croquet and badminton, played country club golf, and could sail with the best of them. After discovering they shared a mutual distrust of Jews, that inflation was playing hell with their wallets, and a belief that Herbert Hoover was a sure bet second termer, it was natural that amiable weekends would be in order.

Walt and Meg were joined in a high mass wedding at St. Marks one year after graduation. A one month biking honeymoon through the Pyrenees concluded with a decadent four-day stay at the Hotel du Palais in Biarritz. They had purposely left themselves incommunicado. In Cherbourg, they went to the Cunard Lines office to pick up their return tickets for home when they were paged to contact the Mauretania's purser. The message was beyond belief. Harold and Suzanne Covington were killed when their Eastern Air Ford Trimotor crashed into a coal-laden barge on the Delaware River. They were on route from Newark to Philadelphia. It was two weeks to the day after their wedding. Burial was a week later. Telegram after telegram bombarded the couple the entire length of the voyage home. It took weeks for Meg to understand the unfathomable, that her two vibrant and loving parents were gone forever. And that as the only child, she was sole heir to two estates, and the mistress of a sprawling home on Court Place.

It took awhile for Meg and Walt to settle in. Her early pregnancy meant a complete overhaul of their social calendar. Trips to Manhattan for theatre parties with college chums became less frequent. At the insistence of Walt's mother they agreed to maintain the two lakefront cottages in Vermont. For Sylvia Spratlin, summers without the lake would be unthinkable. Her mother-in-law's stylized carping often had Meg running for cover. Sylvia would move in for the final months of Meg's pregnancy, and to make sure that baby Billy's cradle would be rocked with the loving care that only a grandmother could give.

Walter was always something of a rebel, and Margaret wondered how he managed to get along in a structured environment like the Army's. He had adapted well to Prudential, but only because he had carved a niche for himself within the mammoth insurance company. Walter had defied family tradition, one that his mother insisted he adhere to, by turning his back on the University of Pennsylvania. Spratlin men had called it their academic home for generations.

Instead, he chose Stevens Tech in Hoboken, of all places. Walter called it "the best engineering school that hardly anyone had heard of." He was a workaholic who chose accounting as his minor. His timing was perfect. The same year he graduated, Prudential was expanding its construction site program. High-rise buildings, both commercial and residential, were going up in cities all around the country. His degree in civil engineering got him a job. He was handed the Chellis Austin Project, a low-rent development in the Ironbound section of Newark. The project bore the name of one of Prudential's most powerful board members. It was also a project that City Hall lusted to get its greedy hands on. City inspectors homesteaded at the construction site. It was a fitting encampment for them, so near the corrosive Passaic River, which in their case did not have to work hard to spread its contamination.

Walter kept them at bay, and the project was brought in under cost. It was hailed as a model for other low-rent, high-density developments badly needed in many of the decaying older cities on the East Coast.

Walter was given a bigger office and a staff of five, and in short order his responsibilities grew. First there was the Douglass Project, named after ex-slave and abolitionist leader Frederick Douglass. Two years later, it was the Harrison Project in the Third Ward, honoring Negro actor Richard Berry Harrison.

From then on, it was bigger things, including bridges. When the war broke out, Walter Spratlin, vice president, became Army Major Walter Spratlin, Corps of Engineers. Air fields, training camps, and new naval facilities were needed, and he was put to work immediately. He followed the war across the Pacific, and with Japan's surrender, Okinawa became American booty. It had to be rebuilt in order to support the huge military complex the United States planned to build there. After it was completed, he'd be on his way home.

Walter would be coming home to a neighborhood that would bear little resemblance to the one he left behind. Margaret never mentioned it in her letters to Walter that an alien world was closing in around Court Place. Nor did she mention that she had made inquiries on how best to unload a Victorian relic that had been the Covington home for three generations. There was no guilt when she decided that the time was ripe to get rid of it.

Margaret had done her homework. She found three large houses near the Seton Hall College campus in South Orange that would be suitable. With Sylvia in her corner, she was certain Walter would approve.

Chapter

33

It pained Margaret that she didn't photograph well. Besides her wedding portrait with Walter, there were few photos of her around the house. Instead there were two large paintings, one in a dominant position at the end of the entrance hall, and the other over the fireplace in the living room.

Each was a gift, actually a payment of sorts, from an artist friend of the family who had been down on his luck during the Depression, and had asked Margaret to model for two of his commercial art commissions.

She got to keep the originals.

Visitors entering the Spratlin home were treated to a brown-haired, bare-shouldered beauty in a satin burgundy nightgown who gazed from her bedroom window at a rolling green landscape. The soap people liked it so well, they used it to kick-off a three month nationwide magazine advertising assault for their new product, LUSH.

Above the living room fireplace was the second portrait of a disheveled beautiful woman sitting up in her rumpled bed. Snowflakes could be seen falling outside the bedroom window. This was the image that the Radiance Corporation hoped would entice well-heeled prospects to purchase their heating system.

Walter and Margaret got a big kick when friends began mailing them the magazine ads. Margaret kept two of them under the glass top of her dressing room table. They were the first things to catch Commander Jacob Feinberg's eye after he and Margaret completed their first sexual bout. They agreed it was a draw, with each of them giving and taking as much as the other. To her surprise, there was no remorse or shame, only a sense of well-earned satisfaction. After all, it had been more than a year since Walter had left for the Pacific.

Billy could hear the soft sound of his mother's bedroom slippers as she glided toward him across the kitchen floor. He braced himself for what he knew was coming. His mother reached the sink just as he was turning off the water and reaching for a towel.

He did not want his mother's attention.

Billy had known about the Navy commander and his Pontiac staff car for some time. His initial reaction to the first night, the night he couldn't force himself up the stairs to see for sure, was self-pity.

He had returned to his room and sobbed into the early morning hours. He wished his grandmother had been there to hold him.

His pity gave way to rage. He thought of killing them both. He would then write to his father. Tell him that everything was okay. That they could begin fresh—father, son, and grandmother.

Why was his mother doing it? This question tortured him for weeks. It was his grandmother who flushed out the answer, the morning after she came home unexpected from New York and surprised the lovers in bed.

That Saturday, Sylvia and Eugenie Kerrigan, a Bryn Mawr classmate and her best friend, had gone to New York for the opening of an off-Broadway comedy. The show was feeble and they left after the first act. Departing as they had arrived in the Kerrigan chauffeur-driven Packard, they retraced their route under the Hudson River, over the Pulaski Skyway, and through the Passaic River stench to Newark.

"Let me out here; my legs are stiff from all that sitting and I need to stretch them out a bit," Sylvia said as the Packard slowed to a halt at the big wrought-iron Court Place entrance. "Let's hope we do better next time. Give William my best." With a brief hug and a blown kiss, she stepped onto the street. She was home almost four hours earlier than usual.

Sylvia's pace, as always, was brisk as she walked through the gate to her home at the far end of the privileged sanctuary. She barely noticed the gray Pontiac with the military plates parked near the entrance. Sylvia wore a black felt Lilly Daché hat, eye-catching but discreet, perfect for the theater. Her black kid-leather clutch bag, midheel pumps, and peacock blue silk dress were from Bergdorf's. The dress was unadorned; a subtle gold necklace and finely crafted Gruen wristwatch completed the ensemble. As she neared her home, she looked forward to having a drink to ease her disappointment.

Margaret would still be awake, if not downstairs in the library then upstairs in her room listening to one of those Saturday-night radio mysteries she loved, Sylvia thought. Once inside, Sylvia found the downstairs dark and empty. Billy, of course, would be sleeping in his room above the garages. She wanted to get into a gown and relax, and as she climbed the stairs to her bedroom she decided to look in on Margaret, quietly opened her bedroom door, and stepped inside.

In the bed, her daughter-in-law's sex-flushed face deepened to crimson. The man who was mounting her turned and stared over his left shoulder. Both were silent, not wanting to prompt any words from the enraged face of the intruder. It took less than three seconds for Sylvia to focus and frame a mental snapshot, develop and enlarge it, and then paste it into the family album.

Not a word had been spoken. Sylvia backed into the hall quietly, closed the door, and with her hand on the doorknob, eased the latch into its anchor in the doorjamb. There was not so much as a click. Since her preschool days with her nanny, Sylvia learned that a lady never raises her voice in anger or cries in pain. This night she passed both tests.

"I'm bored, Sylvia," Margaret said the next morning. The words hissed across the kitchen table. Billy was in the hall. No one knew he was there.

"There's nothing metaphysical about it. No great mystery. I've just been in a mood for a good fuck and I've been getting it."

"Shut your filthy mouth!" Sylvia's soft, measured voice dripped with venom. "My son, your husband. Let's think about him. What happens when he gets back?"

Billy did not want to hear any more. He ran out of the house and picked up speed after turning on High Street, not stopping until he reached St. Mark's.

That was two weeks ago. His confusion got worse with every passing day. *So what do I do now,* he thought as he finished drying his hands.

He could feel his mother's warm breath on his neck as her arms reached around his chest.

Margaret fondly enveloped Billy with her eyes. He was already over five feet tall, just a few inches shorter than she. Her son had his father written all over him—the square, well-formed face with its light skin and freckles, and the thick reddish-brown hair.

"You must be starving. How about a raid on the icebox? A little talk over some cake and milk, how about it?"

"Sure. I am kinda hungry."

Billy went through three glasses of milk, two pieces of layer cake, an apple, and three slices of ham. His mother had some tea. They chatted about school, the new priest, and his friends. Nothing important. Just normal stuff.

During their talk, Billy had completely forgotten what he had come to hate in his mother. Perhaps, without him knowing it, he had even come to understand her a little.

When it was over, Billy and his mother linked arms as they so often did and strode in perfect step until they reached the stairs. Margaret kissed Billy on the forehead and went up to her bedroom, Billy headed to his room—his own private carriage house, his grandmother called it.

In a hurry to get the paint off his hands, Billy had rushed to the kitchen without turning off the garage lights. He checked his father's workshop to see if everything was in order, then walked over to his Schwinn racer propped on its kickstand in the rear of the garage. He felt the tires. They were soft from disuse. He wondered how long it would be before his mother said it was okay for him to start pedaling again. After all, it wasn't his fault that the other kids couldn't afford bikes. He couldn't imagine how rapidly things could change, nor did he know that bikes were the inducement that sucked Richie and Joey into the frontline of a menacing mob war. He turned off the light and headed up the stairs to his bedroom.

Chapter

34

Hensley Parker Bancroft was still pissed off by the news that he would have to start earning his money as the *Clarion* Vice President for Circulation. He had just given his early autumn pep talk to Jim McDuffie and dozens of other circulation managers in the paper's ninth floor conference room. The holidays were coming up and increased circulation meant higher ad rates.

The Bancrofts and the family of *Clarion* publisher, Herbert Bix, went back a long way. Bix and Bancroft were roommates at Princeton, crewed together during regattas on the Delaware, were groomsmen at each other's weddings, and compared honeymoon snapshots from France and Italy.

Bancroft believed that he had nailed down an important slot on the *Clarion*. His buddy Herb tried his damnedest to accommodate him, but it turned out that the tall, blond, blue-eyed Bancroft was, to put it simply, dumb. The coffee break guffaws increased as he bounced from the editorial pages to the city desk, down to the police beat, and finally the obituaries, failing at all of it.

Given the newly minted title of Vice President for Circulation, Bancroft oversaw a department that ran itself. He gave little thought to Goldman's *Beacon*, a morning rag that patronized the great unwashed. That was until yesterday when he sat in with the top brass and learned that David Goldman had the *Clarion* in his sights.

"The audacity of that sheeny son of a bitch," Bix said in a rare burst of temper as he arranged and rearranged several four-by-six index cards on the conference table.

"Who the hell does he think he's fucking with, the *Bayonne Record,* the *New Rochelle Gazette*. It's all right here gentlemen," he said as he tapped the index cards he had shuffled into a neat stack in front of him. "Goldman's renting store front offices in and around our circulation strong points."

"And that's not all," the livid publisher sputtered. "George, take over, fill everyone in."

George Richards wasn't use to all this attention. A third generation printer, he oversaw a pressroom operation that pumped out four editions a day, an award winning Sunday magazine, and special editions when needed. The *Clarion* was distributed throughout the state and read with interest in New York and as far as Washington. He was the only man at the table without a tie and jacket, and who actually worked with his hands.

"Well, to start, there's no doubt Goldman's got big plans for the *Beacon*," the wiry, gray haired Richards said. "We've seen his cut-throat tactics before. This time it's the *Long Island Spectator*. He's closed it down despite the fact that its press, a pre-war Koenig & Bauer, had been completely renovated three years earlier. It's already loaded on freight cars and on its way here."

"Where did you hear that?" City Editor Malcolm Brewster asked.

"From the horse's mouth," Richards said. "The *Spectator's* press boss is an old friend. His last paycheck was for chaining down that beautiful press on an Erie flatbed. He's looking for a job."

"Where's that bastard Goldman going to plant it? There's no room in that squalid piece-of-shit operation of his," Bancroft said.

"He's already knocked out part of the back wall," Richards said, "and to make more room moved circulation into a building he bought next door."

"This is fucking serious," Bix said. "And there's not much we can do about it. Any ideas?"

"Short of hiring a hit man?" legal counsel Wilford Copley said, and what for him passed as humor. "It's no longer a piss-ant David against Goliath. Let's keep in mind the *Beacon's* non-union, and we've got two big contracts coming up. Timing couldn't be worse."

"So what the hell do we do?" Bancroft figured that asking rather than suggesting was the safe way to go.

"I've been giving it a lot of thought," the publisher said as he resumed tapping his index cards on the table and looked squarely at his circulation manager. "Hensley, I've decided you'll be our point man."

"Me?"

"Yes, you. Your minions are on the front line. Get to know them, most of all, get to know what they know. That means getting out in the field, especially to our gold-chip bureaus here in the city. They're most likely where Goldman will have his circulation thugs moving in first."

"That's a big order, I'll have to give some thought to where I start."

"No need to worry about that," the publisher said. "I've checked the map and see that two of your bureaus are in the Third Ward, and four of them are on the fringes. Visit the fringes first, before moving into the Ward."

The meeting lasted another hour, during which it became increasingly clear to Bix that everyone in the room was clueless. Goldman earned his reputation by going for the jugular. The publisher searched the faces around the table and saw there was not a single cutthroat in the bunch.

"Well, that's it for now," Bix soft-pedaled the urgency he was feeling. "We all know that Goldman has bitten off more than he can chew. We'll be ready. Bancroft, I'm sure we won't be seeing much of you for a while. I expect to hear from you regularly."

To be told that he would be on the front line of a circulation war was more than Bancroft had ever imagined. His sour stomach had kept him awake all night.

"Hensley, what in the world is bothering you?" Maude Fahey Bancroft said as she raised her head from her pillow and stared down at her wide awake husband. "You've been keeping me awake with all your tossing and turning, even heard some groaning. It's not like you."

"I've got something to tell you." Bancroft's eyes twitched as he spoke without turning his head. It was as though he were addressing an unseen audience in the dark recesses of their large bedroom. "Starting this week you'll be driving my Morgan, and I'll be taking the Packard."

"Like hell I will. You know how I hate that toy of yours."

"Can't be helped. Got the word only yesterday from Herb himself that I'll be inspecting all my circulation offices, and reporting in directly to him."

"You've never had to do that before. And explain to me why you can't take the Morgan?"

Maude fluffed her two pillows, propped them against the headboard, and reached over to turn on the lamp on her nightstand. She picked up a box of Benson & Hedges and a Ronson lighter, handing the Ronson to her husband as she closely studied the face of the weak man beside her. She had learned early that the charmer who'd swept her off her feet eight years earlier was an empty suit, and that his job at the *Clarion* was no more than a sinecure. Against her wishes, Bancroft had used a sizeable chunk of the cash wedding gift from her father to acquire the powerful two-seat sports car during their honeymoon in Europe.

"Where I have to go, it would be crazy for me to be driving a beautiful machine like the Morgan," Bancroft said as he lit his wife's cigarette, and took one out of the box for himself. "So it's the Packard for me, the Morgan for you. Can't say for how long."

"I'll bear it alright, but I'll be god damned if I'll be grinning."

They spent the remainder of the early morning hours awake, but in silence broken only when Katie, their black cook and housekeeper, brought in their coffee tray. Two hours later, his stomach began to churn when he got behind the wheel of his wife's Packard and headed downtown for the annual meeting with his district managers to kick-off the pre-holiday circulation campaign.

This morning he had to convey a sense of enthusiasm to a rough bunch of streetwise strangers with whom he could hardly be expected to identify. After droning on for almost thirty minutes, he concluded by throwing out the morsel, "Who knows, there might even be a little something extra in your pay envelope."

"The same old bullshit," Jim McDuffie said as he crammed into the elevator that would take him and his cohorts down to Market Street and a world that Bancroft could hardly imagine.

"Call me crazy, but once, just once I'd like to see that fancy son of a bitch show up some Saturday and help stuff the Sunday paper," Bud Morsby, who ran twenty-two carriers in West Newark, chimed in.

"What a fucking joke that guy is," McDuffie said.

Once down on Market, McDuffie and the others who had squeezed into the elevator with him headed back to their cars and the real world.

Al Sweeney, Tommy Spencer and Gino Sharkey had been waiting for McDuffie for almost half an hour when he pulled his green, four-door Chevy sedan to the curb in front of his Avon Avenue office. The three seventeen year old carriers were muscular and mean, the backbone of McDuffie's operation. They had keys to the office, and were lounging lazily on a beat-up brown couch when he walked through the door. The steady rain and dark clouds lent to the gloomy atmosphere.

"Let's cut right to it," McDuffie said. "When you walk out of here, you better damn well know what has to be done."

"So give it to us, boss," Sharkey said, "that's what we're here for."

"The *Beacon* wants a bigger piece of the Third Ward and is already moving in from Frank Marsucci's office on Kinney. What we don't know is what Marsucci's up to right now when it comes to the numbers."

"He ain't into the numbers, not yet," Sweeney said, "but it's comin', you can bet your sweet ass on that. He ain't blind, he knows how we worked over those five coon runners they tried to squeeze into our turf."

"Those three fake, nigger barbers thought they could actually pull it off," Spencer said. "But when we kicked the hell out of the five jigs they sent our way, things got changed real quick. So now they're going after white kids from St. Mark's, really scraping the bottom of the fucking barrel, if you ask me."

"I hear it ain't just the three nigger barbers," Sharkey said as he tapped out four fags from a pack of Luckies, passed out three of them, and lit the fourth for himself. He leaned back on the couch, took a deep drag, and sensed McDuffie's eyes boring in.

These three young punks were McDuffie's information pipeline. All had juvie records, had families with police rap sheets, and as school dropouts for more than a year had learned the hard way how the Third Ward worked.

Gino Sharkey got an education when he sat in with his dad during dominoes at the Sicilian-American Club on Tenth. He quickly learned how the old goombahs hated Zwillman. There might be a truce, but Richie the Boot and Longy's handshake didn't mean shit. Every wop in Newark knew that each wanted mobster control of the city for himself. Arguments at the club, usually oiled by juice glasses of grappa, convinced Gino that Longy's Third Ward was ripe for the picking.

"So what the hell else did you hear?" McDuffie demanded, knowing that he was asking the kid to dishonor a code that said whatever was heard inside his old man's club stayed inside.

"Only that the Boot wanted to take it slow, didn't want to make no waves," Sharkey said. "Even has one of his soldiers working with the three jigaboos to make sure they don't go crazy."

McDuffie decided to push it a little further, hoping that greed would be the tipping point. "Slow, I still don't get what you mean by slow."

"Shit, I don't know, maybe one runner nosing into our turf to test things. Jesus Christ, how the hell am I expected to know?"

"Who gives a damn whether it's one punk or more, they know we'll be waiting," Sweeney said. "First time nearly broke that big coon's arm, howled like a baby. Won't be so easy on them this time."

"The dumb fucks even had two bimbos collecting," a smiling Spencer said as he rubbed the knuckles of his right hand. "Thought it would make things smooth. I got that notion out of their heads real quick."

"So this is the way I see it, and it's the way you're going to see it," McDuffie said. "You got that!"

The battle plan was simple, with the exception of only one apartment, all newspaper deliveries were made via a service staircase or elevator. Excellent ambush territory. The coast must be clear of other deliveries. They didn't want the milkman or daily delivery guy around when they moved in. Make it fast. Don't pull any punches. Then take the *Beacon* and throw it in the apartment trash bin. McDuffie steered clear of giving any cautionary advice when it came to violence. He knew these kids, what they were capable of when angered, and that's exactly what he was looking for, unbridled anger.

He searched their faces looking for any sign of doubt. He discovered more than he had hoped for. All three were leaning forward, elbows on their thighs, as they waited impatiently for what he had to say.

"Nothing out in the open, let's get that straight. Let them push that shitty rag out on the street, but they're not getting into the apartments. If we let them in, they'll be picking your pocket and mine, and I'll be fucked if I let that happen. Agreed!"

McDuffie walked the three kids to the door of his office, watched as they unchained their bikes from around a lamp post, and pedaled away. He knew they were supporting their families up to a point, and salted away a tidy sum for themselves each week. Like him, they had a lot at stake and had already shown how far they would go to protect their turf.

Things are getting too god damn complicated, McDuffie thought. *Can't really bitch about the protection. Switzer said it would be there, and the palooka was right. Longy has the cops in his pocket, there's no doubt about it. If Richie the Boot is moving in like Gino says, things could get ugly.*

McDuffie had turned away just as Sweeney motioned for his two buddies to follow him. Fifteen minutes later, they were on the back porch of the Sweeneys third-floor tenement flat.

"Wait here. I've got something to show you," Al said as he turned and went inside. Gino and Tommy shrugged. You never knew what to expect from Al.

"Take a look," Al said as he untied the strings from around a red and white kitchen towel, and tugged it open. "It's a Beretta, an eight-shot beauty, and this little box has extra ammo. I counted twenty bullets."

"Where the hell did you get that?" Gino said as Al gripped the pistol and waved it back and forth in front of them.

"My uncle smuggled it back from Italy in his duffle bag. It's what the Italian officers used. Here, take a look."

The small black pistol was passed around. Gino and Tommy examined it from every angle. "Not much to it. Not heavy at all," Tommy said. "There ain't no way your uncle gave it to you. Does he know you've got it?"

"Nope. I saw where he hid it under all sorts of stuff in his basement. Grabbed it the last time we visited him and Aunt Lizzie in Nutley. Be a while before he misses it."

"It's not loaded is it?" Gino said.

"Bet your sweet ass it is. What good's an empty gun?"

"Jesus Christ, we've been passing it around like it's a toy, and all the time it was loaded! Are you nuts or something!" Tommy said.

"Not to worry, the safety's been on." Al rewrapped the Beretta in the towel and string.

"So what are you gonna do with it," Gino asked. "Ain't no fuckin' way you're actually going to use it. I'm right, ain't I?"

"Just insurance, that's all," Al said. "Only comes out if those *Beacon* punks cross the line. Just wave it, that's all. They'll shit their pants and run like hell."

Chapter

35

Richie was surprised at how smooth things went with Frank Marsucci. The circulation manager was a punk who picked his carriers' pockets and everyone knew it. But driving around with him in his Plymouth that first weekend, you'd never know it. He helped roll and rubberband the Saturday papers, and inserted *Parade* magazine in the Sunday editions. Marsucci even joked about the printer's ink on both of their hands before sharing a bar of Lava soap with Richie at the grimy office sink. They had spent two mornings together going up and down tenement stairs, apartment hallways, front porches, and assorted shops spread over four square blocks.

"Okay, kid, from here on out, you're on your own," Marsucci said handing over a four-inch locking steel ring that was inserted through cards bearing the names, addresses and amounts owed by each of Richie's fifty-five customers. "This is your bible, don't lose it. If you do, it's extra work for me, and it'll cost you five bucks."

Richie ran his belt through the ring to secure it to his waist at the same time giving him easy reference to addresses he hadn't yet memorized. In his back pocket was a small manila envelope that, at the completion of his daily route, would contain markers picked up from twelve numbers writers along the way. No names, no addresses, each stop had to be memorized before Wilber Fontaine, a.k.a. God's Tall Timber, would let him out the door.

The circulation manager never let on that he knew anything about the policy slips he collected each day, and Richie thought it was strange that a blow-hard like Marsucci didn't know what was going on.

"We'll keep a nice little kitty for you," John Travers, a.k.a. Righteous Reckoning, informed him at the end of the first week. "That's four bucks twenty. Not bad on top of your *Beacon* bread, and your folks don't have to know a thing about it."

It took no more than a couple of days for the gang to overcome their eye-popping surprise when Richie showed up on his Columbia Military long enough for each of them to pedal up and down the block before coming to a skidding stop in front of Milt's. The Pump bitched about how her jumper got in the way the first time around, so came back the second day wearing dungarees and had them all wowing as she zigzagged down to the corner and back.

"Now that's a fucking bike!" a panting Pump extolled. "Like brand new. How'd you get your mitts on it? Bet your sweet ass it cost a mint."

"Yep, you got it," Richie said as he steadied the bike on its kickstand. "Started my *Beacon* route. Got a deal with Simon, paying it off a little each week."

"All of a sudden, ain't it," a disturbed Joey said. "Didn't know you even wanted a route. Marsucci's had my name for months. Still waiting."

"Don't blame me," Richie said, "that's the way the ball bounces sometimes."

From the get-go, Richie was surprised how smooth things were going. But Marsucci had clued him in that a circulation war with the *Clarion* was brewing, and that he'd better be ready. In addition to his paying customers, for two weeks Richie would be dropping off twenty freebies at the doors of non-subscribers. He would get fifty cents for each new customer that signed up.

"It's as new to you as it is to me," Marsucci scanned the faces of the twenty kids who had packed into his office that Saturday afternoon. "It's simple enough, for two weeks you'll be getting extra papers with a list of names and addresses where to drop them off. Then you hit each of them for a subscription. You get fifty cents a pop and a new paying customer to boot. Now that ain't too bad, is it."

"Easy for you to say," a tall, pimple-faced redhead, who Richie didn't know, said. "Ain't no way I can see any new customers along my route."

"That's the point," Marsucci said, "you'll be pushing out into new territory, *Clarion* turf. It's not going to be easy, and there's some job security at stake. Get what I mean?"

"What a bunch of bullshit, if you pardon my French," a stocky older kid said. All eyes turned to where he was seated on a bundle of papers near the front door. Richie guessed he was not much younger than Marsucci. "Bosses like you come and go. You're number four. We'll be the ones bumping heads with the *Clarion,* and who the hell knows if you'll even be around."

"You can bet your sweet ass that Sweeney, Sharkey and Spencer will be waiting," another one of his older carriers challenged. "We all know what they got going, and what they'll do to hold on to it."

"They made god damn sure everyone got the message when they pounded the hell out of those five coons," pimple-face said. "And two of them were skirts."

Marsucci swiveled his chair, propped his feet on the desk, and with feigned indifference leaned back to absorb the bitching and moaning that filled his office. *Who the hell do these kids think they're yapping at,* he thought. *Five hours of grilling by the MPs and provost in Cherbourg didn't break me down, so they can just shove it. There's a big meal ticket waiting to be punched and I'm going to punch it.* He held up both hands to signal for silence, got up and walked to the front of his desk. "Close your traps and listen."

It took less than five minutes for Marsucci to outline all they needed to know. They'd be getting extra papers, a list of where to drop them off, and how a special *Beacon* promotion would give each new customer twenty-six weeks of the paper at half-price. He suggested they take care of their subscribers first, then drop off the freebies. If any of them were caught dumping the freebies into trash cans or down the storm drain, they could take a hike. He let them know that he had a list of more than a dozen kids waiting to take their routes.

Marsucci waited until Richie was about to clear out with the rest of the carriers when he motioned him to stay behind. "Maxwell, I think it's time we talk." He slumped into his desk chair, fished his pocketknife out, flicked it open, returned his feet to their usual spot on top of the desk, and began cleaning his fingernails.

"Looks to me you've got a sweetheart deal going with those three jigaboo barbers," he said. "Don't know how you got it, but from here on I'm in on it."

"I don't get it."

"Easy enough. The big one, God's Tall Timber, Wilber Fontaine, or whatever the fuck you call him, stopped by this morning and we had a talk."

"And…."

"Seems you're Richie the Boot's guinea pig. He's been wanting a piece of Zwillman's Third Ward, and figures that starting small to test the water is the way to go. He'll see if you sink or swim."

"Still don't get it."

"Up to now it's been nice and neat, running from one safe policy writer to another. All tucked away outside Longy's territory. Today I got word that's gonna change."

"How so?"

"Got a new name for you," Marsucci said. "Name's Thelma, Thelma Boyd, runs the newsstand and coffeeshop at the Riviera."

"The Riviera! That's solid *Clarion*. From what I see, there's not one *Beacon* subscriber in the whole place. So that's what you mean by guinea pig."

Marsucci pulled a pack of Camels from his shirt pocket, tapped two out, took one and offered the other to Richie. "Ain't really any of my business, and I really don't give a shit, but do mommy and daddy know what you've got going?"

"You're right, that's none of your damn business."

"Okay, we'll keep family out of this." Marsucci pulled a glass ashtray out of the top right drawer and pushed it across the desk. He studied Richie, looking for any sign the kid was in over his head. He found none. "Only want to be sure you won't be pissing your pants when you run into trouble. I don't mean if, I mean when. You can bet your sweet ass on that."

Chapter

36

The high mid-afternoon sun made Richie squint as he stepped out to the sidewalk and unchained his bike from a light pole, just as an unmarked police cruiser slowed momentarily in front of the circulation office before turning the corner.

"Isn't America great," Nick Cisco said as he cocked his right thumb back toward the *Beacon* circulation office. "Dime to dollar that kid we just passed is running numbers for Richie the Boot."

"Start 'em off young," Kevin McClosky said. "Every business needs a good foundation."

"And in this town, policy parlors are like candy stores," his partner said. "Sweet and innocent. Worst thing you can get if you bite off too much is a toothache."

"Damn Nick, if you ain't a cynic," Kevin said. "That kid back there can't be more than thirteen, give or take."

"Starting out way back when, in the Sixth Ward, they had kids as young as eight and nine," Nick said, "running and collecting for Zwillman. Called it nigger pool back then."

"Barely old enough to add and subtract."

"Talk about adding and subtracting, I bet our boy Gazzi has been counting the hours he's been staking out that tenement. My guess is the whore and her pimp won't be back. We've got an APB out on them, and not a bite so far."

"Let's check it out anyway," Kevin said. "And put Gazzi back on the bricks."

McClosky idled their cruiser to a stop in front of the tenement at the same time a smiling Gazzi stepped from the entrance of the apartment across the street.

"Not raining anymore. Outside of that, nothing new." Gazzi was still wearing his department issue raincoat.

"Neighbors do any blabbing at all?" Cisco asked.

"Not a fucking word." Gazzi shed his raincoat exposing a uniform shirt soaked with sweat. "It's like I wasn't here at all."

"Kept those windows in sight all the time, right?" McClosky said.

"Right, no lights." Gazzi fished a small spiral notebook from his shirt pocket and checked his notes. "The blinds didn't move an inch. Plenty of up and down traffic in the hall, that's about it."

"And you've been here around the clock?' Cisco said.

"You got it, that is except for twice to the call box at the corner and a quick piss and coffee at Bloom's at the same time."

The two detectives reacted in unison, their disbelief turning to anger.

"And how long did each of these trips take?" Cisco asked, his face reddening, the veins in his temples popping to the surface.

McClosky recognized the danger signs and decided he better take over before things got ugly.

"Bloom's is a late night deli. Was one of your piss trips after it got dark?"

"Yeah, let me see here…." Gazzi paused to check his notebook, "It was at ten thirty, just before closing."

"You still haven't said for how long. Five minutes? Ten minutes? Fifteen minutes? How fucking long were you away from your stakeout?"

"Fifteen, but no more than that. It's right here," Gazzi tapped his notebook.

Cisco nodded slightly toward his partner indicating with a deep breath that his initial anger had subsided, but not entirely.

"Frank, does that notebook tell you it might not be wise to leave a stakeout for fifteen minutes in the dark of night in a Ward where everyone hates your guts? Don't answer."

The two detectives unbuttoned their coats, unsnapped their shoulder holsters, and with Gazzi in tow, walked as casually as possible across to Ruby West's apartment. They found her door slightly ajar.

"Police, open up!" McClosky shouted. The command was met with silence. The two detectives drew their snub-nosed revolvers, and pushed their way into a room where the only light filtered through the tightly drawn blinds on the two front windows. McClosky turned to Gazzi still in the hall, "Stand right there, don't let anyone near the door."

Cisco drew open the blinds and found what he had feared. Ruby West, her throat cut from ear-to-ear, was sprawled across a deeply cushioned, purple velvet sofa.

"One down so far. Let's take a look in the back," McClosky said.

Cisco and McClosky cautiously eased their way through a kitchenette and dining area, and into a bedroom.

"Two for two," Cisco said.

A light-skinned Negro, about thirty, was hanging by an electric cord from a ceiling fixture. An ice pick was buried in the center of his chest. There was hardly any blood. He was snappily dressed with a light blue shirt, red tie, gold wristwatch, tan gabardine suit, and highly polished wingtip shoes. Alive, he could have easily been mistaken for a store front mannequin.

"From those deep welts around his neck, it looks like they first strangled this bastard, then strung him up with the same cord," Cisco said. "Forensics will make it official. We'll also need a time. What have you got?"

"All packed and ready to go. And expensive, too," McClosky said.

Two brown leather suitcases with brass fittings laid open amid discarded hangers at the foot of the unmade bed. They holstered their revolvers, bent over and began poking through the contents. The larger of the two suitcases contained neatly folded men's shirts, ties, handkerchiefs, underwear, two pairs of trousers, brown and black belts, and a pair of black Oxfords. A matching leather jewelry case contained gold and silver cufflinks, tie clasps, and an onyx pinky ring.

The smaller suitcase was stuffed to overflowing with assorted women's clothes and lacy undergarments, nylon stockings, garter belts, two pair of high-heel shoes, and a zipper bag filled with tasteful costume jewelry. A nylon pocket sown into the suitcase lining contained an envelope with seven hundred sixty dollars in cash.

McClosky pulled a small beaded purse from under the suitcase and emptied the contents onto the bed. The name and photo on the Georgia driver's license identified the twenty-nine year old woman as Althea Foster, a.k.a. Ruby West, with an Atlanta street address. Tucked into a side pocket were a fancy metal compact, lipstick and rouge. A switchblade also fell out along with two dollars in change.

Cisco straightened, approached the hanging body, used the tip of his pen to carefully push open the left side of the dead man's jacket, and removed a wallet and envelope. He then pushed aside the right lapel, and found what he was looking for, an empty, thin leather ice pick holder clipped to the inside pocket.

"Heartless bunch, string the bastard up and then poke him to see if he's done. I'd say it's poetic justice," Cisco said. "It's a safe bet forensics gets only the stiff's prints, if they get any at all. Here take a look." Cisco handed the envelope to McClosky while he examined the contents of the wallet. "Got a name, Clyde Barton, also a Georgia license, thirty-two years old, and an Atlanta address. Nothing here to indicate a Newark connection. I count nine hundred twenty dollars cash. How 'bout you?"

"Two Baltimore & Ohio tickets. No coach for these two, no sirree," McClosky said. "First class Pullman all the way to Atlanta, with a transfer in D.C."

Cisco took the envelope with the tickets, replaced the contents of the wallet and carefully returned everything to the inside jacket pocket.

The adjoining rear bedroom of the railroad tenement contained only two straight-back chairs, a bucket, wet mop, broom and dustpan propped in a corner. There were five crushed cigarette butts on the floor near the chairs. Its rear door opened to a porch.

"I'd say this is how they got in," Cisco said. "Looks like they were waiting a while."

"Efficient bunch once they got started," McClosky said. "Got to hand it to them, all done in fifteen minutes."

"Dumb shits. They should have known freelance whores and their pimps don't last long in this town," Cisco saId. "Came in the back way, waited until Ruby and her pimp were busy stuffing their suitcases."

"Looks like they were taking care of Clyde, and Ruby tried to make a break for it," McClosky said. "Never got past the parlor."

"Let's call it in, get the APB lifted and a forensic team out here," Cisco said. "Frank, come in and take a look, ever see these two before?"

Gazzi followed the two detectives into the front room where the late afternoon sun bathed the whore's face frozen in a tight, open-eyed grimace.

"Think about it," Cisco said, as he led Gazzi into the bedroom. "Well, ring any bells?"

"The faces, I can't say. But from what they're wearing, especially her with that tight skirt and blouse, I think they're the ones that ran out of the Zanzibar right after the stabbing."

"We'll want your report first thing in the morning," Cisco said.

Chapter

37

A crowd of about two dozen men, women and children had gathered in front of the tenement. They silently cleared a path for the detectives as they made their way back to the police cruiser. Another dozen men and women, drinks in their hands, had sifted out of the Zanzibar Lounge to take in the commotion. The stoop where Gazzi had become a non-person during his long stakeout was now crowded with tenement dwellers enjoying a welcome change in their routine.

Cisco and McClosky watched as the morgue meat wagon, this one a panel truck wide enough for two gurneys, pulled to a stop across the way. The forensic team pulled up behind it. Three uniforms got out of a patrol car summoned from the precinct to help Gazzi with crowd control.

"Let them get started. Make sure they dust the two chairs and doorknobs in the back bedroom. Gives us time to put our heads together," Cisco said.

"It's got mob written all over it," McClosky said. "But it doesn't make any sense. With the mayor, the press and every preacher in town crying about crime, it'd be crazy for either Richie the Boot or Longy to turn their gorillas loose right now."

"Unless the rumors are true," Cisco said, "that the Boot is after a piece of Longy's Third Ward action, probably starting with the numbers."

"You're right, everyone plays them. Win or lose nobody squawks. But hookers, they're something else, more than nickels, dimes and quarters involved. Take Clyde and Ruby, where the hell do they fit in? Let's see what we pry out of the good citizens at the Zanzibar."

There were a dozen patrons, five of them women, scattered about the suddenly silent, dimly lit saloon. A bartender ignored them while wiping down the far end of the bar. A big, muscular black man behind the bar acknowledged them with a wide-toothed smile.

"It's been a long time, a long, long time since Roundy Suggs has had the pleasure," the former Tenderloin bouncer said. "Ever since you two fine men come up in the world. Robbery and now Homicide, you've been strangers to this good ol' boy."

"Come a long way yourself," Cisco said. "But fancy whores and pimps, I'd think you'd leave all that trash behind in the Tenderloin."

"Fancy whores? Pimps? No way Roundy gives them the light of day in the Zanzibar."

The two detectives had taken stools at the bar. They swiveled around to take in the rest of the room. Everyone had suddenly taken a keen interest in the contents of their glasses, avoiding any eye contact with each other or the cops at the bar.

"Okay, let's talk Ruby West. Maybe you know her as Althea Foster," McClosky said.

"No, sir, don't know no Ruby or Althea."

"How about Clyde Barton, a real fancy dude?"

"Nope, don't know nobody by that name either."

"We hear different," Cisco said. "Convince us."

Even in the dim light Suggs could recognize trouble. It was written all over the cops' faces. "Best maybe we move this outside," he said, then turned to the other bartender, "Josh, take over."

Out on the sidewalk, at a safe distance from the Zanzibar entrance, the three men played it casual. McClosky tapped out three Old Golds, offered them around before taking one himself.

"Sometimes a few deep drags jogs things," he said. "Don't you agree, Mr. Suggs?"

"Me and names ain't ever been good together," Suggs said. "Faces sometimes, but not always. Those names again?"

"Let's stop the bullshit. One more time, and it's the last time. Ruby West and Clyde Barton," McClosky said, then threw his cigarette to the sidewalk and crushed it, a clear signal for his partner to take over.

"Big fella, there's a lot at stake here. The Zanzibar, I'm sure you think it's clean as a whistle, but our buddies in Vice, you know how nasty they can be." Cisco noted the black man's growing uneasiness. "I'm sure they'd recognize one or two of those working ladies inside, that's big trouble for you. And we've got a dead black war hero stabbed to death right over there, only a few feet away."

"You don't have to worry about Ruby and Clyde," McClosky said. "They're morgue meat. Got it last night."

Suggs, at least four inches taller than McClosky, peered over the detective's shoulder as the second of two gurneys was loaded into the coroner's van. A crowd of about fifty jeered Gazzi and the other three uniforms clearing a path from the tenement entrance.

"Last night?" a shaken Suggs asked.

"Yeah, last night. It wasn't pretty," Cisco said. "Tell us what you know, and don't fuck around. Ruby and Clyde were spotted in your club about the time our war hero was ice picked."

"Believe Roundy when he says he knows nothing about murders. Those two, never laid eyes on them until maybe last week. Never let them hustle, no sir, didn't want that kind of trouble."

"What about yesterday, around eight or eight-thirty in the morning?"

"They in here at the bar when a good lookin' black man comes in and they join up," Suggs said. "He be a stranger. Had only one drink, left together, and maybe fifteen or twenty minutes later, they come back alone. All out of breath. That's when I hear the shouting and yelling outside. Like I say, don't want no trouble. So I tell Josh to call the police, always keep the number close."

"And the pimp and the whore?" McClosky asked.

"They gone real fast when Josh picks up the phone."

"Anything else? Spill it now," McClosky said. "If we find you've held out, say bye-bye to the Zanzibar."

"Okay, it's coming back now. Those two be new here in the Ward, so it took old Roundy by surprise when they first come in and ordered drinks at the bar, and took them over to a booth. It was like they were waiting for somebody. Sure enuf, a guy comes in, looks around, spots them and says real loud, 'Clyde, Althea, you finally made it.' Then it be party time, lots of laughs. Ruby gets a big hug, and the dudes pound each other on the back. I hear Clyde say 'Buck, big brother, you ain't changed a bit.' When they got going, they sounded real southern."

"Real southern?" Cisco said.

"Slow and easy, not like they talk around here."

Cisco and McClosky were satisfied they had gotten everything they could out of Suggs. They could come up with an accessory rap of some kind, but with three murders on their hands, decided instead to find out just who Clyde Barton and Althea Foster were. And now, they could add big brother Buck to the mix.

The morgue van had pulled away, the forensic team right behind it, and with the entertainment over, the crowd in front of the tenement was breaking up. His work now over, Gazzi crossed Broome to join the two detectives as they were about to get into their car. With the passenger door open, Cisco hesitated as they waited for the patrolman. Maybe the sorry excuse for a cop could be of some help after all.

"Good work, Frank. Could have been trouble, but you handled it well," Cisco said.

"Learning more every day."

"We got three murders on our hands, and think there's a lot going on in the Ward that could be connected," Cisco said. "No need to tell you how easy it is to miss those little tips and clues. We could use your help."

"You've got it." Gazzi's eyes sparkled with the realization that he could be part of a three-homicide headline grabber, maybe even have his name mentioned. "Just tell me how."

"Make your precinct reports as usual, and if you stumble across anything you have a gut feeling about, call me or Sergeant McClosky direct at Homicide. Keep up the good work, Frank."

Roundy Suggs watched the unmarked police cruiser drive away confident he had pulled it off again, playing dumb with an innocent look that bordered on shocked disbelief. He was nobody's fool. Retracing his steps back to the Zanzibar, Suggs recalled the first time Ruby and Clyde paid a visit to the bar. They were obviously nosing around, getting the lay of the land. It was easy to see they weren't part of Longy's stable. He told the cops only enough to get them off his back, but clammed up about what was really happening.

The word was out for months that Richie the Boot believed Longy's Third Ward was ripe for the picking. Would a mobster who shared the front seat of his roadster with Hollywood bombshell, Jean Harlow, give much thought to his old stomping ground. Boiardo was convinced that he didn't. Maybe Ruby and Clyde meant the Boot was already nibbling at the edges. Roundy couldn't take a chance pissing off Longy, so right off he put in a call to the mobster's Political Club and filled them in. The two gurneys he had just seen loaded into the morgue meat wagon convinced him that his call had been taken seriously.

A teletype from the Atlanta police was on Cisco's desk when he arrived at headquarters the following morning. It was no surprise that Althea had a rap sheet that included petty theft, assault, and prostitution charges. Clyde's sheet included burglary, assault with a deadly weapon, gambling and pandering. There were no warrants outstanding, current whereabouts unknown.

Acting on the tip supplied by Roundy Suggs, Cisco also asked if Atlanta or Fulton County authorities had anything on a Negro male, probably in his early to mid-thirties going by the name of Buck Barton. He wasn't surprised to learn that a Leland Buck Barton and two partners skipped town hours before police padlocked numbers banks all across Atlanta. They had been making book from a three-chair barbershop in the front, while running a lucrative policy parlor in the back room. Barton, John Travers and Wilber Fontaine had long rap sheets, mostly pandering and gambling, but had done very little jail time. A postscript suggested that the three men had ties with organized crime, and were somewhere in the north Jersey-New York metro area.

"Quite a bunch," McClosky had pulled a chair over to Cisco's desk in the Homicide bullpen and had just finished reading the teletype. "My guess is that all three are here in town."

"If what we've been hearing on the street is worth anything, it would be only natural. The Third Ward has always been Longy's baby, but he's been spreading his wings. For appearances he keeps digs at the Riviera, hits the Mercer Shvitz for steam, but lives in a twenty room shack in East Orange. It's ripe for Richie the Boot to make his move."

"I agree there's a tie-in here. We just have to connect the dots. It's no secret Boiardo is still looking for payback for the buckshot he's carrying around courtesy of Longy. If we're right that headlines are the last thing these two thugs want, why do we have three stiffs with mob written all over them?"

"You know, there's just something I can't get out of my mind," Cisco said. "And it involves kids, yeah kids. Do you remember when we drove past that *Beacon* circulation office yesterday, and I said it would be so easy for the kid with the bike to be a numbers runner?"

"The Third Ward numbers racket is Longy's baby," McClosky said, "and he's not about to let go of it no matter how big he gets. Are you saying that the Boot figures an easy way to take a bite of the Ward's policy pie is to start small, with kids on bikes?"

"Crazy as it sounds, that's what I'm saying. These kids are hardly choir boys. Been at it for years, many of them are bullies, had to be. Some are outright thugs. If it's true that a *Clarion* and *Beacon* circulation war is brewing, it means that some nasty kids with papers in their baskets and number slips in their back pocket will be butting heads."

Chapter

38

During the three months since his assignment to St. Mark's, Father Terence Nolan realized with ever-increasing clarity that the Inquisition had never ended, only the implements of demanded truths had changed. Mushroom clouds rising above two incinerated Japanese cities provided the punctuation.

True believers of every persuasion were armed and on the move. Long-established fortresses were under siege. Here at fortress St. Mark's white faces peered over the ramparts.

"GLORIA IN EXCELSIS DEO."

The words were an exhortation that echoed through the big, almost empty church. They reverberated off the confessionals along the side aisles and in the rear. The words enveloped, perhaps even imparted meaning, to the baleful expressions of awe on the faces of a vast array of statues transfixed in mute saintliness atop altars and in the shadowy recesses of one apse after another.

"Glory to God in the highest . . ."

Loud and clear. Father Nolan meant it that way. Just let the words go and hope for the best. This was what it was all about. He completed the remainder of the prayer in mumbled Latin. ". . . *cum Sancto Spiritu in gloria Dei Patris. Amen."*

The priest turned to the faces in the pews.

"Dominus vobiscum."

"Et cum spiritu tuo," responded the two altar boys.

Father Nolan glanced quickly at Joey Bancik, then at Billy Spratlin. The priest had been uneasy with Joey all week. His uneasiness was the result of the gibberish of an imbecilic man-child. Eight-Ten had laid yet another unwanted burden on him only last Saturday.

He had just completed hearing confessions and was returning to the rectory when he heard footsteps behind him on the path.

"Faduh. Faduh Nolan."

The priest turned abruptly. Eight-Ten was taken by surprise and bumped into Nolan before he was able to brake to a halt. The rancid stench of the dullard's breath repelled the priest. He backed off a few feet as the stooped man looked smilingly into his face.

"Gotta tell ya sumpin'. Sumpin' ya gotta know."

"Go ahead, I'm listening." Nolan felt that vague uneasiness that the more fortunate cherish when confronted with the outcast.

"Have time, faduh? If ya don't, it'll keep."

"I have time, go ahead."

"It's Richie and Joey."

The priest watched the anxious face as the words spilled out. "Now back up a minute. Just who are you talking about?"

"Aheh, aheh." Eight-Ten smiled stupidly. He didn't understand. With downturned eyes, he intently studied his hands. Eight-Ten had rehearsed his few lines to a point of childish perfection, a perfection that precluded any questioning. He knew what he was talking about. It was all quite clear.

"Let's start again. Richie who?"

Eight-Ten peered questioningly at the priest and remembered the black box. The priest never asked him any questions in the black box. He would listen to him through the screen, then say, "Bless you, my son. May God go with you." Why was he asking things now? Maybe he should have taken his story to the black box. Then he could tell it without anybody asking anything. Eight-Ten dearly wished he had taken his story to the black box.

"Now that's an easy one, Richie who?" A surge of pity overcame the priest as he watched Eight-Ten trying desperately to form the words on his silently moving lips.

Then a smile of shadowy recognition crossed the dullard's face. "Aheh, aheh. Aheh, aheh. Richie who? I gotcha, faduh. Richie who? Richie Maxwell, that's Richie who."

"Now Joey, Joey who?"

"Aheh, aheh. Joey who? Joey Bancik, that's Joey who."

Nolan studied the man-child standing before him in the now-dark path. Even in the dimness, he could see that the dullard's face was no longer beseeching. At that instant, the small, automatically controlled lights that illuminated the church grounds snapped on. One was directly overhead. Eight-Ten's bearded face took on a yellow hue. The dullard's lips were compressed and his head trembled slightly. But he made no effort to say anything. Father Nolan had had enough. "Well, if that's it, good night." He gave one last glance at Eight-Ten, and turned toward the rectory. "Good night . . . my son."

He was brought up short when a strong, calloused hand clamped his left wrist. "Faduh, ya gotta listen." There was no mistaking the look on Eight-Ten's face. Father Nolan could see that this powerful, infantile hulk had no intention of letting him go until the whole story had been told. The priest, simply by raising his voice, could bring Father Schneider from his nearby study. By shouting, he could bring the good sisters from their convent on the other side of the rectory. Either prospect was absurd. With a sigh, he sat down on the grass beside the path. Eight-Ten did not release the priest's arm until he was sure it was not a trick. He was always being tricked.

"Okay, go ahead, I'm listening."

Eight-Ten, his head still trembling slightly, peered at Father Nolan. No, it wasn't a trick. He waddled to the other side of the path and sat down heavily.

"Aheh, aheh. It's bikes."

"Bikes?"

"It's Richie's fault. At Milt's they all love Richie's new bike. Joey has one, too. That makes me so mad. Now they have two bikes to love."

"You should be happy they have bikes. Why are you mad?"

"At Milt's it's not the same anymore."

"I go to Milt's, and I see nothing has changed."

"Aheh, aheh. You don't see what Eight-Ten sees. They don't fool me this time."

Nolan had no idea what this dimwitted hulk was talking about, only that he was deeply troubled, and for some unfathomable reason felt that a priest could help. He decided to give it a try.

"The bikes are good things, are you saying they are being used for bad things?"

"Bad things, yes, aheh, aheh, for bad things. The numbers. Eight-Ten knows the numbers, he plays them with his good friend Gino."

"I don't understand. What are Richie and Joey doing with the numbers? Do they play the numbers like you?"

"Aheh, aheh. Aheh, aheh," the dullard's features softened and his voice took on a superior tone. "They don't play, they run. Don't fool Eight-Ten this time, that they be only paper boys."

The priest wondered if it could be true, that two of his altar boys were numbers runners, using their paper routes as cover. He eyed the dumb oaf who sat opposite him, and to his surprise was convinced.

"Do you know who Richie and Joey are running numbers for?"

"Richie first, and now Joey go to that nigger barbershop on Spruce. The bikes, they be from that cheap Jew's pawnshop. I watch and I know."

"Why does all this make you mad?"

"If everybody at Milt's loves the two bikes, they won't love my pretty pictures the same way anymore. Richie and Joey laugh at my beauties, even push them on the floor."

The priest watched Eight-Ten, who was now crouched on his haunches. His face was curiously immobile, frozen in a dumb but confident leer that seemed almost a jaundiced death mask in the glare of the overhead light. Father Nolan then realized that he was on the defensive, and a thought flashed across his mind. It was a spark zigzagging crazily through the blackness.

Chapter

39

"Keep a tight asshole."

The exhortation was as much a part of each Pacific island invasion as were the Japs who waited patiently. It only took a few months as combat chaplain for Father Nolan to realize that any priestly pre-landing homily of his could hardly match the all-inclusiveness of the profane advisory. It said it all.

How odd, that sitting here, on the well-tended, thick grass beside St. Mark's, he had the same debilitating feeling that he had experienced every time he climbed down a landing net to an invasion craft. He knew that if he were standing, his knees would feel weak. A flood of enervating sensation arose from deep within the muscles of his thighs, knotted his stomach, and bounced heavily off the inside of his ribs. It gurgled up his throat and left a sour taste in his mouth. "Keep a tight asshole."

Father Nolan watched as the hulk backed off into the shadows and shuffled across the lawn. Despite their inadequacies, they had communicated. The kinship was real. The priest felt helpless. What could he do? For the half-man, for the kids? With the realization of inadequacy came fear.

Eight-Ten had reached the sidewalk, where he paused under a streetlight to look back at the rectory.

Terry Nolan remained on the grass late into the night. The light in Father Schneider's study had long since been out when he arose and walked toward the rectory. Several times he could sense the elderly priest's eyes upon him from his second-floor window. He knew that his lonely sojourn had not escaped Mrs. Spiser, who as housekeeper was omniscient. He didn't care what they thought. The encounter with Eight-Ten had brought back memories.

Once again he had relived that day on Saipan, a recurring horror. It had happened only a week before he was to rotate back to the States, after he had spent almost two years accompanying Marines on one island-hopping massacre after another. He performed his vocation in a theater of death, was, in fact, a harbinger of death. What was his purpose if not to prepare a man for dying?

What kind of leaders would perpetuate a sham that bathed the world in blood? An unthinkable thought. So, for almost two years, he performed his vocation well.

That all ended his second week on Saipan. The battle for the island with its weeping soil, lush checkerboards of sugar cane and volcanic juttings, was in its final stages.

Father Nolan had spent a rather leisurely day in and around Charan Kanoa, the site of the original landings. He had received his orders for rotation stateside in plenty of time to beg off this invasion, but had been with the Marines too long to miss the action in the Marianas. The assault would eventually lead to the conquest of Guam, and the first reclaiming of soil taken from American boys by the Japs. He couldn't miss it. It was a decision he would spend the rest of his life regretting.

The battle had moved to the center of the island, and Marines were fighting their way toward the heart of Garapan, the seat of Imperial Japan in the Marianas.

Father Nolan had spent the early part of the day visiting at the tent of chaplain friends with the 4th Marines. They were assigned to the big medical evacuation area at the airstrip near Afetna Point. His orders home were common knowledge before the landings. A bottle of Black and White appeared, and there were toasts until the scotch bottle was empty. It was a nostalgic few hours.

The bottle was drained for the last toast by Father Gregory Fallon, an intense Episcopalian. Flushed from the heat and booze, Fallon arose shakily from his seat atop an empty five-gallon gas can. The sweat on his scalp glistened through his sparse hair. His face was streaked with dirty sweat that ran down to his chin. His fatigue shirt was soaked, and there were wet patches at the knees of his pants. A little, hollow-eyed man with a jutting chin, Fallon eyed his silent companions, all of whom were no less miserable looking than himself.

Father Nolan watched the little guy's eyes as they traveled from one face to another. Then their eyes met, only to be broken off after a few seconds by the mutual consent of two young men trying desperately not to be anachronisms.

"Get your ass home safely, Terry."

They quickly drained their canteen cups, shook Father Nolan's hand, and filed silently out of the tent.

By early afternoon Father Nolan was on his way back to rejoin the 2nd Marines northwest of battle-ravaged Mount Tapotchou, a recently secured thirsty peak that drank the blood of Marine and Jap without prejudice.

The coast road from Charan Kanoa paralleled a railroad that ran the length of Saipan's west coast, what was left of it. The road was a maelstrom of activity, casualties moving south and fresh men and equipment moving north, the grist of war.

Nolan was hot and weary. The few belts of scotch made him drowsy, and the boiling wet sun didn't help. He had gotten a lift on a medical evacuation jeep to the juncture of the road that cut across the island to Tsutsuran. The driver was sorry he couldn't take him any farther, but there were still plenty of wounded who had to be moved from Purple Heart Ridge.

The priest slogged it on foot from there. By late afternoon the crackle of small arms fire could be heard along with the bigger stuff. An occasional round of enemy mortar or artillery fire added to the never-ending chaos always found behind an attacking front line. Nolan knew he would soon be back to work, and he felt suddenly drained. He sat down on an overturned tree somewhat removed from the constant swirl of activity. He took off his helmet and leaned forward to rest his head in his cupped hands. The break didn't last long.

"Excuse me, sir, but are you a Catholic priest?"

Father Nolan looked up through tired, bloodshot eyes. It was a 27th Division GI, about nineteen at the most. His uniform looked fresh, a replacement about to join his outfit. It was all there: blond stubble over a tanned, frightened face, the flat nasal tonality of small-town Midwest, and the clear eyes of a free man. Another young visionary who never loses sight of that Better World at the other end of a rainbow rising from the horrible carnage.

Nolan felt a keen sense of resentment. The boy evoked an endless stream of *Saturday Evening Post* covers, sanitary Americana. Norman Rockwell would have been proud of this kid.

"I hate to bother you, sir, but are you a Catholic priest?" The eager eyes moved from Father Nolan's face to the cross on his collar. "If you are, I would like you to hear my confession. This is my first combat and . . . well . . ."

"Yes, I'm a priest. I understand, no need to explain." Father Nolan arose and reached into his shirt pocket. He removed his stole, wrinkled, stained, and badly worn, but still the symbol of his priestly authority. He put the vestment around his neck as they walked behind a gutted armored troop carrier. The burned-out vehicle partially blocked the sound of the whirling tires of a deuce and a half trapped in loose sand with its heavy cargo of gas drums.

The words of atonement droned on and on. A word here, a word there. A shopping list of sins, real and imagined. It made no difference to the kid; each took on an importance that only the threat of impending death could give. Father Nolan tried hard to concentrate on what the young GI was saying. In the end he failed. Without realizing it, he fell into a doze, awakening when his head began to nod. The first thing he saw when he opened his eyes was the shocked and bewildered look on the young soldier's face.

"Go ahead, my son, I'm listening," he lied in an attempt to recoup his dignity.

"Like hell you are."

The look on the boy's face was unmistakable. He turned from the priest and began to trudge back to the road. He had gotten about fifteen yards when a Jap mortar scored a direct hit on the fuel-laden truck stalled nearby. Flaming gas drums flew through the air like skyrockets. One of them struck the young GI in the head, decapitating him. The gas drum, carrying the boy's head with it, splattered against a palm tree. Father Nolan watched in stunned disbelief as the boy's headless body staggered toward him, took a step, and then collapsed. Blood gushed from the huge wound.

Father Nolan tried to swallow it back, keep it inside, but he couldn't. He vomited all over his boots. He also pissed his pants. He had to pinch it all in to avoid shitting himself.

"Keep a tight asshole."

Chapter

40

P atrick Nolan wanted the best for his son, and in 1930, the best could only be that blending of the temporal and the heavenly found in the Catholic Church. Terence Nolan was thirteen when his father made it perfectly clear which path he would like him to take.

The revelation came at the end of a ninety-minute bus ride from their home in Jersey City to Montclair. Father and son got off the bus and leisurely walked from the candy store/bus depot to Sacred Heart Church. The church was huge. It had flower-bedecked statues on a rolling, well-manicured lawn. This was a far cry from their cramped little parish of St. Anthony's with its church, rectory, convent, and school pinched between an apartment house and Hurley's Furniture Store. The tiny playground in the rear was just big enough for the eight grades to assemble before morning and afternoon classes. At the chancery office in Newark, St. Anthony's had long been recognized as "an asterisk parish."

This mark entitled St. Anthony's to special financial consideration among other "troubled parishes to be closely watched." So to Patrick Nolan, it stood to reason that young Terry would be greatly impressed by Sacred Heart. "Gosh, Dad, this place is big. Is it a cathedral?"

Patrick Nolan smiled. "Not quite, son, but it's close. Lots of money here. Monsignor Flaherty runs a tight ship. I don't know if I've ever mentioned him before. Tim and I are old classmates from Fordham."

Terry had never heard his father mention the monsignor before. In fact, except when the conversation got around to St. Anthony's pastor, Father Joseph, he had never heard his father mention any priest at all.

A big grinning man in a sport shirt and slacks greeted them at the front door. An enormous, brass-plated oak door dwarfed their host, but not his air of authority.

"Pat, it's good to see you. Come on in."

The two men shook hands. It began with each offering his right hand, and ended with the pumping of all four in a tightly clenched grip. They were big men, each over six feet. Almost identical in size. Their faces beamed with the smiles of quickly rekindled memories. Typical Irish Catholic smiles, disarming with their easy flash of teeth, haunting at the eyes.

"And this has got to be Terry. Your father told me about you on the phone. The spittin' image." A huge, hairy hand, surprisingly hard, enveloped the boy's and held it. "Nice to meet you, son."

"Thank you, Father."

"I was sorry to hear about Mary. May God rest her soul. She was quite a beauty, inside and out."

"Thanks," Pat said.

Mary Nolan had been both his and his father's guiding light. Terry tried hard to keep the memory of her final days away, but he couldn't. They flooded back all the time. Even now, as he listened to his dad and the Monsignor talk those painful last days filled his mind.

"I don't know what's wrong with me. That's never happened before," Terry's mom said as he walked into the kitchen for a fast breakfast. She was seated at the kitchen table, no more than five or six feet from the counter on which a shiny new electric toaster was smoking, the smell of the blackened, badly burnt bread filling the room. "I don't know. I just don't feel like moving. Terry, can you please pull out the burnt bread and make your own toast. The butter and jelly are still in the fridge."

"What's the matter, Mom? You don't look well. Can I get anything for you?"

"No, thank you, Terry. If you can just take care of your toast," Terry's mother said. "I'm sorry about the eggs. Have a banana now and take an apple with you to eat along the way to school."

His mother remained seated at the table when Terry got up, grabbed an apple from a bowl on the counter, and turned to throw her a kiss. Her face was bathed in sweat.

"Are you sure I can't get anything for you, Mom?" Terry said.

"No, Terry, your dad is coming home early today, probably before noon," she replied. "He'll take good care of me. Don't you worry. I'll be okay."

That afternoon, Terry rushed home, ran most of the way, to see his mom and dad. The image of the weak and perspiring woman had stuck with him all day. When he reached the family home, he bolted up the four steps to the front porch. His schoolbooks, tightly trussed with one of his father's old leather belts, were tossed onto a wicker swing as he slammed his way through the front door into the parlor.

"Mom. Mom. Dad. I'm home!" Terry shouted. There was no response. The house was silent. He raced through the parlor and dining room into the kitchen, and poked his head into the big utility room. He even peeked into the small bathroom. Fear took hold. "Where is everybody? Mom? Dad?" Terry's stomach was suddenly sick—not vomit sick, but fear and anxiety sick.

Terry took the stairs to the second floor two at a time and headed straight to his parents' bedroom. The door was open, he was confronted with a bed with nothing but a box spring and mattress. The sheets were gone. His eyes jumped from place to place. The blankets were gone. So were the pillows. Where was the quilt? His mother's slippers, always so evenly placed next to her side of the bed, also gone. Terry dropped to his knees and peered under the bed. He had to be sure. Nothing.

From the second-floor landing, his fear increased. At the top of his eight-year-old voice he shouted as loud as he could, "Mom! Dad! Where are you?" Terry gripped the railing as he descended the stairs. He opened the front door and ran out to the walkway. Mrs. Freelander, the next-door neighbor, was waiting for him.

"Terry, your dad asked me to look after you until he got back. He said he would be late getting home, and asked me to give you dinner. " Mrs. Freelander said.

"Where are my Mom and Dad?"

"Your dad said he shouldn't be too late, but if he was later than he wanted to be, I should make sure you're in bed by eight and that your homework was done."

"But where are they?"

"Your mother is sick, dear, and had to go the hospital. Your father went with her. I'm sure it will be fine. Now, let's get you inside."

True to her word, Mrs. Freelander gave him a nice dinner, one that he shared with her and her husband. Every minute was torture for Terry. *When would his folks come back? Why didn't they call? What was going on?*

After he completed his homework at the Freelander dining room table, Mrs. Freelander escorted him back home. He got into his pajamas and she tucked him into bed.

"And my Mom?"

Mrs. Freelander just smiled. "You get some sleep now. Good night, dear."

Terry tossed and turned. He missed his parents. Where were they? They'd never left him alone before. Finally, exhausted from worry, he fell asleep.

He awoke the next morning, jumped out of bed and went downstairs. His father was sitting on the parlor sofa. His hair usually well combed was messed up. His shirt was wrinkled and his eyes were red.

"Dad! What's going on?"

"Good morning, son. How did you sleep? Did Mrs. Freelander take good care of you?" Pat said as he peered intently at his son.

"Everything was good. Where's Mom?"

"She's not here now, but you'll see her soon. She's at the hospital. They said they would call me, and tell me when you and I can come see her."

"What's wrong?"

"Your mother is sick. They say she has spinal meningitis and needs special care we can't give her at home. The doctors are taking good care of her. Let's get you ready for school. Go wash up and I'll make you some breakfast."

That was that.

Every day after school, he waited at Mrs. Freelander's until his Dad came home from work. He asked about his Mom, but his Dad said there wasn't any news yet. Later that week, the phone call finally came late in the afternoon.

"That's was the doctor," his father said, hanging up the phone. "We can see her tomorrow. I'll pick you up from school."

An elated Terry climbed into the front passenger seat of the family's new Chevy the next day. The shiny blue sedan turned from the driveway and headed out of town. The sun was setting when the car turned off a smoothly paved street onto a cobblestone road that ran through thick, high grasses and weeds on both sides. Pat Nolan nosed the Chevy toward a rounded hill that emerged from the dampness around it. They drove through an arched entrance that read SNAKE HILL SANITARIUM, and pulled to a stop in front of a dark, threatening building.

"Stay here, son. I have to talk to the people inside before we can see your mother."

He watched as his father stepped through a glass door and into the lobby where he was greeted by a man in a white doctor's coat. He watched as they spoke, his father nodding. After the conversation, they shook hands.

His father came back and opened the front passenger door. "Your mother is still not feeling well enough to see us. But she can come to the window of her room for us to wave to her." He pointed to the second story of the building.

After a few minutes, the light in the second-floor treatment room came on. Terry and his father walked closer to the building. They had to crane their necks, but they could see clearly through the window. A woman appeared with a man in a white uniform. Her long brown hair was a mess, nearly covering her face. Her lips were moving, and spittle could be seen showering from her mouth. Her head twitched from side to side. Barely able to stand, the attendant held her by the shoulders. She was strapped tightly into a straitjacket.

"Who's that?" Terry said. "Where's Mom?"

"Your mother is very sick, son," he said, holding back his tears. "We better go now so she can get her rest."

"But Dad…"

"We'd better go," his father said quietly. "I'll check in with them later."

For the next three days, Terry asked about his mom, but his father had no news. Then the call from Snake Hill came. Terry was in the parlor when his father picked up the phone.

"Yes, yes, I understand." A pause and then, "Yes, as I told you, all arrangements at my end have been made. I'll call Flannery's as soon as I get off. Their hearse won't take long getting there. Thank you for all that you've done."

Terry began to cry. His father hung up the phone and sat next to him on the sofa.

"It's for the best, son. She is now resting in God's peace."

Terry nodded as his father embraced him. The house seemed so empty and still.

Late the next morning Pat, Terry, and Mary Nolan were aboard a Lackawanna Pullman as it picked up steam and glided out of Hoboken station on its way to Utica, father and son in first class and Mary in the baggage car. His dad explained they were taking her to be buried in Chickapee, her hometown. It was the longest trip of his life.

Pat and Terry bedded down in the stolid, granite McNeese mansion that had been Mary's childhood home. It took only two days for it all to end. Terry knew it was over when his mother was lowered into the ground.

Chapter

41

The monsignor, Pat Nolan, and Terry fell into silence as they walked across a large, thickly carpeted foyer of the Sacred Heart rectory and into a book-lined study.

"A little something? You were always big on Canadian. I think we can find some around here someplace," he said with a wink.

There was no hint that Prohibition had made even the slightest difference in Timothy Flaherty's pursuit of the good life. "Thank the Lord in his wisdom that there is a Canada, and thank him for Father Etienne, a born smuggler," the monsignor said extending his left hand in a sweeping gesture that took in all of the contraband booze on the corner table.

"And I guess a little ginger ale for you, Terry. Scotch for me." The monsignor was already putting ice into Terry's glass at the small, amply-stocked table in the corner behind his desk.

Pat Nolan's first swig of Canadian Club, neat, drained a third of his glass. "Tim, I think you've got it made."

"It is comfortable here, I have to admit. You know, when I went to the seminary, I didn't know parishes like this existed. Sure, I knew the rich had to go to church someplace, but this? It's indecent. There was a time when I would have been satisfied with a parish like our own St. Anthony's. Now that's unthinkable."

It took about ten comfortable minutes for the men to drain their glasses, their small talk mostly about Fordham football. They basked in the warm glow of Tim's expensive booze, and the pride they felt that the Rams had become a national powerhouse. Two Irish Catholics admiring the work of Iron Major Frank Cavanaugh, another Mick, who was bringing sports page fame to their old school.

The monsignor took his friend's empty glass. He then looked at the stupefied boy. "Shame on you, Terry," he said in mock seriousness, his big, heavy hand mussing the boy's hair. "On the wagon or something?"

Terry realized that he hadn't touched his ginger ale. He had been too busy watching and listening to this big, confident man, so different from any priest he had ever seen or imagined. "Guess I'm not thirsty," he stammered.

"It's okay, son, just kidding," the monsignor said. Terry's father chuckled in the background. The monsignor returned from the table with two refills.

"Your phone call really surprised me. You said you had something important to talk about. Important, but not urgent. What the hell does that mean?" The glow of the afternoon drinks was a welcome friend.

The monsignor turned to Terry. "Maybe I better explain something to you, if your father hasn't done it already. If you're wondering about my language . . . well, what can I say? Only that it's the language of friends. Friends who go back a long way. For an opener, I bet you didn't know that we played in the same backfield for eight years, high school and college. Even did a little moonlighting with a semi-pro outfit called the Yonkers Yanks. Your dad was a helluva football player."

"Yes, I know. My dad doesn't say anything about how good he was, but I've seen his scrapbooks. He's working out with me now, over at the park. Still throws a mean pass."

"I bet he does. Now, Pat, what's on your mind?"

"It's about the future, that's why I said it was important, but not too urgent." Patrick looked in Terry's direction, then back to Flaherty.

"I see. Terry, why don't you go to the end of the hall into the kitchen. Our cook, Emily, has a whole shelf full of snacks you'll enjoy while your father and I catch up some more."

Terry rose and put his glass down. "Thank you, Father."

Terry was well into his second cherry tart, washing it down with his third glass of cold milk when his father and the monsignor came into the kitchen.

"Okay, son," his father said. "Time to go."

Monsignor Flaherty walked them to the door. The two men shook hands. "Great to see you, Pat. Don't be a stranger. We'll talk more about the future."

Then turning to Terry, he patted him on the shoulder. "You're a great kid, Terry. I hope to see you again soon."

Terry and his father were halfway back to the candy store/bus stop when Pat Nolan interrupted Terry's enthusiastic questions about the man he'd just met.

"The monsignor will be a bishop someday." Terry felt the heavy warmth of his father's hand on his shoulder. They walked a few more steps. "He's a great role model."

"Dad, I don't follow you."

"You're Irish. You're intelligent, reasonably good looking, and are obviously going to be a pretty big kid. You're well on your way to becoming a damn good athlete. You have everything he had when he started, and look where he is now. It's something for you to think about."

During Terry's final year at St. Anthony's, unfamiliar faces appeared at all of the big games. Terry excelled in basketball and baseball, a key player on the teams, but not one of the stars. Football had become Terry's sport, and behind his outstanding all-around play, the school won the league championship.

A month before graduation, Brother Stephen, a compact little man with broad shoulders and a lisp, was introduced to him in the rectory by Father Joseph. The brother headed the athletic department at St. Monica's Prep, the biggest, most prestigious Catholic high school in the county. It turned out powerful teams in every sport. Most of the athletes came from nearby Hudson County parishes, but others came from as far as ten miles away.

"Well, Terence, I've heard great things about you," Brother Stephen said.

"Thank you, Father. I try to do my best."

"Terence is one of our most conscientious students," Father Joseph added. "And has a terrific jump shot." The two men laughed.

"Have you heard of St. Monica's Prep?"

"Sure, Father," Terry said eagerly. "They've been division champs for years."

"Yes, we've done quite well. And our academic program is one of the top rated in the state. You must come to visit us sometime soon."

"Thank you, Father. I'd like that."

That night, Terry told his dad about meeting with Brother Stephen.

"It doesn't surprise me that you've been scouted. You're a good student."

"Yeah, I guess. But St. Monica's? It seems outta my league."

"Don't sell yourself short, son. You may be surprised. Now go get washed up for dinner."

A week after graduation, Terry got a letter inviting him to attend St. Monica's on a full athletic scholarship, travel expenses included. He would have to take a bus to get there every day, but he didn't care. It was a chance of a lifetime.

"I'm proud of you, son," his dad said when he showed him the letter. "St. Monica's is one of the best. It'll open loads of doors in the future."

Tim came through, Pat thought. *His letter of recommendation for Terry really did the trick.*

From that point on, things went smoothly. Being a jock at St. Monica's did not guarantee preferential treatment. Sure, it might have gotten him into the school, but that was all. He still had to keep up his grades in order to play, and discipline was tough. But he kept his nose clean and graduated.

He was offered full scholarships by Holy Cross and Fordham. Boston College and Villanova offered partial grants, as did William and Mary and, of all places, Tulane. It was no contest. Fordham, besides being his father's alma mater, played a tough national football schedule. Perhaps most important, it was located in New York City, a short trip from his Dad. Their home games were even on the radio.

Chapter

42

To celebrate the good news, Pat Nolan took his son out to dinner at his favorite Italian restaurant in lower east Manhattan. Terry, now eighteen, could legally drink so Pat decided to pull out all stops and share a bottle of Chianti with his son.

"A good choice, sir," the waiter said as he poured a small portion of wine into a glass for tasting.

"I'm sure it is, but the choice was my son's. Let him decide."

The waiter turned to Terry. "I'm very sorry, sir. I'm anxious to have your opinion."

Terry sipped the rich, heavy red wine and rolled it around his tongue as he had seen them do in the movies. His father was grinning. "Fine, just fine."

It was nice. A big fireplace crackled. Two musicians wandered about the room with their accordion and fiddle. Warm, sentimental music filled the restaurant. The spaghetti arrived with meatballs for Pat and sausage for Terry. They ate with relish as they talked about Fordham and the future.

The waiter came by with the bill and emptied the wine bottle into their glasses. Terry looked up from his glass to find his father staring at him. Suddenly there developed that peculiar uneasiness that can sometimes arise when two people who love each other, truly love each other, are mutually overwhelmed by their feelings.

"What can I say?" said Pat. There was a mist over his eyes. "Little, I'm afraid. But, I'd like to make a toast."

Terry knew he would never forget that toast, not for what was said, but what was left unspoken. His father reached forward and they tapped their glasses. "To you, ya big lug." Pat paused, his soft blue eyes bathing his son with all the hopes and anxieties he had for him. "My son."

Terry successfully fought back the tears. "Thanks, Dad." Father and son silently finished their wine.

Terry was never a regular starter during his three years on the Rams varsity. His father took in all the home games despite not knowing whether Terry would get onto the field. As an alum and former player, he got two free choice tickets. Monsignor Flaherty would join Pat for the big games.

The four years at Fordham were good ones for Terry despite his lack of success at football. He dated a lot, mostly girls from Barnard, because they were fun, usually had enough money to go "dutch," and were more liberal than the Catholic girls he met from Marymount College in Tarrytown. Sociology majors from Barnard were the best bet.

One of them was Sarah Green, who took a detached intellectual approach toward her sexual encounters with Terry. Before their split, Sarah had taught Terry the glories of oral sex. Despite her warm smile, Sarah could be direct and oddly impersonal, as though Terry was the raw data for one of her term papers with questions like "How does it feel?" or "Does it feel better when I do this?"

Whenever possible, Terry spent holidays, semester and summer breaks with his father in Jersey City. He was aghast at the rapidly aging face of a strong, Irish Catholic man, a pragmatist who wanted the best of both worlds for his son. His insurance business had collapsed early in the Depression, and with no end in sight, he saw only one viable path for Terry to take after graduation. He enlisted Monsignor Flaherty, and his long-time friend was eager to help. The Monsignor picked up the dinner tab after every important home game, and it took little for Terry to rekindle memories of that afternoon in Montclair and the comfortable opulence of the Monsignor's rectory and church.

"Your studies, still bouncing around for a major?" the Monsignor said after the NYU game his sophomore year.

"Economics."

"Have you given any thought to theology? I know the Jebbies can get your head spinning when it comes to the Church, but theirs is not the only way to go. Have you given any thought to a religious vocation?"

Terry looked at the Monsignor, then glanced at his father. "More often now that I realize I'll be out on the street in a little more than two years."

"No need for me to preach, so I'll only say that the Church in America offers challenges that I believe you'll be more than able to tackle."

So Terry gave it a lot of consideration and decided the Jesuits weren't the answer. They offered a lot of questions, plenty of room for thought, but the seminary in Darlington, New Jersey held much more. A father's dream, a son's future.

Armed with degrees in theology and economics, Terry endured his years at the seminary, where street-smart priests prepared him to go out among common folks yearning for answers where there weren't any. It was Terry's good fortune that tobacco-loving Father Peter Majeski, Father "Ski" to his intimates, was his spiritual advisor. If it wasn't for the big Polish iconoclast, Terry probably would not have gotten through his years there.

It took less than two weeks for Terry to realize that Father Ski would be taking a casual, often back-door approach to matters of the spirit.

"Terry, did you know that I once chewed tobacco?" Father Ski asked as they strolled the seminary grounds one afternoon. "Hell, I did more than chew it, I was addicted to it. The stuff was really awful, but I loved it."

"No, it doesn't surprise me at all that you chewed. You still smoke like a chimney," Terry said. "Can I ask you a question, Father? What in the world are you doing here? You've got the hands, face, and body of a dockworker."

"I got my calling late, six years ago when I was thirty-five," Father Ski said. "Made my family proud when I started wearing that tight white collar. My folks were delighted, relieved really, that I had turned my back on the commies. The Party had been my life after I picked up a sheepskin from Rutgers."

"Communism? You're kidding, right?"

"Hell no. I knew 'em all. Marched with Ellen Dawson during the Garment Strike in Passaic. Took a couple billy club shots from the goons hired by the bosses." Father Ski smiled. "Oh that Ellen Dawson, she was something else. Skinny little thing with freckles, but when she got on the back of a truck and pointed that little clenched fist at you, you'd follow her anywhere."

Terry was mesmerized. As he listened, he could see that his mentor's tight collar would never be able to choke out those happy times.

"I sometimes have regrets about not following her to New Bedford two years later, or marching with her in that bloody Loray Mill strike in North Carolina. The Loray strike was a winner, those mill town bosses would never have it their way again."

"Why did you get out?"

"The pogroms. How can you march under a banner colored red with the blood of millions of Russians? All done by a former seminarian who got ambitious. Stalin knew how to get it done, and that pipe-smoking butcher never forgot his enemies. Just this past year he had Trotsky's head split open with an axe down in Mexico."

They were strolling the seminary grounds late one afternoon when Father Ski motioned Terry to join him on a tree-shaded bench. He reached under his cassock and pulled out a pack of Twenty Grand cigarettes. "Cheapest you can get, and they're proud of it," he said. "You've got to admire that kind of honesty. And now for some honesty between us."

"Where do you want to start?"

"You know, Terry, I was puzzled at the beginning why you were here. Now I'm beginning to get it."

"Fill me in, Father, I need all the help I can get."

"First of all, don't be defensive about why you are here. Vocations are crazy things, no rhyme or reason at all. Take a look at me, a former commie head-knocker. And you, Terry, want to know what I see?"

"I'm listening."

"First, I don't question motivation. If you get through your years here, get out in the world and do good things, tend your flock, so to speak, then I say to hell with why you're here. Your background speaks for itself. I see in your file that you've got a lot of clerical muscle going for you. Play it right, keep your nose clean, and you'll probably go far."

"How far is far?"

"That's completely up to you. I saw that your mom died when you were just a kid. How does your father feel about all this?" Father Ski asked.

Terry flinched and turned from Father Ski to watch without expression a group of seminarians walking on the gravel path. The question took him by surprise, and left him fumbling for an answer.

"My father?"

"Yeah, Terry, your father. How big a part does he play?"

"A big part, maybe all of it."

"The depression hit him hard I take it, and that's a humbling experience for even the strongest of men. He didn't want the same for you. Do I have it right?"

"You got it right. It just about killed me when he became a glorified repo man for a hoodlum auto dealer in Jersey City."

For almost three years, Father Ski and Terry were possibly the most unlikely men you'd expect to see roaming the seminary grounds. Their camaraderie ended when Father Ski left to take over his duties as Catholic chaplain at the expanding Coast Guard boot camp at Cape May. War was coming.

By the time Terry finished his studies at the seminary, the war was raging. He celebrated his first Mass at St. Anthony's and gave Holy Communion to his father and old neighbors in the parish. Then, in a gallant gesture, he became a Navy chaplain and was assigned to the Marines. He was aboard a troop ship enroute to Australia when his father died. Then Saipan.

Chapter

43

Within two weeks of coming home, Father Nolan was assigned by the Archdiocese to fill a vacancy at St. Mark's. He replaced sixty-five year old Father Eugene Koestler, who had suffered a fatal heart attack while delivering the last rites to an unbearably grouchy old woman, who didn't die after all.

Except on holy days, there were two weekday masses at St. Mark's, at half past six and eight. Nolan said the earlier Mass. Within a week or so of arriving, he was reading the sports page over a leisurely second cup of coffee in the rectory dining room when Father Schneider walked in. His pastor nodded silently in his direction, and poured himself a cup of coffee at a huge gothic sideboard, one of the ugliest pieces of furniture Nolan had ever seen. It was replete with carved ogres of every description, battle axes, shields with lacy, crisscrossed bands of questionable heraldry, and even a Byzantine cross or two. Two naked monsters were frozen in perpetual Bronx cheers at the upper corners of the sideboard, their knife-like tongues pointing directly at the beholder.

Father Schneider was of medium height, broad at the shoulder and surprisingly lean at the waist. His step was jaunty, even cocky. He had a full head of thick gray hair, dark eyes and deep furrows on his forehead, probably from aggravation over the years. Terry judged it to be the unaffected swagger of a man who had lost his innocence, but had managed to remain on amicable terms with the world around him.

Father Schneider noted the bemused expression on his colleague's face. "If I read that look on your face correctly, we're off to a good start, a mutual dislike for this gothic abomination."

"Why don't you get rid of it?"

"A good question. It's a gift from the Kramiers, one of our absentee German landlords. I'll give you time before we get into that. For now, let's just say we're stuck with it."

Nolan, although he had been at St. Mark's for more than a week, really hadn't had a chance to talk with Father Schneider. Both men had been busy. There had been a few mumbled words of greeting when he arrived then Mrs. Spiser took over. The housekeeper made it clear that Father Schneider might be his spiritual boss, but she had the final word when it came to running the rectory.

"Well, Terry, I'm going to put you to work," said the pastor as he settled into a chair on the other side of the table.

Father Schneider looked at the young priest and winked, "First, I hope you don't mind me calling you Terry." Without waiting for a reply, he continued, "Good, that's settled. Call me Jim. Makes things simpler."

Terry smiled, "That's fine."

Mrs. Spiser came in with two poached eggs on buttered toast. She poured fresh coffee into their cups.

Father Schneider waited until the housekeeper returned to the kitchen. "She's a spy, you know."

Terry choked on his coffee, his eyes watered and his face flushed.

The older priest sipped his coffee and waited for the spasm to pass. To Terry's surprise, Jim was smiling. "That's right. She's an honest to goodness spy. The cabal of Heinies who once ran this parish lock, stock and barrel, got her the job. I inherited her. I'm sure she reports to them on a regular basis."

"Really? She seems so nice."

"Grumpy as hell, but loveable despite herself. Now let's get down to business."

"I'm ready."

Jim removed a sheet of paper from a file folder he had brought with him. It contained a list of about a dozen names. Next to each were two hyphenated dollar amounts.

"Some of our parishioners complained that they've had their rents illegally hiked. You've been away for a couple of years, so in case you didn't know, it's illegal to raise rents without the approval of the OPA."

Jim paused to fill his mouth with a forkful of poached eggs and toast, washing it down with a big gulp of coffee.

"OPA?"

"The Office of Price Administration. It's been around since the start of the war to prevent rent gouging. With all the returning veterans, housing is hard to find and landlords are taking advantage."

"Are any of them losing their apartments?"

"Some are. I understand they're sending rent collectors around every week now. But even with the higher rents, some of our parishioners feel they're lucky to even have a place to live. Mostly I think they're scared. I hear there are at least two big goons using strong-arm tactics to scare the money out of them."

"But what can we do about it?"

"Not much. We try to steer clear of politics in the parish, but when parishioners seek our counsel, I feel we need to at least follow up as part of our pastoral duty."

"What do you want me to do?"

"Why don't you go down to the OPA office and talk to the director, a fellow by the name of Joseph Daniel Crosswaite. He's a retired insurance company VP or something. He's a nice guy, but overwhelmed. I'll call to set up the meeting. Here's my file with the rent histories," Jim said as he pushed the file folder across the table.

"And that's it?"

"That's it. I'll be anxious to hear how it goes," Jim said as he stood, "Nice to have you aboard, Terry."

Terry was unfamiliar with Newark, and the walk downtown was much longer than he had figured. The OPA office was located in a former Cadillac agency on Broad Street.

A tall, thin man with a salt-and-pepper goatee was explaining something to one of several secretaries when Terry entered. The man looked up, saw Terry, and pulled a gold watch from a pocket of his pinstriped vest.

"Father Nolan? I've been expecting you. I'm J.D. Crosswaite." They shook hands.

Crosswaite led the priest to his glass-enclosed office. Except for his desk, which was a chaotic jumble of complaints, reports, guidelines, and directives, the office was a fine example of austere bureaucratic neatness. There was an American flag on a pole in one corner and a framed picture of President Truman on the rear wall, testimony to how quickly more than twelve years of FDR can become just a memory. There was a clothes tree in the other corner. It held a wooden hanger with a double-breasted pinstriped suit jacket. The gray, snap-brimmed hat seemed out of character.

Crosswaite seated himself at his desk and offered Terry a seat. "How long have you been at St. Mark's?"

"Only a few weeks. I got assigned right after I got back from the Pacific."

"Good to have you here. Now, what's on your mind?"

Terry placed the list of names before him.

"Well, what do we have here?"

"A list of people in our parish, at least the ones that we know of, who are being gouged by their landlords."

"That you know of?"

"Yes, we've got parishioners too scared to complain for fear of being evicted. That's why they've come to us."

"I see. Do you have any rent receipts?"

Terry paused, a bit confused. "Not a one. Everything is done face-to-face, in cash."

Crosswaite exhaled deeply, a sigh that bureaucrats seem to reserve for that moment when they feel particularly put upon by people who have no understanding of red-tape logistics. The sigh came with the job.

"I'm afraid there isn't much I can do without formal complaints." He picked up a blank form from a pile on his desk. "Here's the form. I suggest you get each person on the list to fill one out, attach any documented receipts, then deliver them to this office. We'll follow up, when we can."

"But that could take weeks. These people are suffering now."

Crosswaite reached into a desk drawer and withdrew a thick stack of papers.

"Here are the formal rent complaints we received this past month alone. Each one requires a separate inquiry from one of our staff. We are doing our best with the resources we have. Given the situation, we've got a substantial backlog."

Crosswaite, to this point composed, now appeared self-conscious. He put down Father Schneider's list and leaned back in his chair.

"I'm sorry, I wish I could do more. Perhaps you should put together a petition and send it to the mayor's office, and see where that gets you. Are you prepared for an off-the-record anecdote?"

"I'm ready."

"I can show you complaints that my investigators have been working on for months without being able to run down the owner. One of my men, and I still don't know exactly how he did it, got enough on one big slumlord to blow this town wide open.

"Inevitably, the crooks at City Hall found out about our investigation. There's very little, legal or illegal, that goes on in this city that they don't know about, or have their clammy fingers in. So it wasn't surprising when our regional director called for the entire file on the case. That was six months ago, and nothing's happened."

"So, you're telling me that these people have no recourse?"

"No. I'm telling you that there is a complaint procedure that they need to follow. Otherwise, this agency can't do its job."

"I see." Terry stood. "Thanks for your time. I'll discuss our next steps with Father Schneider."

Crosswaite stood and handed Terry the file he had come in with. "Good luck with your new assignment, Father Nolan. Let me know if I can be of any further assistance."

"Thanks."

For nothing.

Chapter

44

That evening, Terry found Schneider in the sun porch at the back of the rectory. He was wearing a faded gray sweatshirt with the sleeves cut off above the elbows; khaki pants; red, green, and yellow argyles; and scruffy brown leather slippers. His "contemplation clothes," as he called them.

"Got a minute?" Terry said.

"Sure. How'd you make out with Crosswaite?"

"He's a paper pusher with too much on his plate. There's nothing he can do."

Jim nodded. "I suspected as much. Especially now. I hear the OPA is shutting down at the end of year."

"Then it was a total waste of time."

"Not entirely. At least we can say we discussed the problem with the agency. That's what you'll tell the families when you meet with them to follow up."

"Me? I barely know them."

"It's a good way to start. You don't learn much about your flock from the sanctuary, you know."

Terry nodded. He was the "new guy" and had to expect he'd get the tough jobs. At least for now.

"How about a drink?" Jim got up and led them into the rectory. Terry flashed back to his first meeting with Monsignor Flaherty.

Jim lifted a dark green bottle of Vat 69, poured stiff belts into two tall glasses, and dropped in some ice cubes from a bucket Mrs. Spiser provided earlier.

"How do you take your scotch, straight, soda or water?"

"Soda will be fine."

"Cheers."

They returned to the sun porch, both sinking into the wicker chairs. The older man spoke in quick, easy patterns.

"I know it's frustrating, but you need to know the lay of the land around the parish. Our people are struggling to make ends meet. Pure and simple. The women used to rely on their husbands' army checks, but now the war is over. The WPA and other government dole-outs are gone. Jobs scarce. And the Negroes moving in from the South have made a bad situation worse."

Terry looked around the well-appointed porch. "Then how do we survive here?"

"It's not from the offering plate on Sundays, I can tell you that. This is brewery gulch. The German beer makers are gone, but their money lingers on."

"I'm not sure I understand."

"The Krameirs and the Trommers. Both families moved out a few years ago, the Krameirs to a mansion in the hills overlooking the city, and the Trommers to a twenty room seaside cottage. The two families not only competed in beer sales for years, but also in their donations to St. Mark's."

Jim took a long swig of his drink, almost draining the glass.

"Twice a year I make two trips, both just before Christmas. I take the Greyhound to the end of the line in Bay Head where I'm met by the Trommers' Packard. From there we drive along the Jersey Shore, halfway to Atlantic City. I spend the night. I'm asked some questions. I give them answers. The next day I'm driven back to Bay Head. There's a five-digit check in my pocket.

"A week or so later, Anton Krameir and his wife stop by the rectory in midafternoon. We drive to their mansion, and I'm feted like a papal nuncio. Again the unnecessary questions. I supply fatuous answers. Everyone is happy. Mrs. Krameir accompanies me to the car. The chauffeur puts the auto in gear, I wave, Mrs. Krameir waves, her husband waves from the drawing room window, and I pat another fat check as it settles comfortably in my pocket. It's all part of the job. They don't teach that in seminary."

"It's hard for me to understand why they would continue to support a parish where they no longer belong," Terry wondered.

"At first I viewed it as just a big tax write-off on their part. Later I realized it's a legacy, a way for these families to continue to leave their mark on Newark. You'll notice that they are thanked profusely in the Christmas and Easter leaflets. The families feel involved. The diocese is pleased. We get to move forward in relative comfort. Everyone wins."

That talk was the first of many the two priests would have. Father Schneider touched on all facets of the parish's operations.

After a few months, Terry had settled into his duties and got to know his parishioners. He made the requisite house and hospital calls. Said morning Mass. Presided at baptisms, confirmations, funerals, and taught religion in the church school.

He marveled at the diversity of the ward, the hectic face-to-face bargaining of merchants on Prince Street, the synagogues, Greek and Ukranian Orthodox churches, the voodoo shamans whose black magic guaranteed long life and good fortune on Howard Street, and got a different slant on the news from the Negro editors at the *Newark Herald*. Since his recent encounter with Eight-Ten, he began paying particular attention to how numbers runners worked their territories in full view of the police, especially patrolman Frank Gazzi, who seemed to be everywhere and doing nothing.

It was on a Thursday afternoon that he strolled down Spruce where a big, smiling Negro man in a white shirt and trousers waved a greeting from the Peace Barbershop across the street. A perfect numbers drop, Terry thought, just like the innocent-looking policy parlors along Jersey City's Bergenline Avenue that had sucked more than a fistful of nickels and dimes out of his teenage pockets.

It was after Mass the following Saturday that Terry put on a sweatshirt, corduroy trousers, and scuffed loafers, headed back to Spruce, and hit it lucky. Just as Eight-Ten described it, he spotted two of his altar boys, Richie Maxwell and Joey Bancik, pedaling their bikes to the rear of the barbershop. He ducked into a doorway across from the shop, an excellent vantage point for him to see the two kids park their bikes, walk down the alley and enter through a side door. The big imbecile was right, and the question now was what was he going to do about it.

Terry knew he had to take some action, these kids were breaking the law. He decided that, for the time being, he would sit on it.

Although the problem had been eating away at him, Terry did not broach the subject during his next meeting with Jim. Instead, he again voiced his confusion about the racial mix of the congregation.

"You've been handling the eighth-grade religion class for several months now. Any impressions?"

"They're all good kids, but I did notice that the few black families in the congregation don't send their children to our school."

"Yes. What about it?"

"It's just that the Third Ward is mostly black, but St. Mark's doesn't reflect it. Seems odd."

"Not really when you think about it. The church's big brass didn't realize how much it cost to put every Catholic kid behind a desk in a Catholic school. It takes big bucks that most of our parishioners don't have. So we rely on the Kramiers and the Trommers. But there are strings attached."

"Like prejudice."

"Let's just say the schools are kept highly selective. Most black families in our parish can't afford the tuition anyway, but even if they could, their kids wouldn't feel welcomed, and they know it."

"Isn't that our mission?"

"You're right. But there are other factors at work. The powers that be want to maintain the status quo, despite the changes in the community. We're merely the gatekeepers. I make no excuses. Certainly I can rationalize."

"Okay, Jim, rationalize."

"Terry, our parish is made up of frightened people. Most of them speak with accents, some speak no English at all. Most haven't gotten past the eighth grade. They're untrained and unassimilated, trying to survive. Somehow they scrape together enough for the tuition. Then the blacks started moving in. Taking over the tenements. Even jobs. When a man has lost his job to a Negro, how do you ask him to accept that Negro's son into the same classroom with his daughter?"

"That's not the point. It's not in the spirit of the mission."

Jim sighed. "Don't get sanctimonious. That is precisely the point. Thank God that most of the community has another option."

"Like public schools?"

"Yes…and Father Divine."

"You mean that preacher who runs all those stores and shelters?"

"Him and others like him. They give their believers something we can't come close to."

"Cheap groceries?"

"And hope for a better future right here on earth. We offer incense and a promise of some fantastic seven-layer heaven. His heaven is right here. It's heaven filled with ten-cent meals, cheap beds with clean linen, honest stores, and most of all, pride and dignity."

"That's not religion. It's social welfare."

"Maybe, but it's working and his flock is growing. And ours remains as it has been for decades. It's the way of the world these days."

Chapter

45

Terry had just completed the six-thirty Mass, and after removing his vestments and laying them out for the sacristan to put away, he headed for the rectory and breakfast. At his place at the dining table were a few letters and an official-looking manila envelope. In the upper left corner under the OPA logo was a hand-printed "J.D. Crosswaite."

"Mrs. Spiser, how 'bout that coffee?" Terry tore into the manila envelope and pulled out a four-page report prepared by a Marcus H. Cooke for the Central Planning Board of Newark. Attached to it was a typed note from Crosswaite.

> "Father Nolan,
>
> This will undoubtedly be our last contact.
>
> I wish I could say 'read and enjoy,'
>
> but that would be asking the impossible.
>
> If I judged you correctly, you'll soon find what it's
>
> like to have your suggestions to the city's powerbrokers
>
> viewed not only with indolence but with contempt.
>
> You'll probably be talking to Bernard Schein. He's a good
>
> guy and I told him about you. Welcome aboard!
>
> J.D. Crosswaite"

Terry knifed and forked his way through Mrs. Spiser's ham, over-easy eggs and fried potatoes, along with lightly toasted and buttered rye bread. The coffee was fresh and good.

He discovered that the Third Ward contained 26,863 people, of which sixty-threee percent were Negro. He learned that they did most of their shopping along Waverly, West Kinney, Spruce, and Belmont, the so called "Black Belt." There were five grade schools, and white students between the ages of five and twelve had begun transferring to schools outside the ward.

It wasn't until he reached the middle of the second page that Terry felt his anger rise. He fought back an almost uncontrollable urge to curse out loud. Jumping from the page were statements of municipal guilt that more than fifty percent of the Third Ward's housing was in need of major repairs or had no private bath, and that seventy percent of these dwellings were Negro homes. Crowding was endemic.

"Tuberculosis and other communicable diseases thrive under crowded conditions and are more prevalent in the Third Ward than in any other section of Newark," the report noted. When Terry got to the top of the next page, the raw data forced him to put down his knife and fork. "Christ Almighty" escaped before he could control himself. He heard the kitchen door slam as Mrs. Spiser took self-righteous refuge.

Who the hell wrote this thing? he asked himself. *I've got to talk to him.* At the end of the report, he found Bernard Schein's name. He checked the clock; it was quarter past eight. He pulled the phone over and got the Central Planning Board's number from information. He took a chance that someone would be there this early. To his surprise, someone picked up after only two rings.

"I want to talk to Bernard Schein, if he's around."

"This is Schein. What can I do for you?"

"I just had your Planning Board's report sent to me. I read only a few pages, but it was enough to really piss me off."

"Whoa, whoa, big fella. Who am I talking to?"

"Father Terence Nolan, St. Mark's."

"Oh yeah, heard about you from J.D."

"I hope you don't take this call lightly."

"Okay, I don't. If we're going to take this any further, let's not assume anything. J.D. said you just got into town," Schein said. "Still have no idea just how high the bar graph for frustration can climb in Newark. You probably have the report in front of you. Where do you want to start?"

"Here, for example: In the past year, out of 1,245 births, seventy-five percent of the kids died before they were one. Can that possibly be true?" Terry said.

"Yes. True, and it isn't getting any better. What else?"

"Here, out of ninety-eight cases of TB, fifty percent died. How could this be allowed to happen? Why the hell is it happening?"

"I hate like hell saying it, but what in the world do you know about the ward's problems from your vantage point?"

"When are you going to start using the right word? We're talking slum, and from what I've seen, no one wants to use the word," Terry said.

"Damn right it's a slum. The ward is a slum, and much of Newark isn't far behind," Schein said. "Let's take fires, for instance. Every week a tenement house in the ward either burns down or is damaged. We're saying one a week, but that's only a guess. We've gotten no cooperation at all from the Fire Department, the safety commissioner, or City Hall. It's their job to know and tell us what everybody knows, that almost all of the fires are caused by illegal kerosene stoves and unventilated coal stoves."

Schein's impatience was showing and he made no effort to hide it. "Most of the coal for those tenement stoves is sold in twenty-five-pound bags, because that's all they can afford to buy at one time. The coal is bituminous, the cheapest and filthiest stuff you can get. We went to six places along Waverly, Spruce, and Belmont that sell the coal, brought the bags in, cut them open, and found that they all had at least five pounds of coal dust at the bottom.

"Just stick your head in a kitchen burning the stuff and you'll find out why babies are dying and TB is killing everyone."

"This is one time I don't mind being put in my place," Terry said.

"Let's put it this way, Father Nolan, if you try to do anything, get used to being put in your place. And with that starched white collar of yours, the hacks downtown will at least make an attempt to hide their contempt."

"I guess we'll be talking again."

"Good idea. We can meet over borscht."

Terry hung up the phone.

The horrifying statistics in Schein's report submerged a gnawing uncertainty that had been eating away at Terry for the past week. It had been with him since he'd learned from Eight-Ten that two of his altar boys were running numbers. He had not discussed the matter with Jim, and doubted that his indecision was in line with Father Ski's advice to "tend your flock."

Chapter

46

Joey Bancik was surprised when Richie Maxwell approached him with a big smile in the St. Mark's school yard after class the previous Thursday afternoon. They were never the best of friends, so he suspected a trick of some sort.

"Well you finally got it," Richie said. "And if you work it right, a lot more than you'd expect."

"Got what? What the hell are you talking about?"

"A *Beacon* route. Marsucci told me to pass it on to you."

"You better not be shitting me," Joey warned.

"I'm not shitting you, come on, let's go over to the Greek church."

They crossed High Street and parked themselves on the church's steps. Richie leaned back on his elbows and sized up Joey. He found what he was looking for, that crazy look that always crossed Joey's face when he got excited. How he tried to keep it all inside, but was never able to pull it off.

"First, there's more than just you and Marsucci and the *Beacon* to deal with," Richie said. "It's the whole package or nothing."

"The whole package? What the fuck are you talking about?"

"The numbers."

"The numbers. You saying that all along you've been running numbers and telling everybody you're just a paper boy?"

"You want to listen to me or not? Here's the skinny. They said there's room for another kid like me, and asked me for a name. I gave them yours, and they asked me why. I said your family's having it hard and you're always broke, and I told them you don't take shit from nobody."

"Them? Who the hell you talking about?"

"You on board or not? Shake on it, and I'll tell you more."

Richie and Joey extended their right hands, then settled back, and Richie started talking. It didn't take long for him to explain everything, the policy slips, the drops, the pay-offs, and how everything flowed into the barbershop policy parlor. How a bike from Simon had already been arranged for, and how the three bookies would hold onto the loot Joey got from the numbers until he wanted it.

"We're going over to Simon's to get your bike, and just like me you'll be paying it off a little each week," Richie lied. He had never had to pay off his bike, the three nigger barbers had taken care of it. But there was no way he'd let Joey know about his sweet deal.

Eli Simon was alone when they walked into his office. He had been waiting for them. The three black bookies had met with him earlier in the week, and the meeting was anything but pleasant. They had finally spelled it all out. Their policy parlor in the back of the barbershop was too small and had to be moved. They were taking over a large portion of the pawnshop's storage area, walling it off and punching out a door in the rear of the building. Simon knew from the beginning this would happen ever since John Travers, a/k/a Righteous Reckoning, left that silver-plated ladies' hat pin on his desk and promised more to come. He readily accepted their booty, but what choice did he have. It was either that or a burned out pawnshop.

"There it is in the corner," Simon said pointing to a Schwinn with a sturdy carrier rack over the rear tire. "It's seventeen dollars, needed new tubes front and rear. Nothing down, but I'll expect you in here every two weeks with two dollars cash to pay it off."

Joey didn't know what to say, it was all happening so fast. Richie took up the slack. "Thank you, Mr. Simon," he said, then turned to Joey. "Go ahead, Joey, roll it outside and I'll be right behind you."

"And that's it? All there is? Can't believe I got a paper route and a bike all in the same day, just like that."

"Well you do, but don't wet your pants over it," Richie said. "Now let's get out of here."

Outside, Joey rolled up the bottom of his right pants leg, and tested the pedal and brake. Richie straddled the rear carrier rack and grabbed Joey's shoulders.

"It's over to the nigger barbershop," Richie said. "I don't think I have to tell you where it is."

While Joey was doing the pumping, Richie did the talking. He explained that the only way in and out was down the side alley to the door.

Joey pedaled east on Montgomery, slowed as the street veered to the right, then glided past a parked Buick into the alley that ran behind the barbershop.

"Never saw anything like that around here before," Richie said after eyeballing the big, black car.

"Bet it's a rent collector," Joey said.

There were no customers in the shop when they got there, and the policy parlor was closed for the day. The front window blinds were drawn, and the three bookies were in their customary places, God's Tall Timber and Darn Good Disciple relaxing in barber chairs, and Righteous Reckoning in his seat by the door. Joey didn't know what to expect, and as he followed Richie inside, he felt queasy and scared.

"This must be Joey Bancik," the biggest of the three black men said, extending his right hand and smiling broadly. "Ready to talk business, Joey?"

"I'm ready," Joey wasn't sure what to say next. He looked at the faces around the room and decided to keep his lips buttoned.

"I'm God's Tall Timber," the big black man said, "and this fine fellow is Darn Good Disciple, and over there is Righteous Reckoning. Now that you know us, let's talk business."

"Take a seat. Be comfortable," Darn Good said pointing to the center barber's chair.

Joey sat down and waited. His buddy had told him what to expect, but it was obvious he would be no help now. Richie watched impassively from his seat by the door, and Joey knew that from here on, it would be between him and the three bookies.

"Richie tells us that you are smart and tough, and that your family has fallen on bad times," Tall Timber said. "As messengers for Major Jealous Divine we can help, and sometimes that means bending things a little to carry out his mission. You understand…?"

"Yeah, if I run the numbers for you, I'll be breaking the law, and if I get caught, it's my ass in the wringer."

The three bookies laughed and turned towards Richie. "You've got it right Richie, your friend is a smart kid, just what we need."

Jesus, Joey thought, *I wasn't all that funny. I might as well wait 'til they stop giggling before I wade in. This is my only shot at it. So here goes nothing.*

"Richie told me what his deal is, and I want the same thing. Do I get it?" Joey hoped he hadn't pushed too far. "I know I ain't showed you nothing yet, but if I'm caught, the screws at juvie hall don't much care if I'm the new kid on the block or not."

"Of course you get the same deal. The Divine One's fair with everyone," Tall Timber said.

The bookies explained how his ten numbers stops would be folded into his *Beacon* route, now extended into what had been exclusively *Clarion* turf.

"I'm in. What's next?"

"Marsucci, he's waiting for you at his office. Go over and he'll fill you in from his end. You start Saturday. He'll show you around this weekend, and you'll be on your own on Monday. By the way, how do you like the bike?" Tall Timber said.

"I like it fine."

"So will your folks," Reckoning said, "and the money you'll be bringing in. No need to talk about the numbers."

"Sounds good, don't it," Darn Good chimed in. "And it can only get better."

Richie joined the three fake barbers, and everyone was smiling as they all shook hands. The two altar boys walked out to the alley, closing the door behind them.

"You might as well head over to Marsucci's," Richie said to Joey. "I'll walk home. See you around after school tomorrow."

Inside, just as he had when Richie came on board, Vinnie Scarlatti pushed open the door of the policy parlor, strode over to the center chair and got comfortable.

"I see you're still laying on that Father Divine bullshit. I feel like a fucking babysitter," he said. "I hate to admit it, but the young punk sounded pretty god damn good, should fit in. I ain't gonna give these two kids that much time," Scarlatti said. "If they don't work out, you'll be putting your niggers back out there. How long before they butt heads with McDuffie's punks?"

"Should be soon," Righteous said. "Already got Richie picking up from Thelma Boyd, one of our big policy writers. She's a floater. One of her drops is the newsstand at the Riviera."

"Sticking your nose right in there, I like that," Scarlatti said. "But let's make one thing fucking clear, this is gonna be low key, no turf war. The boss is just feeling things out, wants to see if Longy gives a shit anymore about the Third Ward. If not, we move in."

Chapter

47

Joey pushed his Schwinn through the front door of Marsucci's office, lowered its kickstand, and put his hands on his hips.

"Here I am, Mr. Marsucci, at long last!"

Marsucci saw that he would have to put this cocky little son of a bitch in his place right away. He didn't care if the kid was connected to the three nigger barbers. He got up, walked to the front of his desk, and pointed to the bike.

"Not so fast, you have a route when I say so," Marsucci said. "First you got to learn how things are done around here. None of my kids ever bring their bikes in here, they chain them up outside. You better get that straight."

"What am I going to use, my shoelaces?"

"Watch your mouth, I don't need another wise-ass kid around here. You'll be riding with me this weekend, and you've got a lot to learn. I don't want any lip. You got that straight?"

"As an arrow," Joey said. "What time Saturday?"

"Five sharp, you got that, five sharp!"

"See you then."

Joey turned, released the kickstand on his bike and was about to leave when Marsucci pulled him up short.

"Hold it, I ain't finished with you yet." Marsucci walked back behind the desk, sat down and pulled open the bottom right drawer. "What floor you live on?"

"Third. What's it to you?"

"One of those railroad tenements, I take it."

"You don't need to know nothing about where I live. Don't worry, I'll show up on time."

"Gets old pretty damn fast lugging a bike up and down three flights of stairs. Don't want you to burn out before you get started." Marsucci pulled a three-foot length of steel chain, padlock and two keys from the drawer and dropped them on top of his desk. "Take 'em, they're yours."

"Thanks, Mr. Marsucci, I'll pay you back. Take a while, but I will."

"Bet your ass you will." Marsucci knew his reputation and couldn't afford to have this kid think he had a soft side.

Ten minutes later Joey chained and locked his bike to the first floor banister, took the stairs two at a time, and burst into the Bancik apartment with, "I got it! Mom, Dad, I got it, a *Beacon* route! And a bike to boot!"

Josef and Catherine Bancik found it impossible to digest all that Joey blurted out with machine gun rapidity. The route, how much it pays. The bike, and how the greedy Jew Simon wasn't so greedy after all, letting him pay it off a little at a time. How much he would get for each new subscription he signed up. That beginning Saturday, he'd start every morning at five, and that the circulation manager, Frank Marsucci, gave him a chain, lock and keys to keep his new bike from being stolen.

"It won't be much, but at least I'll be bringing in a little every week to help out," Joey said.

"Don't matter how much, every penny counts," Joey's smiling mother said as she placed a plate with stuffed cabbage and potatoes in front of him. "It's just a start, then who knows how far our Joey will go."

"Mom, it's just a paper route." Any further attempt to minimize his job was cut short by his mother's contagious smile. "I waited a long time to get it. Now I got it, and nobody's gonna take it away. You'll all be proud."

Joey's father had been silent throughout the upbeat dinner table exchange. Grandpa Alexander couldn't care less, never once taking his eyes from the food on his plate. Joey looked across the table as his father put down his knife and fork, and wiped his mouth with the back of his hand.

"So you're now our little breadwinner," an unsmiling Josef spit the words out. "Ain't that what you'd be called?"

"Cut it out, dad. I ain't gonna be that at all," Joey said. "I thought you'd be happy, like mom."

"We're all happy, ain't that right Josef. Your son is growing up, that's all it is."

Josef studied their faces then pushed away from the table, and silently stalked out of the apartment, slamming the door behind him as he headed toward the stairs.

"Give your father time," Catherine said as she cleared the table. "There's some coffee left in the pot, want some?"

"Yeah, why not." Joey, who literally flew up the stairs to their apartment a short time ago, suddenly felt mixed up and sad. "What gives with dad? I just don't get it."

"He's not the same since he lost out on that job at Prudential." Catherine placed a half-full coffee cup in front of her son. "It's not that he lost out, but that it's a nigger who got it. That really hurt. I circle the job ads in the paper, but he hardly looks no more."

"Why not? There's got to be something out there for him."

"I know and he knows, but he don't want to ever lose out to a black man again, and that could happen."

The next afternoon Richie and Joey met up in the hallway after their last class at St. Mark's. Once outside, they loosened their ties and undid the top button of their white shirts before heading over to Milt's.

"How'd it go?" Richie asked.

"Good and bad I guess," Joey said. "Good with Marsucci, even gave me a chain, lock and keys for my bike."

"There's a price tag, you can bet on that. Marsucci's not the kind of guy who gives you something for nothing."

"I figured. At home, my mom talked like I was about to buy the *Beacon*, not deliver it. But my dad wasn't too happy."

"Why not?"

"My mom thinks it's because he's been out of work so long, and I'll be bringing in a little something each week."

"He should be happy," Richie slurped the last few drops of soda from his glass. "Hell, my folks think I'm another Henry Ford because I bring in a few bucks each week. I hope you kept your yap shut about the numbers."

"I ain't stupid."

"Probably test you the same as me," Richie said. "After riding with Marsucci, you'll have a few days to nail down your drops, and when they're sure you won't fuck up, you'll start your pickups. By then, you and your policy writers will be on a first name basis. Don't need to tell you how important those slips and bets are, so you better not lose them."

"There's no fucking way that's going to happen."

Richie waited until Joey finished his soda, studied his accomplice's' face and said, "I'm ready to get out of these school duds, how 'bout you? You got any big plans?"

"Nope. From that crooked smile on that mug of yours, I'd say you've got something up your sleeve."

A bright lightbulb of an idea had popped into Richie's head during their walk from St. Mark's. "Are you ready for something a little stronger than soda?"

"Maybe," Joey said cautiously.

"Ale, Ballantine's Ale for 'men with a thirst' so they tell us. You ready to become a man?"

"Lead on, show me the way."

A half-hour later and out of school uniform, they turned down an alley behind the American Legion. An eight-foot, rotten wood fence enclosed the back of the Marauders' Post. Richie pushed aside a few loose boards, and they scampered into a small crab apple orchard.

"Okay, here we go," Richie said. "Keep your head down." When they reached a terraced lawn leading to the rear of the building, Richie stopped and signaled to sit down.

"How many can you handle?" Richie said.

"Same's you, I guess."

"You wait here."

Richie darted to a latticed enclosure adjacent to the rear door. Above the door, surrounded by a painted montage of American flags, and wind-wrinkled pennants, was the inscription: "Lest We Forget." He pulled apart the flimsy latticework, and withdrew four bottles of Ballantine Ale, a bottle at a time. Running back with the bottles cradled against his chest, he slipped on the grass and slid on his backside into the orchard.

"Neat, even fallin' on yer ass, ya looked like a pro," Joey said.

"Go fuck yerself. Here." Richie handed him two bottles. "Follow me."

They duck-walked over to a crab apple tree where Richie pulled a church key from a lower branch. The two youths slumped to the ground under the tree.

"Man, this bottle is warm," Joey said.

"Yeah, but the price is right," Richie said as he used the church key to flip the cap from his first bottle of ale, then handed the opener to Joey.

"Sorry I couldn't make it to the bar and get some of the cold stuff for ya," Richie said. "There's only a few of us in on this. So stop your bitching."

"Who's bitching," Joey said, "not me. Hey warm ale ain't half bad."

They lapsed into silence, the only sound the bubbly gulping of the ale as it cleared their Adam's apples.

Richie and Joey drained their first bottles of ale, leaned back against the gnarled trunk of the crab apple tree, and then, as if on cue, let out a collective burp. They looked at each other and laughed. "Pretty damn good, I'd say," Richie said.

"A real man's drink," Joey said.

Richie and Joey snapped the caps off their second bottle, and Richie carefully replaced the church key in the crook of the tree branch.

"Like my old man says, the first one's for thirst, the second's for pleasure." Richie was beginning to feel the effects of the warm brew.

"I agree with your dad," Joey slurred.

It suddenly dawned on Richie, that except for serving Mass together at St. Mark's, this was the first he had ever spent any real time alone with Joey. Now he and Joey were numbers running culprits who should have their heads examined for falling in with three of the shiftiest niggers they would ever meet. Crazier yet, Richie had put in the good word for Joey, a pissed-off kid he had never been able to figure out.

Chapter

48

There was a distinct hierarchy among the dwindling number of whites in the Third Ward. Richie, who lived at the Exeter, had always thought it weird the way white tenement people behaved. Everyone knew that Joey had strict orders not to talk to any of the colored people in his building.

"Next thing ya know, they'll be borrowin' sugar and bargin' in and out jes like real neighbors, like decent folks," Richie had overheard Mrs. Bancik complain to his mother one afternoon in front of Fishbein's. "They ain't good fer nothin.'"

It was no secret the Banciks were having it tough, ever since Joey's father injured his back. Over forty, he couldn't find work. They poor-mouthed Negroes more than anyone, despite doing all their grocery shopping at Father Divine's Peace Stores because it was the cheapest.

"That's what I call talking out of both sides of your fucking mouth," the Pump had blurted out one day while sharing a booth at Milt's with Carl and Richie. Carl agreed, but Richie kept his trap shut, still guilty that he pocketed forty cents of his haircut money by getting trimmed at the Peace Barber Shop every two weeks.

Richie reached over and poked Joey in the shoulder. They were quiet for a long time, savoring their warm ale. Finally, Richie broke the silence.

"Hic."

"Wash dat?"

"I gotha hiccups."

"No shish. Hic. No shish. Hic."

"Washya say? Ya got hiccups too. Hic."

"Hic."

"A big swig. That'll fix 'em."

"Les go."

They poured down three or four big gulps, the ale drowning their laughter. Richie felt a burning sensation in his head. The ale had gone up his nose and was dripping out his nostrils. A bubble formed on the tip of his nose, then burst in a shower of foamy spray.

Joey, his hiccups gone, was doubled over in laughter. "Sheeit. Bubbles out yer nose. Lookee here, 'nother one." He reached over and popped the bubble with his finger. By this time they were both in hysterics. They fell back limply against the tree, tears streaming from their eyes.

"Sheeit."

"Ya kin shay that again."

"Sheeit."

They polished off their bottles. Richie took the four empties back to the latticed enclosure, and placed them among the other dead soldiers piled next to the back door. He turned and rejoined Joey under the crab apple tree.

"Time to get serious," Richie said. He had gone out on a limb for Joey, and he wanted to be sure that everything was sinking in. "Ready to ride with Marsucci?"

"Five on the button at his office. Same on Sunday." Joey worked hard to push the words past his thick tongue. "Then Monday it's me and my bike."

"Watch your mouth around Marsucci. Not sure where he fits in, but he's made it clear he wants a piece of the action."

"What the hell does that mean?"

"It means right now we're running numbers for three black bookies, and the Jew fits in somehow. It'll be three weeks tomorrow for me, and I still don't know for certain about Marsucci."

"Any problem with the numbers?" Joey said.

"Nope. Clean as a whistle so far, but I know they've been watching."

"They?"

"McDuffie's boys. So far, so good, but who knows. This week I began hitting Thelma Boyd's drop at the Riviera newsstand, and that's right under their noses."

"Any kick-your-ass warnings?"

"Warnings? What the hell you talking about? Sweeney, Sharkey and Spencer don't give warnings, they just kick ass."

"And our asses are next, that what you're saying?"

"You got it, we're guinea pigs, pure and simple."

Still lightheaded from the ale, they stumbled back to the fence, pushed aside a few loose boards, and headed home. Richie and Joey never had much in common, and now, without a hint of guilt, they were criminal comrades.

"Nervous?" Richie asked as they approached the Bancik tenement. "Sure as shit I was on my first day. I didn't know what to expect."

"Thanks for breaking Marsucci in for me. I can handle him okay, no need to worry."

"Blessed be the numbers," Richie said. "Shake on it." They extended their right arms for a tight handshake, pumped four times, and in that moment truly sized each other up.

"Amen to that," Joey said, then turned and pushed his way past four black kids playing on the stoop.

Alice Maxwell witnessed her son's handshake and brief exchange with Joey while on her way to drop some letters into the corner mailbox. She caught up with her son midway down the block, and they walked home arm-in-arm.

"I wasn't aware you were so buddy-buddy with the Bancik boy," Alice said. "You hardly ever talked about him, and when you did, you weren't very kind."

"Things change mom, and even guys like Joey, who can really be a jerk, can come around if you give them a chance."

Richie took their apartment key from his mother, and trying not to let his tipsiness show, unlocked the door and stepped aside to usher her in with a flamboyant wave of his hand.

"Your palace awaits you."

It would be half an hour before Andy Maxwell returned home from work. Richie set the kitchen table for dinner, careful to stay out of his mother's way as she scurried between the refrigerator, the sink and stove. Although the Maxwells were lapsed Catholics in many ways, eating meat on Fridays wasn't one of their transgressions. Tonight it would be filet of sole in a mushroom sauce, mashed potatoes, canned green beans, milk for Richie and coffee for his mom and dad. Dessert would be A&P marble pound cake.

"Ready to start mashing?" his mother asked as she removed several large potatoes from a pot of boiling water. "Grab the masher from the top drawer and don't forget to add the margarine, salt and pepper."

"Mom, I ain't no rookie. I've been doing this for years."

"Don't say ain't. Now let's get back to you and Jocy Bancik. What's going on between you two?"

"For one thing, we're both *Beacon* carriers now. Joey starts tomorrow, and I was kinda filling him in on what to expect from Marsucci. He's had his name in longer than me, and I'm glad he finally got a route."

"So that makes you pals?"

"Not yet, and maybe never. Let's give it some time, and who knows."

"So far it's working for you, let's hope it works out for Joey."

A few minutes later, they heard an enthusiastic "I'm home! And I'm hungry!" echo through the apartment. Andy Maxwell's pre-dinner routine never varied. After a hug and kiss for Alice, he escaped to the parlor with a bottle of Rheingold lager to scan the *Clarion's* headlines, and catch John Wingate's six o'clock radio newscast. There had never been a copy of the *Beacon* in the Maxwell home until Richie had started delivering it three weeks earlier. He was his son's first new subscriber, but except for a pretty good sports section, he rated the paper far inferior to the *Clarion*.

He polished off the Rheingold and joined Richie at the kitchen table. Alice's routine was even more predictable than her husband's. She removed her apron, hung it on a hook in the pantry, and closed the door. True to Emily Post's dictum, a proper wife never wore cooking attire when sitting down to eat.

"So Richie, you got another big collection day coming up," Andy said. "Make sure those three deadbeats who stiffed you last week pay-up. Can't let them think that because you're new they can slide."

"Don't worry, dad, I ain't about to let anybody stiff me."

"Don't say ain't," Alice admonished.

"I see all your *Parade* magazine inserts are bundled and waiting on the landing," Andy said. "I'll help you stuff them tomorrow so you'll be ready to go on Sunday."

"Thanks, dad. Maybe next week I'll have the routine down so I can do it myself." Left unsaid but always on his mind was how best to meld in his policy pickups, and the daily bike ride to the barbershop with his *Beacon* chores. And with Thelma Boyd and Riviera Hotel now part of the mix, things were sure to get even more complicated.

Across the street, after checking to make sure his bike was securely chained and locked to the heavy first floor banister newel, Joey joined his mom and dad at the kitchen table. He could feel a definite change in attitude from the night before. It seemed as though his mom and dad, and even his grandfather, had been waiting for him before starting a dinner of ham hocks, turnips, onions and carrots.

"It's one of your favorites," Catherine said as she ladled chunks of vegetables and a meaty hock into Joey's bowl. "Fishbein had a special price today, and when I told Abe you were starting your *Beacon* route in the morning, he threw in a big bone with all that wonderful marrow. It flavors everything so good."

Josef looked up from his bowl, scanned the table, and thought hard about what to say. The words had to come out right. He had walked the neighborhood the night before, trying to understand his outburst. He knew he had been wrong, but how could he make it right with Joey and Catherine when he had so little to offer. *Starting tomorrow our boy will be out in the dark every morning and for what? A few dollars each week? God almighty, when was the last time I brought in even a few cents. Right now for him, I'm not even here. I have to make him know that things have changed from last night.*

"Josef, you're not eating," Catherine said. "Is anything wrong? I gave you the big bone. It's stuffed with marrow, and you haven't touched it."

"And I won't," Josef said. "Here, Joey, this is for you. Will give you the strength you'll need in the morning."

Josef inserted his fork into the marrow cavity making sure none of the precious fat spilled out, and reached over and placed it in Joey's bowl.

"It's all yours. The best part is digging it out. Makes it taste even better. Get started, before it gets cold."

"Thanks, dad. This is the first time for me," Joey said, then looked around the table and saw that all of them, even grandpa, were watching his every move.

"And it won't be the last," Josef said. "Worth the wait wasn't it."

"I'll say it was," Joey said as his father self-consciously lowered his gaze from his son's face and went back to work on the food in front of him.

Chapter

49

O n Monday, Nick Cisco offered a lazy wave to the smiling young blond at the desk, then pushed opened the door with "Captain Anthony M. Gordo" stenciled on its glazed glass window.

"Tony, things have looked up around here since you took over," Cisco said. "What is it now, about two years?"

"You got it right, and only two months more and I'm outta here." Gordo motioned to one of two leather-padded chairs in front of his desk. "What's on your mind?"

"As you probably already know, those three Third Ward homicides have been dumped into our laps. Got mob written all over them."

"Jesus Christ, Nick. You too? You and your partner have been in homicide for what, less than a year, and you already see Richie the Boot's or Longy's name pinned to every stiff in town?"

"Lay off, Tony. Do you wanna hear what I've got to say, or don't you?" Cisco knew he had to measure every word, that Gordo's three-bedroom, double garage shack and beachfront cottage didn't come from hitting the lottery or a cop's paycheck. "Rumors, just rumors, have it that the Boot thinks the Third Ward's ripe for the picking."

"Where the fuck did you hear that? Nobody wants a shooting war, and that sure as shit will happen if what you're saying is even half-way true."

"More than half-way true. You've seen our report. Ruby West and her pimp boyfriend were freelancers who crossed the line, and Longy cleared that up real fast."

"Bullshit rumors, that's all you've got," Gordo, his jowly face now flushed, almost shouted. "You need more if you want my help!"

Cisco knew that divulging anything to Gordo would be in the pipeline to either Zwillman's Third Ward Political Club or Boiardo's Vittorio's Castle, depending on whose ass he was kissing.

"Just playing hunches, right now," Cisco said. "We're working a lead out of Atlanta that we're hoping goes somewhere. Got three names, one's the brother of our stiff, Clyde Barton. His name's Buck Barton and he skipped out of Atlanta with two partners. The other two are John Travers and Wilber Fontaine. They had quite an operation, a bookie barbershop up front and a policy parlor in the back. They were also running women. They were tied in big with the mob in Atlanta. The authorities in Georgia have long rap sheets on all three of them, and believe they were headed this way."

Gordo's reaction was more than Cisco could have hoped for. The big man shifted uncomfortably in his padded chair. His face was now scarlet, and the fingers of his right hand tapped out a steady tattoo on the desk.

"The three names don't ring a bell. Have anything more to go on?"

"Does the name Jimmy Rossi ring a bell? He's a made man who handles the mob's gambling and vice operations in Georgia. And Atlanta cops say our three guys were his wire into the black precincts. They're here in town, I can feel it."

"I think I got it straight now," Gordo, almost composed, said. "And believe me Nick, I've been playing hunches for more than twenty years, so I understand where you're coming from. Right now we've got nothing on your three niggers. But you're still a homicide dick, and you're asking me to cut loose uniform manpower I don't have. Give me a little bit more, something with meat on it, and we'll see where it takes us."

"Can't ask for more." Cisco got up and reached across the desk to shake Gordo's hand. "And congratulations to you and Veronica on your daughter's marriage. Lucia is a beautiful girl and deserves the best."

"Thanks, Nick." Gordo still grasping Cisco's hand arose and accompanied him to the door. "And our best to that beautiful wife of yours. You couldn't have done better than Connie."

Gordo tried to suppress the painful twinge that surfaced in the back of his neck when he felt threatened. He should have known from the start that nothing good comes out of a phone call from that son of a bitch, Vinnie Scarlatti. The punk's call that night had oozed with phony deference.

"Vinnie Scarlatti here. We need to talk." After several months, murderous rage arose when Gordo recalled that late night conversation. "Hope I didn't wake you up, Captain."

"I'm awake. Get on with it."

"Passing it along from you know who that there are some things you should know about."

"I'm listening."

"I want to be sure you're wide awake now, Captain," Scarlatti made no effort to hide his contempt. "I know I've interrupted your beauty sleep, Captain, so don't doze off on me. It's real important what I got to say."

He was about to explode when Veronica reached over and placed her hand on his chest. His wife knew him like a book, his heart was pounding, as it did during all the nocturnal calls. Her instincts had sharpened over the years and Tony's terse replies told her that it was the mob.

"Easy, honey, don't let them get to you," she whispered as the fingers of her right hand feathered his chest. He cupped her hand in his, tightened it into a fist and gently squeezed. He felt fear and Scarlatti would pay.

"You'll be getting a call from Atlanta from a very important fellow," Scarlatti said. "His name is Jimmy Rossi. He's a made man. He'll give you the lay of the land, filling you in about three jiggaboos coming to town. We don't want any toes stepped on, you can understand that, can't you, Captain?"

"And that's it? Three more crooked coons coming to Newark, no names, no nothing?"

"You'll get them soon enough, no need to worry, Captain. It's all right if I call you Captain, isn't it? If this isn't a good time for you to talk, we'll pass it on to Rossi. We don't want you to give up any of your beauty sleep, do we Captain? *Arrivederci.*"

If Scarlatti had been in the same room with him that night, Gordo would have smashed his face into a bloody pulp. His hatred for the mobster had been seething out of control ever since. A mere beating would not be enough. A solution must be clean and complete, his honor demanded it.

Gordo had begun putting together dossiers on the three book-ies immediately after the Rossi phone call. He didn't like what was going down. Richie the Boot had his eyes on Zwillman's Third Ward. The Boot was convinced that Longy was moving on from his old stomping grounds, and why not take a shot at it. But Longy wasn't giving away anything, not to The Boot and not to the pimp and whore working his turf.

"The boss wants it taken care of tonight," Benny Switzer growled over the private line to Gordo's home late last Monday. "Don't care how the slut and her pimp get it, just get it done. And clean, nothing to connect."

After closing the door behind Cisco, Gordo returned to his desk and punched in a number on his interoffice phone. "Hillary, see if you can run down Sergeants Gamba and Maroni. I want to see them right away."

Had a gut feeling about those three coons from Atlanta, Gordo thought. *Setting up the slut in the Third Ward was dumb, really dumb. And the pimp is the brother of one of the bookies, Jesus Christ, what the fuck were they thinking. This was after I laid it all out for them, so what do they do, they slap me in the face."*

Fifteen minutes later, Lou Gamba and Fabio Maroni were facing Captain Gordo as they took seats in front of his desk.

"Just had a visit with Nick Cisco, and he wondered if I had any thoughts about the Broome Street job," Gordo said. "Thinks it's connected to a Third Ward turf battle that ain't started yet. Wants my help."

"That's a fucking laugh," Maroni said. "What'd you tell him?"

"Said I needed more than rumors to go on," Gordo said. "Now getting back to your job. Fill me in."

"Got a little messy when the whore started running, she didn't get far," Gamba said. "Got it done nice and quiet."

"I saw in the report that Cisco had Frank Gazzi staking out the apartment that night," Gordo said. "He wasn't a problem?"

"Frank Gazzi a problem, you've gotta be kidding," Gamba said. "Spotted him right off keeping dry in the doorway across the street. Already had our trash collector coveralls on. We circled the block and slid into the apartment through the backdoor and waited. Took us about ten minutes, then we got out the way we got in."

"Could just as well've gone out the front. Good ol' Frank was nowhere in sight. He just can't help fucking up," Maroni said. "Still too dumb to handle a stakeout. Never could understand why you keep him around."

"*Stupido Siciliano. Sua moglie,* Maria and my Veronica are very close." Gordo said. "And with your Theresa and Julie, you know how it can be when your wives are calling the shots."

Gordo pushed back from the desk and clasped his hands behind his neck.

"Let's get back to why I called you in. I don't like what's going down. Cisco and his partner are nobody's fools. He's right when he says the pimp and the whore didn't just wander into town like two dumb hicks. And that it's no coincidence the pimp was the brother of one of the nigger bookies."

"So what's it all mean?" Gamba said.

"It means we have to tie up some loose ends."

"What in hell are you talking about?" Maroni shot a quick glance at Gamba before turning to Gordo. "And 'we', where does the 'we' fit in? Unless Lou knows something I don't, it's the first we've heard about loose ends."

"It's the first fuckin' time for me, too," Gamba said.

"Get used to it. We've had a nice run, about twenty years," Gordo's face was tight and grim. He held up his right hand to stifle any bitching from the two rogue cops. "And I got less than two months to go before my pension. You two are right behind me. But before I go there's a couple things eating at me I got to take care of. I want you with me. So why not go out together."

The three crooked cops found it impossible to acknowledge that they were no different than the mobsters they hated and had served so well. The same code of silence that governed the underworld also sealed the lips of the honest cops who looked the other way when the trio planted evidence, falsified reports, justified fatal shootings, inflicted beatings that left victims paralyzed, and when ordered, murders. It was time to get out.

"Are you in or out?" Gordo said.

"If we're in, where the hell does that take us?" Gamba said.

"Scarlatti, I want him to disappear," Gordo said. "And Buck Barton, I want him roughed up real bad, and I mean real bad."

"Why Scarlatti?" Maroni said. "He's nothing more than an over-dressed punk with a big mouth. Is there something we should know?"

"Respect, it's a matter of respect. How many times did I have sit downs with the top *capos* and get nothing but courtesy and respect. We did a job for them, got their thanks in an envelope and moved on. And now this little bastard Scarlatti comes along, and shows no respect...."

"Jesus Christ, Tony, this punk ain't worth it," Gamba said. "I remember him in juvie court for boosting car radios."

"Always smiling, that dandy sticks in my throat like a fishbone," Gordo said. "You know me, never take things personal, but this is different, he's got to go now."

"Word on the street is that Scarlatti is stepping up in class," Maroni said. "That he's been tapped to handle the three spooks running numbers for his boss."

"I don't think you got my meaning," Gordo said. "When I walk away, I want to walk away with respect. I want Scarlatti long gone."

"Okay, Tony, we both get it about Scarlatti," Gamba said. "But why the black bookie?"

"I'll tell you why. I get a call from Jimmy Rossi in Atlanta. He tells me that three nigger bookies had just spent two weeks kissing Father Divine's ass in Philly. Gave him a bundle for his okay to open a Peace barbershop in Newark. Just like in Atlanta, the shop's a front for their bookie operations. He tells me they got big plans for them."

"The coons are moving real fast." Maroni said. "Ain't been in town too long and already their runners are squeezing Longy. I don't get what you're pissed off about."

"It's about respect. I warned them their nuts would be in a grinder if they even thought about freelancing. Buck Barton kept shooting off his fucking mouth. That black son of a bitch was laughing at me all the time, he knew that his pimp brother and the slut were on the way."

"Leave them to us," Gamba said.

The times, places and methods were uncertain, but when Gordo escorted Maroni and Gamba to the door one thing was crystal clear in his mind, that without respect, a man was no more than a piece of shit.

Chapter

50

The following Friday morning, the *Clarion's* Joe Lucio dropped several pages of mimeographed police reports in front of the *Beacon's* Jerry Saunders, then took his copies over to his desk in the press room and began reading. It was the daily chore for one or the other veteran police reporters to go to the front desk at headquarters and return with proof that there was still enough criminal ugliness in Newark to justify their weekly paychecks.

For a decade and a half, they had competed for headlines that would put their stories above the fold on their respective front pages, and had used every trick to get it done. After a few minutes of reading, Lucio looked across the press room and saw that Saunders had also completed the scrawled report at the top of the pile.

"What do you think, Jerry?" Joe said. "Are they at it again?"

"Christ, I don't know. I sometimes wonder if our fair city's thugs don't simply sleep walk from one killing to the next, then wake up patting themselves on the back for a job well done."

"And forgetting what the whole fucking mess was about in the first place."

Saunders and Lucio had survived several city desk coups largely because their editors realized there were no other reporters who knew the city's dark side as well as them. Both were single, profane, drank too much, chased the skirts, but never violated a confidence. A tip given behind the green painted windows of a North Ward Italian social club was treated with the same respect as an inside scoop provided by Police Chief Patrick Riley.

"I see that Cisco and McClosky have the honors again," Jerry said. "Cisco writes a pretty good report."

"He ought to, with all the practice he's been getting," Joe said. "What do we know about the stiff? The moniker, Vinnie Scarlatti, rings a bell, but I can't place it."

"He's one of Richie the Boot's low-level soldiers," Jerry said. "I bumped into him a couple of times, a sharp dresser who fancies himself another Jimmy Cagney. Heard he was moving up the Boiardo food chain, but that's about it."

"Says he got it in the back of the head," Joe said. "Then stuffed him behind the driver's seat of his Buick, and pushed it off that small pier just south of the Harrison Avenue Bridge. Pulled him out yesterday, and it looks like the crabs had been at him for at least two days. Sure looks like a mob hit."

"Could be, I hear that Longy's Third Ward is back in play."

"Heard that both sides are using paperboys as numbers runners to get their points across," Joe said. "Nothing new there, did it myself while still in knickers. How 'bout you?"

"Same here. Dropped my slips off at a shoeshine parlor on South Orange. Only pennies, but sure helped my mom and dad." Jerry picked up his phone and dialed in a three-digit number. "Let's see if we can get Nick and Kevin in here."

Ten minutes later, the pair of exhausted detectives dragged themselves into the press room, and went immediately to the freshly brewed coffee.

"Chrissakes, don't you ever wash these fucking cups," McClosky said.

"Adds to the flavor," Saunders said. "And you can't bitch about the price."

"Can't tell you much," Cisco said, then filled a mug with coffee, and after noting his report on their desks added, "That's all we have right now, but don't worry we'll keep you in the loop."

"I smell a tie-in between Scarlatti and the dead pimp and whore," Lucio said. "Convince me I'm wrong."

"And the ice pick, first the soldier boy and then the pimp," Saunders said. "No way you can tell me it's just a god damn coincidence."

"No way? Do you know something we don't?" McClosky said. "Then spill it, put our minds at rest. You two clowns are doing real good without us. You already got John Q. Public convinced that there's an ice pick killer in every alley."

"Whoa, let's keep our god damn cool," Cisco said. "If you want to listen, we'll give you what we've got."

It took little time to see that these two savvy street reporters weren't about to be brushed off. Lucio and Saunders never shared their sources, but it was obvious they smelled a gangster turf war in the making, and pushed the two detectives for answers. After fifteen minutes of bad coffee and profanity, an uneasy truce was declared with neither side backing off.

After leaving the press room, Cisco and McClosky stopped briefly at their desks on their way to the detective bunk room. They removed their jackets, unfastened their shoulder holsters, kicked off their shoes, and collapsed onto two rock-hard cots. Two and a half hours later, they were back in their car headed toward the Third Ward, with Cisco referring to notes scribbled during calls from Gazzi.

They drove a half-block past the Peace barbershop on Spruce and parked on the other side of the street. It was about the time that policy writers dropped off their slips. Cisco pulled out a pack of Chesterfields and offered one to McClosky. They lit up and waited.

An elderly, white-haired Negro man in patched dungarees smiled in their direction as he strode past, then crossed over and entered the barbershop through its front door. He emerged ten minutes later, nodded in their direction and headed off down the street.

"Well, I'll be god damned," Kevin said, "It looks as though they actually give haircuts."

In about fifteen minutes, a Negro woman walked past the barbershop, took a quick look around, then turned into a walkway along the south side of the building. During the next twenty minutes, six other Negros, three men and three women, repeated the routine.

The pattern was broken when a muscular, olive-skinned kid, no more than fourteen, pushed his bike from the walkway, jumped on and pedaled away.

"Gazzi is right so far," Nick said, then checked his notes. "One down, one more to go."

As if on cue, a clean-cut white boy, about the same age as the first, pedaled his bike out of the walkway and rode off in the same direction.

"That's the kid I pointed out to you the other day on Kinney," Nick said.

"Yeah, the one in front of the *Beacon* office."

"That should be it," Nick said as they watched three black runners enter the walkway, and a few minutes later exit the same way. In less than ten minutes, a matronly, middle-aged black woman came out carrying a brown leather valise.

"There she goes, everything on its way to the bank," Kevin said.

"Well, that's it," Nick said. "Let's give the backroom paper-pushers time to empty out and head home before we move in."

When they stepped into the shop, they were immediately greeted by the larger of two black men impeccably dressed in starched white jackets, matching white trousers and black dress shoes. The man eased himself from one of the three barber chairs, smiled and said, "Welcome. God's Tall Timber, and this other fine fellow is Righteous Reckoning."

"Homicide, not Vice, so you can stop sweating. Lieutenant Cisco, and Sergeant McClosky."

The two detectives scoped the room. Cisco gestured toward an empty barber's chair with an identical white jacket draped over the back, and a barber's cape neatly folded over its left arm.

"We were told there were three of you. I see that it's ready and waiting, so he must be expected. Does he have a name?"

"That would be Darn Good Disciple," the big black man said. "Afraid he won't be among us for a while."

"Darn Good Disciple, God's Tall Timber, and Righteous Reckoning… suppose we throw out three other names for you," McClosky said. "See if they ring a bell. Buck Barton. Wilber Fontaine, and John Travers?"

"This could take a while," Cisco said as he and McClosky eased themselves into the two end chairs.

"Help yourself," Tall Timber said. "We'll just take those chairs by the door."

"So let's connect the dots," Cisco said. "Tall Timber, you're…."

"Wilber Fontaine."

"And Righteous Reckoning…?"

"John Travers."

"Now tell us why you don't expect Buck Barton any day soon?" McClosky said. "And you can drop all that sugar and molasses bullshit."

"Afraid Buck slipped and fell down some stairs. Fractured his skull and broke his right wrist," Fontaine said.

"When did it happen?" Cisco asked.

"Tuesday night, leaving his flat. Treated at County, spent the night, checked himself out the next day, and we ain't heard a word since."

"Give us your best guess," McClosky said. "Hauled his ass back to Atlanta, didn't he."

"There's no way two homicide dicks give a good god damn about a nigger bookie joint," Travers said. "Whatcha want, and what's in it for us?"

"You've got rapsheets a mile long, and we can make it real nasty. So be real careful what you tell us, and maybe we'll look the other way," Cisco said. "Tell us about Vinnie Scarlatti, Clyde Barton and his whore, and what your partner Buck had to do with any of it."

Chapter

51

"Don't need to tell you how things work around here," Fontaine said. "We answer to Scarlatti."

"So you waltzed into town, and all of this just dropped into your laps?" McClosky said, gesturing over his shoulder to the rear door. "That's what you want us to believe."

"Only after Jimmy Rossi, our man in Atlanta, put in some calls," Fontaine said. "Boiardo's people listened. One was to your Tony Gordo. Looking back, that meeting with Gordo might be the reason Buck slipped and got hurt real bad."

Cisco and McClosky exchanged glances across the empty chair in the middle. They were getting more than expected from the bookies.

"Let's get it straight, Gordo's not our man. Where was this meeting? Did he have any other cops with him?" Cisco said.

"It was over on Broadway. We were new in town, and had a hard time finding it, Caffé Palermo. Gordo was pointed out all alone in a big corner booth."

"So no other cops," McClosky said.

"Yes and no," an anxious Travers said.

"What the hell does that mean?" Cisco demanded. "The Palermo's a mob joint."

"There were two guys sitting at a table close to the booth," Travers said. "Big and mean lookin'. Never took their eyes off us, enough for me to think maybe this ain't a good deal after all."

"Ever meet with Gordo or see those mean and nasty men again?" Cisco said.

"Know this is gonna piss you off, but again, we gotta say yes and no," Fontaine said.

"We'll say it just once." McClosky leaned forward in the barber chair, anchored his elbows on his thighs, and jabbed his index fingers at the two bookies. "If you two don't stop fucking around, Gordo and his two goons will seem like choir boys. Start talking."

"First, we never met again with Gordo, not official anyway," Fontaine said. "A week after Palermo, we were cruising downtown. You know, getting the lay of things. Walked out of Swifty's and bumped into Gordo pounding the living bejesus out of this white man. The same two guys at Palermo's that night were holding him up, and man-oh-man, it looked like Gordo was about to kill him. We poked our heads in and out of that alley real fast, nothing there we wanted a part of. We're about to cut out when Gordo spotted us and recognized who we were."

"Christ, this is like pulling teeth," Cisco said. "Our patience is running out."

"They dropped this guy to the ground and turned on us," Travers said. "Gordo warns us we didn't see or hear nothing, and if he gets word otherwise, we'd wish that we'd never hauled our nigger asses into town. They take off and leave us with this guy moaning real loud and bleeding like a stuck pig."

"So you listened real good. What about the guy on the ground?" McClosky said.

"Called the cops and said there was a guy in the alley next to Swifty's, that they better come real quick," Fontaine said. "Then we hauled ass."

"And that's it, you just hauled ass. You never found out who he was?" McClosky said.

"Yeah, nosed around and found out his name was Frank Marsucci, a low-grade punk, lucky to still be alive," Fontaine said. "Did some checking and found he was a pimp who got on the wrong side of Richie the Boot. And that night Gordo was taking care of the problem."

"Anything more you want to tell us about Marsucci?" Cisco said.

"Only that he's working for us and the *Beacon* right now," Fontaine said. "Jes' like our two new runners, white boys on bikes, smart as hell and learning fast."

"That's Vice's problem for now, and whether it bites you in the ass or not depends on where we go with this," Cisco said. "Now tell us about Buck Barton and Gordo at the Palermo."

"Buck's never one to listen, and he got uppity," Travers said. "He wants to know 'why this' and 'why that' and 'why we have to talk to the cops at all.' Easy to see he was pissing the man off."

The two detectives knew that Gordo, a bully with a short fuse, had over the years used his fists to settle scores with other officers. There is no way he would ever suck it up and accept any lip from a nigger bookie just new in town.

"What the hell did your buddy Buck say that put him on a train back to Atlanta?" McClosky said.

"Buck had too many questions," Fontaine said. 'When he asked Gordo why we need to talk to him and not just go to the big man himself, our meeting was over, and I mean it was over real quick. You could see the big, fat cop was really burning."

"Any talk by Buck about moving some working ladies into town?" Cisco asked. "Street pussy can pay real big. Was Buck getting the itch, and invited brother Clyde and Ruby to set up shop?"

"No sir, Lieutenant," Travers said. "Paid pussy is too risky. We can't vouch for Buck, but for Wilber and me, playing the numbers is safer than playing the ladies."

"Tell you about something that's even easier," Cisco said, "It's how you can make us happy. Do you want to hear?"

"We're all ears," Fontaine said.

"All this is Vice business," Cisco said. "If I know Dino and his gang, they're already taking their bite out of your bank. We'll be taking our bite out of you."

"What do you want out of us?" Fontaine said. "We're sliced real thin already."

"We'll make it plain and simple. Information," Cisco said. "Stiffs pile up faster in the Third Ward than anywhere else in town. You and Righteous Reckoning here are gonna be our street canaries."

"Snitches?" a suddenly relaxed and relieved Fontaine said. "Is that all you want from us?"

"Any problem with that?" McClosky demanded. "If not, keep your fucking mouths shut and listen."

"We talked to Lieutenant Peters in Atlanta the other day, and he said that as a trio, you two and Buck Barton, were at the top of the stoolie chart," Cisco said.

"Played both ends against the middle," McClosky said. "What would happen if that got out to any of Boiardo's wise guys? And then back to Jimmy Rossi?"

"Don't need to say any more," Fontaine said. "John and me are singers at your beck and call. You can bet on that. Just need to know how."

"Don't worry, when we want something, you'll know," Cisco said. "The beat cop, Frank Gazzi, will also be poking his nose in on a regular basis. Don't be shy."

"In fact, you should be kissing our asses," McClosky said as he joined his partner at the front door. They walked out, crossed the street, and got back in their car.

It was only a short wait before Travers and Fontaine, no longer dressed in white, emerged from the shop, locked the front door, and after a nod in the cops' direction, quickly stepped it out and disappeared around the corner.

"So, unless they clammed up on us, they didn't know about Scarlatti," Kevin said. "What do you think?"

"I'm not sure, but if they don't, it won't take long," Nick said. "And when they do, they'll probably wish they were with Buck in Atlanta."

"Do you trust them?"

"Hell, no, but we'll use them. They know what happens if they hold out on us."

"Heartless bastards that we are," Kevin said.

"We still have the junk dealer on Quitman," Nick said. "Don't know how he figures in all this, or if he figures at all."

"Gazzi's sure he supplied the bikes to the two kids," Kevin said. "Maybe it was just for a few extra bucks, that's all. Do we really want to mess with him?"

"Right now, I say no. With Scarlatti added to the mix, we have four stiffs on our hands. To go where we have to go with three of them, we'll be tearing the department apart."

"Are you saying free passes for everyone?" Kevin asked, his unease apparent over the prospect of another police cover-up.

"If we take this to Chief Riley, what the fuck do you think will happen?"

Kevin reached for his pack of Old Golds, tapped one out for Nick, and waited until each of them had taken a couple deep drags before answering. "Nothing."

They sat in silence. Each breathing deeply. They stared down the grimy, debris-strewn street that defined the city they had sworn to protect, but at that moment had decided to betray. Nick broke the silence.

"We know the pimp snuffed Sergeant Locklee," Cisco said. "But Scarlatti, the pimp and the whore, there's no way we're gonna be able to stick Gordo with these three. Got anything to change my mind?"

"Not a thing." McClosky took a final drag on his cigarette, tossed it out the window, turned on the ignition, and glided their car from the curb.

"Let's swing past the *Beacon* office on Kinney," Cisco said. "Nothing special, just curious."

Stacked on the sidewalk in front of Marsucci's office were bundles of *Parade* magazine and other material to be inserted in extra copies of the Sunday *Beacon*. Each of his carriers would be picking the bundles up the next day. These would be delivered free to potential new subscribers living in exclusively *Clarion* territory. The turf war to decide who would be circulation and numbers top dog in the Third Ward was about to begin.

"At first I thought it was crazy, but after talking to the bookies today, I've changed my mind," Cisco said. "I'm sure those two kids we saw had just dropped off their policy slips and bets. It's not our worry. We've got enough on our plate."

"What the hell would we do with it anyway, call Dino?" McClosky said. "He and his gang at Vice have been punching their mob meal tickets forever. There's no way that's gonna change."

McClosky pulled their car into a vacant space in the parking lot behind headquarters, and got out as Cisco slid across and took the wheel. He pulled his car keys from his jacket pocket and headed toward his De Soto convertible, then stopped and turned back toward Nick.

"How about a night out, Nick? Gotta good one opening at the Empire tonight," he said. "The headliner's Myrna Dean. God damn if she doesn't have the longest legs in the business. Hell, you can tell Connie I dragged you out screaming and kicking."

"I guess you forgot that we're on weekend rotation. We're back here at six tomorrow morning. I'll take a pass," Nick said. He waited until Kevin drove off before switching on the ignition, turned left out of the parking lot, then headed south to Ivy Hill Park and Grace DeMarco. He knew that his wife had long ago silently rejected his lame excuses for not coming home, and that it was only a matter of time before she confronted him. He also knew he couldn't help himself.

Chapter

52

Earlier that Friday afternoon, Bancroft left the office of *Clarion* publisher, Herb Bix, feeling uneasy, to say the least, about what he had just been told. He had already reluctantly turned over his beloved Morgan to his wife, and with her Packard had canvassed four of his circulation districts around the Third Ward.

"Hensley, I've got some good news," Bix had said, then gestured to the woman seated to his right at the conference table. "You know Wendy, of course."

"Hi, Hensley, it's been a while," the pretty blond feature reporter said.

"Hi, yes it has, I'd say about four or five months." From the start, Bancroft was never comfortable around Wendy Talbot whose desk was across from his during his short tenure in the newsroom. While he labored over obituaries, she turned out one news feature after another with seeming ease.

"I've decided to go all out in our little skirmish with the *Beacon*," Bix said. "Wendy will write a story that profiles a *Clarion* Circulation Bureau, and how the dedication of the lowly paperboy makes it all possible."

Bancroft waited for the inevitable hammer to fall.

"One of your managers and his bureau pops out loud and clear, Jim McDuffie. He runs Bureau 12 in the Third Ward. McDuffie worked his way up from delivery boy, a true-blue *Clarion* man if there ever was one. His bureau includes all those swanky Clinton Hill apartments. It's where all the rich Jews hang their hats."

"Where do I fit in?" Bancroft said.

"Bureau 12 is yours, so you'll lay the groundwork. When we're finished here, give McDuffie a call and set up a meeting, just you and him, for tomorrow. Spend the weekend with him and his boys, get the lay of the land for Wendy, who comes aboard later in the week with a photographer."

"Photographer?"

"Hensley, my boy, I said we go all out, and an important Wendy Talbot piece without artwork is unthinkable. We're discussing the lead feature in next week's *Clarion* Sunday Magazine."

McDuffie was seated comfortably behind his desk when Bancroft arrived at the Avon office. A paperboy, obviously not pleased to be there, was seated next to the desk.

"Mr. Bancroft, glad to see you," McDuffie said as he stepped from behind his desk to greet his boss. "So my humble bureau will be making it big time with a Wendy Talbot story and even some photos."

"That's about it," Bancroft said, hoping that his lack of enthusiasm didn't show. "And I take it this is the carrier we'll be profiling."

"You got it. His name's Jackie Cashman," McDuffie said. "Come on over, Jackie, and shake hands with the big boss."

It was obvious to Bancroft that McDuffie had given considerable thought to his choice. Jackie looked to be about sixteen, tall and lanky with a shock of sandy hair and a confident smile. His handshake was firm.

"Tell me a little about yourself." It dawned on Bancroft that this was the first time he had ever talked to a *Clarion* paperboy, and he suddenly felt ill at ease.

"Been delivering for four years. Took over for my big brother when he joined up after Pearl Harbor. He had the route for, I don't know, maybe six years," Jackie was looking for a way to end it. His family was none of the *Clarion's* god damn business. "It helped us out a lot. Still does, and I'm holding on to it. Need any more, just ask."

"Right now, I can't think of anything," Bancroft said, then turned to McDuffie for help.

"You did great," McDuffie said. "We'll talk more when you bring in your route money this afternoon. Go on now, and just think, you're about to become a star."

McDuffie chose Jackie because the route he inherited included The Breakers, an eight-story gem with an elevator and apartments no smaller than two bedrooms and one and a half baths. Great for a big Sunday feature with pictures. It was at least three blocks removed from the hotels that were the nucleus of his numbers racket. He also knew this made The Breakers a prime target for the *Beacon*.

After the kid left, the two men decided that McDuffie's Sunday routine would remain unchanged, with him canvassing his territory, while Bancroft became a fly on the wall at The Breakers, watching Jackie at work and taking notes for Wendy. Leaving the office, Bancroft found it impossible to erase the thought that his cozy sinecure at the *Clarion* was about to end.

"Did you see and hear it all?" McDuffie asked as Al Sweeney pushed open the door of the backroom and stepped into the office.

"Every fucking bit of it," Sweeney said. "The *Beacon* starts dumping off its freebies tomorrow, and you can be god damn sure The Breakers is at the top of its hit list. I'll be waiting."

"Hope you didn't have shit in your ears when I told you and your two buddies to make it fast and clean. Out of sight, no witnesses. I hear they'll be running in one kid to start. Any ideas?"

"Don't take no mastermind, it's one or the other of those two punks from St. Mark's. Gino even got their names from that big looney that helps him on Sunday. Richie Maxwell and Joey Bancik."

"So you'll be ready and waiting."

"You can bet your ass. Before I split, I've got another idea to throw at you. I think it's gonna get your shit in an uproar." Sweeney walked to the sofa, leisurely took a seat, spread his legs and waited.

"Spill it, all of it. Put my mind to rest."

"I've been thinking, maybe it's time for me to step out on my own."

"What the fuck does that mean?" McDuffie said as he moved across the room and stood looking down at a seemingly unconcerned Sweeney.

"I ain't speaking for Gino and Tommy, but just for me. I figure why do I need your parlor. Been nosing around and I got it that those nigger barbers are looking for writers...."

McDuffie leaped forward and drove his knee hard into Sweeney's crotch. The carrier grunted but before he could raise his arms to protect himself, his boss had him by the throat while raining down a series of vicious slaps.

"You punk son of a bitch. So you wanna be a writer for Boiardo," McDuffie spit the words out as he pulled Sweeney into an upright position. "Here's what I think of your idea."

He yanked Sweeney off the couch and pushed him into a chair in front of his desk where he delivered two final slaps that left him dazed and wide-eyed.

"Now get your ass out of here, and you better be fucking ready in the morning."

Sweeney's cheeks still stung when he got home. He fingered the tender spot where McDuffie had jammed his thumb against his throat, and considered his next move. He wasn't about to back off from McDuffie, but that could wait. First things first.

He had come up with the solution on how to handle his problem. It was crystal clear that he, Gino and Tommy would be the kick-ass guys when the *Beacon* runners started moving in, but his solution would be his alone.

It was fun the way we took care of those five jigs. But they don't learn so good. Now they got two punks from St. Mark's working the streets. Christ, next month I'll be eighteen, and there's no way I should be worried about two snot-nosed kids, but I am, so I gotta fix it.

He stood up, walked to his dresser, and pulled his solution out of the sock and underwear drawer. He dragged a wicker chair to the side of his bed, sat down and carefully positioned it in front of him. He untied the two shoelaces that secured a bundled red and white kitchen towel. He was about to unwrap the bundle and expose its contents, thought better of it, and got up to make sure the bedroom door was locked.

He returned to the bed, pulled open the towel and smiled. In front of him were a fully-loaded Beretta pistol, and a small wooden box containing fourteen 9mm bullets, and six empty shell casings. A week earlier, he had gone to Branch Brook Park to familiarize himself with the gun firing off six shots in a secluded, wooded area. His smile widened as he recalled Gino's and Tommy's astonishment when he showed them the pistol, and let them handle it. He almost laughed at how they nearly pissed their pants when he told them that the Beretta was loaded. When he rewrapped the pistol, he failed to notice that a frayed corner of the towel had snagged the safety catch, leaving it unengaged and ready to fire.

Chapter

53

A day earlier, Profanity Pump was breathing fire when she strode into Milt's, ordered a Spur, then collapsed in the rear booth next to Carl and across from Billy and Marvin. The other booths were packed with kids from St. Mark's, their eyes agog at the spectacle she presented in full Good Counsel uniform.

"Been two weeks, and only now you're showing off that cute little get-up of yours," Carl joked.

"Shove it up your ass," the Pump said, as she loosened the dark green string tie, and unbuttoned the starched collar. "Yeah, hate to admit it, I missed you guys. What's up?"

"Not much," Billy said. "How 'bout you? Spied any guys with balls yet?"

"Not yet," the Pump said. "Hey guys, give me some time."

"Look who's back again," Carl said as he watched Father Nolan step aside to allow a gaggle of students push past him to the street. "He's been around a lot lately asking about Joey and Richie."

"No secret what those two are up to," Marvin said as the four kids watched the priest take a seat at the counter while Milt poured him a fresh cup of coffee.

"I'm outta here," Carl said as he pushed past the Pump. "I'm not up for any dumb questions from a priest."

Father Nolan added sugar and milk to his coffee, and carefully considered his next step. The evidence supported everything Eight-Ten had said during their weird encounter two weeks earlier. Richie and Joey hadn't served mass since then, eliminating any chance he may have had to confront them. He was uneasy about not confiding in Father Schneider, and rationalized it would be imprudent to approach the kids' parents without getting his boss involved. This was his first shot at a real parish problem, a law breaking one at that, and he wasn't handling it well.

He knew the kids' routine, and could have engaged them outside the bookie barbershop, and demand what. Stop running numbers? Give up their paper routes? If they told him it wasn't any of his business, what then? Run to Father Schneider? Call the cops? Did he really want them hauled into juvie court? Or should he confront the parents first? As one of the Diocese's fair-haired boys, anything he did would be carefully noted at the Chancery.

He picked up his coffee and decided to try what might be his only remaining option.

"Do you mind?" he said as he sat down beside Profanity Pump.

"Been keeping it warm for you, Father," Billy said.

They waited until the priest took a few sips of coffee before Pump said, "I hear you're one of our regulars now. That right, Father?"

"More or less," the priest said turning to the Pump. "And you, Mary MacDonough, it's not a lot of bull when I say we miss you. How's it going?"

"Well, it ain't the Third Ward," the Pump said as she reached under her starched collar to scratch her neck, and noticed Father Nolan smiling broadly as he watched her.

Without thinking Father Nolan used his right index finger to tug at his starched clerical collar. "All these years, and I still haven't gotten used to having this board around my neck."

The priest scanned their faces and found an indifferent Marvin smiling back at him.

"Marvin, isn't it?" Father Nolan said. "I've seen you around, and heard you're one hell of an athlete. Anything we've been saying make any sense?"

"Nope. I'm a Baptist."

"Enough said." The priest smiled and got to the heart of the matter. "I've had something on my mind for a while now, and would like to ask all of you some questions."

The priest ordered refills all around, and waited until Milt returned to the counter before shaping his first question. It would be now or never with these kids.

"Can't call myself a regular at Milt's, but when I come around I can't help noticing that Richie and Joey have become really scarce. Have any idea what they've been up to?"

"Well, they're in school every day," Billy said. "Joey's desk is next to mine and Richie sits up front. What more can I say?"

"And I ain't been around," the Pump said. "So can't be much help from my end."

"How about you Marvin? You and Richie are stoopball heroes. Am I right to say you've become friends?"

"Richie and I are friends okay, but don't know about Richie and Joey."

Billy said, "Father, why don't you let us in on what's on your mind?"

"They're picking up slips and bets for three black bookies and using their paper routes for cover. You know anything about that?"

"Like I said, Father, I ain't been around," the Pump said, "so you can count me out. It's been nice talking to you, but it's getting late and I got to go."

The priest stood up to allow her to slip out of the booth. "Let's not be strangers, Mary." He turned to Billy and Marvin, his attempt to ingratiate himself hadn't worked. They had hardly touched the sodas he ordered for them, and the Pump's glass was full. He decided to give it one last try, introducing fear as a possible wedge.

"We've all heard that the *Beacon* and *Clarion* are in a knockdown circulation war. The word on the street is that on Sunday the *Beacon* will be moving into *Clarion* territory, and that could be big trouble."

"What kind of trouble?" Billy asked indifferently, avoiding eye contact with the priest while slowly stirring his soda. "If I understand, you want them to stop running."

"You have it right."

"Then why talk to us, it's Richie and Joey or their folks that you want."

"I don't want a juvie court judge declaring them delinquents," Father Nolan said, "and that's where they're headed. As their buddies, do you have any suggestions?"

The boys exchanged glances then looked at the priest. Marvin went back to sipping his soda, and Billy resumed stirring his drink before breaking the awkward silence.

"Buddies also know when to keep their mouths shut," Billy said, "so I'm sorry, Father, but it's between you, Richie and Joey."

"I had hoped that you could help me out." The priest got up, and dropped fifty cents on the table. "Enjoy your sodas."

Father Nolan waited until he had turned the corner onto High Street before tapping out his first cigarette of the day. He walked to a bus stop bench, and took a seat next to a neatly dressed Negro woman and a boy, obviously her son, who smiled up at him. Two deep drags settled him enough to assess his failure at Milt's. He hadn't realized that these were streetwise kids whose code made no provision for stoolies. Even if they heard him out, what did he expect them to do. It was time for him to talk to his boss.

It was just after five o'clock when Father Nolan got back to the rectory. Father Schneider was relaxing on the porch in his wicker rocker, a tumbler of Vat-69 in hand, and a copy of the tabloid PM on his lap. He had removed his collar and was wearing a faded red cardigan.

"A great Dr. Seuss today," he said, tapping the newspaper, "and Dorothy Parker's piece is wicked as usual. What have you been up to, Terry?"

"I'd like to talk about it, Jim," Terry said as he dropped three ice cubes into a tumbler, poured three fingers of scotch, and settled in for what had become a daily ritual for the two priests. "Would it surprise you to learn that two of your eighth grade altar boys are running numbers for the mob, using their paper routes for cover?"

"Nope. And why should it? You have any names to give me?"

"Joey Bancik and Richie Maxwell."

"I assume you've talked to them. What did they have to say for themselves?"

"Not yet. Frankly, I don't know where to go with this."

"And from me, you want what?" Jim said.

"Advice."

"Then I'd say, leave it alone." Jim leaned over to the small table between them, dropped a couple cubes and some scotch into his tumbler, and leaned back to see what effect his words had on Terry.

"Leave it alone? You mean just walk away when I know that two of our eighth graders are breaking the law? I admit I'm new at this pastoral game. Two years with the Marines didn't prepare me for this."

"Let's get one thing straight, Terry, this is not a game. These kids know exactly what they've gotten into. Do you have any idea how many policy parlors are operating in our parish?"

"No idea," Terry said. "I only know for sure that Joey and Richie make their drops at a Peace barbershop on Spruce."

"There are five that I know of, maybe more. One of the biggest is run by the Grand Knight of our local Knights of Columbus. I doubt if you'd find more than a dozen parishioners who don't play. Let's just call it acceptable corruption."

"Acceptable corruption? What the hell does that mean? I played the numbers as a kid in Jersey City, dropped a lot of nickels and dimes. But I never fooled myself that it was legal."

"Sanctimonious even then," Jim said. "What do you know about these two kids?

"Not much, that's why I wanted to talk."

"The Maxwells I've never quite figured out. The mother shows up with her tithing envelope on Sundays and holy days, and that's about it. I can't remember the last time I saw the father. Richie has kept his nose clean around here, but who knows what he does out on the street. It's no surprise at all that he'd jump at the chance for some real pocket money."

"I met Alice Maxwell last spring," Terry said. "She told me the Prep was too expensive and asked me to see if there was any chance to get Richie into one of the much cheaper parish high schools. I tried, but came up empty. I don't know the Banciks."

"The Banciks are converts, switched from Orthodox, because as Catholics they would be more American. They've had it hard since Joey's dad lost his job. Until now, Joey's never caught a break. Does it really matter where the few bucks he puts on the kitchen table came from?"

"Are you saying breaking the law is okay?" Terry tapped out a cigarette from his pack of Lucky's, lit up, then pushed the pack and Zippo across the table to Jim, collecting his thoughts as he studied the older priest. "Jim, does it matter at all that these boys could end up in front of a judge who doesn't share your point of view?"

"Sure it does, but there isn't much chance of that. Boiardo controls the numbers and just about everything else illegal around here," Jim said. "And he has the cops and a good chunk of City Hall in his hip pocket. Leave it alone."

"So that's it. I just walk away. That's your advice?"

"It's your call. They're eighth graders who will be gone in the spring, so you have eight months to work your magic."

"I'll be talking to Sister Mary Margaret this weekend. I want her to make the principal's office available for a sit-down with Richie and Joey either Monday or Tuesday."

Chapter

54

Jackie Cashman had just completed his Saturday collections, and was sitting on his front stoop separating the bills from the coins when he spotted Al Sweeney headed his way. There was no love lost between them. He knew that Sweeney had poor-mouthed him to Jim McDuffie when his name came up for one of the three numbers slots. So it went to Tommy Spencer, and with it a great chance at some big bucks.

"How'd you like to add a fin to that pile," a smiling Sweeney said from the sidewalk before taking a seat a step below the other carrier. He didn't want to crowd his mark before making his pitch. "Wanna hear?"

"I'm listenin'.…"

"All you got to do is change your route a little, and the five bucks is yours."

"What the fuck does that mean?"

"I know your last stop is The Breakers. Instead, tomorrow morning all you've got to do is start there. It's the easiest five spot you'll ever make."

"Not that easy. The big boss from downtown is gonna be nosing around. The paper is doing a write-up about *Clarion* paperboys, and me and The Breakers got the shitty end of the stick."

"Don't worry about him, just be somewhere else after about eight or so. Simple enough, ain't it?"

"I think it's worth at least a sawbuck."

Sweeney leaned back against the stoop railing, and watched a now confident Cashman calmly fiddling with a stack of quarters.

"Okay, you bloodsucker, ten bucks."

"Hand it over, and we've got a deal."

Sweeney stood up and fished a small roll of bills from his pants pocket, peeled off two fives and handed them to Cashman. "Remember, you're out of The Breakers by eight."

Sweeney was still fuming as he climbed the stairs to the family's third-floor flat. It had been a long time since a mark crossed him up that way. To make his plan work, he needed Cashman to disappear. He had learned from a couple of Marsucci's pissed-off carriers that they were to first complete their route, then come around again with the freebies. It was a do it or else proposition.

He had given his plan a lot of thought and was sure he had all the bases covered. If he dumped McDuffie and Longy to be a writer for the black bookies and Boiardo, he would have to show them he was the man for the job. The Beretta was his ticket. He didn't have to pull the trigger, just wave it around to scare the living crap out of the little punk. They'd see he had the brains to be a writer, that the easy way was always the best.

He twice scouted The Breakers and found that it had everything he needed to make his plan work. Cashman would be gone by eight, taking the big boss from downtown with him. An early start in the morning, and he'd be ready and waiting at the apartments.

Late that afternoon, Hensley and Maude Bancroft were dressing for a rare night out in Newark. Maude hated the city, but knew that it was impossible to turn down a dinner invitation from her husband's boss. With dinner at the stuffy Broad Street Club, followed by Tchaikovsky's Sixth at Symphony Hall, the evening called for full dress uniform.

A silk-robed Maude prepared for another night of banal chit-chat with Penelope Bix by alternating strokes of her makeup brush with sips from her second martini. Her husband and Herb Bix would undoubtedly share a mindless rehashing of Princeton football anecdotes.

"Tell me, what do you think of the good ol' Orange and Black's chances this season?" she asked sarcastically, then turned from her vanity to toss a verbal dart at Bancroft. "Or do I have to wait until you hear from the great man at dinner before I get an answer."

"Are you starting already," her husband said as he stood in jockey shorts at his dresser color coordinating his tie, shirt, socks and handkerchief for his jacket pocket. "And it's only your second."

"With a lot more to come. A night of Junior League twitter from Penelope and 'rah rah sis boom bah' from you and Herb demands plenty of lubrication."

"You better go easy. Herb and I will be discussing a lot more than football. You might even want to listen."

"To hear what. How you're driving around town in my Packard spying on paperboys? What a joke."

"I know you don't give a rat's ass about my job at the *Clarion*, but a brass knuckle circulation war with the *Beacon* is about to start and I'll be in the thick of it. And that, Mrs. Bancroft, is no joke."

"Circulation war, brass knuckles, and you in the thick of it…you're kidding, of course."

"You'll swallow that contempt when I tell you what I'll be doing in the morning."

"And what will that be?"

"I'll be laying the groundwork for an important Wendy Talbot piece in our Sunday Magazine," he said.

"You and Wendy working together, I still think it must be a joke."

Bancroft turned from the busy work he had been doing at his dresser just as Maude's smile tightened into a patronizing smirk. He decided to embellish his story with an outright lie.

"Herb has given me free reign. I'll be shaping what goes into Wendy's article. I've chosen the bureau to be featured and handpicked the perfect paperboy to be profiled, right down to his family, who they are, and what they do. We'll be telling our readers this kid is the heart and soul of the best paper in the state."

"Gosh, oh golly that was a mouth full," Maude said, at the same time freshening her martini from the crystal beaker on her vanity. "Where does the circulation war fit in, you know, that brass knuckle fight you'll be in?"

"Wendy and I, with input from Herb, of course, will be telling the world how unthinkable it is to compare Goldman's slimy fishwrapper to the *Clarion*."

"My oh my," Maude said, "and what exactly will you be doing tomorrow morning?"

"I'll be at The Breakers, sort of a fly on the wall, following our paperboy as he makes his rounds, taking notes and picking out the best places for Wendy's photographer to get shots. That all comes later in the week after I've had a chance to brief everyone."

"This handpicked kid of yours, does he have a name?"

"I've got it written down somewhere. I'll have it when I get to The Breakers, bright and early. I expect to meet up with him about eight-thirty or so."

Chapter

55

Early Saturday afternoon, Frank Marsucci was a deeply troubled man. Lurid front page stories in both papers described in great detail how Vinnie Scarlatti's body was pulled from the Passaic with two bullet holes in the back of his skull.

Joe Lucio's piece in the *Clarion* was headlined: *Boiardo Soldier Murdered*, and speculated that a mobster turf war was about to erupt. Jerry Saunders' account in the *Beacon*, headlined: *Brutal Mob Killing*, left little doubt that Scarlatti's body wouldn't be the last pulled from the Passaic.

So where did this leave him. The more he thought about it, the worse things looked. They've already taken over his office, and he smelled big trouble with the two kids the bookies stuck him with.

He was doing some heavy thinking as he stood at the door of his office, and watched the last of his paperboys collect the freebie inserts for tomorrow. The circulation war would be up and running, a pain in the ass that he had to deal with if he wanted a piece of the numbers action. But the black bookies made it loud and clear a week earlier where he stood.

"Frankie, right now the numbers don't concern you," God's Tall Timber said. "But that could change. Just make sure nothing happens to Joey and Richie. You okay with this?"

"Do I have a fucking choice? You've got me by the balls and you know it."

"Crude, but to the point," Tall Timber said.

"Accentuate the positive," Darn Good Disciple chimed in, "just like our Prophet's been saying all along."

"Don't hand me any of that positive bullshit, just give me the skinny." Marscucci decided it was a good time to clear the air. "You'll be pushing either the Bancik or Maxwell kid onto Longy's turf next Sunday. Ever think of letting me in on it?"

"Take a seat and listen." Tall Timber pointed to the middle barber chair, and waited until Marsucci was seated. "Listen and don't forget."

Darn Good and Reckoning took the other two seats as Tall Timber locked the front door, then positioned himself in front of Marsucci.

"Letting you in on it, is that what you're asking? Time you got it straight, we decide when you're in and when you're out."

"I'm in up to my god damn ears right now. I got two kids working for me, but taking orders from you. You got plans for one of them next Sunday, and I don't even know which one. It don't sit right."

"We're gonna change that." Tall Timber leaned forward, his face less than a foot from Marsucci's. "Next Sunday Joey unloads all his freebies at The Breakers. You make god damn sure he gets in and out okay."

"That means nobody, but nobody, messes with little Joey," Reckoning said as he left his chair to join Tall Timber. "Not a fuckin' hair on his head. That sit right with you?"

"Good as done." Marsucci studied the two black faces hoping to detect an encouraging sign, but got none.

Tall Timber walked to the front of the shop, unlocked and opened the door. "You've had your say, now git."

When Marsucci got behind the wheel of his Plymouth, his hands were shaking. After three misses, he finally inserted the ignition key and turned it over. As he slowly pulled away from the curb, his fear gave way to calculated rage. The three coons underrated him when they sent him packing. They were crazy if they thought he was just another punk always ready to kiss the man's ass. If it didn't work out with them, Longy's wise guys were always looking for street-smart operators. So what if he had fucked up a couple of times, he could show them that he was a new and wiser Frankie Marsucci.

His hatred for the niggers had increased during the past week. His carriers paid the price when they brought in their Saturday collections.

He cut them short when they haggled over the bill, and bellyached about the freebies.

Richie and Joey were among the first carriers to drop off their *Beacon* collections that morning. They ran into each other at the barbershop after handing over their slips and bets. Richie was the only one to have a winner on Friday, his first since becoming a runner. After ten years, it was only the second payoff for Molly Bloom, one of the players Richie had at the Crayton Arms.

"Thelma already got the cash to her," Tall Timber said. "And who knows, there might be a big tip in it for you."

"Just add it to the stash you're holding for me," Richie said as he headed to the side door to join Joey in the alley.

"Notice anything different?" Richie said after they had pushed their bikes out to the sidewalk.

"Sure did. Darn Good Disciple wasn't there. Fact is, I ain't seen him for three, maybe four days now," Joey said. "How about you?"

"The same. I wonder what the hell happened to him."

"Can't waste time thinking about Darn Good," Joey said, "I got a big day tomorrow. Let's head out."

They pedaled in tandem, weaving their way through the solidly black areas of the Third Ward until they reached Milt's.

"Bet you're nervous," Richie said as they slid into the back booth. "I know I'd be with Sweeney and the other *Clarion* punks just waiting to take a bite out of me."

"Yeah, I am. But I'm getting a break with my freebies. They want me to dump them all at The Breakers."

"Your folks have any idea what you're doing? My mom and dad, especially my dad, have really been pumping me. I've been upfront about the *Beacon*, but no way in hell I'm gonna come clean about the numbers."

"Same here, but with me it's my mom, not my dad. She's happy as hell about the money, even jots down numbers to make sure Marsucci's not cheating me."

"Sooner or later they'll be tipped off," Richie said. "Weird it ain't happened yet."

"It's getting close," Joey said. "Father Nolan's been poking around at Milt's. He put the squeeze on Billy and Marvin the other day. Came away with nothin'. And if he knows it, you can bet that Father Schneider and that old cop Gazzi know it, too."

"Heard the same thing, that Nolan don't want us ending up in juvie. My guess is it won't be long before he'll be banging on our kitchen doors."

"And what a fucking mess that will be," Joey said. "My old man sucked it up when I got the route, putting money on the table when he doesn't even have a job. Now he's used to it, even helps me load my Sunday papers."

"Have a chance yet to scope out The Breakers?" Richie said. "If not, you better. You know they'll be watching, maybe try to rough you up."

"Been there the other day. It's got a service elevator so I won't have to fart around with any stairs, get in and out real fast."

"Here's to a fart-free morning." They hoisted their glasses, finished off their sodas and headed toward the door just as Gazzi walked in and took a stool at the counter.

"You kids sure are busy," Gazzi said as he swiveled around in a failed attempt to make eye contact.

"And getting busier all the time," Richie said as he followed Joey out the door.

"That cop's a real loser," Joey said. "He knows what we're doing, but can't do a god damn thing about it."

"It's creepy the way he keeps nosing around," Richie said, "and gets nothing from nobody."

Gazzi watched them leave, then turned and reached for his coffee. *These little punks think I can't touch them. They're in for a big surprise.*

Chapter

56

Saturday morning, Kevin McClosky walked into the homicide bullpen and found Nick Cisco sitting at his desk absorbed in a handheld game of pinball baseball. He knew it wasn't wise to distract Nick as he twisted and tilted the toy in mostly futile attempts to get tiny lead balls into tiny holes.

"Damn, a third out, that's it for today," Nick said taking the toy and dropping it in the upper right drawer of his desk. He reached for the burning Chesterfield in his ashtray, flicked off an inch of ash, and finished it off with a deep drag.

Kevin knew that Nick only played the game when something was troubling him. He waited until his partner lit up another cigarette before pulling over his chair from his adjoining desk.

Nick swiveled around and said, "We've got something to talk about, then it's your call whether you're in or out."

"It's the weekend, and I was looking forward to nothing more serious than coffee, the sports page and comics. What's on your mind?"

"I've been thinking about those two kids at the barbershop yesterday. I'd like to know what they've gotten themselves into."

"Christ, Nick, I thought we decided to leave that mess with Dino's Vice squad. We've already roped in the black bookies as our canaries, and scared them shitless. We're homicide dicks, not priests."

"Want to hear more, or not?" Nick said.

"I'm getting a cup of Joe, how 'bout you?" Kevin said as he got up, retrieved a mug from his desk and reached for Nick's. He returned with the coffee, and planted himself just as Gabby Valentine and Zig Polski, who had just ended their graveyard shift, emerged from the homicide bunk room.

"It's all yours," Valentine said. "Got a couple new ones working, a stabbing in the Tenderloin, and a crazy one in the Third Ward."

"What's that one all about?" Nick said.

"Two broads throwing punches over the big stud who serviced them. Got into it on a tenement stoop on Monmouth. One bimbo was pounding the hell out of the other when she missed with a haymaker, lost her balance and fractured her skull on the sidewalk. Dead when we got there."

"Where'd you get all this?" Kevin said.

"From witnesses," Valentine said as he and Polski turned to leave. "It's all in our report. Have fun."

"We can't seem to shake the Third Ward," Kevin said.

"I had in mind getting back there today," Nick said.

"Why? Unless you've come up with something new I don't know about, I can't see any reason."

"Nothing new, just a hunch...a gut feeling about how those two kids are being used by the bookies."

"Used, how do you figure? Young punks running numbers for the mob goes back a long way. What your gut needs is a Pepto-Bismol."

"Okay, smart-ass, do you want to come along or don't you?"

"And do what? We've got a full plate already. The Scarlatti murder has been a big headline-grab for the DA, and the two papers have jumped on board. Here, take a look." Kevin swiveled back to his desk, grabbed that morning's *Beacon*, and tossed it over to Nick. "And we thought yesterday's headlines were bullshit."

Which Mobster Gets It Next. Jerry Saunders' piece recounted past gangland killings in Newark, tracing them back to the Black Hand murders at the turn of the century. He concluded with: "Newark is a city held hostage by the Underworld."

"And you're worried about two young punks running numbers. Okay, partner, I'll come along, but let's get a grip."

"I want to hear what our canaries have to say. We'll start at the Zanzibar with our old friend Roundy Suggs."

When they entered the lounge, Suggs was pouring shots for two barflies, and a working lady was bargaining with her latest trick in a booth. He spotted them as soon as they came in, wiped down the bar, dried his hands, and walked over with the wide phony smile he reserved for cops.

"Lieutenant Cisco. Sergeant McClosky. Good to see you," Suggs said. "How can I help you? Maybe it be best we talk outside."

"You can cut the charm and the bullshit," Cisco said. "We hear that Richie the Boot is moving into the Ward, and that he's using *Beacon* newsboys as runners to test the waters. So Roundy, fill us in."

"It's real serious, as serious as it gets when one of the Boot's soldiers is fished out of the river."

"Tell us about Vinnie Scarlatti," McClosky said.

"Word is he was the mob's policy boss here in the Ward, and that the three bookies on Spruce were his stooges."

"Scarlatti's history, so who's moved in?" Cisco said.

"A real nasty son of a bitch. It's not for sure, but word on the street is that Carlo Salerno has already taken over."

"Carlo the Butcher?" McClosky said. "You trust your sources?"

"Nobody plays games with ol' Roundy. Yeah, I trust 'em, or it be their asses. I got to get back."

The two detectives returned to their cruiser, and were settling in when Cisco said, "With a cutthroat like the Butcher calling the shots, it's obvious the Boot is sending a message. Let's head over to Spruce and hear what our barbers have to say."

The policy parlor was in high gear when they arrived. Traffic in and out of the side and back doors was steady, and Righteous Reckoning was busy taking bets over the two phones anchored under the rear mirror. Amid all the criminal activity, Tall Timber was trimming an elderly man's hair in what was once Darn Good's chair.

"We'll wait," Cisco said as he and McClosky took seats to either side of the front door. "We want to hear what both of you have to say, so turn off the phones. Your runners know the drill."

The detectives waited until the shop was quiet before McClosky bore in.

"When were you going to tell us about your new boss?"

The bookies exchanged worried glances hoping that the other would be the first to spit it all out.

"Only got the word yesterday, and in person from the man himself," Tall Timber said. "He was trouble as soon as he walked in."

Cisco, with a nod from McClosky, decided to play it dumb. Gazzi had been filling them in by phone every day, and Suggs had just filled in the rest.

"We're waiting," he said, then turned to Righteous Reckoning, . "Maybe you should take over. Spill it, don't leave anything out."

"We got no warning at all. A red Dodge pulls up at the curb and a short, ugly guy gets out," Righteous said. "He comes in and sashays over to the chair like he owns the place. He looks us over and we see nothing but hate, whitey looking down at us niggers."

"Did whitey have a name?" McClosky snapped. "How'd he introduce himself, a business card or what?"

"A name we never heard before, Carlo Salerno," Tall Timber said. "He had this mean little smile, you know the kind that don't show any teeth. He said, 'we're gonna get close, real close.'"

In less than five minutes, the two bookies described how Salerno laid out the new rules. That Richie the Boot had decided to take the gloves off, and with the murder of Vinnie Scarlatti, their gravy train ride was history.

"You remember exactly what he said? Get as close as you can." Cisco said.

"He knew everything. How our runners got roughed up real bad, and we did nothin'. He said that ain't gonna happen again, and how we could bet our 'black asses' on that. Warned us we ain't going nowhere, and we better get ready for what's comin' down."

"Does that mean you're dumping the kids and bringing back your walking wounded?" Cisco said.

"No word about that yesterday," Righteous said. "We let Salerno know that Richie and Joey are already doing good work for us."

"They're just what Richie the Boot asked for," Tall Timber said. "He wanted smart kids tough enough to take the first bites out of Zwillman, and he got them."

"We don't want those two kids hurt," Cisco said. "Anything happens to them, and Salerno will be the least of your problems."

"Not to worry, Joey and Richie are like family," Righteous said as the detectives walked out and closed the door behind them.

Kevin made no attempt to hide his anger inside the shop, and once on the street, his anxiety over how Nick was handling the situation got the better of him. He waited until they were about to drive off when he turned to Nick and said, "So what's your plan? And I've got to tell you Nick, that if we leave it like this, it just isn't right."

"Like I said, it's up to you to decide if you're in or out. I'll be at The Breakers tomorrow morning. You can come along or not."

"The Breakers?"

"Gazzi's tips have been on target all week, and he's convinced that's where Boiardo is going to make his first move. It will either be the Bancik or Maxwell kid dumping free *Beacons* to test the waters."

"And you'll do what, help the kid with his papers? Jesus Christ, Nick, you might just as well be picking up policy slips for Boiardo."

"I want to make sure the kid gets out in one piece. I doubt there'll be trouble, but who knows when a policy turf war is folded in."

"Two homicide dicks playing nursemaid for a snot-nosed kid who's breaking the law," Kevin said. "That's aiding and abetting anyway you look at it. If there's a fuck-up, it's our asses, you know that don't you?"

"You in or out?"

"What time?"

"We'll open shop at headquarters at six, check-in with Valentine and Polski, and give it a couple hours before we head out. I think nine o'clock at The Breakers will do it. Gotta feeling we'll find Gazzi lurking around."

"Wouldn't surprise me."

Chapter

57

By eight o'clock Sunday morning, a state-wide circulation war between the *Beacon* and *Clarion* was well underway. Hidden behind the mastheads of the state's two largest newspapers was a numbers racket that had been flourishing for years. Outsiders would be shocked to learn that it was teenage carrier boys, not mob soldiers, on the battle lines.

An hour earlier, Bancroft finished his second cup of coffee, and was about to push away from the table when his wife Maude put aside the *Clarion's* Sunday Magazine and said mockingly, "Wendy is one hell of a writer, and just think, this week you'll be her Mr. Know-It-All."

"Christsakes, Maude, knock it off. If it works out, I give her all she needs for her article, it could get me back on the City Desk, or maybe even the editorial page."

"You've been down that road before. Have you suddenly learned how to write?"

"Lay off, just lay off will you. This isn't the morning for any of your sarcastic crap."

"What makes it different?" Maude drained her cup and reached for the coffee carafe. "Clue me in, I'm all ears."

"I'll be tracking one of my best news boys, putting together suggestions for Wendy's piece."

"One of your best news boys, that's a laugh. When did you adopt him? Last night you couldn't even remember his name."

"Jackie Cashman. Had to check my notes this morning just to be sure."

"That's my Hensley." Maude put down her cup and tugged at her husband's sleeve as he moved from the table. "Don't go away mad. Come here and pucker up."

As he slid behind the wheel of his wife's Packard, Bancroft was acutely aware of how henpecked he had become. He had long realized that his feeble attempts to save face only fueled Maude's trenchant ability to put the blade in, then pull it out with a smile and a kiss.

Today his wife's toxic wit was trumped by his belief that in the next hour or two he would resurrect his career at the *Clarion*. Everything was in place. The Cashman kid would be waiting for him at The Breakers. He would merely connect the dots, then sit back and wait for Wendy Talbot's article to hit the streets.

Just to be sure, Bancroft decided it would be wise to touch base with Jim McDuffie before heading over to The Breakers. He turned onto Avon Avenue just as McDuffie buttoned his jacket to hide a strapped pouch containing the slips and bets collected by his three runners that morning. In less than an hour it would be dropped at Sy Howard's policy bank.

McDuffie locked up and was about to get into his Chevy when he spotted the big Packard a half-block away. It was the third time since their meeting on Friday that Bancroft had come snooping around without warning and it pissed him off. *What does this useless son of a bitch want now? Why doesn't he just park his ass downtown where he belongs.*

"Up bright and early, Mr. Bancroft," McDuffie said, greeting his boss on the sidewalk outside his office. "Guess you want an early start if you're gonna make me and Jackie Cashman famous."

"Just stopped by to see if everything's in place," Bancroft said. "That Jackie will be finishing up his route at The Breakers, in what, another fifteen minutes or so?"

"Yeah, and you'll be his shadow, just following him around and taking notes for Wendy's piece. Don't forget, I'll be here every day if she needs real inside stuff."

"It's up to her. Just hang loose."

The two men returned to their cars. Bancroft got behind the wheel, then checked his notes to verify The Breakers' address before driving off into alien territory. McDuffie made a u-turn to begin his daily twelve-block drive to the policy bank.

It was the first time ever that Jackie Cashman had reversed his delivery routine.

"You're late, Jackie, it's not like you," Ira Gerber scolded from the front door of his frame house. "Forty-five minutes late, and on a Sunday morning. Can you explain?"

"Sorry, Mr. Gerber, my bike had a flat." Jackie was satisfied that his boldfaced lie had pacified one of his best tippers. He wondered how many more lies he would have to tell before he finished his beat. The ten dollars from Sweeney made everything a lot easier.

He didn't want to know what Sweeney had in mind for The Breakers, but it was a sure bet somebody was in for it. Should he really care, it wasn't his ass on the line, and he was damn glad of that. The job that Sweeney and his two thug buddies had done on those five nigger runners showed everybody they weren't to be fucked with. He rearranged his route so there would be plenty of space between him and The Breakers when Sweeney swung into action.

Starting at five-thirty that morning, a pissed off Frank Marsucci had been driving Joey Bancik to The Breakers. The nigger barbers had made it clear that he should stick to Joey like glue. Two days earlier they had clued him in that Carlo Salerno was his new boss, and he had been stewing in his juices ever since. The brains at Vittorio's Castle had decided that a new soldier was needed to toughen up their Third Ward operations.

Tall Timber had called him at his office, and made it short and sweet. Carlo Salerno was now calling the shots.

"Did you say Carlo Salerno? Jesus Christ, not the Butcher. Is that what you're telling me? Jesus Christ."

"We talking about the same guy?" a confused Tall Timber said.

"It's the same guy, and they don't call him 'the Butcher' for nothin.'"

Marsucci couldn't get that phone call out of his mind as he reluctantly helped Joey complete his Sunday deliveries in record time. He'd dump the kid and his *Beacon* freebies at The Breakers, and then get lost, as far from the Third Ward as possible so he could sort things out. Here he was, the chauffeur for a punk kid who already had more juice with the black bookies than him.

"Here's where I drop you," Marsucci said as he turned onto the driveway that emptied into a large parking area centered between The Breakers and two rows of tenant garages.

"You can drop me at the basement door," Joey said. "Could use some help lugging the freebies over there."

"What the hell you talking about?" a rankled Marsucci spat out. It was obvious to him that this little shit was rubbing it in.

"Okay, okay, don't bust a gut. I'll lug them over."

Marsucci pulled his Plymouth to a stop an arm's-length from the basement door, got out and pulled two bundles of the *Beacon* from the trunk.

"They're all yours kid. You got the list, now get going," he said as he slid behind the wheel of his car, and made a tight u-turn to escape.

Joey made sure Marsucci had hauled ass, then pulled a folded paper from his shirt pocket. It was a list of twenty non-subscribers targeted by Marsucci. Joey guessed that the lazy son of a bitch had pulled the names off the mail boxes out front. He never noticed the dark figure lurking in the shadows of an open garage at the far end of the lot.

The vantage point provided everything Al Sweeney needed, a clear view of the comings and goings at the loading dock, and if anything went wrong, an easy way to disappear behind the garages. He pulled over a wooden box, took a seat and decided to wait until the time was right for him to make his move.

The morning had been a busy one for Sweeney. He hated Sunday, the only day the *Clarion* was delivered early enough for its readers to enjoy over breakfast. He'd started a half-hour earlier than usual making sure McDuffie had his slips and bets by seven. His mom and dad were still in bed when he returned to the family tenement, and he was careful not to wake them. He closed his bedroom door behind him, and went directly to his sock and underwear drawer. He removed the Beretta and a black leather Lone Ranger holster that he had retrieved from a box of long discarded toys stashed away in the closet.

He unbuckled his belt, threaded it through the holster's loop and secured it on his right hip. He picked up the Beretta, and made sure it had a chambered cartridge with a full clip of eight. As he carefully slid the weapon into the holster, he realized that his days of playing the Deadly Desperado game were over. He pulled down his loose fitting sweatshirt as far as it would go to make sure it covered the holster, and headed out the door.

Chapter

58

Father Nolan's sermon that Sunday dealt with concupiscence. He had been toying with the subject ever since he bumped into the two young hookers outside Milt's last summer. "The need to put aside sinful yearnings is with us every minute of every day and you must be vigilant," he told the predictable two dozen or so faithful who attended the early Sunday mass. Among them was Catherine Bancik, always alone and always with a nickel for a votive candle after mass at the statue of St. Francis of Assisi, the patron saint of the poor.

He took his place at the pulpit and explored Matthew 26:11 for his sermon. *For you always have the poor with you; but you do not always have Me.* He had never met Catherine Bancik, but he had no doubt that the woman fingering her beads in the sixth pew, left-center aisle was Joey's mother. Her olive skin, dark scarf and black dress fit the stereotype he had so easily accepted since arriving at St. Mark's. At that moment he decided to ignore Jim's advice that he not poke his nose where it wasn't wanted.

After mass he sped through the ritualistic removal of his vestments, then hurried from the sacristy to intercept Mrs. Bancik before she left the church and headed home. There was no need for haste. She was still fingering her rosary and mumbling at the foot of St. Francis when he sent the last of the other parishioners on their way with a solemn, "May the Lord be with you."

"Mrs. Bancik?" He smiled noting that she averted her eyes while dipping her fingers into the holy water font only a foot from where he stood. "I'm Father Nolan. I thought this would be a good time for us to know each other."

To know each other? What does he mean to know each other? Catherine was puzzled. Never before had a man of authority cared enough to say such a thing to her. *And here I am turning away from him like he isn't here. What will he think and what will he think of my Joey with a mother who turns away from a priest.*

Father Nolan silently watched the strange woman as she descended the first two steps, then hesitated to collect her thoughts, and turned around to face him. She removed the scarf from her head and let it drape over her shoulders. He was stunned by her dark luminescent eyes that captured and held his gaze. He realized he didn't know this suspicious mother, probably never would, but he had committed himself and had to make the best of it.

"What is it you want, Father Nolan? Has my Joey done something?"

"Yes, it is about Joey, something I must talk to you about," the priest said. "Do you have some time to talk, perhaps we can go back inside. Late mass won't begin for another half hour."

Catherine was careful to replace her scarf as Father Nolan ushered her into the church then took a seat beside her in the back pew. She knew it would be uppity for her to speak first, so she would wait to see what this priest had to say.

"I was glad to hear the good news about Joey," the priest said, and uncertain what to say next decided to take it slow and easy. "Your son's *Beacon* paper route had to make you very happy."

"You know about Joey's new job?" she was astonished that with so much church work for him to do he would bother with such a small matter.

"It seems everybody does," the priest said, "and then there's the bike that came with the job. It must make things a lot easier for him."

"So you know about the bike, too," she was now convinced the priest's smile was hiding the real reason for their meeting. "But I don't understand the 'things' you talk about. My Joey delivers papers, that's all, and it helps put food on the table."

"But that's not all, Mrs. Bancik, and that's what we have to talk about."

"I see now what you mean. It's the bike, Father, and I say not to worry about the bike. Joey gives that junk dealer Simon money every week to pay for it. If that's all, I must go." She arose, uncertain of her next move.

Seated where he was, Father Nolan blocked her exit from the short end of the pew. To make her escape she would have to stumble along the padded kneelers to the far end. She hesitated to see if the priest would allow her to pass.

"Please sit down, Mrs. Bancik, this is important," the priest said. "Your son Joey does more than just deliver newspapers. Do you know what the numbers racket is?"

"Everybody knows about the numbers. Joey does nothing with the numbers, he delivers papers."

"His *Beacon* route is only part of his job. He also picks up slips and bets and drops them off at a bookie parlor on Spruce Street." The priest waited until his words sunk in, "Your son's a numbers runner."

"That's not so, he's a good boy. Who told you bad things like this about my Joey?"

"It's been out on the street. Everyone knows except you and perhaps Mr. Bancik. Do you know what juvenile court is? If Joey gets caught, that's where he'll go. Then if the judge decides to make a lesson of your son, it could be reform school. Is this what you want for Joey?"

"You are wrong Father. I know nothing about your court." Catherine pushed herself up and peered down at the seated priest, "What is reform school? Joey goes to your school, to St. Mark's and he is a good student. He needs no reform school."

Father Nolan got up, stepped into the aisle and extended his hand to help Joey's clearly distraught mother leave the pew. She pulled her hand away, turned toward the sanctuary, genuflected and crossed herself. The dignity with which she performed the simplistic ritual washed away any words of wisdom he might have had. He stepped aside and watched as she paused at the holy water font, blessed herself and left the church.

It was time for the Lucky Strike he had been craving since the end of mass. He headed back to the sacristy convinced that for Mrs. Bancik he was a busybody who only wanted to scare her. He had no intention of going through the same thing with Richie Maxwell's mother. His last resort would be a face-to-face meeting with Richie and Joey in Sister Mary Margaret's office in the next couple of days.

Chapter

59

Who in hell did McDuffie think he was talking to, an irritated Bancroft thought as he pulled the Packard away from the curb in front of the *Clarion* office. *The son of a bitch had the gall to put me, his boss, on warning that if Wendy wanted 'real inside stuff' he was the man she should talk to. The arrogant bastard would be looking for another job if I had my way, but I don't.*

Bancroft watched McDuffie's Chevy disappear from his rearview mirror as he turned toward High Street and checked the time. It was ten minutes after eight. He traced his route on the Rand McNally, and saw that the Breakers was close enough for him to get a quick cup of coffee at the Riviera, and still get there by eight-thirty. He found a parking space, picked up the *Clarion* at the lobby newsstand, then took a stool in the coffee shop.

A woman of about forty seemed surprised, maybe even annoyed, when he sat down and opened the *Sunday Magazine*. Wendy's article was a beaut. It profiled George Richards, the gruff, no bullshit pressroom boss he first met during the strategy meeting in the paper's conference room.

Under her byline, he found what he was looking for, a credit that read: *The George Richards story as he remembers it.* He would make damn sure that there would be no Jim McDuffie in Wendy's story, and that the "real inside stuff" would be supplied by Hensley Parker Bancroft.

He finished his coffee, dropped a quarter on the counter, and with the folded *Clarion* under his arm walked out to his car. He checked his watch and saw that it was only eight-twenty, giving him plenty of time to get to The Breakers on schedule. He'd be as discrete as possible, but how inconspicuous could he be if he pulled up to The Breakers in a Packard roadster. It was time for an executive decision, and Bancroft decided to scope the neighborhood for a suitable parking space. He found it down the block and around the corner, safely out of sight. Bancroft saw that it wasn't a great neighborhood and there would be hell to pay with Maude if the roadster was returned with even a small scratch. Couldn't worry about it now, it was time to run down Jackie Cashman.

Jackie was at the opposite end of his route, and after dropping off his last four papers he'd be done for the day. He had busted his ass earning that sawbuck from Sweeney, but a bargain is a bargain and he was finished at The Breakers by eight. He'd skirt around the apartment to stay out of Sweeney's way. He wanted no part of what that mean son of a bitch was planning.

Frank Gazzi had no such inclination. He had worked hard to be Johnny-on-the-spot for the two homicide detectives, and today he was looking for his payoff. He had traded his shift with another beat cop at the Precinct who was more than glad to unload his Sunday. He had cozied up to that scumbag Marsucci to get what he wanted, the time, the place and the kid Richie the Boot would use to make his first move.

As usual, Gazzi had all the information he needed but was clueless what to do with it. The Breakers was at the very end of his walking beat in a low crime area hardly worth patrolling. Street cops in uniform were a rarity so he had been very careful sizing up the layout. He decided it would be best to circle around the garages and find a spot where he could eyeball the loading dock and service entrance.

Then what? He could throw away his career if he fucked this one up. Hopefully Cisco and McClosky would be around and the decision would be theirs. Tony Gordo had twice saved his ass after he screwed up with the two whores, and he had been warned that the numbers racket was off limits. Today he was slapping his friend in the face, and there would be no third chance. He still didn't know why two homicides were involved, and he didn't care. All he wanted was to get the hell out of the Third Ward and back into a squad car. If it took a snot-nose kid to punch his ticket, so be it.

Gazzi found a made-to-order vantage spot behind a large clump of untended shrubbery at the south end of the garages. He settled in too late to spot Joey lugging the second bundle of papers into the apartment and closing the service door to the basement behind him.

Joey was glad he had cased the building last week. This was his second time around and he was just as awestruck as before. If the two elevators weren't enough, one for the swells who lived there and the other for deliveries, there was the thick carpeting in the lobby and halls, and potted flowers on each of the eight landings. Joey wanted to get his ass in and out real quick. He was breathing hard as he pushed the number eight button and began the slow ride to the top. *Bejesus H. Christ,* he thought, *what if Al Sweeney and the other punks from St. Mike's are waiting when I get out?*

He studied Marsucci's list and fingered the small block of wood in his pants pocket. He waited for the service elevator to stop, then stepped into the rarified air of The Breakers' eighth floor. *So far, so good, nobody here. Maybe I'm worrying for nothin'.*

He propped open the elevator door with the block of wood then swiftly walked to number 806, then 804 and 803. There were *Clarions* in front of three other doors, so he relaxed even more knowing that McDuffie's thug had come and gone.

Downstairs Bancroft was surprised that there was no security intercom to screen visitors. He entered the lobby just as a middle-age couple dressed in their Sunday-finest emerged from the elevator, nodded in his direction, and walked out to the street. He checked the layout and saw that a service elevator was tucked away at the end of a hall leading off the lobby. The needle on the elevator's floor indicator had stopped at five. Across from the hall a metal door opened to a stairwell to the basement and the floors above.

The Cashman kid is hard at it, he thought. *Already down to the fifth floor. No sense following him from floor-to-floor, let's give him until the third then take the stairs to meet up with him on the second. That should give me enough notes for Wendy.*

It didn't bother Bancroft to ignore Herb's marching orders to be a fly-on-the-wall recording every move the kid made. *Hell, if you've seen one floor, you've seen them all.* When the needle dropped to three he climbed the stairs to the second floor and waited for Jackie near the service elevator. A quick look up and down the hall told him something was wrong. Three copies of the *Clarion* had already been delivered, but how was that possible with Jackie only down to the third floor? He crossed the hall, sat down in an upholstered chair next to a spider plant and waited.

He had barely taken a seat when the service elevator opened and a kid he didn't recognize walked out with three copies of the *Beacon* under his arm. Bancroft saw that things were not only wrong, but terribly wrong. He realized for the first time he was smack-dab in the middle of a circulation war.

"Who the hell are you?" Bancroft blurted as he got up and approached the kid. "And where the hell is Jackie Cashman?"

"Who the hell are you, mister?" Joey said pushing past Bancroft. "Got work to do and I don't know no Jackie Cashman."

Bancroft was at a loss. He had never imagined that the circulation war would involve hand-to-hand combat. He watched this cocky little son of a bitch make a big show out of checking a list before dropping off his papers. The kid's shitty little grin was telling him 'here they are, mister, and what are you going to do about it.' And where the hell was Jackie Cashman? He was supposed to meet him here, but was nowhere in sight.

Joey knew he was right on target when he figured this klutz wanted no part of what was going on. His fancy duds and the way he spoke said it all. *I'll be god damned if he doesn't know what to do next,* Joey thought. *Might as well push it and see what happens.*

"Taking the elevator down. Wanna ride along?" Joey tossed over his shoulder as he bent down and picked up his wooden door jamb. He turned and saw the guy, whoever he was, disappear into the stairwell, probably on his way to meet up with him in the basement.

Outside Sweeney was getting restless. He figured it was time to get moving. It was at least fifteen minutes since that punk from St. Mark's had hauled two bundles of *Beacons* into The Breakers' basement. Judging from the size of the bundles the kid would be dropping off between twenty to thirty freebies and that should take no more than twenty minutes.

He fingered the bruise on his neck, an unwanted reminder of the beating McDuffie had given him the day before. He considered it a good sign that his eyes had not puffed up. It would be hard for him to scare the shit out of anyone if he had two black eyes. He lifted his sweatshirt and removed the Beretta from its Lone Ranger holster. He hefted the pistol from hand-to-hand like a plaything rather than the deadly weapon it was. He still failed to notice that he had inadvertently pushed the safety bar off.

He hadn't decided yet whether to first slap the kid around before waving the pistol in his face. Or he could come directly to the point, poke the gun at the kid to show he meant business, then kick him in the ass and send him on his way. *Yeah, that would send a message loud and clear,* he thought. *No need to kick the shit out of the little punk, not like the five coons that needed a good working over. God damn it felt good when I nearly busted that nigger's arm. Should have. Damn if they didn't all turn yellow, and now they got this kid doing what they're shit-scared of doing themselves.*

This was a delicious memory and Sweeney basked in its afterglow as he stepped onto the loading dock with an anticipatory smile. He was about to have some fun. He did not see the blue-clad figure step from the shrubbery at the south end of the garages.

From his partially concealed vantage, Gazzi watched Sweeney stride quickly across the parking lot and pause at the loading dock. He knew he had seen this big, muscular teen before, but couldn't place exactly when or where. His cop instinct kicked-in leaving little doubt he was watching a bully up to no good. *That's fine and dandy,* he thought, *but nothing's happened yet so there's not a god damn thing I can do, or is there?*

Gazzi took only a few steps, stopped and stared, not quite believing what he saw. The punk had lifted his sweatshirt and pulled what appeared to be a pistol from a holster on his hip. *What the fuck am I looking at, am I seeing right? Does that punk have a gun? Is it real? A toy? Just something to scare the shit out of the Bancik kid?*

Gazzi waited until the teen disappeared through The Breakers' service entrance and close the massive door behind him before starting out in cautious pursuit. The weight of his Smith & Wesson as it bounced on his hip supplied the courage he needed. He reached down and unsnapped the leather safety flap that freed the revolver's hammer. Gazzi was now ready for action.

He stopped at the service door, waited and listened. Nothing, not a sound. Any pretext would do, just something to justify rushing in with gun drawn, a cop taking control. This was scary territory for a lowly patrolman making a last ditch effort to save a career that had been in the toilet for years. *Cisco and McClosky are gonna be here any time now,* he thought, *and they're gonna see me at my best. You can bet your sweet ass on that.*

Gazzi had no idea what was happening inside. Suddenly he was sweating. It dawned that the only time he had fired his revolver was to qualify at the police pistol range. He cracked the service door enough to hear three loud voices echoing through the basement. One belonged to Joey Bancik, the others he didn't recognize.

Chapter

60

Bancroft was clearly out of sorts as he headed down the stairs to The Breakers' basement. He stopped at the first floor landing to collect his thoughts, but came up empty. The irony didn't escape him. Here he was the *Clarion's* Vice President for Circulation, the big boss himself, on-site to watchdog the opening salvo of a circulation war, and he might as well be invisible. He arose from where he had been sitting on the stairway, brushed the seat of his pants, and started across the landing. Profane shouts from the basement pulled him up short, but only for an instant. He sped down the final flight of stairs and was about to swing open the door, when something in his gut took over. He slowly opened the door, watched and listened to what was happening no more than twenty feet away.

The *Beacon* kid from upstairs, obviously terrified, was backed against the wall next to the service elevator. He was partially obscured by a looming antagonist who leaned over him with his left hand on the wall and the other obviously jabbing him in the chest.

"You miserable little cock-sucker, what the fuck you think you're playing at!" the hulking figure shouted as the *Beacon* kid tried to push himself away only to be slammed back, his head bouncing off the cinderblock wall.

"Jesus Christ, Sweeney, enough's enough, I get it! You don't need no gun."

"Just letting you know we're not fucking around." Sweeney lifted his Beretta and tucked the muzzle under Joey's chin. "You know what the niggers got. This time will be worse."

Sweeney wanted Joey to cower, bawl, maybe piss his pants, but he wasn't getting it. This little bastard wasn't even looking at him, instead he stared wide-eyed at what he saw coming up behind him. He turned with his gun hand poised to be confronted by Hensley Parker Bancroft.

This was all new to Bancroft, real danger, or was it. He stopped in his tracks, his eyes fixated on the Beretta. *Was it real or a toy?* he thought. He cautiously closed the gap between them to ten feet. *Holy shit, it's real.*

Sweeney hadn't moved. He widened his stance as if to brace himself should Bancroft decide to rush him.

"Hold it right there, Mr. Bancroft, we ain't playing games."

Bancroft could see that although the gunman was big, he was no more than a nervous teenager.

"If you know me, then you know I'm not playing," Bancroft said. "Relax, take a deep breath, and hand me the gun, then we can forget this ever happened."

For Joey, it was all happening so fast he couldn't keep track. He didn't budge an inch as he watched Sweeney and the guy face-off. They were frozen in place, each waiting for the other to make the first move. He knew for certain that a nasty son of a bitch like Sweeney wasn't about to hand over his gun.

Then it all fell into place for Joey when he spotted a big janitor's push broom off to the side of the elevator. But he had to be quick, as fast as he'd ever been. They were still jabbering back and forth, but Joey wasn't listening, for him, their words were just noise.

Sweeney was still in a fighter's stance with his feet far enough apart for Joey to push the broom between them, then hook it over one foot and yank. He grabbed the broom, crouched behind Sweeney, and swung into action. He needed every ounce of strength to pull Sweeney off balance so that Bancroft could grab the pistol. *It worked, god damn it worked!* he thought as Sweeney pitched forward.

The bully failed to regain his balance, and with the Beretta gripped in his right hand, he threw his arms out to break his fall. He tightened his grip on impact, his trigger finger squeezing hard, and the pistol exploded in Bancroft's face as he reached down to grab the gun. Bancroft's head snapped back as the bullet punctured his forehead just above his nose, and penetrated deep into the brain. He was dead before he hit the floor.

Joey was stunned. What had he done, what the fuck had he done? Without thinking, he jumped on Sweeney's back and grabbed for the gun.

Sweeney was just as dumbfounded. Now on his knees, he looked down at the blood spreading out from Bancroft's head. He stared at the gun in his hand, uncertain what to do next. First he had to get rid of this little son of a bitch on his back. He pried Joey loose just as the door to the loading dock opened, and a silhouetted figure, gun in hand, stepped through it.

While listening outside, Gazzi had hoped, even prayed, that he would never have to step inside the door, that the shouted obscenities coming from the basement would be the end of it. Cisco and McClosky would show up to see he was as good as his word, that he had kept things under control until they arrived. The gun shot changed everything.

Gazzi took a few steps and stopped to scan the basement. The big teen he had seen in the parking lot was on his knees, one hand with a gun pointed right at Gazzi, and the other arm had a thrashing Joey in a neck-lock. An animal instinct took control. Gazzi fired from the hip, and got off two wild shots. His intended target dropped his gun and released his hold on a suddenly limp Joey.

"You stupid son of a bitch, look what you've done," an enraged Sweeney screamed. "Call a doctor, you shot the kid."

Gazzi holstered his gun as he raced toward the bloody tableau he had helped create. He ignored the dead man, someone he didn't know, and bent over Joey, a likeable little punk despite all his profane, tough talk. The boy's shirt was drenched in blood flowing from a wound in his left chest. His breathing was wheezy, and Gazzi could barely find a pulse.

The shots had drawn an audience of about a dozen of The Breakers' tenants, three of the men still in pajamas, and two women in bathrobes. Most had inched over from the elevator and a few had used the stairs.

No longer feeling a pulse, Gazzi gently lowered Joey's left arm to the floor and looked up. The silent crowd had doubled and he was trapped in the wake of his latest fuck-up. He was strangling in a tightening circle of accusing faces. He returned his gaze to the carnage around him, and tried without success to piece everything together when Sweeney came to his rescue.

"Just don't stand there you mother-fuckers," a sobbing Sweeney spit the words out. "Got phones don't ya, go call, call damn it! Get somebody! The cops even."

As if on cue, Gazzi got off his knees and the crowd, already frightened by Sweeney's outburst, backed away. They bumped into a new batch of voyeurs that swelled the crowd to more than thirty.

"The police are already called," a woman's voice rose above the murmuring. "My Fred made sure of that, he's waiting out front for them."

For Gazzi, her words were a reprieve. A call to the precinct was no longer necessary. He now had time to manufacture a story that would hopefully save what remained of his career. One of his wild shots killed Joey Bancik, how the hell could he explain that? Had he blacked out? Was there a real threat from Sweeney? For sure, nobody pointed a gun at a cop and got away with it. That's the way it works isn't it? He pushed aside the discordant thoughts and confronted the crowd.

"Okay, folks, time to back-off," Gazzi said gesturing with outstretched arms. "Nothing more to see here. You can go back upstairs now. You'll hear all about it on the radio and read it in the papers."

Sweeney fought hard to restrain himself as he watched this useless cop swing into action. Forgotten was the man who laid at his feet in a pool of blood with a bullet in his head. That was an accident and not really his fault. This cop had gone crazy with his gun. Two wild shots, one killed the kid, where the hell did the second one go?

Gazzi watched the last of the crowd disappear then turned to survey the macabre scene. The Beretta was on the floor between the two bodies. Sweeney had dropped to his knees, no longer able to control his tears.

"I killed the boss," Sweeney said. "Didn't mean to, just happened. I tripped, just tripped and shit, I don't know, just don't know why the gun went off. The floor, that's it, the floor did it. Hit the floor and the gun went off. He wanted the gun, grabbed for it."

"Your boss? What in hell do you mean, your boss?" Gazzi's gaze shifted between the sobbing teen and the well-dressed body on the floor. It finally dawned where he had seen this kid before. He was one of the *Clarion* carriers who ran numbers for Jim McDuffie. But who was the dead man?

"Out with it, give me a name!"

"Name's Bancroft. That's all I know. McDuffie called him the big boss from downtown."

"You mean from the *Clarion* office?"

"Think so."

"Get up and turn around, put your hands behind you," Gazzi said as he snapped the cuffs on. "Now get your ass over in that corner and stay there."

Chapter

61

It was shortly before nine o'clock when Cisco and McClosky cruised past the *Beacon* circulation office on their way to The Breakers and saw no one in sight.

"If what we've been hearing is true, it's a hell of a way to start a circulation war," Kevin said. "They must be hiding someplace to ambush the *Clarion* kids."

"That's what has me worried," Nick said. "During my carrier days, there was always a bunch of us hanging out on Sunday morning to bitch with the boss."

"I still don't know why you've got a bug up your butt over those two kids. They know they're breaking the law, and probably don't much give a damn. What do you expect to find today?"

"No idea. Let's take a look at what's come down so far. They pulled Scarlatti from the river, and replaced him with Butcher Salerno. Boiardo's sending a message."

"Scarlatti is ours, but the numbers racket is vice. Let Finelli and his boys handle it. We're homicide."

"I can't really explain it," Cisco said. "It's just something about two altar boys involved in a mob turf war that's already ugly."

They turned the corner and were half a block from The Breakers just as a police cruiser, its cherry top flashing and siren wailing, screeched to a stop in front of the entrance. A shouting man rushed to the car, and pointed to the apartment driveway.

Cisco regretted that he had decided to turn off the police radio during their drive up the hill from headquarters. Now they were in the dark as they followed the cruiser down the driveway to the rear parking area. The two uniforms had already jumped from their car, and were pushing their way through onlookers blocking the large loading dock door when Cisco and McClosky pulled up behind them.

"Hold it right there!" Cisco yelled as he and McClosky flashed their badges. "Homicide. We'll take it from here. Get these civilians away from the door."

The two detectives entered the basement expecting the worst, and had taken only a few steps when their fear was realized. In the middle of a bloody mess stood Frank Gazzi.

McClosky turned to the cops outside the door. "You, get on the radio to the dispatcher and have them call the medical examiner, and you get everybody off the loading platform, keep it clear for the meat wagon."

The scene secured, he joined his partner and an obviously traumatized Gazzi at the murder scene, a dead guy face down on the floor, and Joey Bancik on his back in a pool of blood. While scanning the basement he discerned a shadowy figure standing in a dark corner.

"Okay, Gazzi, start talking," Cisco said, his anger barely under control. "First, who shot the Bancik boy?"

"It was an accident. I had to protect myself. That gun on the floor belongs to that guy over there. He had it pointed right at me…."

"You telling me you shot at that guy and killed the kid? Is that what the fuck you're telling me? Who is he? Got a name? And give me your weapon, wouldn't want another accident."

"Not yet. Happened so fast." Gazzi handed over his Smith & Wesson, and with it his career. "I only had time to cuff him before you got here. I'm pretty sure he runs numbers for McDuffie."

"Get your ass over here where we can see you!" McClosky ordered. "You have a name?"

"Al Sweeney."

"How old are you?" McClosky said.

"Seventeen."

The detectives exchanged glances. Things were going from bad to worse, not only did they have two bodies and a dumb cop on their hands, now they could add a juvenile to the mix.

"Looks bad I know, but I didn't mean to shoot no one," Sweeney said. "Only wanted to scare the kid. Then this *Clarion* guy showed up. I tripped and fell and it went off."

"*Clarion* guy?" Cisco said. "Are you saying you know the dead man?"

"Yeah, he knows him, says he was his boss, name's Bancroft. Doesn't know his first name," Gazzi intruded.

"Shut your god damn mouth!" Cisco said as he fought the urge to grab Gazzi by the throat.

Meanwhile, McClosky was finished searching Bancroft's back pockets and had reached under the body to remove the deadman's wallet from the inside pocket of his jacket.

"Hensley Parker Bancroft. With a name like that, he's got to be important. License says he's thirty-eight, and has a Forest Hill address. A Princeton Club membership card, and let's see here, also a member of the Broad Street Club."

McClosky replaced the wallet and was careful to avoid touching the Beretta and other evidence to be photographed by the forensic team. He arose and turned to the cop standing guard at the door. "Hey you, officer, what's your name?"

"Foster, Officer Foster."

"Okay, Officer Foster, put in another call to the dispatcher and have him call the morgue. Have him relay the name Hensley Parker Bancroft. Maybe the stiff is important enough to get them off their asses."

He looked at Cisco and didn't like what he saw. McClosky sensed the inevitable, his partner was about to lose it, he had seen it before. It was time to take over the interrogation before Nick's rage created an impossible situation.

"You two stay right where you are," McClosky said, then turned to Cisco and lowered his voice. "I think it's time to take a deep breath, Nick. We've got one big, fucking mess here, and it's going to get bigger."

The two detectives realized that their long partnership was about to be tested. They had taken a lot of shortcuts during their years together, but had never turned rogue. Mutual trust and a shared hatred of the crooks on the force made it possible for them to overcome philosophical differences. This time they had turned away from a problem that could have been easily solved, and now there were two bodies to deal with.

"Talk about headlines," Cisco said. "A dead *Beacon* carrier, slash numbers runner, and a *Clarion* executive with a hole in his head. Saunders and Lucio are gonna go crazy."

"Not just the scribblers," McClosky said. "It'll be the whole city. Think about it. Richie the Boot and Longy at it again, black bookies from Atlanta recruiting white kids to run numbers, a Boiardo soldier fished from the river, and we might as well throw in the whore and her pimp ice picked on Broome."

"And Bancroft shot to death by one of his paperboys," Cisco said.

Their morbid litany was interrupted by the arrival of the morgue meat wagon and to their surprise, Coroner Walter Tomokai and his forensic team. Tomokai had the uncanny ability to ferret out the important stiffs from the mundane traffic that passed through his daily house of horrors. Hensley Parker Bancroft must have rung his chimes.

"Detectives Cisco and McClosky, busy, busy, busy," a smiling Tomokai said as he approached with extended hand. Two photographers and a team of medical flunkies trailed behind. The smile faded when he saw Joey Bancik's body. "Christ Almighty, you're never ready for something like this."

The two detectives watched silently as Tomokai put the photographers and medics through their paces. This was an important case and the coroner made sure that every detail was cataloged.

"You two, let's get going," Cisco motioned Gazzi and Sweeney toward the door. "We're going downtown. We'll need complete statements from both of you, so plan on spending the night. The drive will give you plenty of time to dream something up."

Police Chief Patrick Riley was waiting for them at headquarters. After the initial call to the dispatcher, it took less than an hour for word of the shootings to reach him at home. This had headlines written all over it, and he wasn't about to let the mayor and district attorney hog the spotlight. He set-up camp in his office, making sure that all of the celebrity photos on the wall behind him were straight. It had taken only a few minutes for him to shed his golf clothes and pull a freshly-pressed uniform from his private wash room. He was ready.

Cisco and McClosky pulled into the police parking lot and were relieved to see that headquarters was just as quiet as they had left it two hours earlier. McClosky removed the cuffs from Sweeney and dropped them into an evidence bag that contained Gazzi's Smith & Wesson. Forensics had the Beretta.

"The Chief wants to see you," the Desk Sergeant said as they entered the building. "He's in his office."

"Thanks, Sarge, give us the keys," Cisco said, then turned to Sweeney and Gazzi. "You'll get your phone calls after we're finished with the Chief."

They locked Sweeney in a basement holding cell and marched a docile Gazzi to an interrogation room.

"Hold on a minute before we see the Chief," McClosky said. "Let's get it straight where we're going. I know how you feel about the Bancik kid, and how he and his buddy were sucked into the numbers racket. Upstairs I say we talk only about the shootings today. The rest is gonna come out with the D.A. and the press. Agreed?"

Cisco knew that his partner had nailed it all along. They were homicide. They weren't priests and they weren't vice.

"Agreed."

Upstairs they found the Chief had left the door to his office open, a cue that they could walk right in.

"Okay, let's have it," the unsmiling Chief said from his padded leather desk chair, He pushed a large, hand-carved onyx ashtray and chrome cigarette lighter across the desk. "This is a nasty one, and I'll want all you've got before I call a news conference."

"There's not much to it," Cisco said. "The only questions we have concern the charges to be filed, and who files them."

It took less than ten minutes and two cigarettes for the detectives to lay it all out for the Chief. It hadn't escaped their boss, a notorious stickler for details, that the two detectives had no written notes and were winging it.

"So that's it," the Chief said, "You're satisfied with what you've told me?"

"I'd say where we are right now, yeah, I'm satisfied," Cisco said.

"And how about you Sergeant McClosky, do you agree with Lieutenant Cisco?"

"Yeah, I do."

"So that's it for now," the Chief said. "I'll call the mayor and D.A., and set the news conference for four o'clock. Gives you plenty of time to write your reports."

They got up and were heading out when their boss pulled them up short. "And freshen up, you both look like you've been sleeping in your clothes. Put those shavers in the bunk room to use, I want you standing clean and neat behind me when the flashbulbs start popping."

"It's gonna be a circus, and everyone loves a circus," Cisco said outside in the hall. "With an important stiff like Bancroft in center ring, it's up for grabs who'll be the ringmaster."

"My bet's on the *Clarion*," McClosky said. "Everyone will want the frontpage, and they'll be kissing the publisher's ass to get it."

The two detectives wasted little time on Gazzi and Sweeney. They were handed phones and given five minutes to make their calls. Gazzi came close to blubbering while asking forgiveness from his wife, while Sweeney showed no remorse when talking to a father who had been living off his son for years.

Meanwhile, McClosky called Juvenile Court, and was connected to Sweeney's most recent case worker. She'd be there in less than an hour.

"That's taken care of," he said. "And how about you, Nick, I figured you'd want to handle the Banciks."

"I've been thinking about it, and I don't feel I'm the right guy to break the news."

"Got anybody in mind?"

"Yeah, and that's where I'm going now, won't be gone long. Hold the fort, and let's hope there aren't any more stiffs on our watch."

Ten minutes later Cisco was out of his cruiser and at the front door of St. Mark's rectory. Inside, Father Nolan had just polished off his second helping of scrambled eggs, and was leafing through the *Clarion* sports section when he heard the doorbell. He had removed his collar, and was ready to kickback after completing clerical duties that began with the six-thirty mass. He had rebuttoned his collar and stifled his annoyance by the time he opened the front door.

"Good morning, Father. Can you spare me a little of your time?" Cisco said, holding up his badge.

"Certainly, come in," the priest said. "I didn't get your name."

"Lieutenant Cisco, homicide. I'm hoping you can help me out."

"In any way I can, just hope it's legal." The priest was thankful that his lame quip had been brushed aside by the detective. He feared what was coming next. He ushered Cisco toward two overstuffed chairs in the parlor and waited.

"I'm afraid I have some bad news about one of your altar boys, Joey Bancik. He was shot and killed this morning while on his paper route."

"Jesus Christ, Almighty! How did it happen?"

"I'm afraid the story gets even worse, he was accidentally shot by a police officer."

The distraught priest got up and walked to the front window. With his eyes closed, he took three deep breaths in a futile attempt to compose himself. His lips were moving, but the words wouldn't come. He took two more breaths and turned toward Cisco. For the first time, Cisco saw that this priest was different. He was young, tall and muscular, nothing like the aesthetic clerics he was used to.

"What do you want me to do?"

"I want you to break the news to the Bancik family. I think it's the right thing to do, that they get the word from someone like you who can really reach them."

"Lieutenant Cisco, I'm a clerical joke. I've known that Joey Bancik and another one of my altar boys were running numbers. That's right, they were numbers runners for the mob using their paper routes as cover. And I did nothing about it. Only last week I tried to tell Joey's mother what her son was doing, and I couldn't get her to listen. I failed, and now Joey's dead. Tell me, was it the numbers?"

"Yes, Father, and let's leave it at that. If you agree to see the Banciks, then you should take it all the way. Joey is at the city morgue by now. His mom and dad should have someone with them when they view the body. Will you do it?"

The priest could not erase the image of a devout and simplistic woman who dropped to her knees in front of him after last Sunday's mass. She couldn't understand why he didn't really know her Joey. He was an altar boy. He went to school and studied hard, and he would graduate. Her Joey would never run numbers. He was a good boy. He delivered papers and put food on the table. He was a good boy.

Cisco silently studied the young priest who was not only searching for a reply, but for retribution as well. He wondered if he had made a mistake coming here. The priest turned to the window, took two deep breaths, then turned back again and locked eyes with the detective.

"Okay, Lieutenant, I'll do it."

Biography

Steve Bassett was born and raised in Newark's crime-ridden Third Ward and, although far removed during a career as an award-winning journalist, he has always been proud of the sobriquet Jersey Guy. He has been legally blind for almost a decade, but hasn't let this slow him down. He received three Emmys for investigative documentaries, and the California Bar Association's Medallion Award for Distinguished Reporting on the Administration of Justice. Polish on his mother's side and Montenegrin on his father's, with grandparents who spoke little or no English, his early outlook was ethnic and suspicious. It was a world in which cabbage, potatoes, sausage and heavy homemade dumplings reigned. This is the setting for "Father Divine's Bikes."

He has written two nonfiction books, one published by Ashley Books, "The Battered Rich," and "Golden Ghetto: How the Americans and French Fell In and Out of Love During the Cold War," published by Red Hen Press under its Xeno imprint. He lives in Placitas, New Mexico with his wife, Darlene Chandler Bassett.